LET THE DEAD

BURY THE DEAD

ALSO BY ALLISON EPSTEIN

A Tip for the Hangman

LET the DEAD
BURY the DEAD

A Novel

ALLISON EPSTEIN

DOUBLEDAY · NEW YORK

Jacket illustration by Roberts Rurans
Jacket design by Emily Mahon

LIBRARY OF CONGRESS CATALOGING-IN-PUBLICATION DATA
Names: Epstein, Allison, author.
Title: Let the dead bury the dead : a novel / by Allison Epstein.
Description: First edition. | New York : Doubleday, [2023]
Identifiers: LCCN 2022037356 (print) | LCCN 2022037357 (ebook) |
ISBN 9780385549097 (hardcover) | ISBN 9780385549103 (ebook)
Classification: LCC PS3605.P6456 L48 2023 (print) |
LCC PS3605.P6456 (ebook) | DDC 813/.6--dc23
LC record available at https://lccn.loc.gov/2022037356
LC ebook record available at https://lccn.loc.gov/2022037357

MANUFACTURED IN THE UNITED STATES OF AMERICA

1 3 5 7 9 10 8 6 4 2

First Edition

To Grandma Ida,

with love

One must believe in the possibility of happiness, and I now believe in it. Let the dead bury the dead; but while I am alive, I must live and be happy.

—LEO TOLSTOY, *WAR AND PEACE*, TRANS. LEO WIENER

TSARS AND TSARINAS

OF

IMPERIAL RUSSIA

1613–1812

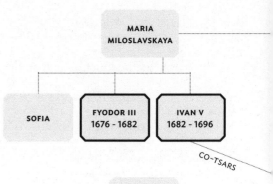

MARIA
MILOSLAVSKAYA

SOFIA

FYODOR III
1676 - 1682

IVAN V
1682 - 1696

CO-TSARS

EUDOXIA
LOPUKHINA

ANNA
LEOPOLDOVNA

ALEXEI

PETER II
1717 - 1730

ROMANOV DYNASTY

- MIKHAIL ROMANOV (1613 – 1645)
- ALEXEI (1645 – 1676)
- FYODOR III (1676 – 1682)
- IVAN V AND PETER I (1682 – 1696)
- PETER I (1682 – 1725)
- CATHERINE I (1725 – 1727)
- PETER II (1727 – 1730)

KOMAROV DYNASTY

- SERGEI I (1730 – 1763)
- CATHERINE II (1763 – 1779)
- ARKADY I (1779 – 1782)
- SERGEI II (1782 – PRESENT)

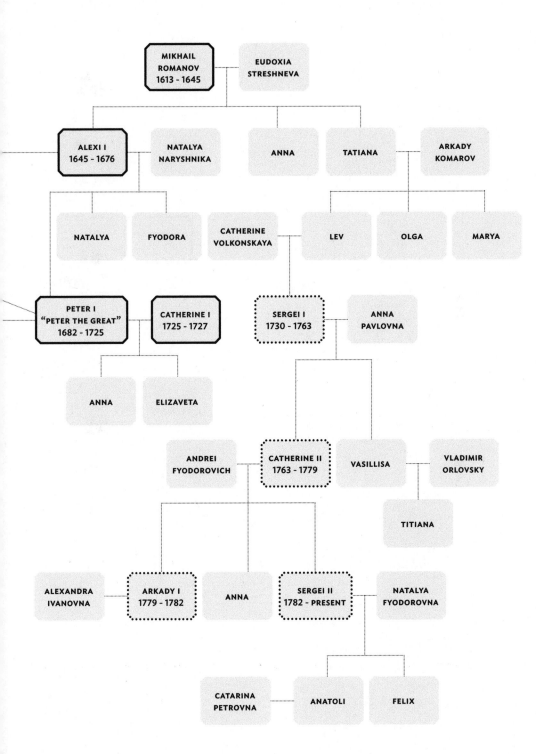

Part I

FIRST

FROST

Sasha

These woods would have run wild, if they'd been allowed to. Not far from here, the forests owned the land—tangled trees, ground rooted up by wild boars and badgers, vegetation-choked lakes that stories said were home to wicked spirits, because what else could thrive in water so black? But the woods outside Tsarskoe Selo were the tsar's woods, and anything belonging to the tsar meant order, regularity, precision. It was winter now, but all year round these trees were as pristine as if a Dutch master had painted them. The only thing out of place was Aleksandr Nikolaevich, who knew he was as far from imperial splendor as it was possible for a man to be.

Long stretches of frozen track and heavy drifts made the trek from Saint Petersburg slow going, and because Sasha's horse was property of the Imperial Army, he'd been forced to leave it at the final outpost and take the last fifteen miles to Tsarskoe Selo on foot. He'd intended to trim his beard before leaving camp, but that hadn't happened either, and so he looked as bedraggled and ill-prepared as he felt with each step nearer to the Catherine Palace. What would Felix think of him, when he stumbled into the grand halls of the imperial estate? Hardly a celebrated hero returning from the wars. A vagabond, rather, begging for a place to stay.

The war was over, Napoleon and his Grande Armée fleeing west pursued by a determined force of regulars who would snap at their heels all the way to Paris, but no one had told Sasha's nerves. Every sense was pricked for anything amiss. The trill of a bird. The creak of tall firs, dusted with snow and ornery with cold. The wind, muffled and hollow through the worn fur of his hat. No sign of danger, not yet, but that was the trick about danger; it seldom gave a sign. The fighting at the end hadn't been like it was before, at the blood-soaked field of Borodino, the disastrous losses at Austerlitz, but it would take more than the retreat of the French emperor to convince Sasha that this was, in fact, a time of peace.

A gap between the trees, and the gilded roof of the Catherine Palace rose through the dusk, bright enough to make Sasha's heart shudder. Its burnished domes were like a cathedral in the wilderness, glittering against the robin's-egg walls. After so long at the front, the palace seemed like a dream, some fantasy one of Felix's cooks would spin from sugar and marzipan. Another step, and it was gone, lost in the leafless tangle of branches. Beautiful, but insubstantial. It seemed impossible that such a delicate structure could exist in the same world where the roar of cannons rattled men's teeth, where the choke of gunfire blotted out the sun. He kept to the path, forcing his thoughts down a different track. A warm fire. A chance to unlace his boots. A smile from Felix, the sound of his voice, not a dream of it but the reality, the true color of which could never be recreated, not even in the most faithful memory. He sighed at the thought, the thick cloud of his breath catching in his hat like frost. *I told you I'd come back in one piece*, he'd say to Felix, when they were alone. *It takes more than a war to keep me away from you.*

Then he stopped.

Without the crunch of his footsteps, the silence was total. And yet he was certain he'd heard something. A small thump. Muted, like a body falling into the snow.

The idea was nonsense. Forests made noises. Snow fell from tree branches. Birds shook dead twigs loose. Badgers raked their claws along tree bark for food to bring back to their setts. He'd been moving since dawn, that was all. Sit down, get something to eat, and the world would start to look like itself again.

The next sound was a soft exhale, distinctly human and not his own.

Sasha looked off into the woods. The woods looked back invitingly.

It wasn't late, but dusk fell early now, and soon it would be dark in earnest. And while he no longer believed the midwinter stories his mother had told around the stove when he was a child, there was still no cause to go looking for trouble. Men weren't meant to walk through woods alone, even manicured woods like these. Too many threats could lurk in the shadows: the scale-crusted vodyanoy, snatching travelers from the banks of its lake to gnaw on their bones beneath the surface; long-haired rusalki, ghostly women luring men to their graves to avenge their own deaths. Nonsense and superstition, fairy stories to keep children indoors after dark, but nightmares didn't die as quickly as belief in them did.

Still.

That breath again, and this time a soft groan. A woman's voice.

Sasha crossed himself and cut sideways into the woods. Despite his better judgment, curiosity remained like the itch of a healing wound, more insistent until every nerve twitched against it. Some instinct—what, he couldn't have said—insisted that whatever had happened here, it was his responsibility.

It didn't take long before the trees opened into a clearing ringed with tall pines. In the center, he saw a woman, lying on her side in the snow.

Had it been any darker, he'd have missed her entirely. Her long, thin coat was the same shade as the snow; in the dying light, she resembled a disembodied head and pair of hands lying in the powdery drift. Her hair covered most of her face, and it was not gray or blond but white—not the white of age, but of feathers, of sun reflected off a frosted window. She lay as if she'd fallen from a great height, one cheek pillowed against the snow.

Sasha's mother always said a vila could change her appearance at will. Cunning spirits of the forest and the air who could assume the female form most pleasing to the man they meant to trap, their sharp laughter ringing as they rent their prey to pieces. He looked up, half expecting to see a grinning demon with silver eyes leering in the branches overhead. But his view to the sky was unbroken, pale gray shot through with red, minutes from sunset. The woman in the snow seemed to shimmer in the fading, otherworldly light. Was this what the painted angels in Petropavlovsky Cathedral would look like if they fell to earth?

A fallen angel, he thought grimly, and yet to his knowledge one angel in particular was famous for making that fall.

The figure shivered, and suddenly she was no longer a fiend, but a woman in need of help. He flinched, thinking of the boys in tattered French uniforms he'd seen lying on the Smolensk road, flesh blue and frozen stiff. He had witnessed enough of that and done nothing—but this was peacetime, this was different. And if Felix's first glimpse of Sasha in months cast him as this poor woman's savior, there were worse impressions to make.

Snowdrifts reached well past his ankles as he forced his way toward the woman. The thick boots of his uniform were ideal for heavy wear, but no clothing in the world was suited for a jaunt through uncleared snow in December. Damp and cold, he knelt beside her, ignoring the wet shock as the snow met his knees. The curtain of hair still obscured her face. He reached out a gloved hand to brush it back.

Her skin, what he could see of it, was nearly translucent and tinged with purple. She barely moved against his touch, but he could see no lacerations, no bruises, no broken bones, and her breathing was easy. He gritted his teeth, then shrugged off his overcoat and draped it over the woman, allowing winter to pierce the weave of his uniform. Lifting her was easier than he'd expected, as if her bones were hollow. As he forged a path back to the road, the woman's heartbeat matched his, seemingly sympathetic to his shivering. In a few minutes, they'd both be inside, a soldier and a stranger in a palace of royals. What happened after that was outside his control, and things past control were past concern.

Soon the woods gave way to cleared paths and neat grounds, carefully manicured beneath the snow. He held the woman close and quickened his pace toward the Catherine Palace, that great hollow building with its five spires catching the last flares of the sun. Marzipan dream. Gilded prison. Either way, warm, and out of the wind.

The woman stirred in his arms; in shock, he nearly dropped her. It had only been a twitch, but that was enough. Alive enough to move. Thank God. Entering the palace holding a corpse wasn't the effect he'd been aiming for.

"It's all right," he said under his breath. "We're nearly there."

The woman gave a soft hum and cracked one eye open, the lashes barely separating. One golden eye. A rich tawny yellow, bright as a coin.

He blinked, and her eyes were closed again, pale lashes against lilac skin. The inhuman color was gone, as if it had never been.

Because it *had* never been. Now was not the time to let his imagination run wild. Without his coat, the cold set in deep. He could feel his numbed hands falling slack around the woman, threatening to drop her at any moment.

When he kicked the side door in lieu of a knock, it gave way at once, which annoyed Sasha but did not surprise him. For all that he was the younger son of the tsar, Grand Duke Felix was startlingly lax in matters of personal safety. If Felix hadn't left every door of the palace open in Sasha's absence for robbers and brigands to stroll through and help themselves to imperial heirlooms, he supposed he should count himself lucky. Sasha set off in the direction of Felix's private apartments. At the very least, he'd find a servant there to direct him. And to lock the door behind.

The Catherine Palace was the same as when he'd last seen it six months before, and for a hundred years before that. Time moved slowly for the imperial family, however quickly it passed for their subjects. Take a stroll down Krestovsky Island in Petersburg where Sasha had grown up, and barely one building in twenty was older than he was. Homes and taverns and shops bloomed and died like crocuses, progress cycling through and leveling anything that had outlived its utility. But this hall hadn't been altered since the last tsar had walked through it, or the tsarina before him. Polished mirrors capped with gold, marble floors, portraits of severe-looking men draped in military medals looking down their noses at Sasha and the woman. Avoiding their eyes, Sasha watched the gentle ripple of the woman's breathing instead. He was thirty-one years old, and yet the disdain in these paintings made him feel like the awkward youth he'd been when he'd first seen the imperial family, a new cadet with an ill-fitting uniform and hungry eyes. His boots left heavy prints of mud and snow along the marble, but that would be a servant's task to deal with later. This garish palace could stand a brush of something natural.

Around another corner, Sasha at last came upon a footman, who stopped in his tracks with wide eyes and his mouth half open. Evidently he hadn't expected an army captain and a half-dead woman to let themselves in at this point in the evening.

"The grand duke?" Sasha said tersely.

The footman blinked, taking in Sasha's uniform, his familiarity with the palace, how little good arguing with him was likely to do. "With the musicians," he said.

So this was Felix's idea of security without Sasha to direct him. God grant him patience. "And where are the musicians?"

This second prompting seemed to jar the footman back to himself. "In the east parlor. Do you require—"

"No," Sasha interrupted, already setting off. "I know the way."

The footman, thankfully, did not pursue him.

Each step along the marble floor soured what remained of Sasha's hopeful mood. It had been foolish to expect a private audience, but when he'd pictured this homecoming, he'd allowed his imagination to get the better of him. More than once, he'd dreamed up the scene: Felix would be alone in his bedroom, absently watching the snow fall through the window, only to look up at the faint sound of Sasha's entrance. The distance separating them would shrink to nothing, and Felix would be in his arms again, and they could fall together into bed for as long as they chose to stay there. It was a pretty thought, but not worth the minutes he'd spent dreaming it.

Because the door to the east parlor was in front of him now, and though he could not see inside, the door was ajar, and he could hear. The careless dance of two violins in harmony, playing with more finesse than Sasha had heard in months—since the last time Felix had brought in a band of musicians from Petersburg, no doubt. And there, above the complex weave of the music, a tangle of voices, raised in song and smoothed along the edges with drink. One voice that, even in a chorus, Sasha would recognize anywhere.

The woman nestled closer against his chest, as if to remind him of her presence. He shivered, imagining long hair, cold fingers dragging him through a crack in the ice, in the earth. The sooner this woman wasn't his responsibility, the happier he'd be. And if that meant interrupting this band of midwinter idlers, so be it.

Without the benefit of his hands, Sasha shifted his balance, then kicked the door open.

As if they faced such interruptions every day, the musicians didn't miss a note. They were scattered across the parlor as if it were any peasant barn or bonfire, their unhandsome faces alight with drink. Beyond the violinists Sasha had heard from the hall, there was a young woman with a clarinet and a boy of perhaps fourteen with a hand drum, who alone looked up as Sasha entered. A grand brocade sofa sat near the center of the room, with two beautiful women sprawled along it, their skirts vibrant and their cheeks flushed, voices raised in song. One, the blonde, had a near-empty glass of wine in her hand. The other, the dark-haired one, sat on Felix's lap, trailing one finger through his hair.

Sasha had hoped—had feared?—that the tsar or the tsarevich or the pressures of wartime would finally have forced the grand duke to grow up. But no, this was precisely the same Grand Duke Felix he had left. Tall, strong shouldered, and slim waisted, he still looked like a storybook prince, his pressed jacket slung over the back of the sofa and his cobalt-blue waistcoat carelessly unbuttoned. When Tsar Sergei had banished Felix from Petersburg to Tsarskoe Selo two years ago, the understood intent had been to cool his son's wayward spirit, or at least shame him with a taste of exile from the business of the capital. What he had done instead was give Felix a pleasure garden and the privacy to make the most of it. Sasha could have laughed, if not for the weight in his arms, and the curious twist in his throat as the dark-haired woman's fingers trailed down Felix's cheek.

Jealousy was familiar territory for Sasha, but Felix had always lacked the insecurity needed to comprehend it. The moment he caught sight of the curious pair in the doorway, Felix's dark blue eyes flashed with delight, and he extricated himself from the tangle of limbs on the sofa.

"Sashka!"

The musicians stopped playing and turned to Sasha, standing there awkward and unannounced with a half-dead stranger in his arms.

"Sashka," Felix repeated, slightly puzzled now. "And you've brought a wife with you. Good God, war *has* changed you, hasn't it?"

The woman shifted in Sasha's arms, and her hair fell away from her face with the smooth movement of water poured from a height. "Be serious," he said, and he was briefly thankful that if he couldn't get Felix alone, at least he'd come upon him in this careless company, a time and place where he didn't need to bow and murmur "Your Imperial Highness" like any common man called before a Komarov. "Help me, would you? She needs a doctor."

"Who is she?"

"How should I know that?" Sasha said tersely. "I found her on the grounds."

"Aleksandr Nikolaevich, model of Christian charity," Felix drawled. "I'll recommend you for sainthood." Authority blended with amusement as Felix gestured at one of the violinists. "Right then. Arkady, you can hold a person as well as an instrument, can't you?"

"So I've been told, Your Highness," the musician said with a wink, earning a laugh from the women on the sofa and a blush from the clarinetist.

Felix grinned. "Good. Take her to the bedroom at the end of the corridor. And send for my physician once you get her warm. We'll want to know who she is and how in hell she wandered into my park, but that's a question for tomorrow."

"Yes, Your Highness," Arkady said, as Sasha carefully transferred the woman to him. Sasha's arms seemed to hover beside him, suddenly unburdened by the weight. He watched as Arkady carried the woman away, in search of a soft bed and a safe place to rest. He'd done his duty, but even so, he didn't like the idea of turning his back on her.

"And you," Felix said, spinning Sasha around to face him. All thoughts of the woman vanished with the warmth of Felix's hand on his forearm, and that brilliant smile. "Well done, you. I suppose you're the one to thank that Napoleon turned tail and ran."

Sasha frowned, tasting gunpowder. "General Kutuzov won't like you giving me the credit, Felya."

"And when have I ever cared what that swaggering drunk likes?" Felix said, and God help him but the gleam in Felix's eye seemed even wickeder now. That rumpled waistcoat, and his dark hair messy, and his attention fully, entirely, intoxicatingly on Sasha. "You've just won a war, Sasha, and saved a helpless maiden besides. Let me embellish a little. Enjoy the fairy tale for a night."

He led Sasha toward the sofa, which the two women had already vacated. Their job was not to seduce the grand duke. It was to make sure Grand Duke Felix had everything his heart desired. And tonight—as Felix guided Sasha down onto the cushion and sat beside him, his mouth so desperately close to Sasha's throat—what Felix's heart desired was Sasha.

"Where are your manners, you good-for-nothings?" Felix said to the musicians, though the jab had no bite in it. "Get the hero something to drink."

The softness of Felix's fingers. The sight of Felix's brilliant grin. The familiar chill of a glass pressed into his hand. It wasn't at all how Sasha had imagined his return.

Not that he was complaining.

2

Felix

Felix woke late the next morning with a dry mouth and a headache. He gave a soft, irritated mumble and rolled over to nestle against Sasha's shoulder. Effects of last night's drinking notwithstanding, he intended to enjoy waking up this morning, and that meant making it last. It had been ages since he'd shared a bed with Sasha, and he'd missed it, the solidity of the soldier's body against his own. His bed hadn't stayed empty that whole time, of course, but there was a safety in Sasha's presence that no countess or courtier had been able to match. Those encounters had been entertainment; Sasha in bed beside him was home.

"You're impossible," Sasha murmured, though he did not push Felix away.

The vibrations of his voice rumbled through Felix's body like a wild horse. "I beg your pardon. I have it on good authority that I am a delight."

Sasha hummed, though if the way he carded his fingers through Felix's hair was any indication, he didn't entirely disagree. "I missed you, Felya," he said, his voice still more sensation than sound.

There was such comfort in being held like this, by someone who would tease him with one breath and kiss him with the next. Sasha's broad shoulders looked like granite against the fine sheets. "Nonsense. All those rugged grenadiers in those fine, tailored uniforms, you must have been in heaven. I'd be surprised if you had half a thought to spare for me."

Sasha scoffed. "And I suppose you and your harem of musicians were all sitting with your noses pressed to the window pining."

Felix laughed. "Come now. If I'm to be judged by what I say and do, there's no hope on God's earth for me."

He sat up and ran one hand through his hair, letting the sheet fall to his hips. Sasha mirrored the motion as if by instinct, keeping the distance between them the same. All the while, Sasha's eyes never left him. It was a beautiful, shining sensation to be seen like that, not as the disgraced son of the tsar or the lord of the Catherine Palace but as *Felix*, a man of twenty-eight with a sharp wit and a zest for grandeur. He'd forgotten, when Sasha left for the front, how much he loved being seen this way. He cupped Sasha's cheek in one hand and leaned in to kiss him, soft and slow and careless.

"Do you know what I'd like to do this morning?" Felix said. His lips were still very near to Sasha's, and he enjoyed Sasha's shiver like an actor accepting applause. "I'd like you to stay right here with me. We have months of lost time to make up for."

Sasha smiled, which felt like a success. But then he swung his legs out of bed and reached for his shirt, which felt like a categorical failure.

"That is the precise opposite of what I *just* said, Sashenka."

He didn't stop, though he did laugh. "You ought to come spend a week with my regiment. It'll teach you that sloth is a vice."

"I know it is," Felix said, folding his arms. "I'm collecting vices. Trying to complete the set. Come back to bed."

"You have a guest, Felix."

Felix cocked an eyebrow at him. This was no time of day for riddles, even without the lingering headache. "What, do we expect a visit from the American ambassador? Mr. Adams can wait until we're finished. Or he can join us if he's so terribly eager—"

"Felix," Sasha interrupted. His expression was severe, but Felix could tell he was trying not to laugh. "That woman."

Ah. Felix had forgotten the unconscious stranger Sasha had brought back to the palace the night before. An enthusiastic homecoming celebration had a way of overshadowing such details.

"I'll bet you fifty rubles she's sleeping," he said. "The state she was in? And unless you're encouraging me to loom over strange women while they sleep like some kind of night demon . . ."

Sasha had fully dressed by now. The morning sun caught him through the window in the corner, making the trim of his jacket gleam. His black eyes and sober expression made him look like an icon hung for worship, and about as easy to argue with.

"Trust me, Felix," Sasha said. "I don't think you should leave her alone."

"You sound like my nurse," Felix muttered, though he did lean over the side of the bed for his trousers. "Afraid of the women in the woods. Are you going to tell my future in the mirror next? Drop some candle wax in a pitcher and see who I'll marry?"

"I'll come with you, if that will get you out of bed faster," Sasha said. "Or I could leave you to do it yourself and see whether any of those handsome grenadiers are stationed in the village—"

"All right, I'm coming, stop *hectoring*."

⸻

Felix sent a maid ahead to the east bedroom to alert the stranger to their presence and give her a chance to dress properly. The necessary nod to formality had additional uses: it gave him time to splash his face with cold water and send for a servant, who returned with enough scalding-hot tea to chase away the worst of the fog still drifting about his brain. Sasha remained near the doorway while Felix made himself presentable, watching the production solemnly. Felix, who had never once objected to an audience, made no effort to hurry.

At last, the maid returned and, with a faintly alarmed look at Sasha, led them to a small sitting room at the far end of the corridor, where the woman was already waiting for them.

She sat in an armchair beneath the window, her legs tucked up beneath her, watching the falling snow. The posture gave her a curious look: small but not weak, like a coiled animal before a strike. She wore a simple navy-blue gown with cap sleeves and a square neckline—something the maid must have unearthed from deep within one of the palace's unused wardrobes, as Felix didn't recognize it as anything he'd lent to other women who'd stayed the night. The color became her, throwing into relief the strange gold of her eyes.

In the clear light of both morning and sobriety, there was no denying it: she was the most beautiful person he'd ever seen. Striking in a categorically different way than Sasha was, like trying to compare a deep-rooted pine and a flash of lightning. He wasn't one for embarrassment, but Felix felt the blood rush to his face looking at her, this remarkable woman who sat in his chair like a snake, waiting for him to speak.

"You can come in, Felix," she said.

Startled and not a little embarrassed, Felix took a step forward. For the way she'd addressed him, "inappropriate" was an understatement. The correct form of address was "Your Imperial Highness," followed by a deep obeisance that would connect her forehead with the ground. She threw out his given name without thinking, the way Felix might address a servant. Something twitched within him at this—anger, at first, and then something else, rich with excitement and utterly forbidden.

"Obviously," he said. "It's my house."

He sat on the edge of one of the upholstered armchairs opposite her, leaning back onto his hands. Sasha remained near the door, his hand at his belt where his pistol would have been. For all he had treated it lightly before, there was no question, Sasha was afraid of this woman. In her presence, it was easier to see why.

"You may go," the woman said, dismissing the maid with a wave of her hand.

The maid stared, clearly stunned at the notion of leaving a woman unchaperoned with two men. She was hardly alone: Sasha looked positively indignant about it. Then again, Sasha could be indignant if a horse in the palace stables looked at him rudely, so long practice made that easy to ignore. And Felix had to admit, the woman's boldness had caught his attention.

"You heard the lady," he said, nodding to the maid, who closed the door behind her with great trepidation. Alone now, Felix cleared his throat, though the cough sent reverberations through his headache. "I hope you slept well, mademoiselle," he said politely. "You looked as if you could use it last night."

She rested one elbow on the arm of the chair. "Yes. Thank you for the valiant rescue."

"It's Captain Dorokhin you should thank," Felix said. "He's the one who pulled you from the snow."

Captain Dorokhin, from the door, seemed to be sincerely regretting that decision.

"Do you have a name?" Felix asked.

"Sofia Azarova."

Felix regarded her with his head tilted. "And what exactly were you doing in my woods, Sofia Azarova?"

Sofia shrugged, rustling the soft fabric of the gown. "I am sorry about arriving unannounced," she said. "I'd have called on you properly, but the journey was more difficult than I thought."

This had not answered his question. "Because you flew here, I expect," he said waspishly. "And fell out of the sky."

"Your Highness, if you want her gone, I—" Sasha began.

"Not yet," Felix said, raising one finger. He leaned forward, resting his palms on his knees. Sending her away would have been safer, but something in her had sunk its claws into him and refused to let go. It was so rare, in his position, to find a person whose next move he could not predict. "I've been patient with you until now, mademoiselle, but if you've forgotten who you're speaking to, I'm happy to remind you."

"I know who I'm speaking to," she said. "I wonder if you do."

Felix's eyebrows arched. "I have some ideas," he said, striving to imitate the dry detachment with which his father received petitioners. "A peasant girl. A charlatan. Someone trying to work her way either into my bed or my purse, or both if she's lucky."

"That's not quite how I'd put it."

"You tell me, then," Felix said. "I don't have time for games."

Sasha took a step forward, with the apparent intent of removing Sofia bodily from the room.

But Sofia only smiled. And then the corner of her mouth wasn't all that moved.

The casement window flung open behind her, as if a hand had seized it from outside and pulled. Cold, piercing and immediate. Felix leapt to his feet and scrambled away as curls of snow thundered into the room, translucent and untamable. Had it even been snowing a moment before? He couldn't recall. Couldn't think of anything but the snow that danced and swirled in tight spirals before settling on the imported carpets, dusting and melting against the candle flames. And at the center of it all, Sofia Azarova. The wind caught her hair and sent it fluttering like a saint's aureole. Her golden eyes, flashing.

The sound that escaped from Felix was very nearly a scream. His body moved on its own, scrabbling backward like a grasshopper, nearly tripping over Sasha. The woman might have leapt from the chair and torn out his throat. Instead, she let out a soft laugh. The floor under Felix's feet trembled with the force of his heart.

Power. The marrow of his bones knew the feel of it, and the roots of his hair. He knew it as surely as he knew anything.

And then, as suddenly as the storm had come, it was gone.

With one last swirl, the snow lost its momentum and settled to the floor in a soft powder. The window banged against the frame, once, then once again, and stilled. Sofia's hair fluttered, then drifted to her shoulders just as it had been, not a strand out of place. Merely a woman dressed in a borrowed blue gown, perched on a chair that now reminded Felix of a throne. She said nothing. Waiting for a response he wasn't sure he'd ever be able to give.

"You can shut your mouth, Felix," she said drily.

Felix snapped his jaw shut. His boots crunched against snow as he stepped forward. "Who *are* you?"

Sofia grinned. "That's hardly a polite question to ask a lady."

"Felix," Sasha began, reaching toward Felix's shoulder, "I wouldn't—"

"Yes, I know you wouldn't," Felix said, shrugging him away. "Mademoiselle Azarova, you can stay at Tsarskoe Selo for as long as you wish. I think we have a great deal to talk about."

"Thank you," she said, in the tone of someone who hadn't been waiting for permission.

"If you need a chambermaid to help you with—" Felix began, ignoring Sasha's indignant splutter at the idea of giving this stranger access to servants.

But Sofia cut him off. "No need," she said. "After long enough making do for myself, I prefer it that way. But thank you for offering. It's kind of you."

Felix nodded. He should, he knew, have had any number of reactions. Confusion, the kind of horror that would immediately precede his running from the palace grounds and never looking back. What he felt instead was fascination. A hint of fear. And beneath that, a hunger. Not for this woman, not precisely. But a hunger to know her—to understand her and her command of the world.

"Of course," Felix said, with a small bow. "You should rest, mademoiselle. Might I come speak with you later?"

He couldn't remember the last time he'd asked permission of anyone for anything, let alone entering a room in his own house. Still, he felt an unaccountable relief when Sofia nodded. "I'll take a walk later, I think," she said. "Explore the house, build my strength back. But this evening I'd be happy to talk further."

"By all means," Felix said, before Sasha could protest. "The Catherine Palace is at your disposal until then. Come on, Sasha. Let's leave her be."

Sasha glowered at Sofia, then turned on his heel and left. His boots left firm prints in the snow covering the carpet. Behind him, the storm continued to swirl beyond the window, shadows of white against the glass, directed by God knew what.

Felix closed the door, his blood like lightning. Despite the door between them, he thought he could still see Sofia, those sharp eyes looking into him, past him, through him. Even if their encounter had been mundane in every respect, he'd have known there was something different about her, something special, from those eyes.

"I'll call the guard," Sasha said, turning to go.

Felix shot out a hand to stop him. "What?"

Sasha pulled away so fast Felix flinched. His disbelief was as complete as Felix's own. "You saw that. Don't you see what she is?"

Through the window on the opposite side of the corridor, the snow fell faster than ever. Felix could hardly see the park through the cloud of white. It was as if the sky itself had come down to Tsarskoe Selo, claiming the palace and everything inside as its own. It was impossible that she'd called up this storm, but the thought presented itself regardless, insistent.

"What is she, exactly?"

Sasha swore. "I don't know, but it's not natural. You know the stories. The vila, the rusalka, witches and spirits. What she's just shown us isn't half of what she can do. It's too dangerous to let her stay here."

Felix stared. "Are you mad?"

Sasha squared his shoulders, and in a moment he was an army captain again, not the grand duke's lover, not a frightened peasant startled by a storm. There was a way of standing when you wanted your orders to be obeyed. There was a way of speaking when you expected your audience would pay rapt attention. Felix had been raised in the imperial family; he knew them both. Sasha had led soldiers to their deaths; he knew them, too.

"Don't laugh at me, Felix. I know what I saw."

A witch. Here. In Tsarskoe Selo. If not for the deathly seriousness in Sasha's posture, Felix would have thought the captain was joking. Some ancient spirit of the land or sky that drew her power from the forests and mountains and lakes, who could magic herself into a great predatory bird and with a word control the snow and the lightning. A spirit who had chosen heroes among the ancients and given them gifts of glory beyond measure. A cruel queen who betrayed her heroes, soaring away over the woods, leaving scorched earth and bone behind. Resting in one of the unused sitting rooms in the Catherine Palace, wearing a spare gown, while below the kitchen staff determined the menu for supper.

"Sasha. Listen to yourself." He laid one hand on Sasha's shoulder. Sasha flinched as though at a great weight. Aleksandr Nikolaevich, the fearsome captain of the Sixth Corps, afraid? "She's different, I'll grant you that. But I thought we all gave up believing in witches when we were children."

The soft edges of fear in Sasha's eyes hardened. He stepped back, broad shouldered and heavy browed, his familiar face cold and unyielding.

"I don't trust her. Send her away."

Felix hesitated. He'd known of her existence for less than a day. He could send her off and return to the beautiful comfort of this morning, with Sasha's fingers tangled in his hair, content and untroubled. The war was over. There was no reason to create new battles out of nothing.

He opened his mouth to agree, but a different answer came out, the one he'd known deep down he would give.

"No, Sasha."

"But—"

"She stays. That's all."

The authority felt strange on his tongue. He rarely flaunted his power, detested the way his father and brother wore their rank like an ermine mantle. But he was second in line to the imperial throne, and in this, he would settle for nothing less than having his way.

Sasha's expression melted away, and he turned and left Felix alone in the corridor. As if he couldn't trust himself not to say what was on his mind.

It wasn't too late for Felix go after him. Soothe the hurt he'd caused, make it right. Send Sofia away to make peace and then later, when their nerves had settled, persuade Sasha to tell him what had frightened him so deeply, what superstition had leapt from the heart of such a practical, levelheaded man.

Felix glanced once more at the closed door separating him from Sofia. With that look, he was decided. Sasha's hurt feelings could wait.

The captain was, suddenly, no longer Felix's most interesting companion at Tsarskoe Selo.

3

Marya

Fifteen miles from the Catherine Palace, in a cramped neighborhood where the Neva split Petersburg like a seam, Marya
Ryabkova leaned against the pane of the second-story window
and kept a sharp eye on the street. Behind her, Isaak worked at
breakneck speed, his thin body bent over the printing press like
some sort of fantastic insect. Another copy of the pamphlet they'd
spent two weeks rewriting emerged from the press, the close-set
type bold against the page. Two hundred copies, they'd decided
that morning before setting out. Two hundred would be enough
to get their message in front of the Petersburg citizens most likely
to respond to it: students, shopkeepers, soldiers fresh back from
the front, the drivers and messengers and menial laborers whose
bent backs kept the city breathing. Those two hundred would tell
two hundred more, and before the week was out, the Koalitsiya's
message would have spread like wildfire. Yes, some would ignore
it, caught up in the wave of patriotism the tsar had nurtured
throughout the war. But others would see that the fabled prosper-
ity of Russia spent more time at certain men's tables than it did at
others'.

And those people—the ones who saw matters the way they
did—might be ready to seize the moment.

"Divide them in half once you've finished," Marya said, glancing
back at Isaak. "You can start at the harbor and work east. I'll start
by the Haymarket."

Isaak grunted, whipping another printed copy from the press. "When did you start giving orders?"

"The writing was your job," she answered, "just like the speaking will be. Let me do the one thing I'm good at."

Isaak rolled his eyes but didn't argue. The words they would distribute today had flowed from Isaak's brain to the page with only a layer of polish from his fellow members, spinning a rationale for the proposed general strike so compelling it had stirred Marya's blood, even though they'd discussed almost nothing else for weeks. His speech at the upcoming rally would do even more to win hearts than the printed words could. He would bring the patchwork collective of discontented citizens together under the Koalitsiya's banner with a skill that was his alone, uniting them around the cause: legal protections for workers and peasants, a reformed imperial council, religious freedom, a clear path to emancipation for the country's twenty million serfs. But the way he knew the cause was the way Marya knew Petersburg. Its streets were as natural to her as the flow of blood through her veins. She hadn't earned her place at Isaak's right hand by having nothing to contribute.

Down in the street flashed the green of a familiar uniform.

"Soldiers," she said sharply, easy banter forgotten.

Isaak swore. In a moment, he'd rolled what pamphlets they'd printed into his satchel, while Marya sent the movable type scattering like mice across the floor. They'd kept the pamphlet short, as most of their audience could read only with difficulty, but a single page had the added benefit of being easier to hide. Tracks covered, Marya peered through the window, checking the progress of the soldiers. Six uniformed members of the Semyonovsky Life Guards Regiment stood outside the door to the printshop. The first had already taken a step up the stairs.

Marya locked the door to the staircase, though it wouldn't hold for long under pressure, and turned back to Isaak. It wasn't the first time they'd found themselves with armed soldiers too close for comfort, and she allowed a clear-eyed focus to shove away her fear. They were in danger, but she could manage it. If she moved fast.

"How did they find us?" she said, though her attention was already focused on escape routes.

"The same way they find everyone," Isaak said grimly.

Technically charged with maintaining order in the city, the Semyonovsky Regiment, like Ivan the Terrible's *oprichniki* before them, had one task that rose above the others: to track down opposition aided by a scent on a breeze, a single footprint in the snow, a suspicion and nothing else at all. More pernicious than any fairy-tale monster, a multiheaded dragon with ears in every wall. The regiment might have had informants placed in any den in the city, any *traktir* or market or back room where the Koalitsiya dared to meet. Of course Marya and Isaak had been found. It had only ever been a matter of time.

The locked door shuddered under the kick of a booted foot. In moments, Marya and Isaak would be face-to-face with at least seven soldiers, armed to the teeth and under orders to shoot those deemed traitors on sight. The dozens of pamphlets in his satchel would only seal their death sentence. Isaak had an old dueling pistol tucked into the pocket of his greatcoat, and Marya's hunting knife hung where it always did at her waist, but the tsar's men were trained from the cradle to kill when orders commanded. If it came to a fight, it wasn't one Marya and Isaak expected to win.

The second dirty window at the back of the room hadn't been opened in years, judging by the unbroken layer of paint that splashed across both sill and glass. Still, desperate times.

"Stand back," Marya said.

"What—"

With the birch handle of her knife, Marya struck the center of the window, smashing the cheap glass into tiny shards. Her knuckles hummed with pain from a dozen small cuts, but there would be time in the future to worry about those. Punching out the remains of the window with the knife, she unwound the long scarf that covered her hair, then secured one end to the window sash. She could feel, from a great distance, her mother's weary disapproval—*A respectable woman of your age never goes bareheaded in public, Masha, think of your reputation*—but if Vera Ryabkova had known the full extent of her daughter's activities with Isaak Tversky and the Koalitsiya, proprieties of dress would have been the least of her worries.

"God in Heaven, Masha—" Isaak began.

"Watch your hands," she said, climbing through the window. Holding tight to the scarf, she braced herself against the wall some fifteen feet above the alley below. It wasn't an impossible drop, and the scarf would help her belay down partway. She took a careful step, then another, feeling the grip of the wall through the soles of her boots.

Just above her, the door gave way under a soldier's rifle. Isaak scrambled through the window, and Marya, startled by the quavering of her makeshift rope, let go.

She hit the ground hard and rolled, swearing loudly. She hadn't broken anything, as far as she could tell, but there would be a bitter bruise on her hip come morning. Isaak kept his feet through the landing and extended a hand to haul Marya to hers. Behind them, Marya's scarf fluttered like a pennant of war, urging their next move.

A tactical retreat. And quick.

"Go," she hissed, jerking her head toward the river. Isaak had always been the faster between them. If he left her behind, he could get out of sight before the soldiers—no doubt already aware their quarry had given them the slip—formed an organized pursuit. And the Koalitsiya needed Isaak more than it needed her. She had long ago decided how much she was willing to give for the cause.

"Don't be a hero, Masha," Isaak said. "That's my job."

He dragged her down the street. Each step in their halting run made her grit her teeth in pain, but she refused to slow. She knew what would happen if the soldiers caught them; they both did. A cell in the Trubetskoy Bastion, where men whose life's work was making others talk would coax out every last secret they possessed. Where the Koalitsiya made its headquarters. Which members made up its ranks. Who spoke on behalf of the dockhands, who for the discharged soldiers. How their forces were organized, how news passed from one member to the next, how far they were willing to go. There was no question how it would end: with every soul that had ever so much as thought the word *Koalitsiya* buried in a shallow grave on the outskirts of the city, the ground too frozen even for carrion birds to peck through.

They cut sideways through an alley and emerged onto Kronverkskiy Prospekt, a wide boulevard glittering with the fading afternoon light. Citizens went about their business on both sides of the snowy street, their bodies swathed in rich furs and heavy fabric. One or two sent a disapproving glance toward Isaak and Marya—a young woman in the company of a man, unchaperoned and bareheaded, limping, blood dusting her knuckles, would be a scandal in most neighborhoods—before turning up their noses and keeping their distance. Their sneers meant nothing to Marya. At present, the only thing she cared an inch for was the sledge driver guiding his horse south down the boulevard, bearing a paltry load of root vegetables.

Isaak, spotting it at the same moment, raised a hand to hail the driver, but Marya was faster. She put two fingers in her mouth and let loose a piercing whistle, sharp enough that the horse nearly skidded to attention. The driver glanced their way, his beady eyes suspicious beneath his wolf-pelt hat.

"I don't run a charity service, *devushka*," he said coolly. "You keep to your business, and I'll keep to mine."

"Preobrazhenskaya Square," Marya said, hauling herself onto the open back of the sledge and watching Isaak clamber in after her. "Please. We'll pay double if you're fast."

That was all it took. The driver flicked his whip, and the sledge took off down the icy boulevard, leaving the district and their pursuers behind.

Marya slumped down against a wooden crate of what seemed to be turnips, her chin practically resting on her breastbone. Everything hurt. She'd be limping for days, and her heart still had not resumed its usual pace. Even the edges of her vision had begun to shudder, and she wondered if she might faint. But they were free. Away. And they'd achieved what they set out to do.

Beside her, Isaak reached into his satchel and produced a single copy of the pamphlet, with which he gestured at the driver.

"Think our new friend is interested in a strike?"

Marya looked at him in disbelief for three uninterrupted seconds. Then, with the near madness of two people who had been until recently running for their lives, they both began to laugh.

———

They left the driver with a sum of money twice as large as either of them could readily afford, along with a copy of the pamphlet for good measure, then set off. Their destination was several minutes' walking from where the sledge had left them, but they knew better than to lead anyone to the Koalitsiya's current sanctum, even someone as seemingly powerless as a driver. Everyone in Petersburg talked. Let one fact slip, and in three days there was no telling who else might know it.

"You're all right?" Isaak asked, watching her hesitant steps.

Marya winced. "Oh, just grand," she muttered. "Come here."

He offered her an arm, and she leaned heavily on him, letting his thin frame take half the weight off her leg. This close, she could sense the tension in his jaw and the firm set of his shoulders. Their narrow escape had shaken him, and it touched her that Isaak trusted her enough to let her see. She could count the number of people who knew that Isaak Mikhailovich felt fear on one hand.

Moving like one awkward three-legged creature, they ducked into a narrow building in the line of tight-packed town houses, taking the back courtyard entrance up to the third floor. The stairs were too narrow to walk two abreast, so Isaak followed behind, prepared to catch her if she fell, though she had no intention of doing so. Even from here, she could see the faint haze of warm air from the stove. Her sore bones yearned for the heat.

The sound of raised voices as she opened the door was decidedly less welcome. So much for a calm place to retreat to.

"I won't tell you again, Ilya," Irina was saying. "You can think whatever you want, but the moment you start saying it out loud, that's when you put us all in danger."

Isaak's wife stood at the central table in the lone room. Beside her was a tall dark-skinned woman in a soldier's coat, her face turned away. Even from the back, Marya felt a familiar warmth in her stomach at the sight of Yelena Arsenyevna—tempered with faint unease at what Lena would say when she learned of their escape. Marya knew Lena loved her, but she was also familiar with Lena's predisposition toward lecturing, and she certainly deserved the traditional "What did I tell you about being careful" speech on this particular occasion. But circumstances had conspired to spare her. Both Irina and Lena had their full attention on the wiry, bearded man in the flat cap who leaned forward with both hands on the table. Marya sighed and sank into one of the remaining chairs. Isaak, it seemed, hadn't come back a moment too soon.

"Just because you don't like it doesn't mean I'm not right," Ilya said. His voice, as ever, was well oiled with vodka, but Marya didn't hold that against him. Ilya Zherebetsky had had a hard war, and the two fingers missing from his left hand were a constant reminder of it. Cut off by a senior officer for dereliction of duty, Ilya had told them—attempted desertion before the slaughter at Smolensk that summer, Marya had learned later. "Keep wasting your time on this and you'll have just enough strength left to flinch as the tsar's boot crushes you."

"And you'd rather we what, exactly?" Irina said. From beside her, Marya could see her advancing pregnancy through her unbuttoned overcoat, but God forbid a small concern like growing a human inside her should cause Irina Aaronovna to sit down and let someone else do the fighting. "Storm the Winter Palace and cut their throats one by one?"

"It's no more than they deserve," Ilya said. "I don't expect you to understand, but I've seen what they've done. Death is too good for them."

Marya winced. This was not the way to convince Irina of anything. Lena, noticing her at last, moved behind Marya and laid a hand on each of her shoulders. Her fingers kneaded Marya's tight muscles, a pleasant pain that couldn't fully distract her from the fight brewing between Irina and Ilya but went some way toward softening its edges.

"You think I haven't lost anything?" Irina fired back—Marya's arrival certainly wasn't enough to dissuade her when she'd made up her mind to argue. "Maybe we have lost less than you, Ilya, if we still have brains enough to know a stupid idea when we hear it—"

"All right," Isaak said, raising both hands and stepping between his wife and Ilya. All the weariness from the street was gone now. This wasn't Isaak Mikhailovich the man anymore. This was Isaak the general: determined, inspired, unquestionable. To most of the Koalitsiya, this Isaak was the true one. The legendary commander they'd follow anywhere. It made Marya tired just to watch him, knowing the effort it took to become the leader they wanted.

"You tell her, then," Ilya said, thrusting one finger toward Irina. "Tell your wife what the Komarovs are capable of, and see if she's still so set on her damned half measures."

Isaak's dark eyes hardened. Even Marya, who knew him better than almost anyone, was afraid of what he might say next. She reached her right hand up to her left shoulder, and Lena took it. "My wife knows what we're working for," Isaak said coldly. "She came here from the Pale with me. Believe me, she knows."

Ilya scowled but changed tack instead of pressing the point. "Oh, I don't doubt you think you're doing what's right, but all this talk of striking? You know them. You can't think we'll get what we're after by asking kindly."

Ilya's conciliatory tone was too little, too late. The power had come into Isaak's posture now, and the fire into his eyes. In this mood, he wasn't only the leader of the Koalitsiya; he was liberation itself. He had the kind of vision that would live on in songs and legends, that made him impossible to argue with.

"You're a soldier, Ilya," Isaak said. "You think a battle's ever been won by rolling straight into enemy lines with the biggest cannon in your artillery and not caring who you hit on your own side? Just because we're not making a grand suicidal gesture doesn't mean I'm afraid. Can you say the same? It's the frightened dog that bites first."

Ilya lowered his eyes. Contrite for the moment, though obviously not convinced. Marya, however, was of Isaak's opinion on that subject: conviction could come later, so long as they had obedience now.

"Come on, man," Isaak said, and the sternness in his voice melted away, though the strength did not. "Enough of this. I need your help planning a watch over the rally, keep out any unwelcome ears. Put your tactical mind to work on that, and afterward we can talk about the future."

He drew Ilya aside, into a small alcove of the apartment where they could speak privately. Marya could see Ilya's pride ratcheting upward with each step, relishing the attention of being consulted personally. Isaak had that effect on people. Even if you disagreed with him, receiving his attention was like being smiled on by the sun in the dead of winter.

"One day," Irina grumbled, "I'm going to punch that man."

"If he doesn't come for you first," Lena said, shaking her head. She kissed Marya on the cheek, then took the remaining chair at the table, leaning forward to keep hold of Marya's hand. "Honestly, Irochka, you have to be careful with Ilya and his people."

"You don't have to like him, but we do need him," Marya agreed. "And if you keep antagonizing him, he'll walk, and take his soldiers with him."

"Don't do that," Lena said, her brow furrowing in what seemed to be both amusement and severity.

"Do what?"

"Try to pretend you're the reasonable one here. What happened? You and Isaak look like you just fought Bonaparte."

"Complications," Marya said wearily. "Don't go near Kronverkskiy Prospekt for a week or two, to be safe."

Irina swore and closed her eyes. "Did they see you?"

"I don't think so," Marya said. "They knew someone was there, but I don't think they'd recognize us by face. It could have been worse."

"Could have been better, too," Irina muttered.

"Take that up with your husband," Marya said. "Printing them up was his idea."

"Oh, I intend to. Once he's finished dealing with this disaster, I'll shout at him about the next one."

Marya laughed. No matter how dire matters got, Isaak and Irina would always be like this, each as annoyed with the other as they were in love with them. Lena had taught her how to understand that sort of love. Rolled eyes and an embrace could mean the same thing, from the right person. Exhaustion washed through Marya, kept at bay until now by adrenaline, and she allowed her eyes to droop. Lena drifted toward the window, where a basin of water rested on the ledge next to the Tverskys' silver sabbath candlesticks and three of Isaak's prized, battered books. Returning with the basin and a handkerchief, she nodded, and without being asked Marya placed her shredded palm in Lena's lap. Lena swirled the handkerchief in the basin, then washed away the blood and dirt with an artist's care. The water in the basin took on a pinkish tinge, reminding Marya oddly of poppies. Love could look like this, too. A bloodied handkerchief and a soft touch.

"It's not as bad as it looks," Marya said, though the chair made her bruised hip ache.

"It had better not be."

"We got what we went for. Other people would call that a success, you know."

Lena scoffed. "I'll congratulate you when you come home to me in one piece, which is all I've ever asked you to do."

This, of course, wasn't quite true. Lena and Marya had both asked a great deal of each other, those long nights they'd stayed up hours past midnight spinning utopian fantasies across the weak light of the candles. Those things, Marya had been only too happy to provide, and with only the slightest thought for her own reward.

Anything for another beat of affection from this statuesque woman with the short black hair that curled around her ears, her kind eyes, the future they were working for together.

"You'll let me have a look at that leg?" Lena asked.

Marya laughed. "What, take off my skirt in the middle of the room? Ilya might get the wrong idea, Lenochka."

Lena scoffed and swatted Marya with the damp cloth, which only made Marya laugh more. "Fine. Limp, then. At least you won't be working tomorrow."

Marya winced and shifted her weight. "Not tomorrow, no. The day after, maybe."

From the look Lena and Irina gave her, Marya was quickly running up on the line dividing "exasperating" and "the most stubborn creature on two legs." "We don't need the money as badly as that," Irina said.

"Really, I don't want you standing on that leg," Lena said.

"I won't be a burden," Marya said stubbornly, at a volume she mistakenly thought they couldn't hear.

"You aren't a burden, *kotik*," Lena murmured, the playful term of endearment landing sweetly on Marya's ear. "Maybe someday you'll accept that and let someone else take care of you, just once."

The softness in Lena's face, and the quiet worry in her deep-set eyes, was enough to wear down the last of Marya's defenses. She hadn't allowed herself to admit it until now—and wouldn't have to anyone but Lena, under pain of death—but the arrival of the soldiers had unsettled her. The Koalitsiya wouldn't achieve its goals without risk, but once the risk had been run, there was nothing to lose by letting down her guard for an evening and allowing herself to be cared for. She wasn't Isaak, wasn't the pure flame the Koalitsiya turned to for light. She was a piece of the machine, a secondary actor playing her part. And what ordinary person wasn't allowed to enjoy life's little pleasures when they happened along?

"Fine," she said, shifting the hem of her skirt. "Have a look at the leg?"

Sasha

Sasha paced the north hall of the Catherine Palace, his veins feeling as though they'd been traced with needles. He'd heard the stories before: his mother had told them, and his grandmother before her. All manner of wicked spirits roamed the world. Lake spirits, forest spirits, house spirits. Those that blessed, those that killed, and those that did both. By God, a demon had fallen from the sky, and he—like a damned fool—he'd brought the creature into the tsar's palace, given it a bed and a warm meal. Felix could laugh and deflect and call him a superstitious peasant all he wanted, but Sasha knew a threat when he saw one, and he'd turned it loose on the imperial family. He deserved to be taken behind the palace and shot.

But not yet. Felix had been brought up in the palace, coached to speak four languages and master the most fashionable dances known in Paris, but he'd never been given the slightest notion that anything might exist beyond what his European philosophers could explain. Sasha knew better. He knew that songs and tales persisted across the centuries for a reason.

As a warning, and as instruction.

The Catherine Palace seemed to close in around him, each high door concealing an adversary. At the front, it would have been different. Threats there were simple: hunger, cold, an enemy at the opposite end of the field with a rifle in hand and cannon fire beyond. Here, there was no telling what might come next. He paced like a caged creature, anxiety clawing at his skull, achingly aware of the woman somewhere in these same halls, preparing God knew what.

He paused at the end of the corridor, where a tall window over-looked the grounds. The Church of the Sign wasn't quite in view from here, but even a slow-moving petitioner could reach Tsar-skoe Selo's parish church within ten minutes.

There might be one place still the devil didn't dare go.

The first blast of cold hit him hard as he emerged onto the grounds, still pulling on his coat. He cursed through his teeth, his exasperation rising in a mist. A wind curled around him through the trees, like a man's soft hand against his cheek, late at night, in the lazy glow of a fire. What was it Felix had said, back in his private quarters at the Winter Palace, when he'd been the most shameless scoundrel in Petersburg and Sasha the young soldier given the impossible task of keeping him out of mischief? *You can be exhausting, Sashenka*, Felix had said, *but I know in the end you'll keep me safe. Whether or not I want you to.*

That was years ago, when Sasha was twenty-five and hungry for glory, and the idea of moving from his lonely regiment stationed in Novgorod to a post in the Komarov family's personal guard spoke to the part of him that yearned to be important, to matter. He'd stood in Palace Square with two dozen other soldiers under the hot July sun, blinking beads of sweat from his eyes as the impe-rial family passed in their inspection. The tsar, lofty, barely spar-ing a glance for the men he surveyed. The tsarevich, the picture of dedication, practically trembling with desperation to impress his father. And then Felix—Felix, who met Sasha's eye out of all the guardsmen standing there, and let the look linger, and smiled.

When the news came a week later that Grand Duke Felix had requested Sasha for his personal service, Sasha accepted the post as if in a dream. He fell into Felix's confidence with the sweet inevitability of drowning, following him far beyond duty into dark-curtained clubs and opera boxes with nothing more than a look for his invitation. The first time Felix kissed him—late at night, in a private room in the back of the English Club, into which God knew Sasha would never have been allowed without Felix at his side—it was simultaneously a stunning flash from heaven and the least surprising thing in the world. Sasha had lost control of his life the moment he saw Felix, the moment he fell for this shooting star of a man who burned bright and impulsive and heavenly.

When he'd enlisted in the Imperial Army at seventeen, he'd sworn to give his life for the safety of the Komarovs. But that night, the taste of wine he hadn't drunk on his lips, Sasha had sworn to do more than that for Felix. He'd give Felix every last drop of his strength and gladly, for the impossible pleasure of being useful, wanted, necessary.

And God, was his strength needed now, whether Felix could see it or not.

The Church of the Sign wasn't large: built like a two-story Petersburg town house, with a modest bell tower tacked onto the roof for a finishing touch of holy grandeur. Painted in soft peach and white, it had a charming, provincial look. Like a nobleman's idea of a country church, Sasha thought distantly, pulling the door open. He'd passed through enough villages at the front, seen enough peasant churches decimated and smoking from the French cannon. It might please the tsar to imagine that his people lived like this, but it would never be more than a pleasant dream.

Inside, the scent of incense hung heavy, left over from matins. Sasha crossed himself with three fingers as he entered, taking comfort in the ritual. The gilded faces on the iconostasis looked around and past him, rising floor to ceiling, solemn and flat and distant. So unlike Sofia, those golden eyes laughing, alive with challenge. The icon of Our Lady of the Sign had never hummed with such silent power as that woman had. Was that a fault of the painter? Or was it merely a reflection of the different sources of the women's strength: the one rooted in the divine, the other a wild, untamable energy?

No. God was his anchor, and he would hold to that. During the war, Sasha's religious devotion had drifted: there hadn't seemed much point in praying at the front, where the only evidence of God was that you were still alive to curse him. Now, though, the church had a strength to it, an iron core to support him. Aleksandr Dorokhin the infantry captain could count on his own strength in any earthly contest, but when Sasha the mortal man saw a woman command the snow and wind, stronger intervention was required.

Another man might have chosen to address his prayer to a different icon, one more suited to the task at hand, but for Sasha, one saint had always seemed more likely to listen to him than the others. He drifted to the left of the iconostasis, where the golden face and stern brow of Saint Aleksandr Nevsky regarded him at a sharp, almost disdainful angle. The icon was beautifully made, though beginning to blacken and fade with age and heavy use. The great man—Russia's grandest military hero, the legendary savior of medieval Rus'—was dressed for battle even in his holy portrait, a fur cloak draped across a glittering breastplate, his gauntleted right hand over his heart in a pledge of fidelity to God and tsar. It was not an uncommon portrait, but even so, Sasha felt power flutter through him at the sight of it.

This man was his namesake. This man rescued his country from unimaginable danger. This man let nothing frighten him. If Sasha could derive only one quality from his patron saint, let it be that: the courage to look danger in the face and make a stand.

He took a burning candle from the rail beneath the icon and lit another with its flame. The candle flared as the light absorbed a second wick, a quick hiss of searing brightness that settled into two self-contained peaks of light. Something from nothing. Wasn't that the nature of a miracle? Each movement here was prescribed: how many fingers to cross with, when to kiss the hands of the painted saint, when to bow, the proper cadence of the prayer. He bent his head to the icon, breathing deeply the thick air of the silent church. Ordinarily he would pray in quiet, but the empty space seemed to beckon his voice, thin and lonely though it was.

"Saint Aleksandr Nevsky, Holy Mother of God, and all the

saints, please, pray unto God for me, for the tsar, and for Grand Duke Felix."

Felix would have laughed to know Sasha prayed on his behalf. *You're wasting your breath*, he'd have said. *I sin so many times before breakfast God must have deafened Himself to my name by now.* That amused, mocking smirk on the grand duke's face, the same one that had tugged at his lips when he dismissed Sasha's warning as superstition. The common man with his mindless faith and his ancient tales, leaving crumbs out at the stove to feed the domovoi. A ridiculous, unenlightened way to live.

The memory of a window flung open, glass rattling against iron. Snow spread across a carpet, across Felix's shoulders. Sofia's sharp bright eyes, intent as an owl, waiting.

If Felix thought him ridiculous, so be it. That didn't stop him from being right.

"Saint Aleksandr Nevsky, please, defend the imperial family from this creature, protect them from—"

A shiver, and then every last candle in the Church of the Sign went dark.

The temperature had plunged in the space of a breath; even his overcoat was no longer enough to ward off the chill. Heavy curtains covered the windows, and though outside the morning sun must have shone as brilliantly as ever, the shadows were as thick as evening. And through the darkness, a whisper, as though the speaker were just behind him, close enough to touch.

"Protect them from what?"

Sasha whirled away from the icon, reaching for his pistol. But there was nothing at his belt, and nothing behind him. Only a frightened, unarmed man with trembling hands, and the vast expanse of an empty church, preternaturally dim, utterly silent.

This wasn't the first time Sasha had wondered if he was going mad. Nightmares no longer did him the courtesy of waiting for sleep before rearing their heads. The smallest disturbance could call them up, stronger than a memory and too real to ignore: the scent of rotten flesh, the thunder of cannon. This was the same, nothing more. Sasha had slept poorly the night before, and now with Sofia consuming his unsettled thoughts, little wonder he would hear her voice. He'd imagined it, that was all. His mind was still rattled from fighting and from shock.

And the candles?

Candles were objects of fire and air, not of spirit. A candle in a church might gutter out for any number of reasons.

A candle, yes. But fifty . . .

Sasha turned back to the icon. "Saint Aleksandr Nevsky," he began again, his voice firmer now, more determined. "Hear my prayer, and protect the tsar and the grand duke from any and all evil. Show me what I must do to protect them, in your name—"

"No one is listening to you."

The voice was closer this time. And when it spoke next, the sound was as close as if the speaker had rested their chin on Sasha's shoulder to whisper in his ear.

"No one but me."

Sasha flinched, shielding his face with a hand. Nothing there but the empty church. His breathing rasped loud in his ears. Every shadow might have held a thousand spirits. He grasped at the frayed ends of his prayer, but the words danced away, vanishing in the face of these thick shadows, that invisible voice.

A flicker of movement from behind the iconostasis, smooth and light as a woman's footfalls.

Someone else was here.

Sasha crossed himself and ran to the door. The thin slice of light between the door and the floor promised freedom, promised breath, promised silence, where whatever sought to drive him from the church could not touch him—

He flung the door open and found himself less than a foot from Sofia Azarova.

It was all he could do to tamp down a cry. Sofia was dressed for the weather now, with a black fur-lined coat that fell to her ankles and thick gloves. Her pallor made her look like a breath of snow in a pool of darkness, cut through by those amber eyes. She smiled to see him and gave a half curtsey, lowering the bottom of her coat into the snow. Her fresh-woven plait hung over her shoulder like a general's ceremonial braid.

"I'm sorry to interrupt, Captain Dorokhin," she said. "A servant told me the Church of the Sign was a marvel, so I thought I would look for myself. But if you were at prayer, certainly I can leave you to your devotions."

Her voice was light and easy, nothing like the horrid whisper he had left behind. Even so, Sasha's skin crawled at the sound of it.

"What do you want with the grand duke?" His voice emerged rough and breathless.

Before, Sofia's smile had been pleasant. Now it was colder than the bitterest wind. "What a question, Captain," she said. "I can't think what you mean."

"You know what I mean. You—"

The laugh Sofia gave then was more unsettling than any whispering movement from the depths of a darkened church. "Oh, my dear Sasha," she said, and she rested one gloved hand on his forearm before he could jerk away. Her touch, even through the gloves, was cold enough to burn. "That's quite enough of that, don't you think? I'll attend to my business with the grand duke, and you will attend to yours."

She squeezed his forearm once, then brushed past him into the dark church. No, not dark—the candles were aflame again, and their light sent sparks dancing across the gold crowning the saints' faces. He had only another moment to look for the stern brow of Aleksandr Nevsky in the depths of the church before the door closed behind Sofia, and he was left alone, staring at inexpressive wood.

Mad.

Was it possible?

Ice flooding from a woman's upturned palms. Footsteps through the darkness. A demon, whispering in his ear. If a man had approached him at the front and said he'd heard the voice of a vila in an empty church, he'd have had the soldier requisitioned for insanity, sent to some adjunct position behind a desk where he could do no harm.

But no, it was not madness. Felix had seen it too. The threat of the Grande Armée had been neutralized, but this power that faced them now was no less real, the possible threat even more serious.

Felix would never forgive him if Sasha followed through with what he was considering. For all the tumultuousness of Sasha and Felix's—what? relationship? entanglement? affair?—neither of them had any desire to hurt the other. They shared the same potent secret, which created a kind of faith that cut deep when broken. Felix thought Sofia was his guest, a fascination, a visiting power to be entertained. And Sasha would go behind his back to expose her, destroying not just the laws of hospitality and rank, but trust too.

Sasha had sworn to keep Felix safe no matter what. If this was what it took to keep that oath, so be it.

As he crossed the park back toward the palace, it felt as though the church itself watched him go.

5

Felix

It became clearer by the day that Felix had never met anyone like Sofia before. Her presence helped to offset Sasha's sudden absence, for it seemed that the mere mention of the pale-haired woman was enough to make him vanish. It was all deeply irritating, and irrational on top of it. The old stories were full of spirits—the domovoi, the banniki, the vila—but they were *stories*, not descriptions of everyday life. Felix knew that war had made Sasha prickly at best, but the least he could do was be civil to the woman. Fortunately, Felix knew enough about being an impeccable host for the both of them.

He spent most days alone with Sofia, their afternoons together melting into evenings that became night with a thief's secrecy. She never spoke about where she'd come from, and Felix considered it impolite to ask, but she adjusted to palace life as if its luxury were as mundane to her as it was to him. By the second day of her recovery, she was sitting sideways in a silk-upholstered armchair, her long hair tossed into a loose braid, smoking an ivory pipe like a common muzhik while they talked about the French novel she had borrowed from the palace library or Felix's two-year-long quest to find a satisfactory chef. At her request, Felix had gathered the simplest garments his servants could scrounge from the palace's wardrobes, loose-fitting morning gowns in black and dove gray and pearl, the kind of heavy shawls that would have made anyone else look like a grandmother but on her looked as if they'd come from an expensive couturier. When she was nearby, the richness of the palace seemed pathetic. Felix felt that he might punch a fist through the finery of his own sitting room and send the whole production crashing to the floor, like the scenery of some provincial play. Before long, they began to move their conversations outdoors. The park surrounding the Catherine Palace was no less artificial, but at least it imitated nature more skillfully.

Today, their walk led them south, along the rim of the great pond that marked the formal border of the tsar's private estate. It was a beautiful day, clear and cold, the new snow on the pond undisturbed by bird or beast. A companionable quiet sat comfortably between them—a novelty for Felix, who had always considered silence a sort of failed conversation—until Sofia, gradually guiding their steps east, spoke first.

"Kutuzov drove the last of the Grande Armée out of Vilnius a few days ago. They'll be fully across the Niemen by now, though they won't stop running till Paris."

This was news to Felix. The conflict between his father and Emperor Napoleon had lost all interest for him now that Sasha had returned. International politics was his father's concern and his brother's pet interest. The last time Felix had shown any enthusiasm for the business of governing Russia, the tsar had all but taken Felix by the collar and dragged him from the council chamber for having the temerity to agree with the chairman of the State Council that the tsar's current approach to rationing could lead to popular uprisings before the year was out. Of course, the opposite approach had done him no favors either: he'd gone directly from the council chamber to the servants' wing, and—Sasha attending to other business at the time—thoroughly distracted himself with two of the better-looking palace laundresses. Which led to quick detection, the dismissal of both laundresses, and Felix's undignified exile to Tsarskoe Selo, in that order. So in a way, Felix reasoned, it was displaying an interest in politics that had gotten him exiled in the first place. It wasn't a mistake he intended to repeat.

"Bravo, General Kutuzov," he said. "I hadn't heard. It takes more effort to keep up with the news when I'm so far from the city."

Tsarskoe Selo was fifteen miles at most from Petersburg, and from Sofia's scoff, she didn't intend to let him forget it. "And I'm sure you put in so much effort when you lived in the capital."

"Have I mentioned I like it when you shout at me?" Felix winked. "It's quite stirring."

"I'm glad one of us enjoys it. Come on," she added, gesturing along the road. "How do you feel about warming up?"

Felix followed her gesture until he sighted the bathhouse ahead of them, a respectable-looking building painted white and pale orange, within shouting distance of the palace. He laughed. "Together? Well, of course. I've wasted the day if I haven't scandalized an entire court before the end of it."

He expected her to ignore this as she'd ignored his prior insincere flirtation. Instead, she frowned. "I didn't think you cared what others thought about you."

Felix swallowed an indignant reply. Of course he didn't care. He couldn't afford to, not after his father had banished him from court, out of sight and out of trouble. Caring what people thought only promised disappointment. Tsarskoe Selo was practically his own kingdom, and here no one's opinions mattered but his.

Except for Sofia. He cared deeply what she thought of him.

Not in that way—or at least not *only* in that way. Yes, she'd be one of the most beautiful people he'd brought to his bed, if it came to that. But his attraction to her had been brushed aside after a few short minutes. What he wanted now was simply to be around her, with her, part of her, dissolving the barriers between them any way he could. And if social convention was one of those barriers, well then, adieu convention.

The bathhouse door opened onto a small antechamber with fine linen towels folded on a stool and pegs along the walls for bathers to hang their clothes. There had been an attendant at one point, but Felix had shifted him to a different post a year ago—with the kind of activities Felix tended to use the bathhouse for, a spectator was explicitly not wanted. He looked at Sofia, intending to pace the extent of his disrobing against hers. Just outerwear, perhaps, if she seemed concerned with modesty . . .

He quickly turned away. Sofia had already begun to peel off her clothes and showed no intention of stopping. He followed her lead. Gloves first, then coat, her fur hat left on the floor like a small animal that had crawled in from the cold. Boots, stockings, then— with increasing hesitation—Felix pulled off his waistcoat, and cautiously undid the buttons at the cuffs of his Parisian shirt.

Christ. And now what?

Nudity had never bothered Felix; Sasha used to joke that Felix spent at least a quarter of his waking life naked. Add in the steam of the bathhouse and the outcome seemed inevitable. But for the first time in many years, Felix found himself uncertain. He frowned, irritated. Nerves were ridiculous, he told himself, stripping the rest of the way and hastily wrapping a towel around his waist. This was a bathhouse; this was what people did. The fact that he'd reached for a towel at all would be considered unbearably prudish in most circles. Besides, he'd sweat to death in ten minutes otherwise.

"Can I—" he began awkwardly.

"Of course," she said. "You took your time."

Red-faced even before the steam, Felix turned. Sofia wore nothing but the towel. He found his eyes lingering on her exposed knees, the length of her calves, then forced himself to look at the single spider crawling along the joint between wall and ceiling. He felt like he'd been caught pissing outdoors by a priest.

In the central room of the bathhouse, the air felt luxuriously thick, each breath slow. The stove at the center of the room was alive with heat, and Sofia doused the hot coals with water from the bucket beside it. A rush of steam spilled upward, followed by a smooth waft of warmth in defiance of the gut-piercing cold outside.

Felix sat on the bench beside Sofia and leaned his head against the wall. The steam rose around them, blurring her edges and adding a veneer of anonymity to the encounter. He couldn't stop thinking of the half foot between his unclothed body and hers. When was the last time Felix had felt *flustered* like this? Surely not in adulthood. This feeling belonged to a fifteen-year-old boy.

"I'm surprised your father didn't invite you back to Petersburg," Sofia said. "Given the victory." The words seemed almost disembodied, drifting through the steam. It was the first time since her arrival that Sofia had raised a subject he did not want to discuss.

Felix wiped his palm across his mouth, brushing a trail of sweat from his upper lip. "Why on earth does that surprise you? My father wants nothing to do with me. Frankly, I'm surprised he only exiled me here and not to Sevastopol."

"I know you don't get on," she said—Felix laughed, genuinely amused by the understatement of his father's disdain for his existence as "not getting on"—"but you've won the war, haven't you? Flaunted the Komarovs' control of every handful of dirt in the empire? Aren't they celebrating in the capital?"

No doubt they would be. Felix's father had an inexhaustible supply of money and a fearsome pride in his country, which inevitably added up to celebrations on the grandest scale. Felix could picture it now: the capital alight with lamps and fireworks, a ball in every ballroom, women in impossibly brilliant gowns packed four to a carriage. Tsarevich Anatoli and his beautiful Prussian wife leading off the first dance, the empire's golden children, the promised future. The Winter Palace was at its best during a party, every facet of its gemlike face polished to a shine. Petersburg had been built from nothing overnight to give the wealthy somewhere to peacock. And Felix would be here, in exile. A dozen miles away, but it might as well have been a thousand. Rotting here alone, while the country rejoiced.

Sofia leaned forward, her forearms on her thighs, and watched him intently. She watched him in a way no one had ever watched him before. He was no stranger to people looking at him, but that sort of attention was for a performance, the character of Felix rather than his essence. Sofia looked at him now, not at a grand duke. With a blend of respect and curiosity, as if he had earned his power but not yet revealed his next move.

"You could do it yourself, you know," she said.

"Do what myself?"

"Celebrate the victory," she answered. "Be the strong, triumphant prince they want. Don't you think your people deserve that?"

Under other circumstances, Felix's response would have been a thoughtless and immediate yes. He loved a party the way he loved anything else that made him feel purely and utterly alive, and it had been so long since Russia had anything worth celebrating. He could host a victory ball like no one else in the country, one to rival his father's.

That, of course, was the trouble.

"My father would never allow it," he said. To his disgust, he found himself jogging his left foot against the floor.

Sofia shook her head, and her hair—damp from both melting snow and a trickle of sweat that beaded down her cheek—rippled with the movement. In its loose strands, Felix saw feathers, saw fur, saw scales. "I don't recall asking your father," she said. "I asked you."

The thought was foolish, dangerous, but tempting. It was ridiculous, after all, for someone within arm's reach of the throne to hide and cringe at his father's will. He was nearly thirty now. No longer a child.

"You have the Catherine Palace," Sofia said, as if she knew his thoughts. "It's not Petersburg, but it could be so much more than what you've made it."

A capital of his own. As if his father's banishment had been a test and not a punishment. He could take the reins of this little secondary court, and the people here might see him as a person worth listening to. Instead of shame, they might associate him with victory, heroism, triumph.

"The people would be thrilled to see it," she said casually, though there was nothing at all casual about the light in her eyes, which sliced through the steam like a saber. "First, the grand duke commanding the Catherine Palace. Then, who knows? The council chamber?"

The thoughts in Felix's head didn't feel like his. But they fit there so neatly, as though Sofia had carved a place for them to live. In her eyes, he could see himself reflected back, the wings of the double-headed eagle sprouting from his own shoulders. A man who governed for his country and not himself, one who put domestic concerns before foreign wars. One who could help the people when they needed it. One the people loved as well as feared.

If Felix were tsar, he'd be a man worth respecting.

A coal clattered to the bottom of the iron stove. Felix flinched, and they were only two people again, sitting together in the swirling steam of the bathhouse. He blew out a long breath, then stood, securing the towel at his waist with one hand. It must have been the heat. Sending his thoughts into corners they had no business exploring.

"A ball," he said, as if nothing they'd spoken of since that idea had been worth mentioning. His voice seemed to bring them both back to earth. "Yes. It's a good thought."

Sofia grinned like a mischievous schoolchild as she stood up. "I know," she said. "I don't have bad ones."

He laughed and followed her into the antechamber. His back to her, he reached for his shirt, hastily pulling it over his sweat-damp chest. Dressing was no less awkward than undressing had been. He laced his boots and waited a great deal longer than necessary before turning to face her.

"Would you help me with the planning?" he said. "Since you're possessed of so many brilliant ideas."

"I'll be here if you need me," she answered. "But I don't think you will. As far as I can tell, you're perfectly equipped to manage this yourself."

"Time will tell," he said wryly, and he opened the door to a gust of freezing air.

Almost immediately, a sharp voice rang out across the park. "Felix!"

Sasha. Dressed in his dark green overcoat, he veered off the path, taking the most direct route through powdery snow in their direction. Felix turned toward the door to the bathhouse, but there was no one behind him, and the only footsteps in the snow were his own. Felix craned his neck back just in time to see a snowy owl beat its wings, gaining altitude as it soared north, above and past the palace. It filled him with a strange urge to cross himself.

Was it—

Certainly not. Sasha was the superstitious one, not him. *Mère de Dieu*, but foolishness must have been contagious.

"Good afternoon," Felix said cheerfully, sweeping the unease from his mind as easily as a layer of dust.

Sasha emerged from the snow onto the path. The powder clung to the coat, forming tiny clumps along the hem. "What were you doing with her?"

"With whom?" Felix made a great show of checking over his shoulder. Sofia did not materialize—frankly, if Felix had known an irritable soldier was waiting for him on the threshold, he wouldn't have come out either.

Sasha clenched his jaw so tightly a single vein rose along his temple. It must have taken all his strength to keep his voice as level as he did. "Felix, I mean it. I don't trust her. I don't know what she wants with you, but it can't be good."

Irritation flicked in Felix like a cat's tail. Surely it wasn't madness to think that another person took Felix seriously, and believed the rest of the country might too. "Sasha, it's all right," he said testily. "You don't have to like her. But at least trust that I know what I'm doing?"

With one last, cold look at the bathhouse, Sasha turned back to the Catherine Palace. He walked slowly, clearly expecting Felix to follow but too proud to turn and make sure of it. Felix watched him go. With every step, Sasha became smaller and less familiar, until in less than a minute Felix felt he was looking at a man he hardly knew at all.

When Sasha was nearly out of sight, Felix turned north, along the cleared path running through the park. The cold had already sunk its fingers into him, but he had no desire to return to the palace just yet.

Sofia saw him, not the way he was now, but the way he could be. No one else had ever done that.

Privately, and with a fervor that startled him, he hoped her vision was right.

PRINCE IVAN AND HIS HORSE

Long, long ago, beyond the high ridges of the Carpathians, a king ruled over his kingdom with unyielding severity. His people felt little love for him, and under his reign the crops struggled to grow, and snow remained on the ground until the spring was nearly gone. It was thought that the spirits of the clouds and sky and sea had turned their backs on the king and left the kingdom in darkness. But on the day when the queen bore the king a son, it seemed the spirits smiled again. By fifteen, the young Prince Ivan could wield the sword and bow with more skill than men twice his age. His mother glowed with pride, but his father watched him warily, for he was jealous of the prince's strength and wisdom, and he knew that the kingdom loved its prince in a way it would never love its king. So it happened that when the boy came of age, his father sent him out into the world to make his fortune, with the unspoken hope that his son would never return.

Prince Ivan wandered far and wide in the woods, and despite the many dangers, he felt no fear. The wolves and bears knew better than to cross him, and so he walked easily, meeting no one but birds and martens and mice. He went undisturbed until the seventh day, when he heard the snap of a branch behind him. He turned, and there at the end of the path stood a vila, framed by the trees. Her long white hair was loose, and she wore no shoes. She had just landed from flight—her wings folded into her back and disappeared as he watched.

"We knew you'd come, my prince," said the vila.

"What do you know of me?" Ivan asked, for he had never seen a vila before, and it seemed impossible that he could have been expected—he himself did not even know where he was. The thought crossed his mind that his father had sent this creature to test him, perhaps hoping he would fail—perhaps hoping the vila would tear him to pieces. But if the vila wanted to attack him, would she not have done so by now? Instead, she remained where she was, merely watching.

"Oh, we all know of you," the vila said, with a laugh like the rustle of leaves. "You were born in our city, in our forest, under our clouds. And you have nearly everything you need to be the hero you were meant to be."

Ivan frowned, for he was a prince and did not at all like the thought of having *nearly* everything. "Why, what am I missing?"

The vila smiled and gestured behind him. "What good is a prince without his horse?"

Ivan turned just in time to see the fallen tree limbs and pine needles and crushed leaves that littered the forest floor move, like a dog's nose twitching at a new scent. And then they rose, and knitted themselves together, and before his wondering eyes they became the most magnificent horse he had ever seen. A grand piebald beast, fully seventeen hands, with brilliant glittering eyes and a coat like the view of the sky through the forest canopy. Quivering blue flames curled from his nostrils with each breath, and though his hooves raked the forest floor, he was silent as the shadows.

"Treat him well," said the vila, "for he was made for you."

The prince reached out tentatively, and the horse bent as if bowing, permitting the prince to stroke his muzzle. The horse's skin was impossibly soft, finer than the finest velvet. Ivan had never felt so close to another being, as though the beast were an extension of his own soul.

"Why have you given him to me?" he asked.

The vila fixed the prince with a look he would never forget, not for a single day of his long, long life. "Because your people are suffering, my prince. They need a hero. And I have decided that it will be you."

Before Ivan could protest, wings sprang again from the vila's shoulders. Color paled, fabric shredded, limbs shrank and nose sharpened in a flash of cloth and skin and feather and bone. The vila was gone, and in her place a snowy owl, who took wing and disappeared between the gaps in the trees.

The vila, as all lovers of tales know, had not chosen wrongly. The adventures of Prince Ivan and his magnificent horse are known throughout the wide world, far beyond the craggy tops of the Carpathians. But what the prince thought as he stood alone with his horse in the forest that day, the creature's breath sparking against his hand, is not recorded in those tales.

6

Marya

Early morning was the best time to pay a visit to Alevtina Vladi-mirovna. The clientele of the dusty pawnshop on the edge of the Apraksin Market shifted by the hour as the day went on. Tired mothers and young men who'd tried and failed to make a fortune at the card table filled the shop by afternoon, giving way to less-savory characters looking to earn a coin off ill-gotten gains by nightfall. Marya's weekly meeting with the pawnbroker gener-ally wasn't illegal in the strictest sense, but she still appreciated the quiet of the shop just before sunrise, when scattered candles cast a bronze glow over the shelves of marooned possessions and gave them the dignity of artifacts in a museum. Besides, Marya had learned through experience that Alevtina's mood tended to sour the longer the day went on, and the price she was willing to offer dipped accordingly. The slight annoyance of waking before the sun paid double.

A bell above the door tinkled her arrival as she entered the shop. Brushing a film of snow from the shoulders of her deep-pocketed coat, Marya wove through the mess of tea tables, chiffoniers, and paintings of dubious authenticity that littered the shop-room floor. Mediocre quality, all of them. Alevtina's wasn't a shop for the well-to-do; it was for working-class people pawning the last of the family heirlooms for enough money to make ends meet for one more week. There was a sadness to it, the familiar illogical mel-ancholy of lost objects, but also a kind of ragged dignity. This settee had once served a proud, capable woman, and with any luck it would do so again.

Marya crossed the shop without disturbing the merchandise and rested her elbows on the counter. Behind it, in a chaotically arranged kingdom of her own making, sat Alevtina Vladimirovna, nursing a cup of tea and swathed in so many scarves it was impossible to approximate the shape and size of her body.

"*Dobroye utro,*" Marya said when it became clear Alevtina would not greet her, and she began to empty her pockets onto the counter.

Alevtina didn't look up. The pawnbroker tended to reserve visible displays of interest for large items—the kind Marya had to sling over her shoulder in a canvas bag, or recruit Isaak or Lena to help her haul across the length of the city. They both knew the rule as well as anyone, though: the size of a find had no bearing on its value.

"How much is stolen this time?" Alevtina said into her tea, which no doubt contained more than a healthy splash of spirits despite the hour.

"Not much," Marya responded hotly. "Barely any."

Alevtina scoffed, but Marya wasn't lying. In truth, the only item she'd stolen that week was the savonnette pocket watch, which she laid now on the counter with not a little pride. It was lovely, with an intricate sunburst design etched into the case, and she felt a pang of regret as she set it down. This beauty had been hanging from the fob of an unobservant gentleman chatting in Nevsky Prospekt late Monday afternoon, and Marya sincerely doubted the fop had even noticed its absence.

The rest had been obtained in the usual manner: by barter, favor, or luck. The city's aboveground economy was a harsh mistress, but Marya knew how to navigate the underground one like a harpist plying the strings. A harried mother of three would pay a packet of tobacco for someone to hold her place in line for bread while she kept an appointment. Then, a soldier itching for a smoke would offer up a pair of his lover's silk gloves, and a ballet dancer hoping to impress a gentleman in one of the finer opera boxes would trade for the gloves, offering a fur coat another suitor had once left behind, and who in Petersburg didn't know someone in need of a good fur? It was a quick-moving business that paid Marya's keep, and if Alevtina Vladimirovna raised a thinly penciled eyebrow at one or two of the more brazen wares she tried to pawn, well, at least the proprietress rarely questioned an object's provenance if she could make it turn a profit.

It was a way of evening the stakes, she told herself. Connecting the dispossessed with the resources they needed to live. And there were worse ways to make a living. The Tverskys insisted she could stay with them for free, that her contribution to the Koalitsiya's political activities was enough, but pride was a fierce animal, and it had to be sated somehow.

"How much?" Marya said, as Alevtina turned the watch over and back in her hands.

The pawnbroker brought the watch to her ear, listening for the steady heartbeat of a tick. Marya knew it sounded regularly—the fop had taken fastidious care of his possessions, though he'd failed to keep a careful eye on them when it mattered. "I can give you a hundred for this," Alevtina said, "and for the rest, eighty together?"

"You'll give me two hundred and fifty for the lot, or I'll take it elsewhere," Marya said.

She reached for the watch, but Alevtina snatched it away like a dog guarding a bone. Marya smirked.

"I'm already giving you a better price because I like you," the pawnbroker said. "Learn to settle for good enough."

"I'm asking what it's worth, and you know it," Marya replied. "Two hundred fifty or I walk."

Alevtina sighed, then took a long swig of her rapidly cooling tea. "Two hundred ten. It's the best I can do."

"Done," Marya said. It wasn't worth that—Alevtina was right, the original offer had been generous—but the only way you kept your head above water in this world was by knowing how to drive a hard bargain. After so long working this connection, she knew exactly how far she could afford to push.

She passed the remainder of her items across the counter, and Alevtina whisked them away as fast as a conjurer. Her hands slowed considerably in the act of counting out the money. Marya watched each banknote as Alevtina extracted them from her clip, feeling their value like a physical weight at the base of her ribs. It was good for a week's take. Enough to make up for the slow week that had come before and to take some of the pressure off the week to come. But the deal wouldn't be over until the door had closed behind her.

"While I have you," Alevtina said, as she laid the last of the banknotes on the dirty counter. "There's something I wanted to ask you about."

Marya snatched up the money and tucked it into the pocket of her coat before Alevtina could change her mind. "If Nikolai still wants someone to nick the brass globe from Baranovsky's shop window," she said wearily, "I've told you both, I'm not in that business anymore, and I don't appreciate the insinuation."

"Not that." Alevtina clicked her tongue, then took an object from beneath the counter, wrapped in creased paper. "This."

The object, divested of its paper, proved to be a beautiful sphere-shaped snuffbox with the imperial double eagle etched across the lid. Marya suppressed the urge to whistle. Had Alevtina found a supplier with a direct connection to the palace? Their working relationship was strong, but if a disillusioned footman had taken to pocketing odds and ends from the Winter Palace, Marya's usefulness in Alevtina's eyes would quickly lose its luster.

Alevtina, however, took the snuffbox back and replaced it under the counter, then pushed the wrapping paper across the counter toward Marya.

She recognized it instantly. It was one of the copies of the pamphlet they'd made at the printer's, before the Semyonovsky Regiment sent them scrambling. It was true, what Irina said: you couldn't count on anyone for anything in this life, but you could count on salacious news to spread, and Alevtina Vladimirovna would always be quick to lay hands on a piece of information that could benefit her. Marya read slowly and with difficulty, but they'd taken care to make this paper shout its opinions to the world, and the words leapt out at her now in the dim shop. *Your work sustains this city, but you receive nothing in return. Make yourself heard. Strike, and demand what every citizen deserves. Wages. Safety. Bread. A choice.*

"I don't suppose that fancy-talking man who isn't your husband has anything to do with this," Alevtina said, tapping one square fingertip against the word *strike*.

"As Isaak isn't my husband," Marya said airily, "I wouldn't know. Why? Does it interest you?"

Alevtina clicked her tongue, but her dark brown eyes glinted. "You know me, Masha. Anything with a potential for profit interests me."

It wasn't a yes, but it wasn't a no either, and by now Marya knew whom she could trust. Marya was one of Alevtina's best runners. She wouldn't hand Marya over to the soldiers, no matter what reformist tendencies she suspected her of. There was too much money to be made in looking the other way. And she wouldn't have asked if the notion hadn't appealed to her. A pawnbroker knew better than most the lengths working people were driven to in the city to stay alive.

"It isn't the first I've heard about this striking business, either," Alevtina added, creasing the paper neatly down the middle.

Marya's heart didn't stop so much as trip on its way from one beat to the next. "You know this city loves its gossip," she said lightly. "Can't believe half of what you hear. Some people will accuse their neighbors of anything to make themselves look loyal to the tsar."

"At ease, Masha," Alevtina said. "I get all sorts here. Former soldiers, mostly, and those fellows who were professors before the war shut down the university. Two groups that can't keep secrets, as you well know."

She sighed. Ilya, no doubt. And she'd wager fifty of her new-earned rubles that at least one of the professors had been Pyotr Stepanovich, a well-meaning middle-aged philosopher who dealt out rumors like they'd burn his palms if he held on to them too long. She'd have words with Petrushka next time he turned up at a meeting, that much was certain. Pointed words about the value of discretion.

"Enough to make you wonder why we tell men anything of importance," Marya said. She had already begun to do up the buttons of her coat, signaling with each flick of her wrist that the conversation was drawing to a close. "But if you wanted to get a clearer picture of the situation, I've heard the fellow who printed up those pamphlets will be speaking on Vasilevsky Island on Friday evening. Ten o'clock. Kadetskaya Liniya, the old university hall. If you think you might see profit in what he has to say."

Alevtina narrowed her eyes. "Do you?"

"I'm sure I have no idea," Marya said breezily. "You're the one with the eye for what things are worth."

As she left the shop, the bell above the door tinged merrily. A good omen, she hoped.

The sunrise was beginning to crest the rooftops of Petersburg as Marya crossed Sadovaya Street and made her way back west toward the Neva. She rubbed her hands together, relishing the resulting warmth even through her gloves. More than two hundred rubles, and another body at Isaak's rally on Friday to boot, plus all the people the well-connected—and, more importantly, cautious—Alevtina Vladimirovna might bring with her. It wasn't at all bad for a morning's work. Still, the unchecked spread of what she'd considered privileged information would have to be addressed. The Koalitsiya might have achieved its aims in a week if it really was the united coalition its name suggested, rather than a ragtag collection of people who, apparently, couldn't be trusted to keep their mouths shut. Passing an invitation to Alevtina was all very well, but it only took one poor judgment of character for everything to collapse.

Marya wove her way back through the increasingly crowded streets. Shopkeepers and servants were setting about the true business of the morning, and more than one messenger skidded on slick streets in their haste to pass a letter from one count or prince to the next. Illicit trysts were planned, business dealings argued over, family quarrels escalated to the point of duels at dawn. In a way, the messengers carried the lifeblood of the city in their pockets, hidden in folded and sealed letters they themselves would never read.

In another, much more real way, the lifeblood of the city hummed through Marya's veins, and through the ink of the pamphlet now hidden beneath Alevtina Vladimirovna's counter.

Bolstered by her success, Marya tilted her head back and admired the pale gray of the morning sky. Overhead, the clouds shifted in the wake of an easterly breeze off the harbor, alluding to snow more than threatening it. Far off, Marya could see the brilliant white of some great creature—an osprey, perhaps, or an owl, with a majestic wingspan, each feather catching the light of dawn as if they'd positioned themselves perfectly to do so. An incomparable hunter, giving the city one final salute before retreating to her darkness to wait out the day. Marya felt the urge to salute.

Instead, she jammed her hands in her pockets, feeling the reassuring crunch of banknotes against her fingers. The day was young, and there were more deals to be struck before she was through.

7

Felix

Sound and motion spilled from the Hall of Lights. From within, the string quartet Felix had brought to the Catherine Palace from Petersburg conjured up the strident rhythm of a polonaise, the stern line of the cello emulating the rumble of an army on the march. Felix took a step toward the open double doors, examining his reflection in one of the countless mirrored walls. His navy-blue jacket had arrived the day before from one of the choicest French tailors in Petersburg, and his waistcoat was edged with thread of gold, which caught the light at every turn. Each of the Grand Dukes Felix in the endless recursion of mirrors looked handsome, well-dressed, impeccable. But he didn't just want to look good. He wanted to look stunning. Like a man who deserved the glory of victory.

"This is what you were born for," he said to the phalanx of reflected selves in the mirror. "Show them." The acoustics were good in this part of the palace, making his voice sound authoritative. Almost confident enough to convince himself.

He took a breath, then entered the ballroom to a swirl of color and light.

High ceilinged and vast, the Hall of Lights still felt intimate—a testament to the long-ago architects who'd built it, and to the staff he'd set to work arranging the evening. The arched floor-to-ceiling windows showed only the night sky blanketing the grounds, the park itself lost to view, but every sconce and candelabra housed expensive wax candles that gave the room a soft, warm light. Vases overflowed with flowers brought in from Tbilisi, bursts of purple hyacinths and yellow crocuses. Above them, a grand fresco commissioned by Felix's grandmother depicted the foundation and expansion of the Russian Empire in artistic allegory, cherubs and seraphim arrayed shoulder to shoulder with the most powerful men of Russia's past. Small wonder his grandmother had given the room its name: the candles and the gold baroque ornamentation that covered the walls sent up a glow that fluttered with each brush of skirt, each breath. It was like he'd walked into a palace in heaven itself, an enchanted place where impossible beings might live.

The guests—representatives of the finest circles in Petersburg, Sheremetevs and Shuvalovs and Naryshkins and Volkonskys and all the families that had peopled Felix's childhood—spun to a halt, and a wave of applause greeted him like the pattering of spring rain. The room rippled with silk and velvet as woman after woman dipped the lowest curtsey her knees could bear, and men sank into bows that were veritable feats of acrobatics. It gratified him, and he wasn't above letting it show. At past balls, he'd been accustomed to trailing at the end of such welcomes, letting his father catch the lion's share of the room's adoration. Genuflections and applause had always been the tsar's prerogative, Felix's participation in the ritual purely incidental. But tonight, this was his court, his guests, his power.

Felix bowed in acknowledgment to his audience, then gestured to the quartet in the corner.

"Play on!" he said, his voice echoing through the high-ceilinged room. The violinist nodded to the other musicians, and strains of music again filled the air, the polonaise giving way to the smoother triple time of a mazurka.

It felt alive in here. It felt the way the Winter Palace had in Felix's childhood, before his mother's death, when a ball had still been a cause for celebration. He'd attended his first at five years old, during which he'd gorged himself on almond tea cakes, charmed the wives of four ambassadors, and fallen asleep during the ecossaise, so that his nurse had been forced to spirit him away to bed. He allowed himself a small smile at the memory. Yes, there was still room in this world for celebration. They'd won the war. They were safe, and Russia was strong, and France was gone, and Sasha was back, and Sofia was here, and Felix was home among friends, ruling over a court of his own.

Felix snatched a glass from a passing servant. The wine sloshed like a golden wave, gone in a moment and warming him deliciously from the inside. He set the empty glass aside as Sasha approached, parting a sea of people without effort. The gleaming dress uniform made him look like a hero from a poem. It made him look like a wolf walking upright. It hadn't occurred to Felix to ask whether Sasha owned any other presentable clothes, but it didn't matter—he wouldn't have deigned to wear them even if he did. He approached a formal engagement the way he approached an armed skirmish: something to charge stoically through and endure.

"Look at you, polished up to a shine," Felix said, with a sweep of a hand. "Remind me to commission a portrait of you like this. I'll hang it like an icon."

Sasha scowled. "Don't do that."

"What, speak to you?"

There was a hair of amusement in his sigh, though the greater part was still exasperation. "I have a reputation to protect."

From the corner, the quartet reached the final notes of one piece and picked up another, this one a minuet with a statelier tempo than the previous mazurka. The violin led the tune, bright and confident like a gull over waves.

Felix gave Sasha a mischievous grin. "And the kind of reputation I have is very difficult to damage. Shall we dance, Sashenka?"

Sasha would have shoved him had they not been in public. As it was, he had to settle for rolling his eyes, which only drew out Felix's laughter. "Go to hell, Felix," he said, stalking off, his dignity perhaps a little damaged but his precious reputation intact. Poor man; he never knew how to breathe easy. Perhaps one day Felix would manage to teach him the trick of it. Happiness wasn't an accident, it was a conscious decision, one Felix had been making each day of his exile.

Sasha might refuse to take part in a celebration, but there was no need for Felix to follow his lead. It was a Komarov's right to be pursued and desired. There were plenty of other beautiful people here to dance with, all hoping to catch his favor for the space of a song. It was empty attention, but even so, it gratified him to be approached by these gorgeous women from the capital, these eager, fawning socialites with their uncomplicated needs. And it had been so long since he'd properly danced. The night spun away in a flurry of careless flirtation, shifting skirts, fine music, and the fuzzy halo of too much wine crowning it all. It might have gone on forever, time compressed to the blink and breath and bow between dances.

But then Sofia entered, and the rest of the room seemed to vanish. When she wanted you to notice her, you did.

She stood in the doorway of the ballroom, commanding attention the same way Felix had. Her gown was a triumph—Felix would have to pay the modiste double. The delicate bodice and sweeping skirt were made of tiny scalloped pieces of white lace, more like scales than fabric. As she moved toward Felix, the lace rippled, revealing endless gradations of white in carefully tiered layers. The sleeves stopped just over the curve of her shoulders, leaving her arms bare against the candlelight—not unheard-of, but daring, especially for winter. She had braided her hair as usual but accented it with a silver comb studded with sapphires, striking as a single jewel on a diadem. She looked like an empress, even more so after the borrowed skirts and peasant's clothes he'd grown accustomed to seeing her in.

When she stopped before him, he bowed, and she curtsied in return. Warmth flowed through Felix from his core at the sight of her, more potent than the wine.

"*Vous êtes ravissante, mademoiselle*," he said.

"The best way to honor our victory," she said wryly, answering him as she always did in Russian. "Looking spectacular."

It might have been a taunt, but Felix didn't mind it. This new elegance hadn't changed her. Her presence was comforting in a way he found both unfamiliar and natural, as though he'd wanted it all his life without knowing.

"Shall we show these dull people how to dance?" she asked, extending an arm.

Felix stared, taken aback for only a moment. Women did not ask the grand duke to dance; he selected them himself, and they considered themselves honored by the choice. But the spark in Sofia's eyes pushed aside the small part of Felix that adhered to the rules of propriety, that tiresome whisper of *What would your father think*. She wanted him. And tonight, he was content to be wanted.

He took her arm. "If you think you can keep up."

Every head turned toward them as he led Sofia to the center of the ballroom, attracted to their passing as to a falling star. Standing near one of the high windows, Sasha scowled, then took a heavy drink from a glass that did not contain wine. Felix ignored him. Sasha's area of expertise was the battlefield. Here in the ballroom, Felix had the tactical advantage.

"Let's give them a show," he said, and the violin led them into the dance.

Felix didn't recognize the music—something new the quartet had prepared for the occasion. It was slow, ethereal, in a seductive minor key. But more importantly, it was in three, and if there was one thing Felix could do with absolute confidence, it was waltz. Sofia followed beautifully, more floating than dancing. With her skirt brushing against him as they turned and spun, the music guiding him, and Sofia's hand on his shoulder, there was no need to think as the candlelight whirled and blurred.

Was he even moving anymore, or was the floor simply revolving beneath him? He had never felt this way as he danced, like a spectator watching his own body perform from high above. And Sofia in his arms, his partner and his guide, her skirts rippling outward like scales, like feathers, like water. A blink, and he snapped back into himself again, moving through the steps as though this were a dance like any other. He was out of breath, thrilled, alarmed but not frightened. Sofia's golden eyes held such a knowing expression that he laughed, the sound escaping from his lips like sunlight.

How long since he'd laughed like that? God only knew. It was the innocent, thoughtless sort of laugh he and Anatoli had shared as children, when he and his brother would run wild through the halls of the Winter Palace. Tearing around corners, sliding down banisters, sending the servants into paroxysms of anger, terror, or amusement, depending on the case. When Tolya had been willing to bend the rules and their mother had indulged two young boys' wildness. When Felix slept easily, dreamed of nothing in particular, and woke in the morning to his mother's embrace and the arrival of his nurse with breakfast. Happiness, or something like it.

Sofia gripped his hand tighter, and he realized he'd drifted again. The music had changed while his attention was elsewhere. Another dance in three, but faster, wilder, with notes skittering in all directions like the legs of some iridescent beetle.

"Congratulations," she said. "I don't know how you managed it."

"Managed what?"

"To celebrate so completely you almost forget what it's about."

And then Sofia shifted her hands so that she was leading. Felix was caught on the back foot, and he almost stumbled in the effort to change direction. She led as capably as she followed, but Felix had never learned how to take the secondary position, and his footwork was awkward and uncomfortable.

"What do you mean?"

Sofia's teeth, exquisite white, were bared in laughter. "Is this what you think the outcome of war is?" she said. "Toasts and music and fine clothes? Ask that captain of yours. I think he'll tell you something different."

Felix held tight to her shoulder. The air in the hall was thick with bodies and candles and drinking, and warm, terribly warm. It seemed to Felix that he might dance all night, dance until his feet melted to bone and left bloody tracks against the marble. What was it they said in the fairy tales, about the beautiful creatures who would dance away your life until decades had slipped by?

"It's nothing at all like this," she whispered, so that he could barely hear her over the music. "And I think you know it."

It was as if the moment had been split in two. He could see himself still, circling with Sofia through the sweeping rhythm of the waltz. The golden ballroom still surrounded them, Petersburg's finest around the perimeter, ladies whispering behind their fans about the impossible scandal of Grand Duke Felix Sergeevich being made to follow. Painted angels and soldiers watching from on high. Uninterrupted, enclosed like two gilt figures in a music box. But while she spoke the room seemed to darken, until nothing existed but her words.

"I wish I could show you the battlefield, Felix. Could make you hear the screams, coming from nowhere and yet clear as anything. Feel the snow piling up around your ankles, and beside you the steam rising from the sliced-open body of a horse, with crows picking at the entrails. You'd taste blood on your tongue, and you'd have no way of knowing whether it was yours or someone else's. You'd look up through the smoke, and you'd see the battle flag in the distance, and you'd wonder, because how could you not wonder, was that what your friends had died for? Was that what they were still dying for? That silly little scrap of a flag?"

There was an edge to the music now, a madness, the kind that would leave a man crying out in the dark. Felix felt the outer rim of his vision blur, as if a great cloud had belched from an iron cannon, from the gaping mouths of rifles. The room was too large, the ceiling too high, and whether it was suggestion or truth, Felix did taste the tang of blood—he must have bitten the inside of his cheek, but he felt no pain, only sensed it thick and hot.

"That's over now," he murmured.

"That part, yes," Sofia said. "But it doesn't end so easily as that."

He gripped her shoulder, and it seemed as if the ballroom's shadows shifted closer, licking at his heels. "Show me."

Her eyes glinted like embers in the dark. "You think it doesn't change a country when it decides it can afford to shed the blood of thousands? It changes everything. Nothing wholesome can grow from a place like that. Twisted trees, withered crops, riverbeds that give way to flood and unbury the shallow graves of the dead. A country like that can't be expected to recognize the truth of what's happening. To hold itself responsible."

"I don't—" Felix began.

"Picture a family, Felix," she interrupted, the dance now more like the movements of a swordsman. "Poorly dressed and terrified, the mother balancing a newborn on one hip as she runs. Behind them, their house burning, and soldiers swarming the ruins, taking everything left worth owning. Picture a woman starving in the streets, because the French blocked shipments of food from the countryside and the tsar hasn't lifted a finger to help. Picture a man standing against a stone wall, cloth bound around his eyes, and the mouths of six soldiers' rifles taking aim at his chest. Picture a man dragged from his bed at night by soldiers, hauled to prison for the crime of protesting his own misery. Picture it all, and know that this is Russia, and that men like you made it this way."

She spoke, and she spoke, and it seemed to Felix that the two split moments of his life blended together, figures layering into a palimpsest of human life, Countess Yusupova's lace fan fluttering in front of a limping prisoner, ribs stark through his tattered tunic, fingertips blackened with frostbite—

Felix stumbled as the last chord of the waltz gave way to silence. He caught himself with one hand and one knee on the ground, halfway to a genuflection. Sofia stood straight above him. The floor was ordinary again, and the room was bright with candles and pearls. No one here but the aristocracy in their finery, gathered to celebrate.

He staggered to his feet, breath coming in gasps. Sofia took his hand and curtsied, low enough that her skirt spread around her like the petals of a lily. She kissed the back of his hand, and it was all he could do not to flinch.

"Do you understand?" she said, so that only he could hear.

He nodded, unable to speak.

"See you don't forget it," she said.

She let his hand drop, or rather Felix snatched it away. In the corner, the musicians gathered themselves for the next dance, as though nothing had happened, as though the very frame of Felix's world hadn't been cracked.

"I couldn't," Felix said. "Even if I tried."

"Good," she said. "Someone in your family ought to remember, don't you think?"

Think. He couldn't bear thinking. He turned away and pushed through the crowd ringing the dancers, guests scrambling to make room for the tsar's son. A shaky breath brought the remnants of strangers' perfume to the back of his throat. This was the world. This crowd, its giddy wave of jewels and feathers and bare flesh. The present. His world, as he'd made it. The world of exile in Tsarskoe Selo. Not—not whatever that had been.

Truth. He had seen truth, no matter how his mind revolted at the thought.

He leaned against the window, gesturing to a servant for another glass of wine. It burned on the way down—perhaps this vintage had gone sour. Snow raged outside the window, battering the glass, piling in drifts along the grounds. It would be no easy feat for his guests to return to Petersburg in the morning. Perhaps they'd all simply stay here, tonight and every night after, slowly growing ragged and mad as the house closed in around them. He felt frozen and flaming, wild as the snow against the window. Everything felt too close, too much, too strong.

"Felix, what in hell—" began a voice he knew well.

Felix turned away from the window. Sasha stood behind him, thunderstruck. His hand hovered near his belt—where his pistol would be, if this were the kind of occasion where men were permitted to bring pistols. Felix had frightened him. Well, good. Someone else in this room ought to feel a little fear.

"I'm all right," he said hoarsely. "Only warm. From the dance."

Sasha didn't believe this for a moment, but Felix didn't need him to. He needed Sasha to accept the lie and leave him alone until the world became itself again. Anyone could have taken the hint—Felix knew he looked pale, if not positively green. The taste of blood hadn't left his mouth, blending horribly now with the sickly perfume and the rancid flavor of the wine.

"Let me call for a physician," Sasha said. "You look—"

Felix pushed away from the window, but he'd misjudged his balance. Light-headed, stomach turning, he stumbled over nothing, and if not for Sasha's hastily offered arm, he'd have fallen. Furious, he twisted from Sasha's grasp. He'd be damned if anyone touched him. Not with the smell of smoke still lingering in his mind, and the screams, how could he remember so clearly the sound of something he'd never heard—

"Sasha, I swear to God," Felix said quietly, "if you don't leave me alone this minute, I don't know what I'll do."

Before Sasha could respond, he fled the room, and did not stop until he reached the sanctuary of his own bedroom and locked the door.

The anodyne familiarity of the room was a salve to his shredded nerves: the four-poster bed, the bearskin tossed over it—one his grandfather had hunted—the cream and gold damask wallpaper Felix loved even though Sasha had once remarked it made the room look like a French pâtisserie. There would be no sleep for him tonight, not for hours. Felix slouched into a chair beneath the window, which backed up against a sideboard holding a crystal decanter half full of rum. He slung his legs over one of the arms of the chair and filled a short-stemmed glass, from which he took a heavy pull. The night drew on, and he sat awake and alone, watching the snow through the window, tossing back drink after drink.

If he dreamed that night, he didn't remember it.

8

Sasha

If Sasha had been a braver person, he wouldn't have let Felix out of his sight that evening. He'd have taken Felix somewhere safe from prying ears and said what needed saying, which was *What were you thinking?* and *Now do you see what I meant about her?* and *For God's sake, Felix, tell me what happened, I can only help if you tell me.* If not for the wildness in Felix's eyes, he'd have done it. But there had been anger in that look as well as fear. Sasha and Felix cared for each other, loved each other even, but since Sofia's arrival, the trust between them had become fragile, and the wrong move could shatter it.

Tomorrow, he told himself, stalking away from the Hall of Lights. He would be braver tomorrow.

The next day, the Catherine Palace stumbled through its routines in a hungover half dream. It seemed as though the air surrounding Felix's guests had been replaced with last night's golden wine, their movements slowed to swimming more than walking. Each parlor and corridor hosted Petersburg nobility in clumps of three and four, slumped napping on divans or halfheartedly writing letters to the capital to describe the festivities of the previous night. *The event of the season, but* mon Dieu, *the spectacle the grand duke made of himself with that strange woman. What is her hold on him? I can't fathom. I shouldn't wonder if she's carrying his child.*

If only he could have shouted at them, turned a pack of dogs loose in the halls, anything to get the vapid crowd to disperse.

The Catherine Palace, less than welcoming at the best of times, had become unbearable. Sasha wasted an afternoon on the edge of the park, firing bullets into trees in what he told himself was practice, but was more accurately his own worry thudding into bark again and again. Finally, when the rest of the palace prepared to sleep—or to make a dent in the remaining stores of wine and rum and vodka, the apparent motto of the aristocracy being *Waste much, want not*—he traveled the familiar path to Felix's bedroom. The door was closed, which he'd expected. It was locked, which he hadn't.

He knocked for what felt like a full minute until, at last, he heard Felix's muffled voice.

"All right, *mon Dieu*, who is it?"

"Let me in, Felix, or I'll have the guard break the door down."

Another moment's silence, and then Felix opened the door, barefoot and in shirtsleeves. His eyes were deep-set and shadowed, and his hair stuck up wildly in the back. "You *are* the guard, you idiot," he said hoarsely.

"Captain now, remember," Sasha said, straight-faced. "I have people to break down doors for me."

Felix rolled his eyes and stepped aside. His quiet irritation, so familiar, was a relief—Sasha had half expected to find Felix dead in this room, or blank faced and silent as if the vila had siphoned out his soul. Sasha sat at the end of the bed, trying not to think about the rumpled bedclothes, the empty decanter on the sideboard, how Felix had clearly not left his bed until Sasha knocked at half past nine in the evening. The room smelled stale, like a long-abandoned traveling trunk. Felix sat beside him with his back against one of the high bedposts. Sasha could see then, as he sometimes did in rare flashes, what Felix would have been like if he'd been born into any other family. Like this—hair askew, face drawn, clothing unremarkable, silent—he didn't look like a son of the tsar. He looked like a vain, frightened man, confused and alone. A man like that would never have survived a youth like Sasha's, a fact that only nurtured his feeling of tenderness. Loving Felix was like cultivating an orchid in a hothouse, the specimen made more precious because of its impracticality, its delicate beauty that had no right to exist in such a place.

He had to say something. Now, while Felix was quiet, shaken, desperate to be guided. *After what happened*, he should have said, *we have to get rid of her, surely you see that now*. But then Felix leaned forward, the back of his hand brushing Sasha's thigh, and the words died on his tongue.

He was being foolish. Allowing himself to be distracted by that touch was putting Felix's safety, the safety of the entire imperial family, at risk.

So be it. Everyone had a weakness they couldn't fight, and Felix was his.

Sasha nested one hand into Felix's hair, pulled him close, and kissed him with fondness and desire enough that he thought his heart might stop from it. Felix exhaled as if he'd been holding that breath for days.

They had always been passionate, the two of them. Stolen moments of intimacy would do that, as would Felix's insatiability and—since the outbreak of war—the clock placed on their time together by Sasha's brief periods of leave. Urgency and scarcity: two factors that spurred them to seize any moment left to them. But tonight, there was more than passion in their kiss, more than hunger. There was affection. There was fear.

And there was a strong sense that, beautiful as this was, it wouldn't last.

Sasha rested his forehead against Felix's, then sighed. The fire in the hearth had been recently stoked, and its warm glow spilled across the bed, catching the shine of Felix's hair and the faint flecks of silver in the bearskin beneath them. Did Felix even know how to stoke a fire? Sasha tried and failed to imagine Felix's fine hands occupied with a task so mundane.

"Are you all right?" Sasha said softly.

"Yes," Felix said, though he shook his head. "It was just . . ."

"Did she say something to you?"

Felix pushed one hand through his already-erratic hair, worsening its disarray. "Several things," he murmured. "Was it terribly stupid, do you think? A ball?"

It wasn't like Felix to question the propriety of a party. "It's good, isn't it? Peace?"

"Is it?"

Dread pooled in the pit of Sasha's stomach. He took Felix's hands and held them so tightly his knuckles flashed through the skin. "What did she say to you?"

Felix tugged his hands away, and Sasha let him. Felix was already jumpy as a hunted rabbit, and frightening him further would not help anything. "It's all falling apart," Felix said bitterly. "All of it. The war's over, but none of it's changed, and there's just as much pain as there ever was, just as much danger. My father thinks it's a victory, but it isn't, not with a cost like this."

He didn't know what Felix was talking about, and in a way, it hardly mattered. If Felix suddenly wanted to take up a philosophy of charitable pacifism, let him, but not until Sasha had ensured his safety. "You're the son of the tsar, Felix," Sasha said. "It's your responsibility to look after your people. You have to do something." *You have to get rid of her*, he thought, but did not say.

"I know," Felix said. "And I will."

Relief soared through Sasha's chest. He ran one hand thoughtlessly down Felix's thigh, tracing the familiar muscles. A terrain he knew well. All of it, from the bite of Felix's narrow hip to the diagonal scar along his calf, barely raised but still discernible to the touch, from a bad fall from a tree in childhood. Even the air in the room seemed lighter now. "Good," he said. "I'll spread word among the guard."

"Do," Felix said. "Tell them we leave in three days."

Newborn relief curdled into dread. "Leave?"

"For Piter," Felix said, surprised. "Where else? I need to speak with my father."

"About what, for God's sake?"

Felix twitched away from Sasha's hand and stood up. "Didn't

you hear me?" His voice was cold enough to make Sasha draw back. "My father's been so intent on winning his war that he can't open his eyes to what's happening to his country. I have to show him. He'll listen to me." He shook his head with a rueful laugh. "Granted, listening hasn't been his strongest suit in the past, but this time will be different. I'm different now."

It was all Sasha could do not to shake him. Whatever Sofia had said to Felix last night, it had planted this impossible notion in his head and encouraged it to take root. "Felix," he said, rising from the bed, one hand outstretched in either placation or desperation. "Stop, for one minute, and think this through."

"You think I haven't?" The break in Felix's voice might have been frustration, might have been fear. "I've thought plenty. I'm a Komarov, Sasha, not some peasant off the street. The safety of the empire is my family's sacred trust. If I see what's best for my people, I have the right—I have the *duty*—to say it."

And to think Sasha had imagined Sofia was the only threat to Felix's safety. If Felix spoke that way in his father's presence, he'd get himself exiled somewhere far less pleasant than Tsarskoe Selo. Recovering himself, Sasha grabbed Felix's wrist, hard enough to hurt. "You know what that sounds like, don't you, Felya?" Sasha said, the affectionate diminutive utterly failing to temper the anger in his voice.

"Leadership," Felix said tightly.

"Treason."

Narrow eyed, Felix shoved Sasha's hand away. Sasha's chest tightened until his brain seemed to shudder from lack of air.

"You think the tsar will welcome you into the Winter Palace with open arms and embrace your proposals for reform?" Sasha pressed on. "Think, Felix. The last time you tried to share your views, he exiled you here. And has Tsar Sergei ever thanked a man for telling him he was wrong?"

Felix laughed, a wild laugh that frightened Sasha. "You don't think I can do it? Silly little Felix, without a brain in his head, not like you, Saint Sasha who's never once been wrong—"

Sasha hadn't let himself be properly angry in months. Years, maybe. In the Imperial Army, a single crack in his self-control was enough to get a man disciplined or discharged. Enough time swallowing your rage and you start to think you no longer feel it, when instead it coats your throat and fills your lungs, infuses itself into everything you do. He grabbed hold of Felix's shirtfront and yanked him closer, until they stood nose to nose. Close enough to kiss. Close enough to spit in his face.

"Right now? Right now, I'm not wrong. You think the tsar will let you do whatever you like because you're his son? Yours wouldn't be the first imperial blood spilled in the Trubetskoy Bastion. Would you forget what she's told you, just for a moment, and *think*?"

Felix twisted from Sasha's grip. His eyes were like chips of glass, frozen and razor sharp. "Maybe you should think about who you're speaking to," he said. "Keep this up and it's not my blood you should be worried about."

These last words punched Sasha past the point of anger, leaving him hollow and windswept and empty. Felix wasn't just daydreaming about wielding the power of the Komarov dynasty. He was brandishing it in Sasha's face. Using it as a weapon, as if Sasha were nothing but an obstacle in his way. Well, and what else *was* he? Felix was right: he was a Komarov, and a Komarov took what he wanted. Sasha closed his eyes and lost himself in the blankness inside him, the void that had carried him through every day of Tsar Sergei's war. Feeling was weakness, and he'd been stupid to forget it. Sasha's duty was to Russia, not to Felix. If this empty-headed prince was intent on sealing his own fate, it wasn't Sasha's responsibility to stop him.

"Very good, Your Imperial Highness," Sasha said with a sharp bow. "I'll inform the guard we leave for Petersburg in three days' time. And when everything goes to hell, remember that I warned you."

"Sasha," Felix began.

Sasha shut the door behind him with a sharp click.

Well then, he thought, long strides carrying him rapidly away from Felix's bedroom. Matters were out of his hands now. If Felix wanted to command his household and drive them to the edge of ruin, let him. No doubt Felix would bring half of the Catherine Palace's staff with him. Enough to people a small city, if the city's only exports were pleasure and entertainment. Felix would want to make an entrance into his father's household, like potentates in centuries past who once traveled with all their furniture, carpets, and wall hangings in tow. And Sasha would go with them. As if that had ever been in doubt.

Felix might command Sasha to follow him, but while the grand duke could control his actions, he couldn't control his heart. And now, more than ever, Sasha knew that strange, cruel woman with the silver hair had to be done away with. For Felix's own good, and for Russia's, even if he couldn't see it.

"Captain?"

Sasha turned. A startled-looking servant hovered in a nearby doorway, watching the soldier's rapid progress with apprehension. Sasha had no doubt he looked alarming—he could already feel the ache rising in his clenched jaw.

"Is everything all right, Captain?" the servant asked.

"Tell the master of the household to start packing," Sasha said, already walking away. "We leave in three days for Petersburg."

9

Marya

The hall off Kadetskaya Liniya was full to bursting. Once, this vast amphitheater had been the beating heart of the university, with a small stage at the front for a lecturer to preside from and rows of wooden chairs sweeping up through the remaining space where students would hang on every word. After the university shuttered during the war, the room had fallen into disrepair. The chairs had long since been cleared away, either sold or burned for warmth, and stains from an old leak in the roof discolored what Marya could see of the floor. But that hardly mattered, in the face of a crowd this size. The room hummed with its own natural resonance, and she could see it as it must have been thirty years ago, people whispering radical philosophy from ear to ear, ideas flowing like wine.

Marya and Lena sat at the front of the room, their legs dangling over the edge of the stage, Lena's right hand interlaced with Marya's left. Their own nerves buzzing like the crowd, they scanned the room for familiar faces, seeing which connections they'd made over the past week had borne fruit. They'd relied on the whisper network of Petersburg to spread word of the time and location, knowing that committing such details to the printed pamphlet would all but ensure a visit from the tsar's soldiers, and in the end the news had roared through like-minded Petersburg like fire through rye. Marya recognized a half-dozen people whose belongings she had bartered for or sold over the past month. On the other side of the room—she noted with amusement—stood the driver who'd rescued her and Isaak from the Semyonovsky Regiment. He was engaged in conversation with Ilya, but when the driver caught her staring, he tipped his hat in her direction; she nodded before losing track of his face in the crowd. It was a better number than she'd dared to imagine: bitter whispers and isolated acts of defiance rippled through the city everywhere one looked, but before the Koalitsiya had begun uniting that dissent under a shared name and common cause, they had never amounted to anything more than a mote in the tsar's eye. It was their efforts that had pulled these threads together, their months of work that had strengthened isolated whispers into a crescendoing unison. It wasn't perfect by any definition—Ilya wasn't alone in doubting that they'd selected the right means for their ends. But for tonight, Marya succumbed to the temptation of optimism. Whether or not the Koalitsiya agreed on every point, they agreed enough to come.

"How many, do you think?" Lena said.

Marya grinned. "Enough."

"Too many, if the tsar catches wind of it."

The warning was reasonable, but Marya had already warded off one bout of gloominess just now and was in no mood to face down another. She rested her head on Lena's shoulder, nuzzling in like she'd seen puppies do for warmth. "If I'd known you were going to be dour and negative all night, I'd have gotten you properly drunk first."

Lena shoved Marya off her shoulder, but the response was playful, not annoyed. "We'll have plenty of time for that after, Masha," she said. "Plenty of time for all sorts of things, in the new world we're building."

Marya raised her eyebrows, mock scandalized. "Are you making a lewd insinuation, Yelena Arsenyevna? In a hallowed hall of learning?"

"I most certainly am," Lena said, before leaning in to kiss her.

Marya hummed her pleasure into the kiss, then pulled back as a wave of silence descended across the amphitheater. Other than the slight shifts and throat clearings usual for a crowd this size, all movement had stopped. Marya and Lena turned, angling them-selves toward the center of the small stage. It felt like the hours before a festival, the time separating you from the celebration simultaneously unbearable and part of the attraction.

Like an actor taking his place in a scene, Isaak emerged onto the stage.

Marya tried to imagine what it would be like for the new mem-bers of the crowd, seeing Isaak Mikhailovich for the first time. More than likely, the first look disappointed them. There was noth-ing outwardly remarkable about this young man of about thirty, his serious expression sporting the patchy stubble of an accidental beard. On the face of it, a person could pass him in the street and not remember him the next minute. But this crowd was discovering now what Marya had the first time she heard Isaak speak to a crowd of a half-dozen sailors along the docks: that appearances could be deceiving. With the first word that passed his lips, his voice filled the amphitheater like a choir. It was an impressive sound, confident, measured, clear. The kind of voice that could pierce a crowd and force you to listen, make your understanding of the world tremble.

"Brothers and sisters," Isaak said. "I know what you're risking by coming here. So thank you, from the bottom of my heart, for risking it."

When he spoke, Isaak was no longer the awkward printer's assistant with whom Marya had recently climbed through a win-dow. There was something classical in his profile now, something marble in his posture. When he spoke this way, Isaak became a statue carved by a master, every line of his body designed to awe. Marya gripped Lena's hand harder, hungry for what he would say next, although they both already knew what it would be.

"We now have one month of peace behind us, brothers and sis-ters," Isaak continued. "One month with the bulk of our soldiers returned home. One month of Russia's glory restored, the tyrant Napoleon forced west, a new dawn, or so the tsar tells us."

He paused, fixing the crowd with a glance sharp as an arrow. It seemed they could feel his attention traverse each of them in turn.

"Tell me. Does this feel like peace to you?"

A murmur rippled through the room. Isaak hadn't rehearsed this speech verbatim—a voracious devourer of books, he nevertheless shunned the idea of reading a prepared text—but Marya could feel every syllable of it land.

"Does it feel like peace, with our soldiers brought home to starve, huddled together twelve to a room? With the lines for bread winding farther than you can see, and the price higher than you can pay when you finally make it to the head, if there's anything left at all? With the land of this country locked in the strongboxes of the tsar's favorites, and our families reduced to working what ruined fields we can, or running to the city to make half a living from doing five men's work? With soldiers around each corner listening, ready to silence any man, woman, or child who so much as thinks a word against them? Is that the peace you and your brothers and fathers and husbands and sons fought and died for?"

He had the crowd exactly where he wanted them. Even Marya felt her pulse racing. She'd heard the argument before, of course, from him and from others, a hundred times. She'd said it herself. At twenty-nine, Marya had lived more than long enough to know what life had to offer the people of her country. She'd seen it from the docks to the markets, heard it in the report of her father's death on the battlefield at Austerlitz. She knew what it was to hurt. For most of her life, she'd been thinking up ways to stanch the bleeding, each more far-fetched and vainglorious than the last. But it was different, somehow, when Isaak spoke of changing it. Nobody else could paint a future like he could.

"The tsar and his ministers think they have us trapped," Isaak said—he was pacing now, too much energy for words alone. "They think because they control the army and the bread lines and the prisons, we can't challenge them when they make life less bearable by the day. But do you know what I think?"

He paused, letting the silence swell with possibility. Marya could have spoken the next words aloud with him.

"I think they've forgotten this city is nothing without us."

This was the essential moment. This was when Isaak's words had to become more than an attractive idea well expressed. This was the point where theory became action, and if the crowd didn't feel themselves propelled as one toward what he said next, then all the speeches in the world would do them no good.

The assembled faces were no less weary, no less weather-beaten, shoulders no less slumped beneath the weight of accumulated days. But every nerve and fiber of every person in that room was taut with the effort of listening. Two middle-aged men, one with his left arm in a sling, exchanged a significant look, and they flashed each other the faintest hint of a smile. See here now, those smiles seemed to say. This is a man who knows what he's talking about.

There was hope in that smile.

"Imagine it," Isaak said. "The sun rises on another day in Piter, and the people, as one—do nothing. No shops open their doors. No servants cater to their masters. No bakers bake, no butchers sell, no soldiers raise their arms. What can the tsar in all his majesty do then? What can any of them do? They told the city what they thought of us, what they reckoned our value to be, but what if the city, with one voice, in one moment—what if the city said no? What if we showed them they need us to survive, and we expect to be valued accordingly? We'll work, we'll tell them. As soon as they let us have a life worth working for."

At the far edge of the crowd, Irina leaned her shoulders against the wall with one hand at the small of her back, smiling. Isaak, with his natural showmanship, had been the clear choice to take up the public face of the strike—that same public's general unwillingness to take direction from a woman six months pregnant being the other reason. But the pride in Irina's face was as clear as though she'd been the one speaking.

The unfamiliar woman next to her, however, appeared to be thinking something entirely different.

It was as if God had silenced Isaak with a look. Marya could no longer hear him, though she sensed him building to the speech's climax, somewhere beyond the level of her consciousness. She no longer had eyes, ears, heart, mind for anyone but the tall silver-haired woman standing near the front of the crowd, dressed in a black fur-lined coat that fell to her ankles, her impossibly bright eyes focused sharply on Isaak.

It wasn't merely that the woman was beautiful. Marya had always considered herself to have an artist's eye for female beauty. She'd noticed Lena that way, the first day the arresting woman with the soldier's posture had arrived in the Tverskys' parlor pledging her commitment to the Koalitsiya. Marya had heard the strength in Lena's voice, seen those hands as comfortable around your waist as on the reins of a horse, and she'd known then that she wanted to intertwine Lena's life with her own. She wanted to know Yelena Arsenyevna like a painting, a wash of color and feeling. It had been a flood of affection and connection and a sense of being understood, like reaching out a hand in the dark and knowing someone was there to take it.

The feeling rising in Marya now was not at all like that.

This was fascination, and it was terror, all in the same moment. The woman was at least six inches taller than Marya, though to be fair many people were at least that, and the color of her hair seemed to belie her relative youth: her narrow face was unlined, and she stood with a dancer's confidence in the strength of her body. She was easily the most beautiful person Marya had ever seen, in a way that was almost inhuman—in a way that made her something beyond an object of attraction, beyond what any person could be bold enough to desire.

As if aware she was being watched, the woman in black turned to where Marya stood on the other side of the crowd.

Her eyes—perfect amber, round as gemstones—met Marya's.

The impossible woman smiled. Marya would have torn open her own rib cage, presented her own heart in two cupped hands, if the woman had asked it of her, if only to earn that smile again.

"Masha," Lena said sharply.

Marya blinked, and the world flooded back into focus. She could hear Isaak's voice again, the crowd around them rising in a swell of agreement. The speech was nearly finished, only the grand call to action left, and yet the strike had never been farther from Marya's mind. The woman's eyes were trained again on Isaak, who closed his speech with a voice that echoed like the ring of trumpets.

"The twentieth of January. That's the day it starts, brothers and sisters. The first step toward a new future."

The future indeed, Marya thought, as she watched the woman applaud.

The speech couldn't possibly have gone better. Isaak had given it every drop of persuasion he had, and the crowd had drunk it all and stood thirsty for more. Even so, they knew when it was time to leave. Lingering in large numbers was a danger none of them could afford, not when they'd already defied the odds by escaping the tsar's notice for so long. Marya bid farewell to as many people as she could on their way through the double doors. The twentieth of January, she reminded the mass of humanity as it gradually separated into individuals, loose-knit twos and threes. Don't forget, *brat*. Tell your family, *sestra*. Before long, the humming energy of Isaak's speech had been tucked into the pockets and under the hats of the crowd, who hurried out into the street with bent heads. Only core members of the Koalitsiya itself remained, Isaak and Irina at their center. It made Marya smile to see the Tverskys in ebullient discussion, reliving the thrill of Isaak's speech word by word. Two more determined, serious people were difficult to imagine, but when the mood of triumph took her friends, she saw how they might always have been in a different world: unburdened, excited, his arm around her with the easy affection born of long partnership.

But she'd spent years thinking about the Tverskys. Tonight, it seemed, she was destined to think about something new.

She'd been sure the pale stranger would disappear with the crowd. There was no reason for her to stay—whatever connection Marya had imagined between them was just that, imaginary, certainly not enough to risk arrest for. And yet, the stranger still stood alone against the east wall, her arms folded. Noting Marya watching her, she gave the ghost of a smile.

God help her. That feeling again. Hunger and terror. Both unfamiliar sensations, as though the woman had placed them in Marya's bones herself. She wanted to run, and at the same time never to move from this spot.

"Masha," Lena began warningly.

"Sonya!" Isaak said, addressing the stranger. "You came after all." He clapped his wife on the shoulder before hopping off the stage, and the white-haired woman opened her arms as he embraced her. The intimate diminutive only underlined the genuine affection that seemed to flow between them, though they acted more like brother and sister than old lovers.

"Silver-tongued Isaak Mikhailovich." The woman's voice was lower than Marya had expected, and rougher around the edges. There was none of the polish of high society in it, despite her poise. Another riddle to join the rest. "That was a speech worth raising a glass to."

"He can't help it," Irina said with a shrug—her journey from the stage to the floor had been more cautious than Isaak's. "Why say something simply when he can move a man to tears?"

"Certainly the more stylish way to undo an empire," the woman said.

Marya couldn't quite place her tone, somewhere between ironic and earnest. It was enchanting, the way this woman could speak lightly about the cause they had all pledged their lives to and yet never seem for a moment like she didn't believe in it. Without meaning to, Marya drifted toward the woman. Her mouth opened, though there were no words on her tongue. The woman, noticing, let the side of her mouth curl in amusement. There, too, that irony that cut to the heart, but without disdain.

"Isaak," Lena said, with a hand on Marya's wrist. "Your friend still hasn't introduced herself. Although evidently that isn't supposed to worry me."

Somewhere, distantly, Marya knew Lena was right to be cautious. The Koalitsiya couldn't risk a stranger getting too close and asking questions. And Lena's judgment had never been wrong before. Perceptive, steadfast to a fault, Lena was her rock. Lena's opinions could be trusted.

And yet.

The woman didn't seem put out by the sharp question. "Of course," she said. "In these times, it's impossible to be too careful. Sofia Azarova."

"We met at the printshop some weeks ago," Isaak said. "Had a most interesting conversation, once Kyril finally left us to ourselves. Didn't I tell you it would be worth hearing?"

"If I'd known I'd stumbled into the shop of the second coming of Pugachev, I'd have signed on with you straightaway," Sofia answered.

Isaak grinned. He didn't dispute the comparison to Russia's most famous insurrectionist; on the contrary, Marya knew, the jab amused him. "There's plenty to do, as you can see," he said. "We could use a mind like yours on the matter, if you like what you heard."

Sofia shrugged and plunged her hands deep into the pockets of her coat. "A strike? Very well, my friend, it's a start."

She grinned, and her sharp eyes drove through Marya like a nail, pinning her to the spot.

"But I think we can do better than that."

Marya intended to leave the university hall with Lena. Still possessed by the spirit of the evening, there might have been a beautiful night ahead, one that might carry them to any *traktir* or teahouse or other haunt that offered privacy and plenty to drink. But when Sofia Azarova touched Marya's elbow and gave her that sideways, ironic smile, all thoughts of leaving fled her mind. Lena, still standing at her side, scowled, but Sofia either missed or ignored the slight.

"I won't tell Isaak," Sofia said.

Marya blinked. "I'm sorry?"

"That his speech didn't quite hold your attention," Sofia drawled. The touch on Marya's elbow had been light, but she could still feel the outlines of Sofia's fingers. "We all have our moments of distraction."

Sofia had caught Marya staring. That was it. Marya would perish, and the sheer power of her embarrassment would melt her body into a puddle. But Sofia didn't seem offended. If anything, she seemed amused, like a cat receiving an overture of friendship from a mouse.

"I helped him plan that speech," Marya said, her tongue feeling ungainly in her mouth. "I knew where it would land."

"A politician, then," Sofia said. "And full of surprises. Your name?"

It seemed unwise to give it, as if surrendering that much of herself would give Sofia power over her. Even so, Marya heard herself answer before she'd decided to. "Marya Ryabkova. Isaak's right hand, or at least that's how he puts it."

"A title I'm sure Isaak doesn't bestow lightly," Sofia remarked. "Will you walk with me, Marya?"

"Masha," Lena said warningly. "I don't—"

"I'll find you later, Lenochka," Marya said without thinking, following Sofia out into the night.

Clouds had dimmed the sky when Marya arrived at the university hall, but they must have cleared while Isaak was speaking, for stars now shone brilliantly over the streets of Petersburg. It was the kind of night Marya loved best, when she felt as if she could see forever. Standing beside Sofia, every breath of clear air felt charged, incandescent. Like a drug that might kill you in the end, but would first give you a taste of the purest, coldest, most impossible clarity anyone had ever known. She kept a few careful inches between them as they walked toward the river, side by side under the starlight.

"Might I ask you a question?" Sofia said, almost idly.

"If I get to ask one in return."

Sofia laughed, sharp against the quiet. "I didn't realize we were bargaining. All right. What brought you to the Koalitsiya?"

It was a loaded question, which Sofia must have known. The answer would have wound through a lifetime, through scraped-together meals and crowded apartments, from the breadline to the battlefield. Marya had always kept her reasons for fighting close to the chest—most of the Koalitsiya did, and their companions knew enough not to pry. The softness at your center was both the fire that drove you on and the easiest spot for someone to sink a knife into. And though Marya's urge to lay herself bare before this woman was strong, she remained wary enough to keep a safe distance.

"The Komarovs took something from me that I want back," she said finally.

"And what is that?"

Marya stopped walking. So did Sofia. It seemed as though the entire city had stopped in anticipation of her answer, one that was too complicated to ever give. Her father. Her dignity. The land her family had once worked. Her friends' homes. Their families. In the end, she chose the simplest response. "My future," she said.

Sofia nodded. They had nearly reached the bank of the Little Neva, the wooden expanse of Tuchkov Bridge spanning the ice not far from where they stood. The night was bitterly cold, and yet a curious warmth spilled through Marya's hand, up her arm, taking root in her chest. A warmth that seemed to spring from Sofia's bare palm, so near to her own it would have been no effort at all to touch it. She thought of lost animals drawn into a strange den in the dead of winter, of moths pulled toward flame.

"My question now," Marya said quietly.

"I did agree to that, didn't I? Go on."

"What did you mean, when you said we could do better?"

"Exactly what I said. No change ever came about through caution, you must know that."

Deep irritation rose within Marya. "It's easy to say that, harder to do it. You don't know how long we've worked to come this far. To get the city behind us. You don't—"

She cut herself off mid-thought, as Sofia began to laugh. Forget fascination—she was no longer sure whether she wanted to take Sofia's hand or shout at her.

"If it's funny to you, we don't need your help," Marya snapped. "You haven't been part of this. I have."

The laughter died at once, though the amusement in Sofia's eyes did not, and she took Marya's hand at last. The heat was undeniable now, as if a candle burned in each of Sofia's fingertips. Marya wasn't certain she was still breathing.

"I know you have," Sofia said, and though her voice was low, it was strong as a chain of iron. "And I think you've driven this movement from behind as far as you can. But if you want to shake this city to its roots, you need to hear what I'm telling you. All this power at your fingertips, and you're so afraid to use it."

"I'm not afraid," Marya said.

Sofia's grip on her hand tightened. "If I told you everything you could become, you would be."

Marya took one more step forward. The hem of her skirt brushed Sofia's coat before settling around her own ankles.

"Try me," she murmured. "I'm harder than that to scare."

She watched Sofia watch her, the progression of thoughts visible on her beautiful, almost harsh face. *I can't possibly tell her*, followed almost immediately by *Unless, of course, I can*. And mere moments later, the flicker of something almost amused, a careless fatalism. *And why not? What is there to lose, if she knew?*

"Perhaps I will," Sofia said. "In time."

Should she have been frightened? She was alone, with a woman she knew nearly nothing about—a woman who, from the power that radiated from her, might have been capable of anything. It wasn't unreasonable to think this might be the last night she spent alive. And she was frightened, but not in a way she'd ever felt before. It was the life-giving terror of walking to the very edge of a cliff and looking down into the river below, when every leaf and stone and blade of grass sharpened with impossible precision.

On a whim, she turned Sofia's hand over, palm up to the night.

Sofia's palm was warm and smooth, the lines spidering across it so pale they were almost invisible. Shadow lines, Lena called them. The marks left by a fate passing above and around you, a fate that might have been yours. No surprise there. Sofia looked as if she moved around time, not through it. Any number of fates might have brushed against her without taking root. Sofia's fingers curled slightly back toward her palm.

"What are you doing?"

"I'm going to read your future," Marya said. "If you'll let me."

Sofia leaned forward, never taking her hand from Marya's. It felt like stretching an arm into the mouth of a bear. "Please. You'd be the first."

Marya let her fingers walk the lines of Sofia's hand, tracing their paths, their depth. The last time she'd done this, Lena had been beside her, watching as Marya recalled the rules and patterns she'd taught her, making soft noises that weren't quite a rebuke, but were enough for Marya to know when she'd made a mistake. Now she had only her own instinct to guide her. Still, the lines in Sofia's palm unfurled themselves in perfect order. Disconcertingly clear, as if they'd been written in ink instead of skin.

"What do you see?" Sofia said.

Marya forced herself to focus on the lines and not the feel of Sofia's hand in her own. "The heart line," she said, tracing it. "It's broken here, you see? Tragedy, maybe. But the main branch is long, and it forks up from the small one."

"Which means?"

"A change," Marya said. "Either things are about to get better, or they're going to get a great deal worse."

They were closer than Marya had allowed herself to be to anyone but Lena in a long time. This felt nothing like being with Lena. Lena was safety, was comfort, was home. This was power.

This was a woman who could change the shape of the world with a thought.

"Did you learn anything else about me?" Sofia asked.

Where the boldness came from, God knew, but they were so close, and Sofia's golden eyes were warm as candles, and before Marya could stop herself, she'd taken Sofia's other hand as well.

"I don't think I'll ever learn everything there is to know about you. But I'd like to try."

Sofia laughed, and though Marya had never thought herself to be particularly clever, she found she desperately wanted to be, to earn that laugh again. Marya stroked her thumb down one of the deeper ridges of Sofia's palm.

"I should go," Sofia said. "You all have work to do."

Of course. Their work came before everything else. No matter how intoxicating it was to receive Sofia's full attention. No matter how frightening and beautiful and impossible it was to touch her hand. *If you want to shake this city to its roots.* A torrent of power that left nothing unchanged in its wake. *If I told you everything you could become.*

"Will I see you again?" Marya asked.

Sofia flexed her fingers, the lines in her palm brightening with the stretch, until she tucked her hands away inside her coat. "Sooner than you might think," she said. "I didn't come all this way for nothing."

Marya must have blinked. One moment, Sofia was standing on the corner, a half smile on her lips, and the next, Marya was alone. She saw no one down the length of the narrow street, though the shadows were deep enough to conceal anyone who did not wish to be seen. The only other living being was a snowy owl, which hung briefly against the dim moon before wheeling west toward the docks, where the harbor's frozen shallows eventually gave way to frigid whitecaps of deep water. Marya stood there as the owl drifted away, and then long after it was gone. The night, clear as before, seemed infinitely darker now.

THE HOUSE IN THE WOOD

In a distant kingdom, in a distant time, a young
woman lived with her cruel stepmother and her two
spiteful stepsisters in a tiny house on the edge of the forest.
Her mother, before she died, had given the young woman
a splendid wooden doll, with a face carved exquisitely and
hair of yarn as soft as the finest coverlet. Each night when
she held the doll to her, she vowed to be industrious and
strong, so that she would deserve her mother's blessing.

Every night, the stepmother gave the three young
women a task to keep the household neat and earn enough
money to sustain them there on the edge of the forest. The
stepsisters would knit or make lace or embroider in the
firelight, and the young woman would spin the flax they had
gathered throughout the day. She worked hard while her
sisters gossiped and idled, the creaking of the treadle her
only contribution to their conversations in the dark, dark
night.

But one night, the fire went out, and the little household
was plunged into darkness. They must have light to work,
but they knew the only place they could find it was in the
heart of the wood, where, it was said, a witch lived in a
house that glowed with a never-dimming flame. In no time,

it was decided that the young woman would go and plead with the witch to lend them light—for, said the stepsisters, if the young woman was lost, it would be no great hardship.

And so, holding her doll like a talisman, she ventured into the woods, whose roots and branches lapped the edges of the little house, and the forest swallowed her whole.

She had never gone more than a few feet beyond the edge of the woods, warned off by her stepsisters' stories and the distant baying of wolves. It took only minutes until she had lost her way entirely. Even the path had disappeared beneath a carpet of fallen pine needles. Frightened, she felt herself on the verge of tears, and she would have choked out a sob were it not for the firm, clear voice that addressed her from the darkness.

"Do not weep," said the voice, and the young woman nearly cried out, for the voice had unmistakably come from the doll in her arms. "Your mother's blessing will see that you come to no harm. Move forward, and follow the light."

She blinked, and before her rose a house in a clearing that had not been there moments before, surrounded by a curious fence. As she drew nearer, she saw that the fence was made of human bones, each bone capped with a bleached human skull. The house, too, was formed of bones, interlocked so cunningly that it seemed like the skeleton of some great creature. And from within the house, exactly what the young woman had come in search of: a steady, warm glow.

Though she was still frightened, she steeled herself and walked to the door, which opened before she could knock to reveal a powerful witch, dressed all in black, her pale hair glowing. The rumors had always said that the witch who lived in these woods was hideous and forbidding, but the young woman saw now they had been nothing but lies, for she had never seen a woman so strikingly beautiful as this.

"Who has come to my home in the dead of night?" demanded the witch.

The young woman quailed, but as she knew she could not return home without the light, she clutched her doll and spoke as courageously as she was able. "Forgive me, sister. I have come to beg a gift of light from you, if you can spare it."

The witch considered, and then, with a quirk of her brow, stepped aside, beckoning the young woman in. She did as she was bid, and the door snapped shut, the sound of grinding bones confirming her fear: the door was locked and would not open again without the witch's word.

"You are bold to come here and ask a favor of me," said the witch, "but I am not in the habit of giving something for nothing. By tomorrow sundown, you are to clean my house, wash my clothes, cook my dinner, and spin all the flax in my storeroom into thread. If you do this, I will give you the gift you have requested. If you fail, you will not leave my house alive."

And with that, the witch vanished, and the young woman was left alone.

The first tasks were not difficult. The young woman was used to hard labor, and the witch's house, though in disrepair, was put into order without much difficulty. But when the young woman entered the storeroom, she was alarmed to see a mountain of flax, stretching from floor to ceiling and reaching every corner of the room. It would take her weeks to spin this much flax into thread, and she had only hours. The young woman sank to the floor and began to weep, for she knew she would meet her death in that house.

"Do not weep," said the doll, which stood behind her now in the doorway as if it were a living being. "Your mother's blessing will see that you come to no harm. Go and cook the witch's supper, and leave the flax to me."

The young woman did as she was bid, and when she had finished preparing the witch's supper, she peeked into the storeroom and could scarcely believe her eyes. There laid neatly on the floor were balls upon balls of the finest linen thread, without a scrap of unspun flax. The doll sat motionless at the treadle, and it seemed to the young woman that her familiar carved face had begun to smile.

Just then, the witch reappeared in the center of the house. To her evident surprise, everything had been done as she commanded. The young woman stood near the stove clutching her doll, waiting for judgment.

The witch smiled, then ran one hand through the young woman's long hair. Her fingers were softer than the young woman had supposed, smooth and cool as bone. She leaned against the witch's palm—she had never been so close to anyone so beautiful.

"You have done as I asked," said the witch, and there was a smile in her words now, "and so I shall do as I promised. Take the light and go back, and you will find your home much changed."

The young woman was not at all certain she wished to

leave the witch, but disobedience seemed dangerously unwise, and so she did as she was bid. In another blink she was at the edge of the forest, looking at the little plot of land where her small house had stood. But in its place was a fine two-story dacha, with a garden in full bloom despite the thick snow that blanketed the ground. As the young woman drew closer with her light, she saw that the yard was encircled by a curious fence—the gate ornamented with three human heads that, she realized, once belonged to the cruel stepmother and the spiteful stepsisters. And when she opened the door to the dacha, the young woman saw the witch waiting on the threshold.

"Do not weep," said the doll in her arms. "This happiness is the blessing your mother sent you. Bring me inside, and live in peace."

With gladness in her heart, the young woman followed the witch into the dacha. The house they shared was filled with warmth and happiness, and the doll sat always in a place of honor above the stove, the light from which never went out.

10

Felix

Complaining about living in Petersburg had been a fashionable pastime since the city was built, but Felix had never managed to summon the traditional disdain for its frequent floods and lack of basic necessities. He loved the city, honestly and without irony. Its cosmopolitan soul appealed to him, that sense of something diaphanous and rare just beneath the surface. It didn't stagger under centuries of tradition the way Moscow did. Petersburg was a child among cities, little more than a century old, and that meant light, meant freedom, meant life. Exile from Piter had been more than a cause for shame—it had been a true loss, as though he'd been ripped away from part of himself. So while the prospect of confronting his father left Felix nauseous as the coach dragged forward from Tsarskoe Selo, wheels threatening to stick in the packed snow, the feeling that swept through him loudest of all was anticipation. This was home, after all. Good things had happened here, as well as the bad.

The coach heaved over the next hill, and there it was—Saint Petersburg.

Brilliant as a dream: sweeping boulevards and a diamond-crusted river that cracked the land into dozens of minor islands, the massive Bronze Horseman surveying the capital from the summit of its mountainous pedestal. Domes and multicolored rooftops, the glittering spire of Petropavlovsky Cathedral from within the heart of the tsar's fortress, and not far from it the Winter Palace, grand enough to make Tsarskoe Selo look like a child's retreat. Between the shimmering rooftops, the Neva and its tributaries wound their infinite paths toward the sea, the slick gray surface of the water shielded by a layer of ice thick enough to drive a troika across. This would always be Felix's city, no matter how long he spent away: beautiful, delicate, full of possibility.

The coach descended into a maze of streets and boulevards, grand town houses and gated parks, until at last it reached the wrought-iron gates that led from Palace Square to the interior courtyard of the Winter Palace. Through the window, Felix kept one wary eye on the golden double-headed eagle that loomed over him from the gates. It was only a carving, only ornamentation, and yet he couldn't help but feel that the eagle's two sets of eyes, though facing opposite directions, were both fixed directly on him. He bit his tongue and held his breath like a field mouse hiding from a bird of prey.

Muffled shouting from outside the coach, the scrape of iron, and then the gates opened wide, allowing them to move through the grand neoclassical arch and into the courtyard. Felix hopped out the moment they halted, not waiting for the servant to come round and open the door. If he allowed himself to hesitate, he'd retreat into the coach and order the driver to disappear into the city, and no one at the palace would ever see Grand Duke Felix again. The air was so cold it felt like the inside of a scream.

Welcome home, he thought.

Even from outside, the palace was so lavish it seemed impossible that anything shy of seraphim might be allowed to live inside it. The three-story structure stood as if it, too, were an emperor, regal and disdainful in white and yellow, with gold capping every window and the base of every pillar. Felix saw no faces in the windows that surrounded him on all sides, but even so, the sensation of being watched was inescapable. No doubt three dozen servants had their eyes on him from behind the curtains. He hooked his thumbs in the pockets of his overcoat and tilted his head back, wondering absently whether he could hide on the roof, or whether his father's servants would track him down even there.

Half of Felix's household had arrived at the palace before him, the other half still filing through the gates. Up ahead, Felix saw Sasha dismount with the grimness of a cavalry soldier resigned to capture or death. Sasha handed the reins to another guard before approaching, each step striking the packed snow heel first. Felix turned his back on the captain. This visit was risky enough without the tsar discovering he'd fallen for a common soldier in his time away from the capital.

Sasha, evidently, could take a hint. "We'll have your trunks sent up to your rooms, Your Imperial Highness," he said, as stiffly as if he and Felix had never met. "For now, it would be best if you . . ."

"Ah! Felix! Returned from the ends of the earth at last."

Sasha fell silent.

Felix sighed. "All right," he murmured to himself. "No turning back now."

Tsarevich Anatoli Sergeevich Komarov, Felix's elder brother and next in line to the imperial throne, descended the stairs into the courtyard, his wife, Catarina, only a step behind. Some four or five servants hurried after, though what his brother intended to use them for, Felix couldn't fathom. The epaulettes of Anatoli's uniform gave his shadow an almost eerie angularity. He must have shaved only minutes ago: his close-cut beard was sharp as a knife's edge. It made Felix, clean-shaven and permanently tousled, feel even younger than he was, like a child playing at the idea of a prince. His sister-in-law, meanwhile, had dressed with the same care for her clothes that a soldier paid to his weapons. Her gown, though simple and half concealed beneath a brocade shawl, was precisely the same pale yellow as the palace. As if to remind Felix that though she had begun life as the daughter of the king of Prussia, Catarina Petrovna was now more a member of the Komarov family than Felix would ever be.

"Tolya," Felix said, leaning into the casual diminutive. "And dear Katya." He kept his hands behind his back and cracked each knuckle in turn.

"We have enough staff here to attend the whole family, *mon petit frère*," Anatoli said. He clapped Felix on the shoulder so hard Felix almost buckled. The two brothers had a similar build, but Anatoli was stronger, a consequence both of his conscious training and his brief military career. "You didn't need to make your people travel all this way."

As if Felix was meant to turn up in the back of a farmer's wagon, one carpetbag in hand, and beg his brother the loan of an irritable manservant to scowl at him every morning over the shaving mirror. "Comfort of the familiar," Felix said, weaving away from his brother's touch. "They know what I like."

Anatoli raised his eyebrows. "I should think everyone knows what you like by now."

"Don't be a beast," Catarina admonished. She extended a hand for Felix to kiss, and when he stood straight again, she was smiling. Out of practice with reading her expression, he couldn't be sure if she was mocking him or glad to see him. "*Vous m'avez manqué, vaurien.* Court is terribly dull without you."

"Though I've come to quite appreciate dullness, really," Anatoli added.

Felix's lips tightened, but he kept his tone light. "There we differ, clearly. Can you show me to Father? I assume he's expecting me. We're already a little later than planned."

Anatoli frowned. "I'm sorry about that," he said. "Papa is in council with the British and Swedish ambassadors. With the alliance in its current state, even I don't dare interrupt him. Have your people start unpacking, and he'll send for you when he's ready."

Two years gone, and yet nothing at all had changed. He was every bit as capable as Anatoli; surely he deserved at least the same deferential audience as some overdressed diplomat from Stockholm. And yet here he was, left to cool his heels like any second-rate noble. No doubt the tsar had done it on purpose, to remind Felix of his place. Under the tsar's control, utterly, and not important enough to necessitate any change to the daily schedule.

"Excellent," Felix said crisply. "Sasha, when Mademoiselle Azarova's carriage arrives, please see to it she finds a comfortable room. I think my brother wants me to make myself scarce, from the look he's giving me."

Anatoli's smile never wavered. "Isn't it possible I missed you?"

"Tsarskoe Selo is fifteen miles away, brother," Felix said darkly, stalking past his brother and sister-in-law into the palace. "If you'd really missed me, you'd have survived the journey."

———

Some days later, Felix stood in his suite of rooms in the Winter Palace and scowled at his reflection in the mirror. Behind him, three trunks' worth of clothes lay scattered across the floor, the bed, the chair. What he'd finally settled on still felt wrong—no doubt it *was* wrong, in a dozen ways he wasn't yet aware of, but he'd exhausted both his options and the time to explore new ones. The jacket was a deep royal blue that skimmed easily along his shoulders, with the lighter blue sash of the Order of Saint Andrew slicing his torso diagonally in a way that made him think of a bayonet wound. He didn't have Anatoli's medals and honors to ornament himself with, which made the sash feel like a joke, leaving him simultaneously under- and overdressed. With more than a little petulance, he flicked one section of hair deliberately out of place.

That first afternoon at the Winter Palace had stretched into more than a week, and Felix was still no closer to securing an audience with his father. There had been a different excuse provided at every turn: ministers to converse with, ambassadors to manipulate, generals and nobles and ministers to consult, a splitting headache to cap it off. And beneath all of it, one inescapable truth: that Tsar Sergei would rather do practically anything than speak to his second son.

Sofia sat in one of two armchairs flanking the tea table at the center of the room. She watched him examine himself in the mirror, her posture flawless and her expression unbothered. She had been his near-exclusive companion during his time in Petersburg, aside from the legions of servants populating every corner of the Winter Palace, whom Felix could not entirely avoid despite his concerted efforts. Sasha had kept his distance, for which Felix was privately grateful. They still had not addressed their quarrel at Tsarskoe Selo, and there simply wasn't enough room in Felix's head to confront that along with everything else.

He sighed once again and turned away from the glass. "I look ridiculous," he muttered. "Go on, you can say it."

"I wouldn't say ridiculous," Sofia said. Her smile hinted that whatever replacement word she'd have selected was no more complimentary. "But really. All this for the tsarevich?"

It was a fair point, but Felix refused to rise to the bait. Any move Felix made in Anatoli's company would be relayed directly to their father in excruciating detail. Besides, given that even Anatoli had been avoiding him since his arrival, a meeting with his brother was at least a step in the right direction. Best to overprepare.

"Don't think of it as me dressing for the tsarevich," Felix said with a wink. "Think of it as me dressing for you, then having to spend an evening with my self-righteous brother instead."

Sofia laughed. "A tragedy," she said, "when you put it like that." She rose from the chair and wandered toward the window, where the sun already dipped behind the rooftops of Petersburg. With her back to the room, Felix could only read her mood from the set of her shoulders. Impatient, but not yet angry. "Don't let him intimidate you. You know how they are, they crush anything they see as a challenge." She turned from the window, and her eyes were shadowed, beads of amber ringed in silver. "Show them you're harder than that to get rid of."

He grinned without meaning to. He was Grand Duke Felix, and there was nothing he couldn't do. For the first time in many days, the plan that had been so urgent at the Catherine Palace began to seem possible again.

"If I cause an incident," he said, turning to go, "there'll be no one but you to blame."

Anatoli waited for Felix in one of the west parlors, which backed up against the interior courtyard. Though it had been years since he'd walked these halls, Felix didn't need the two footmen who had arrived to escort him: he could have found the room blindfolded. It was one their mother had liked to use, one where Felix used to come and sketch while Tsarina Natalya Fyodorovna answered letters or spoke in her native German to her brother and servants. Felix himself had never been permitted to speak his mother's language in front of his father, who'd considered it impertinence bordering on treason. Still, his ear had known it well, and though it had been fifteen years since the tsarina had died, he could still feel her sharply angled German consonants in his memory. The parlor was an eerie place out of time, the words of his childhood preserved in the hang of its curtains. If Anatoli had wanted to make Felix feel small and unsteady, he'd chosen the perfect setting. The inside of his throat felt alive, as if an animal were trying to wriggle out of him. Enough of this. Petersburg was his home, and Felix was certainly able to stand up to Tolya, of all people.

Felix swallowed hard as the footman opened the door.

"His Imperial Highness Grand Duke Felix Sergeevich," the footman said, with a bow. It was the proper form of address, but in front of Anatoli, the title held the hint of a sneer. It was the same disdain that hid in the ceremonial sash, the fine clothes, the artificial cheerfulness of his welcome. *You don't belong here. You never have.* Felix entered the parlor like a chess piece, straight forward across the parquet.

"Come in," Anatoli said, well after the fact.

His brother sat near the end of a rectangular table, flanked on both sides by sofas upholstered in blue damask. Behind him, at the sideboard, another two servants manned the samovar, both directing their gaze into the middle distance with the studied emptiness of someone trying to pretend they were not eavesdropping. A porcelain teacup hung easily in Anatoli's hand, empty now. Though his silver jacket was absurdly elegant for an evening spent among family, he looked more effortlessly in command than Felix had ever managed. Felix sat stiffly, causing the chair to creak.

"I assume Father's still in council," Felix said coldly.

Anatoli set the cup aside and shrugged, as if to say *What did you expect?* "I asked him to join us, but he's been cornered by the chairman of the State Council. You know how Bezkryostnov is when he gets in a snit."

Felix nodded, though of course he didn't know: the last chairman had been dismissed for the same display of liberal-minded impertinence that had gotten Felix sent away, and Bezkryostnov was the latest replacement. He bit his lip, watching his brother as the silent servants poured them fresh cups of steaming tea. Was the old Anatoli still somewhere inside this fine prince? The brother who had taught Felix all the best places to hide in the Summer Garden, who would brag to their mother on his behalf—*You should have seen how Felya skated today, Mama, faster than anything, he'd have frightened a Cossack.* That brother had to be in there somewhere: an entire person couldn't vanish without leaving some trace behind. But ever since their father had begun supervising the tsarevich's education in earnest, Felix could only spot the kind older brother he remembered in certain unconscious gestures, the way Anatoli held his cup between both palms, the tilt of his head. They sat sipping oversteeped tea hot enough to scald, with nothing more to say to each other than a pair of strangers.

"Katya's well?" Felix asked, purely to break the silence.

"Wonderful," Anatoli said. "Hoping to travel to Berlin in the spring for her brother's marriage, now that the war is through."

"Assuming we've chased Napoleon far enough away by then."

"Yes. Assuming that."

Another long silence. The sound of the clock in the corner was torturous.

"I've been thinking it over since the moment you arrived," Anatoli said finally, setting aside his cup, "and I still can't work it out. *Franchement*, that's why I asked to see you. So you can help me understand."

Felix did not move. There was something in Anatoli's voice more alarming than curiosity. "Understand what?"

"Why you're *here*."

Anatoli stood and paced toward the window, hands folded behind his back. The disdain shone clearly even in his posture as he studiously looked away from Felix, watching the shadowed snow filling the courtyard that divided one half of the palace from the other.

"If you'd burned through your allowance already, you could have dealt with that in a letter. You know Papa would gladly make sure you had everything you needed." *Everything you needed to stay as far away as possible*, Anatoli meant, but did not add. "Instead you come here, now, just when the damned war is over and Papa can finally start solidifying the stability he's created. It's as if you want to hurt him, though what he's ever done to you to deserve it, I have no idea."

Felix's sip of tea served like oil to a fire, fanning his indignation higher. "Solidifying the stability he's created"—a fine phrase, and true enough, so long as you closed your eyes and thought only of foreign ambassadors and trade negotiations and paid no attention to the city just outside these walls.

"I wonder what the people of Piter think of the tsar's stability."

When Anatoli turned back around, his lip had begun to curl, a cold and foreign anger coursing through him. Anatoli's anger had always been hotheaded, impetuous, easy enough to dodge or wait out. This was their father's rage, the kind that aimed before it fired. "You have no idea what the people think, Felya. Don't pretend you do."

Felix shoved his cup aside, his hands forming fists without his meaning them to. The sneering diminutive—little Felya, *mon petit frère*—pushed him past the point of being careful, and he spoke without thinking. "You tell me, then, if you've been listening so carefully. I never had you down as a defender of the people, but it's been two years, and who's to say? Men change. Maybe you're fast friends with your servants now, even remember their names."

Anatoli scoffed; both servants gazed expressionlessly ahead. "*Soyez pas con.* If you'd been here for more than ten minutes, you'd know yourself what they're saying. God knows they're saying it loud enough. If the people only understood they have the tsar to thank for bringing them peace." He strode back toward the table, as if the citizens of Petersburg were arrayed just outside the window, clawing to be let in. "There are demonstrations and riots every other evening. Idiots demanding wild sums of money, land they have no right to, the onset of anarchy. You know why Father is with Bezkryostnov right now? Because there's another assembly planned at the Andreevsky Market for the end of the week, and we need a way to tear out this uprising at the roots. Meanwhile, you're out in the country, hosting balls and seducing chambermaids, and you think that qualifies you to give the tsar advice?"

Riots in Petersburg. And he, less than twenty miles away, unaware. Sofia had told him that the country had begun to slip out of control, but it was already so much worse than he'd imagined. Felix gritted his teeth and tried to remind himself that the ignorance wasn't his fault, that his father had been the one to send him away, but there was no use lying, not to himself. It was his family's duty to lead the people of this vast, aching country. And he'd willingly set aside that responsibility at the first obstacle.

Enough. No more.

"I thought that's why we stood against Napoleon," Felix said. The room felt colder than ever, the long table separating the brothers like a vast plain. If Felix measured its length in steps, how many would he count? Enough for a duel? "So our family could rule our own people. Is the job not as attractive now that some French usurper isn't fighting you for it?"

"You don't understand, Felix," Anatoli said—the emphasis on his name cruelly condescending. "What it's like in the city. What people are thinking. What they're starting to want."

What the people wanted, the tsar would have said, was immaterial. What the people needed was a strong voice to tell them what to want, and a stronger hand to guide them away from any alternatives. It had always been this way, in all the lessons Felix had sat through in his youth, tsar after tsar firm and decisive and final. Even he, who had avoided his tutors until one of them enlisted half a dozen guards to search the palace for him, knew that much. But now the people had known the end of the war. They'd known the privations of rationing, the French army bearing down on Moscow, setting their ancient city ablaze with their own torches rather than shame their country through surrender. They'd known all of that pain, and they'd fought, they'd proven themselves as brave as the officers they'd died beside, and for them, what had changed? What had the tsar's famed peace done for them?

That was what Sofia had wanted to make him understand, back in the Hall of Lights. Small wonder the people of Petersburg were rioting. Hopelessness was a dangerous infection, and it could come to one of only two ends. Either the people would sink down, exhausted, into torpor and blind obedience—or a single spark would catch the dry tinder of their despair, and the city would go up in flames.

"Help me understand, then," Felix said, leaning across the table toward his brother. "Let me help you."

"We aren't interested in the kind of help you have to offer," Anatoli snapped. "You want to help us? Do the minimum we've asked of you and marry whichever German princess you can stand to speak to. And the sooner the better. Your reputation is making it less and less likely every day."

A mad laugh bubbled up in Felix's throat. His brother had no idea what Felix was capable of, the tactical skill and strategic brain behind the façade of the decadent prince. Tolya didn't understand—as Felix did, perhaps for the first time—that their father had sent him away not because he was a fool, but because he was powerful enough to be listened to. He had no idea of the voice in Felix's ear right now, the voice of a woman who believed in him, her faith as old and powerful as Russia itself.

The voice whispering, *Stop waiting.*

"You said Father is with Bezkryostnov?"

Anatoli blinked. "Yes. For hours yet. Are you listening to me?"

"Oh, I'm listening," Felix said. "But charming as this has been, I didn't come to Piter to meet with you. In fact, I might just pay Father and the chairman a visit. They're in his study, I assume? He always liked the comfort of his own rooms for a good haranguing."

"Felix," Anatoli warned. "Don't. You know what would happen."

But it was too late. Felix was already halfway to the door, and the servants did not dare stop him.

The tsar's study, dead center of the imperial apartments, was a straight shot along the *bel étage* from the late tsarina's parlor, its door firmly closed. Not far—certainly not far enough for a shocked Anatoli to overtake and stop him, and none of the palace servants had worked up the daring to challenge a grand duke. A voice murmured inside the study, one Felix didn't recognize. The chairman's, no doubt—it lacked the tsar's decisive cadence. A month ago, before Sofia's arrival, Felix might have hesitated, frozen by the danger of what he was about to do, but not now. Now, the voice in the back of his head pushed him forward with the cold surety of the north wind.

Stop waiting.

Felix flung open the door and stepped into the tsar's now deathly silent study.

11

Sasha

The vila was everywhere, and Sasha couldn't bear it.

He couldn't take a breath in the Winter Palace without sensing her nearby, feeling her over his shoulder, seeing icy hair flash around a corner. A palace the size of a village, staffed by hundreds, should have been an easy place to keep one's distance from an enemy. And yet Sofia existed in every shadow, in every room. She wasn't living in the palace so much as possessing it, and Sasha felt her haunting like a sickness.

It had been a mistake to ever let it get this far.

He stood at the edge of the Concert Hall, leaning against the high arched window overlooking the Neva. The room was dim and silent at this late hour. The palace was large enough that a vast space like this could be left vacant, aired out only for chamber music performances held perhaps once a month. The towering arched ceiling was supported by massive Grecian columns, atop which perched carvings of classically dressed women Sasha assumed, based on the nonsense poetry Felix used to spout when in a good mood, must be the Muses. Their stone faces looked eerie from this distance and in such shadow, sharp and unyielding. The tremendous chandelier, four tiers of polished crystal, seemed a ghost of itself without light and life swirling beneath. Through the window, the frozen band of the Neva glowed dark purple against the faint light of the city.

A flash of movement on the other side of the window. The unmistakable flutter of feathers.

Sasha stumbled back. If not for the expensive plate-glass window between him and the night, he'd have drawn his pistol and fired at the shape. It passed again, this time catching starlight against its feathers, and Sasha could see it clearly before it darted off across the river. A goldfinch, no larger than his palm. Nothing more. A family of goldfinches had nested outside his window as a child. He'd watched them chase one another over the fields during the war.

This massive hall, empty as a mausoleum, and still she wouldn't stop haunting him.

He stood straight, folding his hands behind his back. If the Muses had cared to observe the soldier beneath them, they would surely have believed Sasha to be in perfect control of himself, but Sasha had never felt so far out of his element. His thoughts swirled like the hidden eddies beneath the frozen river, a submerged disturbance that looked, to the uninitiated outsider, like quiet.

You brought her here. You found her in the snow and brought her inside, and as thanks she sunk her claws into everything that ever mattered to you. Your country. Your faith. The man you love. She holds all of it in her talons now, ready to tear, and it's all your fault. Everything that happens next will be your fault.

He shook his head so hard his brain seemed to rattle. That was weakness. That was like a soldier weeping in the night because he blamed himself for the bayonet through his captain's gut, when no quantity of tears would ever bring the man back. Sasha had never permitted himself to be that person, and he didn't intend to start now. There was always an enemy in every war; no reason to become your own.

It isn't your fault. A man can't control the devil. And that's who sent her, whatever she says. You've heard the stories since the day you were born. The vila blessing their heroes and then shredding their flesh with cruel hooked beaks. The rusalki whispering sweet promises to men before dragging them into the depths. They all have the same roots, the same master. Pray all you like, but the devil's servants never listen to prayer. She'd have found a way in even without you.

But she didn't have to find a way. You let her in. She's here, in the home of the tsar, because of you.

He snarled and drove his fist into the wall.

Because of you.

Delicate wallpaper and plastered wainscoting lent the palace a misleadingly fragile face. Its walls were more than strong enough to take a single blow without flinching. Sasha swore and clutched his hand. A smear of blood from his knuckles had left its stamp on the wall, dark copper in the shadow. Everywhere he turned, it seemed, he left blood in his wake. What was a man like him meant to do in peacetime?

"I don't understand," he'd said to Felix once, early in their acquaintance, one of those otherworldly summer nights that never darkened, the pale midnight sun casting curious shadows through Felix's bedroom. "You chose me to serve you, and for the life of me I don't understand why."

And Felix, his brow damp with sweat, shirtsleeves pushed past his elbows, Felix had laughed, and he'd said, "The truth? For all I'm certain you know three dozen creative ways to kill me, you made me feel safe when I met you. I can count the number of people who make me feel safe on one hand."

The corollary of violence was safety. The other side of blood was a vow of service. Love wasn't love unless it came with responsibility. Felix had made him see it then, but Sasha suspected he had always known it.

A beam of light flashed through the Concert Hall from the open door, piercing and inescapable as a great eye. Sasha flinched, drawing back instinctively from the glow. But it was only a servant, crossing the gallery with a lamp in hand. Toward the imperial family's private apartments, where the tsar and his two sons would spend the evening as royals did, surrounded by luxury and power.

Where that miserable creature with sulfur for eyes would be creeping through every shadow, pouring her poison into Felix's ear.

Sasha had tried behaving like a man who understood peace, but war was in his blood, the only truth he knew. Those who sought a reason to delay would always find one: a general's lingering cough or an ill-omened cloud on the horizon. And every moment's delay gave the enemy the chance to better position itself. Christ hadn't waited for a tactical advantage to challenge the devil.

Come on, then, said a voice on the other side of the glass, where the goldfinch had flown. *Enough talk. Show me the power of your conviction.*

Sasha ran one hand along the grip of his pistol, then disappeared through the door into the gallery.

12

Felix

Against the sumptuous adornment of the rest of the Winter Palace, the tsar's private study was startlingly ascetic. It was the one room Tsar Sergei had free rein to decorate as he chose, unconstrained by the weight of tradition or the need to create a conspicuous spectacle of wealth to intimidate foreign leaders. If Felix's father had his way, no doubt he would have outfitted the entire palace in this manner: polished oak furniture, forest-green velvet curtains, not a single cornice or column beyond those integral to the structure of the room. Sober. Practical. Felix had always privately believed his father would be happier far away from the excesses of Petersburg. Perhaps living in a small hunting dacha near Novorossiysk, dressed in furs and stalking an elk.

Reality, of course, had other plans for the Komarovs.

Bezkryostnov must have been speaking before the door opened: the man's owlish face bore the unmistakable affronted expression of someone halted in the middle of a phrase. The wire-thin chairman stood in front of the vast rectangular desk at the south end of the room, staring at Felix in incomprehension. Felix ignored him entirely.

Behind the desk sat Tsar Sergei Alexeevich. His uniform was flawlessly creased, as though it hung in a wardrobe and not on a man. Those deep blue eyes—Felix's eyes, one more part of the Komarov legacy that had carried forward—coolly sized up his son with neither anger nor surprise, only a faint undercurrent of disappointment. The welcome was even worse than Felix had feared.

"Good evening, Felix," the tsar said. "I did not send for you."

Felix swallowed, feeling his courage quail. Anatoli must have entered behind him; his father glanced toward the door as if expecting an apology to emerge from that direction.

"No," Felix said. "I wasn't sure you ever would."

The tsar sighed, then made a swift gesture toward Bezkryostnov. "Nikolai Semyonovich," he said wearily, "I'll send for you in the morning to finish this discussion. For now, I think you had better leave us."

Bezkryostnov did not wait to be told again. He bowed rapidly to the tsar, then darted around Anatoli and out of the room as if the hounds of hell were in hot pursuit. The tsar's stern, handsome face looked wearier than Felix remembered it. Was that a consequence of his own arrival, or had years of on-and-off war with the French weighed more heavily on his father's shoulders than he'd expected? They'd certainly left their traces in his hair. None of Felix's memories of his father included the strands of silver that now shot through the tsar's hair and beard.

"It may surprise you to hear this," the tsar said, "but being tsar does not afford me an inordinate quantity of leisure time. When I ask Anatoli to tell you I'm otherwise engaged, I expect you to believe it."

"I do believe it."

"Then why are you here?"

Felix had heard that voice before, many times. It was the voice with which the tsar had addressed his wife, the single time Felix could remember Natalya Fyodorovna daring to raise a dissenting political opinion in front of the tsar's ministers. It was the voice with which he'd banished Felix from the council chamber and then from the city. It was the voice all Komarov men were meant to have mastered so that it became as natural as breathing, the one that said, *I value your opinion less than dirt, less than nothing at all.*

The dread in his bones lasted only a moment before he squared his shoulders, surprising himself with his own boldness. It was as if Sofia's words had dripped from his memory into his skeleton, steeling his spine. He was a Komarov. They might crush anyone else who attempted to challenge them, but it would take more than a curt voice and a stern brow to turn him away.

"We need to talk, Father," he said. "We've needed to talk for years."

The tsar exhaled and leaned back in his chair. His overall air was that of a man preparing for a theatrical production he had not wished to attend. Confronting his father still felt like squaring off with a bear, righteous determination or no.

"Talk, then," the tsar said.

Felix cleared his throat. "The tsarevich told me about the assembly in the Andreevsky Market. I want to know what you intend to do about it."

"Papa, I tried to tell him—" Anatoli began, but fell victim to the tsar's silencing look.

"You can't be surprised they're starting to agitate," Felix said. He was speaking too fast now, gesturing too broadly, but who was he to try to stem the tide? "What do you expect them to think, when they stop freezing in the streets long enough to see a fire blazing in every window of the Winter Palace? You think they look at pictures of their tsar done up in gold and all they think is, 'Well, thank God the tsar is thriving,' while they're still shivering in clothes shredded by French bayonets?"

The tsar stood; Felix dropped back. Contained behind the desk, the tsar's physical power had been masked. Now, in the open, he looked fully the man Felix remembered, all six feet three inches of him. This was the tsar who had broken a fox's neck with his hands when the bullet had failed to kill the hunt's quarry, who had drunk straight through the endless winter nights and spent the entirety of the next day riding as if sleep were for lesser beings not touched by God. Nothing could stop that man.

"And I suppose you know better than anyone what the people think," the tsar said. "You've been chatting with them over tea, I expect. In the drawing room of the Catherine Palace. Every bedroom full up with beggars and prostitutes."

Felix flushed but gave no further ground. "I know it."

"How, exactly?"

He'd seen it in the shadows of a ballroom, a second reality creeping like a smoke screen over the first. Bloody wounds and mouths torn open in endless screams. He couldn't possibly tell his father that. Was he mad after all? He must be, to think he could argue with the tsar and win.

The insistent echo of Sofia's voice pushed him forward, shoving away his doubts. No, he wasn't mad. He was the only member of this family who knew how to *listen*.

"Trust me that I know," Felix snapped. "You would, too, if you ever set a toe outside your dozen palaces. When's the last time you spoke to a person who isn't a baron or a princess or a minister, Father? A few hundred of them can't outweigh the three hundred thousand in the streets of your city."

The flat of the tsar's palm slammed against the desk, and Felix flinched as if he himself had been struck. Neither of the tsar's sons dared to speak. This was the sort of silence one did not break without permission.

"You," the tsar said, "are a child. A coward. And though I won't dishonor your mother's memory by suggesting it, there are days I wish you were no son of mine. Now get out of my sight, before I expend the very last of my patience."

"You've been in this palace so long you've forgotten what your people—"

"Exactly." The tsar's voice fell like thunder, striking Felix silent. "They *are* my people. I've led them through everything. War. Uncertainty. Famine. Thirty endless winters, one after the next. And still they turn to me to set the country right, after every calamity that sets us back. Me, and the dynasty our family began. Do you know why?" The pause was long enough to invite a response, the silence too thick to permit it. "Because they know who I am. And in the darkest hours of this country, they turn to the Komarov on the imperial throne to steer the way with a strong hand and turn aside any threat. That is what General Kutuzov and I did with Napoleon's Grande Armée. That is what Chairman Bezkryostnov and I are doing with the rioters in the Andreevsky. And it is what I will do with every agitator who thinks his own ideas are worth more than the safety and stability of my empire, whether it's a band of lawless rebels in the street or my own son. *Tu comprends?*"

It was the longest sustained speech Felix's father had deigned to deliver to him in years. Even in the months before his departure for Tsarskoe Selo, their conversation had been limited to terse, utilitarian exchanges: *Good morning, Hand me that notice, Your brother is in the gallery.* When the tsar turned his attention on Felix with this much force, it was hot enough to melt under.

"I understand you perfectly," Felix said. "That doesn't mean I agree."

"Felix," Anatoli said again, "for God's sake—"

Felix turned to his brother, pivoting his anger without effort. Anatoli didn't care what Felix had to say. All the tsarevich wanted was for their father to see him as the reliable son, the one who could be trusted with the throne in due course. The good son, who had not failed their father.

"You know I'm right. If you looked farther than your own nose for one minute, Tolya, you'd see it, too."

The rest of the thought died on his tongue. Anatoli's dark blue eyes were wide, his expression pleading. This wasn't the disapproving, conservative brother he'd expected to chastise him for holding wayward opinions. This was how Tolya had looked at twelve, bending over him when Felix had fallen from that tree at the palace at Gatchina, anxiously checking his leg for a break before sprinting back to the house to call for help. His brother was frightened for him. He knew what their father was capable of.

A flicker of parallel fear danced through Felix, there and gone in an instant. If Anatoli didn't have the stomach to point out their father's mistakes, he didn't need to stay here. Felix had never asked him to come to his defense.

"A strong hand is one thing," Felix said. "But it only works so long as the people consent to be led. What happens when they change their mind? Push a brittle branch too far, and what happens when it snaps?"

A terrible silence followed.

"If you were not my son," the tsar said slowly, "you would already be dead for what you've said to me tonight."

Chilled but not daunted, Felix stood his ground. This was why he'd come. He'd argue all night, fight with everything he had, if it would make a difference. He would be the kind of man he knew he could be. The man Sofia believed in.

The unmistakable sound of a gunshot broke through the silence, followed by the crash of shattering glass.

Father and both sons looked at one another blankly.

"What . . ." Anatoli began.

Felix was already sprinting for the door, his brother's protest fading to nothing in his ears.

13

Sasha

He heard her soft whisper ahead of him, breathlike and always moving. No matter how fast his pursuit, she was always just ahead. Taunting him. The Winter Palace was a maze, corridors spilling outward and doubling back, a staircase where he expected to find a wall. Mirrors, mirrors everywhere, reflecting back his own haunted face. All around him this impossible beauty, like a poisoned jewel one still longed to touch. And there, just over his left shoulder, a flash of movement, the tail of a braid—

Sasha turned, met by a blank wall.

The voice sounded again, farther down the hall now, mocking. Just out of reach, or never there at all?

"Come now. Is this how you made your name in the field? The fearsome Captain Dorokhin, who stalked and killed every Frenchman on the Smolensk road, who led men to their deaths at Maloyaroslavets. Prove yourself, then. Find me if you want me."

He'd never wanted anything more.

It had been two years since Sasha had served in the Winter Palace, and his knowledge of its halls was not what it had once been. The part of his brain suited to navigation thrived under the open sky—here, every priceless painting and gold-plated vase looked the same as the next. Even so, the internal compass honed over months in the field pointed him west, away from the suite of public ballrooms where he'd been lingering, deeper into the private apartments of the Komarov family.

Toward the tsar.

As he quickened his pace, his footfalls echoed against the walls, as if he were being tailed as well as the one tailing. This was why hunts were meant for the open air. A man would go mad like this. He thought he saw a scrap of black fabric flash around a corner, but by the time he made the turn, the hall was as empty as the one he'd just left. Surely there should have been guards here, this close to the tsar's private rooms. Had the vila dismissed them somehow? The stories gave them power both of prophecy and persuasion— she might have turned them away with a word. Whatever the cause, it did not matter. She would not get away. She might be driving him entirely, fully mad, but in the end, mad or sane or lost somewhere in between, he would find her.

Around the corner, the long hallway running through the center of the tsar's private apartments stretched before him. The corners were shadowed, despite lights shining from each room lining the hall. He recalled Felix once describing this part of the palace as the "dark corridor." When Felix had been small, he'd said, he would hang back at the edge of it, frozen, until one of the servants came with a light to guide him through the shadows to his mother's chamber. Felix had laughed when telling that story, self-deprecating, and Sasha had dismissed it as a simple childhood fear. Now, seeing the corridor yawn in front of him, he understood. This was the kind of hall where anything could hide.

And it was here—of course it was here—that she waited for him.

Insubstantial as a ghost, dressed in black that made her skin seem washed-out, fainter than white. There could be no breeze within the corridor, every window well-sealed and locked, yet her spun-silver hair seemed to ripple from her shoulders, fluttering like the feathers of a bird in flight. Though she was too far away for Sasha to see her face, he felt her eyes sharp as teeth, and the cruel curve of her smile goading him onward.

Before he could think better of it, Sasha drew his pistol and fired.

The mirror at the end of the dark corridor shattered, sending lightning strikes of broken glass through Sofia's reflected face. He whirled around, but she was already gone, if indeed she had ever been there at all. Only the fractured mirror remained, and the shards of glass littering the floor.

Without thinking, Sasha took off in pursuit, frightening a scream from a maidservant as he tore past. It was unquestionably stupid. It was all he could think of to do. Whatever kind of creature Sofia was, she still breathed, and still lived by bread, and still slept when she was weary. Blood still filled her veins. A bullet ought to kill her, the same as any other beast.

Around the corner stretched the corridor that led to the tsar's study. And there, in the glow of secondhand light from an open door, stood the vila.

Her hair had come loose from its braid, strands haloing around her face, and her lips were parted, but not in fear—in their curve, Sasha saw the cruel, laughing taunt of a predator. This wasn't the woman Felix thought he knew. This was a monster of nightmares and ghost stories, the vila who fought alongside the bloodiest warriors, a growing pile of corpses at her feet. This wasn't a spirit you longed for; it was one you locked your doors against and prayed never to meet. And he would never get a cleaner shot than this.

Aleksandr Nikolaevich was known for one thing in the Imperial Army, and it was his unholy ability never to miss. He'd picked off fleeing soldiers from more than a hundred yards with a single shot. The woman stood barely twenty feet from him, armed only with a smile that could freeze a man's blood. His aim was perfect. He sighted without hesitation, both eyes open, and fired again.

"Sasha!"

Despite himself, he turned. Felix burst out of the tsar's study, frozen half in, half out of the doorway.

"Get back!" Sasha said, spinning around again.

The shot had been flawless, but there was no body on the floor, and no blood. Only a gaping hole in the window at the end of the hall, a cold wind rippling through it into the corridor. If he squinted, he thought he could make out footprints in the snowy courtyard, but with the wind as it was, they would be gone before he could follow where they led.

And there, gliding northward into the city, a pale white shadow, a massive snowy owl with its wings fully extended, riding the Petersburg night.

The arm holding the pistol sank to his side. With the other, he crossed himself three times, flowing through the prescribed movements with something nearing desperation. *Lord God, save and protect me,* he thought. He'd seen dead men before, hundreds of them, mutilated in ways beyond imagination, but the terror that rose in him at the sight of that bird was unlike any terror he'd ever known.

"What is the meaning of this?" roared a voice behind him. "Guards!"

Sasha's heart froze. Time itself seemed to stop. Slowly—very slowly—he looked.

In front of him stood Tsar Sergei.

The tsar looked as if the towering portrait in the Catherine Palace that Sasha passed beneath daily had stepped through its frame: not a brushstroke different, not a hair out of place. The resemblance was unnerving. As if a character from a fairy story had escaped from the page into the real world. The tsar stood a few steps in front of Tsarevich Anatoli, whose face—so like Felix's, and yet nothing like it—was alive with fear. The tsar, on the other hand, had overleaped alarm in favor of rage. His voice echoed in the corridor like cannon fire. An ivory-handled penknife glinted in his right hand, likely the only item in the study resembling a weapon. Not that it was apt to do much damage except at close range, but one could not fault the tsar for nerve.

"Who are you?" the tsar demanded. "Who sent you?"

Sasha dropped the pistol to the ground with a clatter and fell to one knee. The protocol for presenting oneself to the tsar had been drilled into him since the first moment he entered Felix's service, but terror made the specifics impossible to remember. Should he have bowed instead? Genuflected? All he wanted to do was run.

"Captain Aleksandr Dorokhin, Your Imperial Majesty," he said quietly. "No one sent me. I'm here to protect you." The full severity of his situation dawned on him all at once. *You colossal idiot, you fired a* pistol *ten feet from the* tsar, *in his* house, *if you wanted to invent a way to get yourself executed by firing squad you'd have given up on this as too obvious.* He raised both hands, palms spread wide. His hands shook, and he was certain the tsar could see it. "I beg you to understand, Your Imperial Majesty, there was a woman, she—"

"I should have known," Felix snarled.

No. He wouldn't.

But of course he would. Sasha could only watch helplessly as the tsar turned to his younger son, though not before he snatched up the pistol that Sasha had let fall. There was terror in Felix's eyes now, undergirded by resolve. It was a look Sasha had never seen in the usually artless grand duke. That look, he knew, was Sofia's doing.

"You," the tsar said. He advanced slowly on Felix, his hand clenching the pistol. "This was you. Sending your man after me, armed, to threaten me into giving your childish, radical ideas credence."

"No," Sasha breathed, on the brink of true panic now. "Your Majesty, I've only ever tried to serve you—"

Before he could finish, a pack of three guards rounded the corner. Weapons drawn, they spread out across the corridor, eyes darting to evaluate the threat. Sasha saw the moment determination mixed with confusion in their eyes. Expecting a black-garbed assassin, they had instead come upon the tsar, the tsarevich, the grand duke, and a sworn soldier of the empire. And the tsar, at present, was the only one armed.

"Your Majesty," one of the guards began, "what—"

"That is what I mean to determine," the tsar said. "Felix. Start talking. At once."

Felix took a deep breath, followed by a trembling exhale. He glanced first at Sasha, then at the armed guard arrayed behind him.

"Believe me, Father," he said quietly, "Sasha is the most loyal soldier you could wish for. I know who he fired at. And it's as he says. He thinks he's defending you."

Sasha had known Felix for years, better than he had ever known anyone else. He knew the exact moment when the grand duke decided to say the most awful thing he could.

"But he's wrong."

Sasha had stopped breathing. This imperious man might be Felix's father, but he was still Tsar Sergei. Russia's Little Father before all else, ready to bring any of his children into line should they happen to stray. It was like watching a stranger climb on the railing of a bridge and prepare to jump: horrifying, but impossible to turn away from.

Felix's voice was rising in pitch and tempo now, sounding simultaneously more fervent and less convincing. "*Je t'aime, Papa.* I would never hurt you. But it's because I love you that I'm telling you this. Sofia is right, and you're wrong. And if you give your soldiers permission to fire on every person who dares to tell you so, you won't like what might happen next."

"I see," the tsar said quietly.

It was as if a wall had risen behind the tsar's eyes. The towering rage that had made him seem like a divinely inspired warrior moments before had been locked away, vanished as suddenly as extinguishing a candle. This impassivity, to Sasha, was infinitely more frightening. He did not dare rise from the floor.

"Devyatov, Erdenko," the tsar said. Two of the guards snapped a salute, awaiting orders. "Find the grand duke's companion, that peasant woman. Search the palace, the grounds, anywhere she might have fled. Confine her to the Bastion when you find her."

"Yes, Your Majesty," came the inevitable chorus.

"Kopenkin," the tsar said to the remaining guard. "Go with Captain Dorokhin. Escort Grand Duke Felix to his rooms and ensure that he stays there."

Sasha and Felix both froze.

"In what capacity is Captain Dorokhin coming, Your Majesty?" Kopenkin said.

The tsar looked down at Sasha, still kneeling. The pause that followed felt interminable. "As a guard," he said at last. "But without his weapon. And if he attempts to aid the grand duke in any way, shoot him."

Sasha's skin felt too tight, as if woven for a different body. But now was not the time to think, or to feel. The tsar had given him an order, and his reason for being was to follow those orders when they were issued. He could consider their implications later, when there was time.

"Father—" Felix began.

But the tsar half raised a hand, and Felix snapped his mouth shut. Whatever else, the tsar had trained his sons well. "If you were anyone else," he said coldly, "I'd have Devyatov and Erdenko drag you to the Bastion along with your friend, and you'd be executed before the week is out. I ought to have you arrested regardless. Out of a father's generosity, I choose to believe that you've simply gone mad. But that doesn't mean I intend to take chances with you."

"Your Imperial Highness," Kopenkin said to Felix. The guard's light brown eyes were stern, faintly worried. "If you would follow me."

Felix stared at him for a pregnant moment, daring him to back down. Kopenkin barely blinked. He reached out and took Felix by the wrist, leading him at a rapid clip toward his chambers. Sasha followed automatically, mind blank. Anatoli and the tsar stood motionless behind them, surrounded by cold air and broken glass.

The moment they were out of sight of the tsar and tsarevich, Sasha watched Felix's veneer of self-control vanish. A wordless noise escaped the grand duke's mouth, and when he spoke, it was with a waver that would break Sasha's heart if he let it.

"*Sang du ciel*, you can't be serious."

The only way Sasha could do this was not to feel anything,

and this kind of numbness demanded action to fill the space left behind. He did not look at Felix, focusing on keeping in step with Kopenkin. "Move."

Kopenkin dismissed the servant standing outside Felix's rooms with a curt gesture that forbade questions, then flung the door open. "Your Highness," he said. "I would suggest you cooperate. I don't wish to use force."

Narrow eyed, Felix stood unnaturally still in front of the open door. His fear had transformed into something far easier for Sasha to identify, because he knew it well, had long ago learned how to use it. Anger.

"How could you," Felix said—and God, it was so much harder for Sasha to remain detached now, hearing the hurt in Felix's voice. "Sasha, you know me, you know I'd never hurt him."

"I know that," Sasha said, painfully aware of Kopenkin's intent expression only steps away. "But the tsar doesn't. And you can hardly fault him after what you said. You ought to be begging for his forgiveness, not fighting me about—"

"Forgiveness." Felix shoved Sasha in the chest with both hands. "How dare you. I'm not the one who needs to be forgiven."

It was a pathetic blow, capable only of irritating. Sasha barely moved in its wake. But at the sensation of Felix pushing him away, something in Sasha snapped shut. The strength of the tsar's express order straightened his spine and steeled his resolve. It simplified everything. All that remained now was the cold of his own heart, steadily hardening until he couldn't feel betrayal, or pain, or fear. Only certainty.

Felix had decided to turn his back on his family, his country, the only person who had ever truly cared for him, to throw in his lot with a madwoman, a demon, on the basis of a few pretty words and a promise of power. So be it. Sasha served Russia and the tsar. He served God. He did not serve Felix. If Felix wanted to play this game, let him try it. After harrying the French down the Smolensk road, Sasha knew a thing or two about keeping an eye on the enemy.

"That's for the tsar to decide," he said coldly. "Kopenkin, if you would?"

He had only a moment to witness the shocked, almost childlike hurt in Felix's wide eyes before Kopenkin forced the grand duke through the open door and slammed it in his face, locking it from the outside.

Sasha's hands trembled—he curled them into fists to still them. Just through this door, he could almost see Felix sinking down onto the bed, taking his head in his hands. Sasha wanted to take Felix in his arms and protect him from everything, from himself, to kiss the back of his hand and apologize in every language under the sun. Instead, he stood straight. Feet firmly planted against the floor, six inches apart. Arms folded behind his back. The model soldier, executing orders. He knew this pose. The space between focus and dreaming. A middle distance, one that narrowed the larger world to a single task, one responsibility, one thought. Keep Felix where he was. He would do that, and only that.

"I haven't forgotten what the tsar said about you," Kopenkin said, standing beside Sasha in an identical posture.

Sasha did not look at him. "Neither have I."

Around them, the corridor glowed with honeyed lamplight, thick and stultifying. When he closed his eyes, he saw the jagged lightning strike of the shattered mirror, bisecting a woman's face, and that hungry twist of her smile.

Eyes open, he saw nothing at all.

A SONG UNWISELY SUNG

In the thrice-tenth kingdom, beyond the thrice-ninth land, a captain and his lieutenant rode together through the woods, enjoying the quiet of the afternoon. They were returning home from a campaign in which they had served bravely and secured many riches, and both were in high spirits as they listened to the birdsong and the whisper of the wind.

"Come, my friend," said the captain, "it's only right that the world shares in our victory. Sing with me, one of the drinking songs from the camp."

The captain expected the lieutenant, an exuberant fellow, to toss back his head and break out in song. Instead, the lieutenant turned pale and avoided the captain's eyes, as if some great fear had taken him.

"I would, without a second thought," said the lieutenant, "if we were anywhere but in these woods."

"Why, is there something to fear among these trees?"

The lieutenant hesitated, but at a severe look from his captain, he sighed, then began to explain. "Once, when I was a youth, I came into these woods with my sweetheart, and we drank too much wine and made the whole forest ring with our song. Then a vila appeared to us from out of the shadows. Out of jealousy of our voices, she swore that if she ever heard me sing again, she would pierce my heart and my throat with her silver arrows."

The captain was troubled, but refused to let the soldier see it, for he was the man's superior and knew he ought to be above such superstition. "I didn't take you for a child who still believes in tales," he said, with a hearty laugh meant to convince them both. "Sing with me, and don't be afraid. Haven't we faced more terrible foes in the field?"

And the lieutenant trusted the captain with his life, so he began to sing a bawdy song they had both loved from their days in the camp, their two voices rising high and clear.

A rustle came from above, in the treetops. The lieutenant stopped singing.

"Merely a bird," said the captain. "Sing on."

The lieutenant swallowed his misgivings and continued. Another rustle disturbed him, but before he could stop his song to inquire, his body sagged from his horse and fell to the forest floor below. Two arrows jutted from his motionless body, blood glittering at their tips.

One through the throat, and one through the perfect center of his heart.

The captain let out a cry and galloped off in pursuit of the rustling in the trees, which he knew now beyond doubt to be the vila. He chased her through the woods and across the streams, down treacherous paths and into the depths of shadow. The vila flew fast and would have escaped him, but the captain was driven by inhuman fury, and with one throw of his powerful club, he struck the vila between the shoulders and felled her to the earth.

Stunned but not killed, the vila tried to escape, but the captain had pinned her to the forest floor with his boot.

"God defend you, creature," cried the captain, "you've killed a fine man, and for what? Your own whim, your jealousy? Come with me and heal him with your arts, or I swear by all that I hold holy, you shall not carry your head upon your shoulders another moment."

The vila cringed, knowing that she had been bested, and the captain dragged her back to where the lieutenant's body still lay. With a touch from the vila, the wounds healed themselves as if they had never been, and the lieutenant sat up, untroubled by his ordeal save for a pounding headache. The captain turned to finish his revenge on the vila, but she had already fled back into the trees, where her sister spirits waited for her in great consternation.

"You're lucky to have escaped with your life!" they exclaimed.

"It's that captain who is lucky to escape," said the vila grimly. "But I won't forget the shame he brought me today. He thinks my hatred is a whim, but he doesn't know me. He doesn't know how long I remember. And he doesn't know I always get my revenge."

14

Felix

Fists clenched, face burning, he stood as seconds became minutes, staring at the door that had just slammed shut in his face. He wanted to scream, but he wouldn't give Sasha the satisfaction of hearing it. He would be silent, unmoved, while the wreckage of his life fell around him. At last, he sank onto the end of the bed, surrounded by the clothes he'd flung across it in what felt like another life. He'd always known his father thought him foolish, impulsive, useless. But this—that the tsar would think him capable of treason.

To think that in the moment, treason had been exactly what he'd meant.

A flash of movement at the corner of his eye. Outside the window, a shock of white against the black. The wings of a great snowy owl, slicing a path through the night away from the Winter Palace. Even through the glass, Felix thought he could hear its screech. It felt like a sign. He stood up and ran his hand along his mouth. He wasn't trapped, not yet. The palace couldn't hold him if he refused to let it. This went in the face of everything that should have been dear to a Komarov: family, country, loyalty, authority. Everything that had governed his education, his morals, his reason for being. But the two sides of the question had made themselves clear, and there was only one path he could choose. He couldn't stay here and prostrate himself in front of his father, begging forgiveness for speaking a truth he was the only one brave enough to see. And if he refused to recant, he'd find himself left in a prison cell to rot, or worse.

He had to escape. Now, or he would never get another chance.

He pulled open the wardrobe and rifled through for the least obtrusive articles of clothing he'd brought with him. Curse the Winter Palace for its formality. Practically nothing he had would help him remain incognito, but in terms of fashion at least, he'd always been able to improvise. A simple black shirt with silver stitching, dark blue trousers with white piping down the leg, an unremarkable black overcoat. He would hardly pass for a common workman, but a vaguely Europeanized man with modest clothes and social aspirations was as remarkable in Petersburg as a monk in a monastery.

Just outside, Sasha would be standing with his back straight as a bayonet, shutting out all thoughts except for his duty. Ever the loyal subject. Felix had seen him that way a hundred times before. He'd never hated it until now.

The window opened easily, as it always had. It was almost enough to make him laugh, despite it all. If the tsar didn't want Felix to break out of the palace, best not to lock him in the same rooms he'd spent the better part of his childhood sneaking out of.

He crouched on the sill, feeling the full danger of what he was about to do. It was a thirty-foot drop if he missed, and the darkness made it even more difficult to find the right footing. Besides, his father's guards were already on the hunt for Sofia, and he was as good as condemned if they caught sight of him. Curls of snow whipped through the open window until he felt the cold drench his bones. The trick had seemed significantly easier at twelve than it did at twenty-eight. Then, it had been the start of an adventure, with only his mother's disappointment to face in the morning if he was caught. Now, it felt like a circus act, one he hadn't practiced in more than a decade. Of all the ways to die, this had to be the stupidest.

He shook his head—it was only air, only snow, only winter—and secured his grip. Every moment he delayed might send one of his father's men after him, ending with him chained in a cell or with a bullet in his back. He took a breath, then eased himself down, carefully, silently, to the balcony below. The curtains had been half drawn against the French doors, but through the opening he could see an empty room, and the weak hinge he'd doctored himself as a teenager. It was the work of a silent minute before he was back inside the palace, stealing from alcove to alcove to keep out of sight of the servants. The service stair wasn't far, and he took it as quickly as he could, not leaving time for the fear to freeze him. Between his nerves and the tight circles of the spiral staircase, his head soon began to swim. He gripped the rail at the bottom and braced himself, gathering what courage he could find. Then he shouldered the door open and stepped out into the night, praying for safety under cover of darkness.

The palace loomed over him, each window lit, shedding a soft glow behind drawn curtains. It reminded him of the magic lantern his mother had brought him from his parents' diplomatic trip to Sweden, back when he was very small and still seduced by lies told sweetly. The images that projected from the lantern were bathed in light, wild beasts and mounted hunters coursing across his wall, detailed yet lacking any depth. The palace, too, looked thin, like pasteboard and paint. Like it might stand for a thousand years, and at the same time like a stiff wind might send it crumbling.

Inside that palace sat the tsar and his loyal son, who would soon discover that Felix was no longer where they'd left him. And when they did, it would unleash a storm of wrath on the imperial court. An escape in pursuit of a vanished intruder, on the heels of a dangerous outburst, after predicting the collapse of his father's reign. Even a forgiving tsar could not have ignored such a threat, and Tsar Sergei was anything but lenient. No, the great administrative beast that was the Winter Palace would lurch into action the moment it discovered he'd escaped, and it would not rest until Felix was captured, disarmed, brought to heel.

But for that to happen, they'd have to catch him first.

He saw her then, as if she'd known what he would do and had waited here for him. Sofia stood at the palace gate, still wrapped in her long black coat. She reached out a hand, and he took it, desperate for anything that felt like safety. His gloved hand trembled in hers, but with the strength of her grip, a breath of his own courage seemed to return.

"You're full of surprises, aren't you?" Sofia said.

"You as well," he said. "How is it there aren't guards?"

"If I don't want us to be seen," she said simply, "we won't be. Are you sure about this?"

"I'm sure," he said. "You're the only one who understands. I'm with you, no matter what."

She smiled, and then—the gesture seeming to surprise her as much as it did him—pulled him into a tight embrace. He could feel his own heartbeat screaming between them, nervous as any hunted animal. Sofia's pulse was perfectly steady.

"And I'm with you," she said.

He glanced over his shoulder. The palace glowed behind them, stately and vast. Home. Perhaps. Nothing seemed certain anymore, least of all that.

"Now come on," he said. "We have to run."

Part II

A

GATHERING

STORM

15

Marya

That night, Marya and Lena had the Tverskys' apartment off Preobrazhenskaya Square to themselves. Irina had spent the past few nights in the safe house on Krestovsky Island with Ilya—nearer to the dockyards where the two had been spreading word of the strike among the working men of the district, despite Isaak's repeated warnings that Irina shouldn't overexert herself, that someone else could go in her place. Isaak himself was finishing a last-minute order at the printer's shop, invitations for some high-society affair. The others, the dozens of transients who spent two nights at this house and three at another—Pyotr Stepanovich, Vaska, pretty Oksana with the scar along her left cheek—all weathered the dark somewhere else tonight. In other words, it was as close to a romantic evening as Marya was likely to receive, and she intended to make the most of it.

They'd been trading stories in the glow of a single lamp, half old tales and half anecdotes from their day in the city, alternating the role of storyteller and listener with the ease of a couple fluent in each other's rhythms. Marya could spin up a story about Alevtina Vladimirovna's gossipy antics that left Lena breathless with laughter, but it was Lena's memories she hungered for, the little golden pictures she painted of her childhood in Riga. It never failed to fill her with pride and fondness that Lena would take off the determined mask every member of the Koalitsiya wore and let Marya see her, the adult woman who had once been that child, who had bathed naked in the Baltic Sea and baked full loaves of bread to leave out for the domovoi.

"Wasn't your mother furious?" Marya asked. "Mine would have broken the switch over my back for wasting that much food." She plunged a needle into a scrap of dark gray fabric, pulling the thread through. Irina's child wouldn't be born for months yet, but the city would still be pierced through by cold then, and the little one would need all the warmth they could find. Even in moments of rest, neither she nor Lena had ever liked being unproductive.

"Oh, I wish you could have seen it," Lena said brightly, as if her mother's anger were a fond memory. She tied off a stitch, completing the hem of the infant nightshirt she'd been sewing, then adopted such a terse, irritated voice that Marya could almost see Lena's mother in front of her. "Yelena, where do you think rye comes from? Do you think it's the domovoi who feeds you? No supper for you, unless it wanders out from behind the stove and decides to thank you with a meal."

Marya laughed, both at the impression and at the thought of Lena as a child, so determined even then to ensure that no one went hungry, the Arsenyevs' house spirit included. "I'll bet five rubles you didn't try that again."

"You owe me five rubles," Lena said with a grin. "I was a terrible child."

"You still are," Marya said. "Fortunately, I've always found breaking the rules to be extremely attractive."

Such nights were like wrapping herself in the warmest, softest blanket anyone had ever woven. Marya had always been indifferent to the idea of sex itself, never felt any great sweeping rush of physical desire for any woman or man, but flirting with Lena was one of life's great joys, and being close to her in this way was a pleasure beyond any other she knew. If there was any justice in the world, she would be able to stay here, just like this, until the Tverskys returned or the sun rose.

The knock at the door ended that fantasy.

The two women exchanged a glance. Perhaps Isaak had come

home early. He could work at a devil's pace when the mood took him, particularly in the warm glow that had surrounded him since the successful speech at the university hall. And if it wasn't Isaak—if their unexpected visitor took his orders from the tsar and was on the hunt for illicit activity to report—well then, they were simply two women, stitching an infant's clothes by lamplight.

Marya opened the door, and two people looked back at her from the landing. Neither of them Isaak. And one of them not unknown.

"Sofia," Marya said, stepping aside to let the white-haired woman in. "And . . . friend."

It had been days since she and Sofia had stood together in the street, tracing the lines in Sofia's palm and speaking of the future. It might have been only seconds. Marya remembered every plane of the woman's face, every strand of her hair, every quirk of her mouth. It was as familiar as looking at her own face in a mirror, but her own face had never made Marya's chest ache the way Sofia's made it ache now. Sofia's sideways smile clearly found amusement in Marya's speechlessness. It was a smile that said, *I told you I'd be back*. Marya felt that smile brand itself on the backs of her eyes, a perfect image to be called up and remembered in the loneliness of night.

What was this? She wasn't like this. Lena had teased Marya about it a hundred times, the almost academic way she'd always expressed her opinions of other women's looks. And yet here she was, staring like a fool. It was an entirely unfamiliar feeling, and one that frightened her. She had never before wanted so badly to be seen.

It was difficult to pay attention to anyone when they stood beside Sofia, but her companion was doing his best to hold his own. The tall man was dressed well—better than anyone had any business dressing in this quarter of the city, where stepping outside with silver buttons like those was as good as an invitation to robbery—and his face, though narrow and visibly nervous, was handsome. Familiar, too, as though she'd seen a variation of it before. From the bright flush of his cheeks and the tips of his ears, he hadn't expected to be outside that night, or at least hadn't dressed for it. His clothing was hardly warm enough for the drafty apartment, in which Marya and Lena both kept their overcoats on, let alone the unprotected street he'd just left. Beneath the usual suspicion that came with the arrival of a stranger, Marya felt a flash of sympathy, like she might feel for a kitten found half drowned during a flood.

"Forgive me," Sofia said, and her amber eyes did look genuinely sorry. "I wasn't sure where else we could go."

"And we're the usual haven for lost souls," Lena said tersely— she'd set aside her work and come to stand beside Marya, one hand on her shoulder. "You vouch for him?"

"I do."

"Then he can stay, though he'll have to abide by the rules."

Sofia smiled at the man beside her. "I told you they were kind."

"I never said they wouldn't be." The man's voice was refined, as though he'd be more comfortable speaking French than Russian, and he tilted his chin up proudly.

"I assume you're the one who's in all the trouble," Marya said, nodding at him.

He clearly meant his gaze to be defiant, but the effect didn't quite succeed. "Who says there's trouble?"

Marya laughed. "I know a man on the run when I see one. Oh, don't be offended," she added, sensing he was on the verge of a retort. "You aren't the first man who's run afoul of the tsar to sleep on these floors, and you won't be the last. Just mind you don't antagonize Lena, or she'll fillet you in your sleep."

The man swallowed hard. Had that been the first real threat he'd ever received? He seemed profoundly unused to them. With a visible effort, he let out his breath and relaxed his shoulders. In one dancer-like motion, he sank down onto the cot against the far wall, on which each member of the Koalitsiya had stolen a night's sleep at some point in the past. It had been a long time since she'd seen someone move so gracefully, as if he inhabited another world entirely from her own. One thing he and Sofia had in common.

Marya's eyes lingered for another moment on Sofia, the way she had not looked away from Lena's hand on Marya's shoulder, the smoothness of that knowing smile.

"Thank you," the man said, and he rolled his neck with an audible pop. "I'm getting too old to be climbing out of windows. And damn but it's cold out there."

Marya tightened her focus on the man, his curious clothing, his casual form of address. Maybe that way, she wouldn't have to think too carefully about what it meant that Sofia's eyes were still lingering in her direction, or that she had not for a moment stopped feeling their power.

"It's Piter in January, my friend," she said. "I'm not sure what you expected."

"All the more reason not to spend a moment more outside than I need to," the man replied. He was a talker, this one. Isaak was the same: finding comfort in uncomfortable moments by filling them with the sound of his own voice. And he was clever, too. The Koalitsiya was full of idealistic, determined people who had bravery in spades, but few of them had much by way of a sense of humor.

"Sofia said a man lived here?" The stranger glanced toward the corner, as if Isaak might be hiding behind the stove. No question this fellow was wanted somehow—he had a prey animal's need to know the exact position of every threat. It hadn't escaped Marya's notice that he'd sat with his back to the wall.

"At work," Lena said. She'd returned to the table and took up her sewing, but her eyes—narrow, now, and still narrowing—never left the man. Marya had seen that look on her face before. The look of someone determinedly trying to place a memory. "He'll be back before long."

"And he won't mind that I'm . . ." The man gestured with one arm, indicating his general presence.

"You can trust Isaak," Sofia said. "He won't—"

"My God," Lena snarled. "I don't believe it."

Marya flinched. Lena had gone stiff all the way to her shoulders, and she looked at the stranger as if a rat in human clothing had joined them in the room. Lena's anger could be a source of terror, a cold and dreadful poison, but it was never impulsive. It took a long time to earn her hatred. Except for this man, who had managed to do it in an instant.

He edged as far back as he could, his spine now flat against the wall. All the color had drained from his face. Still, when he spoke, his words were even. "Is there a problem?"

"Masha," Lena said—as if she couldn't bring herself to look either Sofia or the man in the face. "I tried. I tried to give her a chance. But *this*? This is what we get for trusting?"

"What—"

"She brought us a *Komarov*," Lena said.

Marya gaped. Sitting alone with his knees drawn up, the man still didn't look like a threat. His face was as drawn as ever, weariness dripping from every muscle. But his clothes were finer than Marya had ever seen. His smooth, polished accent. Those deep blue eyes—that was where she'd seen them, the same eyes that had looked out at Marya from a thousand portraits of the tsar, hanging on a thousand walls in a thousand homes. Of course. It was impossible now not to see it.

"Not just any Komarov," Sofia said with a smile. "Grand Duke Felix Sergeevich."

Lena never took her eyes from Felix, impassive as the Bronze Horseman in Senate Square. The grand duke's pedigree, to her, was certainly not an asset. But Marya turned to Sofia, who only shrugged, still smiling that quiet smile. This was Grand Duke Felix, in the heart of the Koalitsiya. It was only a matter of time until the tsar's men followed after. It was the end of everything. It was a bullet in their chests, a shallow grave chiseled out of the frost.

Unless, of course, it wasn't. Because Sofia had announced his presence like it was a gift.

There was no reason to trust Sofia. She'd brought their deepest enemy into their midst without a word of warning. But something in Marya—or in Sofia, something sweet and bitter and wicked that tempted stronger than the devil could have done—made her doubt. A doubt that, if tended properly, could spark and grow into faith.

"He's still our guest, Lena," Marya said quietly. "At least we can let him say his piece."

"His piece?" Lena repeated. "The only piece I want him to say is a quick prayer before I cut out his—"

"I know," Sofia said. She hadn't moved, hands still carelessly shoved in the pockets of her fur-lined coat. The humming tension seemed to amuse her, like watching a dog chase its tail. "Just listen."

Marya could almost hear Lena gritting her teeth, but her patience won out in the end. Lena turned, facing Felix. "You have five minutes, princeling, and then I'll put the bullet in your heart myself. So talk."

Felix flinched. Little wonder he was jumpy. Two pairs of unimpressed, distrustful eyes stood between him and the only exit from this little room. Fine words might have let him skate through life with most of Petersburg society, but there was no way he could flatter his way out of this. No, for this, he would have to become very convincing, very quickly.

Felix let out a decisive breath and stood. Lena's hand twitched toward the pocket of her overcoat, where Marya knew her pistol waited, longing for an excuse to fire. Felix must have known it, too, from the way he followed the movement of Lena's hand, but he stood as straight as ever. Marya could see the ghost of his family's authority in him, the men and women whose every word was God's law. Whatever he intended to say next, Felix believed it as deeply as any Komarov had ever believed what they proclaimed.

"You don't trust me," he said. "Of course you don't. If I were you, I wouldn't trust me either. I know my father. I know how the war was. I know how he's crushed demonstrations after it, and how much more damage he still intends to do."

"You know all that," Lena repeated tonelessly.

Felix raised both hands, palms outward. "I don't know all of it. How could I? Not like you do."

Marya didn't know what she'd expected him to say, but this wasn't it. During the weeks and months they'd agitated for a reprieve from the tsar's severity, it had never occurred to her that people inside the Winter Palace might agree with them. People like the tsar's own son. It changed everything. She couldn't think fast enough to keep up with what it could mean.

"One of the only true friends I've ever had was from Petersburg," Felix went on. He was talking faster now, and though his face darkened at this, the energy in his words didn't fade. "At least, I thought of him as a friend. He grew up poor, not far from here. He didn't tell me much about what it was like, but I paid attention. I saw how each proper meal at the palace looked like a miracle to him. I saw the old scar down his back from when soldiers raided his mother's home looking for agitators. I saw the way the war changed him. I saw that no matter how close Sasha and I were, there would always be that line between us, that line that made it impossible for him to trust me, because of what my family had done."

Felix turned away, and Marya pinched the bridge of her nose, as if to contain the thoughts swirling inside her. She didn't know who had sparked these memories in Felix—some servant from the Winter Palace, or a guardsman who'd managed to coax some friendship from the grand duke—but that didn't matter. What mattered was the guilt she could hear in every word. That was guilt they could use.

Isaak had been so adamant that change would come from the streets, but surely it could come faster from within the palace. With Felix on their side, they could infiltrate the halls of power, start to work from the inside, advance the reforms they'd been demanding. A sympathetic voice on the tsar's council, a Komarov with the authority to sway ministers and shape orders. Only a second son, true, but if God had decided to bless the Virgin Mother with another child, the younger messiah would still have been a friend worth having.

"I don't know what to do," Felix said, and the slight break in his voice was perhaps the most honest emotion Marya had seen in days, in this world of hardened people trained to conceal their own doubts. "I don't know what to do about any of it. But I know I need to do something. And I'm hoping you might know what that is." His voice faltered, and he looked down to his finely made shoes, dirty with slush.

Ignoring Lena's indignant splutter, Marya stepped forward and laid a hand on his shoulder. He was more fragile than she expected—she could feel his bones under her palm.

"You're right," she said. "You should have done something years ago. But it's not too late to choose a new way. And I'm glad you have."

"Masha," Lena snapped, "I swear to God—"

Marya turned to face Lena, who had still not released her grip on the pistol in her pocket. They rarely fought, the two of them, and even more rarely about anything serious. They'd fallen for each other in part because they agreed so entirely, so completely that it was like falling in love with yourself seen from another angle. But this was different. Marya was the right hand of the Koalitsiya now. She'd promised to do what it took to succeed. And she knew the chance they'd just been offered.

"Think about it," she said. "If he's telling the truth, then we have a direct link to court. He speaks for us, changes his father's policies, saves lives without a fight. It's what we've been dreaming of, can't you see that? A chance to speak and actually be heard. Isn't that what you're always telling Ilya you want?"

"And if he's lying?" Lena said coldly.

Felix inhaled sharply but did not speak.

"He's lying, then we have a hostage," Marya said simply. "The tsar's son, even if it's the disgraced one. That's another way to be heard."

The emptiness following this seemed to stretch forever. Felix remained frozen, watching the silent conversation humming between Marya and Lena. Debating the wisdom, weighing the risk. After so many years together, neither of them needed to say a word to be understood. Finally, Lena took a step toward Felix. She was nearly his height, and with her broad shoulders in her soldier's greatcoat, there was no doubt between the two of them which one was the warrior.

Lena extended a hand. "I don't like you," she said. "I don't expect I'm going to like you. But I will give you one chance. Just know that if you even think about betraying us, I will kill you myself, and I will very much enjoy it."

An admirably short pause, and then Felix took the offered hand and shook it. "Agreed," he said.

Near the door, Marya saw Sofia smile.

———

Isaak returned not long after, and to Marya's surprise, he saw immediately the value of what she had suggested. Whether because of his trust in Sofia, the strength of Marya's explanation, or his belief that Felix wasn't dangerous enough to cause any real harm, he agreed that Felix could stay—provided he never left the apartment without the close supervision of at least one member of the Koalitsiya. Felix didn't protest the restriction. As the son of the tsar, he'd likely spent precious little time unsupervised in his life, so perhaps the order didn't grate on him as it would have Marya.

Over a late meal of slightly cold meat pies Isaak had brought from a vendor near the printer's shop, the awkward quintet did their best to make conversation. Isaak and Lena pointedly did not bring up the latest news from their efforts—the way the workmen and artisans Lena had spoken to that morning hungered for a general strike, the eager students prepared to add their voices to the sea of protest at any minute. Spirits ran high in the capital, the vision they'd tried to paint finding a willing home among people who had seen their rations slashed once too often. It was all Marya wanted to speak of, but knowing better than to do so in front of

Felix, she concentrated instead on the spiced lamb inside the flaky pastry. As busy as the work kept her, she constantly forgot how hungry she was until she took the first bite of suddenly available food.

Isaak seemed to consider philosophy to be safe conversational ground, which at least kept Felix entertained. As was his nature if given permission, Isaak leapt from Fourier and Saint-Simon to Rousseau without pausing for breath, and Felix—no doubt thanks to a battalion of palace tutors—knew enough to keep pace, challenging him here and there on points of logic. What little familiarity Marya had managed to glean through long proximity to Isaak had never been nearly enough to support a sustained conversation of this nature, and Isaak latched on to his new discussion partner like a burr to a man's trousers. Lena listened silently, scowling at her dinner.

"If a man could change the world by talking about philosophy," Marya said to Isaak, "you'd be a god, my friend."

"Or there would be no God," Felix offered. "You'd have philosophized the Lord himself to death."

Isaak laughed, visibly surprised that the son of the tsar could make a joke. Marya smiled, satisfied. She'd been right—this man had something they could use.

Sofia swallowed the last bite of pie with the force of a bird of prey, then touched Marya on the shoulder. All thought died in the face of that touch. "Walk with me a moment?" Sofia said quietly.

"Masha," Lena said.

If she ignored that warning, there would be no going back. She'd have shown clearly what she would choose if pressed. But there was nothing for it. Marya handed the remainder of her pie to Isaak and followed. Lena didn't say a word at her leaving, though Felix did look after her nervously. It almost made Marya laugh, that Felix had decided to consider her his protector. As if she was the least dangerous member of the group. Though, admittedly, she hadn't been the one to threaten him with a bullet through the heart.

Sofia led the way down the narrow stairs and into the courtyard, where snow packed tight by dozens of footprints glowed almost blue in the darkness. Marya's breath fogged around her in a thick cloud, and she shivered, but Sofia seemed not to feel the difference between indoors and out.

"Thank you," Sofia said simply.

Marya stared. "For what?"

"For standing up for him." Sofia didn't look at Marya, but let her gaze wander down the alley. If she could see far enough in that direction, Marya knew, she would find the façade of the Winter Palace, broad and stately as a warship on the bank of the river. "I hoped you'd see his use, but I wasn't sure. Clearly I should have trusted you."

A rush of warmth spilled through Marya at the praise, in wild defiance of the cold. She wrapped her arms across her chest nonetheless, not for heat but in self-recrimination. She had never felt the need for approval so strongly before. Or maybe Sofia simply knew how hungry Marya was to be seen, properly, for what she could do. *Be reasonable*, she told herself severely. *This isn't you.*

"Yes, you should have," she said, laughing at her own daring— apparently *be yourself* meant *be as rude as possible*. "I don't trust his family, but all that matters is whether he can help. And I think he can."

Sofia nodded, and those impossible eyes were entirely focused on Marya now. Had she ever truly been seen before? Never like this.

"I knew that about you from the first time I saw you," Sofia said. "At Isaak's speech. The way you were listening to him, I knew you were willing to do what it took to change Petersburg for the better."

Where her daring came from, Marya didn't know, but she took a step closer. The light of distant stars caught in the lines of Sofia's long coat, until it looked like the sable fur at the collar had captured part of the night itself.

"You're right," Marya said. "And I'll tell you this: we're going to win. It's people like him that will help us do it. He can carry our voice to the places that matter. I meant that."

Sofia stepped nearer, closing the distance between them. Her beautiful face had twisted slightly, into something just shy of scorn. Marya had never felt smaller than in that moment, nor so desperately powerful, for being the target of Sofia's attention. "You're starting to sound like the rest of them, Masha. Change the world with pretty words, keep your ambitions within limits. You know better than that."

She raised one hand and brushed Marya's cheek, and the protest half formed on Marya's lips extinguished like a snuffed candle.

"There is no change that follows the rules," Sofia said. "That's why people like us don't believe in any."

And Sofia Azarova—holy terror, slanted smile, coat made of stars—leaned in and kissed every thought from Marya's head.

Sofia's lips burned like liquor at the back of her throat. She leaned into them, unable to stop thinking for every moment it lasted—*There are no rules, only desires, only this, only want.*

And she wants me.

The kiss made her lips tingle and her breath catch, like inhaling peppermint. She had been kissed before, but never like this. Never kissed until her mind was blank of thought, her whole being nothing but this kiss. Every part of it was freezing, and she hoped she would never feel warm again.

She shivered, and they pulled apart. Sofia's eyes flashed, pupils blown like black pearls. Her laugh—soft, not quite cruel—was invisible in the cold, unlike Marya's shallow, translucent breaths.

"I'm glad I found you," Sofia said. "You're just what I need."

How could she respond to that? Words had vanished along with the rest of her thoughts. Nothing seemed real but the taste of Sofia on her lips, and her own heart frantic in her chest.

"Tell Isaak I'll call on him tomorrow afternoon," Sofia said. "And keep an eye on Felix for me."

"Both eyes," Marya agreed, barely hearing herself.

Sofia smiled once more, then squeezed Marya's hand and turned away. Marya blinked, and the courtyard was empty. Perhaps Sofia had turned down one of the alleyways that spidered off it to fracture the heart of the city. Perhaps she had leapt into the air and ridden the wind into the clouds. A single feather, white and sparkling like the vila's hair in legend, fluttered across the snow, until the tip caught beneath the toe of Marya's shoe. She bent down and held it up against the stars, considering.

16

Sasha

It wasn't yet sunrise, but the midnight shadows had begun to turn pale, and still Sasha and the guard Kopenkin stood at Felix's door, waiting for new orders. Servants had drifted by throughout the night like figures in a dream, but they avoided Sasha's eyes, and he in turn pretended not to notice their passing. He was no stranger to long nights, but at the front, he'd been able to ward off the dark by imagining what Felix might say about the events of the day, by imagining that the soldier sleeping in the bedroll opposite was Felix, by spinning one impossible future after another. Throughout this endless night, Kopenkin had not said a word to him, and Sasha hadn't dared break the silence, leaving no voice in his head but his own. And his was not a mind he cared to spend much time alone with.

He ran a weary hand across itching eyes, then straightened his back as he saw the tsarevich approaching from the end of the corridor.

Evidently Sasha wasn't the only one who'd passed a rough night. Anatoli's usually straight carriage had slumped into what must have been his natural posture, head forward, shoulders slightly hunched. It made the resemblance between the two brothers so powerful that Sasha forced himself to blink, fighting to differentiate the Komarov on this side of the door from the one beyond it.

"Your Imperial Highness," Sasha and Kopenkin said in unison, with matching salutes.

Anatoli sighed and nodded toward the door. "Has he said anything?"

"Not a word, Your Highness," Kopenkin said. "I think he fell asleep."

"Good," Anatoli said bitterly. "At least one of us will be well rested today." He shook his head, then paused, looking Sasha over. "Dorokhin, *n'est-ce pas?*"

"Yes, Your Imperial Highness."

"I've heard of you," Anatoli said. "You had command of the Sixth Corps at Maloyaroslavets?"

Stunned, Sasha nodded. There was no reason on earth for the tsarevich to know that. Even Felix hadn't always remembered where and with whom Sasha had fought, and Sasha had told him at least a dozen times.

His surprise must not have been as subtle as he intended. "I didn't see much fighting myself," Anatoli said, rolling his neck. Sasha heard his vertebrae pop and shifted his own shoulders in sympathy. "My father wouldn't permit it, and even if he had, my wife would have shouted Kutuzov's brains to jelly if I'd come within twenty yards of a bullet. But I was in the camp in the general's entourage for parts of the campaign. Papa thought it would teach me something."

It was unnerving, seeing a man who looked so much like Felix speak of the war as an event he'd witnessed, not an abstract inconvenience. Sasha rarely attempted to share memories of the front with Felix. Trying to shape his nightmares into plain language only made them sharper, and he saw no reason to invite that kind of pain with the one person who had ever truly enabled him to forget it. But Anatoli might understand. He might not have killed, but he had at least seen. There was something to be said for a witness.

"A turning point, Kutuzov called it." Anatoli shifted his weight, casting an anxious glance at his brother's door. "The beginning of the end for Napoleon. I know my father wants you to prove yourself, but I'm inclined to trust a man who won us such a brilliant victory."

Any imagined connection between Sasha and Anatoli vanished. The tsarevich didn't understand. Maybe, knowing just enough to be dangerous, he understood even less than his brother. General Kutuzov had considered the Battle of Maloyaroslavets a victory, and strategically, it had been. With six thousand French soldiers dead and the Grande Armée's safer southern retreat cut off, the general had publicized the battle as the moment Napoleon's doom was sealed. From then on, their foe had been condemned to the slow, deadly, frigid western march, a natural assault more deadly than any Russia's men could have launched.

Even so, the night did not live in Sasha's mind as a cause to celebrate.

He thought of it often—had been thinking of it for much of the long night he'd just weathered, watching the shadows on the wall lengthen and retreat. The pitch-black sky over Maloyaroslavets had been cold and moonless, but in its way, the dark had been a blessing: anything outside the circle of the campfire had been lost to sight. Sasha had sat with his gloved palms to the fire, watching the dance and snap of the flames with the single-minded focus of a wandering holy man speaking to God. The bayonet gash along his thigh was superficial, and he'd bandaged it already himself, knowing the camp doctor had his hands full with worse crises. Standing would be an act of will for a week or so, but he could tell it would heal neatly, leaving only a scar behind. He barely noticed the pain. It was nothing compared to the voices. All he could hear, in every direction, was the moaning of doomed men from the shadows. Every sound burned into his mind.

"Please," begged a voice not far off—a voice he knew, Fyodorov, a towheaded private Sasha had drunk under the table not two days before. The medic tent must have been nearer than Sasha thought. "Please, just finish it, I don't care, I can't . . ."

All the drink in the world wasn't enough to drown out the soldier's voice. Nor was it enough to mask the unearthly howls from deeper in the darkness. The screams of men blended with the cries of the wolves, and Sasha knew beyond doubt that when the men went silent, the wolves would circle closer, mouths watering at the chance to take their portion of the spoils of war. The commanders would close their eyes and let it happen. There was no time to dig proper graves, not with the French already on the move. In some ways, though no one would ever admit it aloud, the wolves were a mercy. The army would have to return this way, those who did return, and no one wanted their final march to be paved with frozen corpses. Pistol in one hand, flask in the other, Sasha sat in front of the fire, listening to the screams, and waited.

"Does the tsar have new orders, Your Highness?" Sasha said to the tsarevich.

Anatoli frowned, but he did not press Sasha on the change of subject. "To be frank, he spent all last night arguing for sending Felix to the Bastion, but I convinced him they should speak first. It won't go easily for Felix no matter what happens, but if he can grovel enough, he might escape with another exile. This one not so near at hand."

The tsarevich clearly meant this to be reassuring, but Sasha didn't find much hope in it. In all the years they'd known each other, he'd never once seen Felix grovel.

"Would you like to speak to him, Your Highness?" Kopenkin said.

Anatoli nodded grimly. "No good in waiting."

The room, when Kopenkin unlocked the door, was quiet and bitterly cold. A dull fire smoldered in the grate, in its last embers. The bed was unmade, articles of clothing still strewn about in the careless way the wealthy treated their possessions. The window had been flung wide. A sheen of frost dusted the sill. Felix was nowhere to be seen.

Sasha knew immediately what had happened. Behind him, he felt the dancing flames of the camp at Maloyaroslavets. His breath rasped like the panting of wolves.

Oh, Felix, he thought. *What have you done?*

The tsar received the news that his son had fled the way Sasha had seen generals learn of deserting soldiers: coldly, without any display of extraneous emotion. Sasha stood stiffly in the tsar's study with his back to the window, side by side with Anatoli, and waited for a wave of rage that did not come. The only sign the tsar had even heard what Sasha had told him was the rapid rhythm of his fingers drumming against the desk, a steady roll like a marching snare.

"So," the tsar said, after a long silence. "Tell me where you think the traitor who used to be my son has gone."

Sasha's heart told him to say nothing. He had sworn to protect Felix with his life, and Felix had never been in as much danger as he was now. The tsar's tone promised vengeance, even if the shape of it was yet to be determined. To keep Felix safe, he had to keep Felix away from his father. But Felix was no longer the only one who needed protecting, and Sasha's head knew better than his heart.

His duty was to Russia, not to Felix. For years, serving one had been the same as serving the other, but the calculation had shifted now, and if there was a choice to make, his vows of service only left one option. And that was without considering the consequences of disobedience—consequences that, for those without royal blood, were likely to prove fatal.

"You know the grand duke better than I do now," the tsar said. "Help me find him, prove your loyalty to me, and I will see you rewarded. Hinder me, and I will see that you are dead before dawn. It is as simple as that."

Nothing could be simpler. Sasha wrenched the doors of his heart shut and let his head take the lead. The words rolled off his tongue with the clipped precision of tactical orders. "He's gone after that woman, Your Majesty," he said. "Sofia Azarova. There's no question."

"He has to be brought back," Anatoli said. "With or without his cooperation. With the city as unsettled as it is, one word in the wrong ear could set the streets alight. The rebels will have him murdered, or worse."

The tsar shook his head. The drumming fingers had stopped, replaced by the certainty of a flat palm. "Felix's safety is no longer my concern. What matters is the security of Petersburg. You're in agreement, Captain Dorokhin?"

Sasha bowed deeply. When he rose, his face was a mask of perfect agreement. The tsar did not need to know the doubts fissuring through him, threatening to crack him in two. What the tsar needed to know was that Sasha was a loyal soldier and servant of Russia, one who would give his last breath in defense of the imperial throne. He would protect Felix if he could, however he could. But the grand duke had made one too many mistakes, and the web they had spun could only be untangled with slow, careful movements. He would do his duty, and he would carry out the tsar's orders, because there was no alternative. But he would have his own aim as well—not in opposition to the tsar's, but in parallel, twin wills strengthened by adjoining resolves.

They were connected now, Sofia and himself, as if a thread had been knotted to link her heart and his own. No matter how labyrinthine the city, no matter how devilish her plans, she would never escape him. Her hold on Felix could not continue. Either Sasha would die or she would.

"Yes, Your Imperial Majesty. I am in your service. And I will find them."

—————

Nearly fifteen years had passed since Sasha had seen the neighborhood where he'd been born. He'd traveled the country since then, seen distant corners of the tsar's empire, and through it all his memory of Krestovsky Island had remained a touchstone, reminding him of himself. Crowded apartments and the shouts of dockworkers, families with too many mouths to feed and no energy to spare for wishing life were different. The façades of its buildings and the faces of its people were shakier in his mind, but externals didn't matter. The essential nature of the district, the heart of the people who lived there, that was part of his history. It was *him*.

That night, as he walked along the back alley that led to the neighborhood's cheap rear apartments, a small band of the tsar's soldiers at his side, he saw that either his memory had warped something essential or the streets themselves had changed. The island looked the same, but it no longer felt like the one he'd known. Each curtained window seemed to hold him in suspicion. Once this had been home, but now it felt more like a crouching creature than a welcome. Now anything could happen here.

When the soldiers he'd consulted from the Semyonovsky Regiment had shared their suspicions, he'd wanted to tell them they were wrong. Despite everything, it seemed unthinkable that Felix would take such drastic action. But according to the tsar's eyes and ears in the city, there was only one group of agitators with the authority and the motivation to shield the kind of traitor the grand duke had become. The Koalitsiya had dozens of dens across the city, only a handful of which were known to the tsar's spies. And so the first thing to do—the only rational thing—was to work his way through them, one by one.

The tsar was in agreement, when Sasha shared the name of the street he planned to search with Kopenkin, Devyatov, and a hand-selected group of soldiers from the Semyonovsky Regiment. "He won't have gotten far," the tsar had said. "My son would be slinking back to the palace within the hour if it wasn't for that woman. And even she can't survive in this city without help."

Sasha might have said that the tsar didn't know his son at all if he thought Felix was helpless outside of palace supervision. He might have mentioned the nights they'd spent together in Petersburg's seedier clubs, running up monumental tabs under an assumed name and paying it all off the same night with the money Felix won by cheating at faro. He might have said that Felix's particular talents meant he could charm his way into free passage on a schooner with a smile, and by week's end he was as likely to be in Copenhagen as at the palace gates.

But Sasha had said nothing. His job was no longer to defend Felix. It was to find him.

The buildings in this part of town had pleasant-enough façades overlooking the main street. But back here, where no one ever went but the city's poor, the architects had chosen not to expend effort on ornamentation. No call for originality when speed and cost were the primary concerns, and all that mattered was housing the greatest number of people at the smallest possible expense. This was the true city, the one behind the grand Italian-inspired architecture that drew the eyes of Petersburg's wealthy. The grim skull beneath the painted face. Sasha stopped behind a house that might once have been his own, where he and his mother had shared an apartment with two other families. He glanced up toward the second-story window overlooking the alley and wondered what its new inhabitants might keep on the windowsill where his mother had placed her cheap icons of Saint Nikolai and Elijah, faded from worship and candle smoke until the saints' faces were barely distinguishable from the background. From the street, he could see nothing. The building might have been abandoned. A dozen families might have had their noses pressed to the glass, watching.

"Captain?"

Andrei Suvarin, one of the Semyonovsky soldiers assigned to Sasha's service, waited with one hand on his belted pistol. He wore the uniform's dark green greatcoat as if he'd been born to, and his blond mustache gave him the air of a Cossack warrior, dashing enough to turn heads. Looking as he did like an engraving on the base of a statue, it was easy to forget how young Suvarin was, until his hand caught that way on his pistol, until his voice hitched on the word *Captain*. He was a good soldier; Sasha had known that at once. Suvarin would do what was needed. But he wouldn't act until Sasha gave the word. He would not take responsibility for what came next. And who could blame him? If Sasha could have hidden behind the authority of a commanding officer, he'd have done so. But this was his task now. His opportunity to prove his loyalty.

Fists clenched, Sasha jerked his head toward the door. "Keep your guard up," he said. "Assume they're armed."

They ascended the narrow back stairs in single file, a thin snake of soldiers moving silently as a wicked thought. Through the deathly stillness, he could hear the murmur of voices, impossible to distinguish through the closed door. Sasha's breathing sounded like a death rasp. He kept his hand on his pistol. It should have felt like a comfort, instead of what it did feel like, a curse. *Dangerous rebels*, the tsar had called these people, and perhaps they were. But they weren't the ones skulking in the shadows with a loaded pistol. Sasha gritted his teeth, then threw his shoulder against the door. It crunched open under the weight, splintering in places as if under cannon fire. Sasha led the small company into the room, Suvarin and Devyatov flanking him, the others fanning out to cut off any possible escape.

He stood in a small, dimly lit apartment, afforded natural light through the smallest of vented windows, which could be cracked to let out smoke from the stove. It didn't seem as if anyone lived here regularly. What furniture there was looked to have been scavenged—he recognized the twin lions of the Sheremetev coat of arms carved into one of the chairs, though the wood was battered and water stained. The half-dozen people in the room reminded Sasha of the furniture: any inherent beauty now weather-beaten and cracked, hardened over for protection. A roughly equal mix of men and women, underfed, seemingly unarmed, drawn faces turned toward the door with wide eyes and tight mouths. Sasha felt as if he'd kicked aside a stone and revealed a colony of mice waiting for the blow that would crush them. But Sasha had seen many times the kind of damage people like this could do. If this unassuming group of people truly belonged to the Koalitsiya—and if the Koalitsiya knew where Felix could be found—then he would see this through with the caution and attention due to any military matter. He had underestimated his enemy before, when it had been only Sofia. He would not do so again.

Sasha stepped forward, fingers still resting on the end of his gun. "Which of you is in charge?"

A man sitting straight-backed at the edge of the Sheremetev chair stood. He was wiry and clean-shaven, with a flat cap pulled low on his brow. His hand closed as if around an invisible pistol; Sasha noted the two missing fingers. "None of us," the man said, with startling defiance for someone on the wrong side of armed soldiers. "Are we under arrest?"

Suvarin started to speak, but Sasha silenced him with one raised finger. In the army, one acted first and asked questions later, but this was civilian life. Here, he would see what words could do.

"No one's under arrest," he said, in the same tone he'd used to reassure a horse spooked by cannon fire. "I have a few questions, that's all."

The eight-fingered man laughed and raised both hands. "A few questions. Would you look at that, my friends? We've found a saint in a soldier's uniform. Ask your questions, then, Your Holiness."

"I'm looking for someone," Sasha said—aiming for the midpoint between reassuring and threatening. "Two someones, in fact. The first is a fugitive. An aristocrat, in the tsar's closest circle. We have reason to believe he's sought refuge with you."

One of the other bedraggled occupants, a brown-haired pregnant woman with a splatter of freckles across the bridge of her nose, laughed aloud. She sat on a low stool with her hands folded on her belly, as casual as if soldiers strolled into her home every day. "Look around," she said. "Does it look like any of us are dear friends of the tsar?"

Sasha might have liked her grim sense of humor, under other circumstances. Still, shabby surroundings didn't mean anything. Even Felix might have seen the wisdom of keeping a low profile. Dressed in common clothes, under an assumed name, Felix Sergeevich could have slipped into this band of agitators and no one would have been the wiser. He'd seen it himself: those moments when Felix, frightened and desperate, looked almost like any other man.

Sofia, though. No disguise on earth would allow her to blend in.

"His companion, then," Sasha said. "A woman. White hair. Golden eyes. If you've seen her, you'd remember."

The silence told the truth for them. The woman exchanged a

glance with the eight-fingered man, whose mouth had thinned to a slit. Don't tell him, said the woman's wary glance. I don't know what he wants, but don't tell him a word.

Devyatov, at Sasha's side, drew his pistol, the movement of metal against leather deafening through the quiet. This time, Sasha didn't stop him. He gripped his own, still dormant at his hip, and the cold metal reminded him of the brass buttons on Felix's waistcoat, how his calluses had brushed them as he gently helped Felix undress, in what felt like another life entirely. *I know your darkest secret*, Felix had whispered, late one night, when Sasha was in an indulgent enough mood to let the grand duke curl into him, aligning the curve of their bodies as if together they made up one person. *It's that you're a good man, and you're terrified that someday the rest of the world is going to know it.*

Then, he'd suspected Felix was wrong. Now, he was certain. No good man could have felt the rage that darted through Sasha like lightning shattering the trunk of a pine. Unhesitating. Unstoppable. Worst of all, familiar.

Sasha seized the eight-fingered man by the lapels. The man stumbled, caught off guard. This close, Sasha could smell the bite of alcohol spilling from the man's pores. The worn wool of the coat threatened to tear in his hands. This was not a lonely back-street apartment in Petersburg, this was a battlefield, and if there was one thing Sasha knew, it was how to finish a fight he'd vowed to win.

"Listen to me," Sasha said, his voice low.

The injunction couldn't have been less necessary. Every person in that room—civilian and soldier alike—seemed barely to be breathing.

"I'm not a man you want as your enemy," Sasha said. "The things I've done, they'd freeze your coward blood in your heart. I've killed more men than I can count, burned a village to the ground, fired a bullet between the eyes of a boy bleeding out at my feet, and afterward? I sleep soundly at night."

There was only one lie in this recitation, and under the wave of his own rage, Sasha barely even noticed it.

"You think your life would weigh on my conscience? You think if I crushed your throat with my own hands, I'd spare it a thought in an hour, a day, a week? You know what I need to know, and you will tell me, or you will live every moment looking over your shoulder, wondering when I'll put an end to your miserable little life. And by the time I finally do, you'll be praying for it."

He flung the man backward, and the woman surged to her feet, with surprising speed, catching him by the shoulder before he fell. Her dark brown eyes pierced through Sasha like a narrow beam of light sharpened through a crystal. He saw himself then, the way he must have looked to her. A soldier inured to death. A mad dog set loose. A murderer, one whose body would be buried facedown at the crossroads to keep its sin from polluting other corpses. The inside of Sasha's mouth had gone very dry, and his tongue felt like a foreign object behind his teeth. The rage had evaporated in an instant, and in its place was something colder and more poisonous still. This had been the tsar's test, but he could not say whether he had passed or failed. He couldn't be here another moment, couldn't bear one more glance at himself twisted through those eyes.

"I know where to find you now," he said, and in some sort of black miracle his voice was as deadly as it had ever been. "I'll give you one day. And if you don't tell me what I need the next time I see you, it'll be the last mistake you ever make."

He turned to the door, only to see Suvarin's shocked face behind him.

"Captain—" he began.

The objection was obvious. Petersburg was a thief's warren, with an endlessly multiplying supply of places for men to hide. Turn his back on this group tonight and they'd scatter like rabbits, and nothing short of sorcery would bring them back under his power again.

"Move, Lieutenant," Sasha snapped.

Suvarin moved wordlessly aside, and Sasha swept down the stairs, into the wind-blasted courtyard, where the winter air struck his face like a pitcher of cold water after a night drinking. He leaned against the wall of the building and sank into a crouch, resting his head between his knees. Sweat had soaked through the weave of his uniform; he felt it freeze, leaving his undershirt stiff and sharp against bare skin. His breath rattled on the inhale and smoked like a dragon as it left him. Smoke that thickened into a bitter cloud as he cast aside the last of his self-control and let the cry building up inside him fly free, a shout in a voice that sounded nothing like his own, equal parts fury and terror.

He already knew the reasons to fear the vila. But now, he had something worse to fear: what he already felt himself becoming.

17

Felix

When they were children, Anatoli used to tell Felix that his inability to think ahead would be the death of him. He'd always been at least half jesting, whenever Felix had gotten in trouble with the palace's pâtissier for stealing intricately frosted *mignardises* intended for the tsarina's tea, or when he'd nearly fallen through ice that Anatoli had said a dozen times was too thin for skating. *You don't think about anything except what will make you happy in the moment*, Anatoli would say, *and you think you'll enjoy it forever, but what about when your luck runs out? What are you going to do then?*

Outside this run-down *traktir* on the corner of Sredny Prospekt and Kadetskaya Liniya, his brother's voice worked in tandem with his nerves to keep him frozen outside the door. That question, over and over, insistent and unanswerable—what on earth was he going to do?

He leaned the back of his head against the narrow red door of the *traktir* and closed his eyes. The air was frigid, but each breath made him uncomfortably warm, or maybe that was just the fluttering of his heart. He'd wanted to make his father listen, to claim his birthright and make a difference, but he hadn't prepared himself for hiding from soldiers, standing side by side with a band of dangerous commoners who thought they could pressure the tsar himself into reforming an empire. The memory of Sasha's disgust flashed before him, that deathly chill in his father's expression.

He'd made his choice, and the betrayal in that decision had cut deep. Deeper, maybe, than Felix could ever mend.

Felix took a long breath and let a different memory fill him. His mother, leading him by the hand as they walked the lower halls of the palace, pausing at the kitchens, the laundry, the scullery, for her to greet the servants by name. How they'd spoken to her like she was their own mother, the *matushka* the tsarina was always purported to be: with respect, yes, but with an affection Felix could never imagine them directing toward the tsar. Felix and Sasha, together in the back room of a public house on a jaunt to Moscow, Felix midway through his second pipe and Sasha remarking almost dreamily through the smoke, *When do you suppose someone in the tsar's family last set foot in a place like this? Before or after Nestor the Chronicler?* The hard flat of Sergei's hand across the back of Felix's head when he lingered a moment too long outside the Winter Palace, bending to give a ruble to a beggar. Standing outside the *traktir*, Felix was eight, and twelve, and twenty-four, and as old as Russia itself, old as the canyons dug between the ruling class and the people they ruled.

Felix was making a choice. He was thinking ahead. And possibly for the first time in his life, he knew the right course of action.

The door opened a crack, and the black-haired, almond-eyed Marya Ivanovna stuck her head out into Sredny Prospekt. Felix had liked her at once, and not only because she'd been the first to argue against killing him—though, he had to admit, that played a not-inconsiderable part in it. "Are you coming?" she said. "Or should I tell them you've frozen to death in the street?"

Felix huffed. "Most of them would take that as good news."

"I talked Oksana into leaving her knife at home, I promise."

"You do know how to reassure a person," Felix said drily.

"I try," Marya said. "They're waiting."

Nothing else for it, then. Felix took a last steadying breath and followed her in.

As a rule, the Komarov family wasn't known for its extensive experience with Petersburg public houses, but Felix had never much cared which doorsteps he was and wasn't meant to darken. This *traktir* was the kind of drinking hole where people in all cities passed their free evenings, heat rising from the fire until it fogged the windows and concealed the city from view. The front room was painted a rich ochre almost like saffron, with uncovered wooden tables packed close across the scuffed wood floor. Low light rose from oil lamps balanced on the unstable tables, which reflected off the gold-rimmed mirrors and the icon of Saint Juliana, her hair dutifully covered and her dark eyes overseeing the tavern with amusement. The smell of *kvass* and *shchi* and black bread gave the room the sense of a space well lived in.

Marya gestured toward a door at the far end of the room, beneath which a light flickered. "This way."

There were no windows in the back parlor. Oil lamps and smoky candles clustered on the one long table, around which a small crowd of men and women sat with papers and books and maps spread before them. They were dressed poorly, drab colors and cheap fabrics, wire-rimmed spectacles balanced on more than one nose. Felix spotted Lena at the head of the table, her thick black hair coiled into a scarlet scarf. She scowled as she watched Felix enter, but Isaak—seated beside her—cut her off with a look, and Lena swallowed her protest along with an irritable spoonful of what smelled like the worst-made *shchi* Felix had ever encountered. Sofia shot him a reassuring smile as he sank into an empty chair to her right. It wasn't enough to dispel the impression that most people in that room would have liked to see him dead, but it was better than nothing.

Lena cleared her throat, drawing the room's eyes—if not its attention—to her. "As you can see," she said, "we have a guest. Tell him what he needs to know, nothing more."

He'd expected this sort of lukewarm welcome, but it rankled nonetheless. Felix was risking as much as any of them by coming here—his life was in as precarious a position as any of theirs. More, even: as far as he knew, he was the only one among them specifically wanted by name. Still, he was in no position to demand greater respect than what was on offer. He nodded for Lena to continue.

"Now then," Lena said, her voice as curt as any commander Felix had ever met. "Oksana. As you were saying."

"Right," a small woman with tan skin and almond eyes said from near the window. She was a full head and shoulders shorter than Felix, but he said a silent prayer of thanks for Marya's reassurance that this fierce-looking person was indeed unarmed. "Yulia and I spent yesterday at the Bolshoi Kamenny, and the entire Imperial Opera is with us. Every chorus member, every stagehand, all of them. Name the day, and they'll join the strike. It was easy as breathing, honestly," she added with a laugh. "The most dramatic lot you've ever met, and tired of pretending there hasn't been a war going on. They're leaping at the chance for some heroism."

"Excellent," Isaak said, but his satisfaction quickly melted into a frown. Felix sank down, attempting to dodge the anger Isaak directed at the woman seated to his immediate left. Sofia had slouched forward with one elbow rudely on the table and made barely any effort to conceal her laughter. The shift in the room's mood at the sound did not trouble her in the slightest.

"Something you'd like to mention?" Isaak said coolly.

Sofia shrugged, and for a wild moment Felix was jealous of her daring. He'd been bold enough with his father, but the courage it took to laugh in the face of a man with a gun was beyond him.

"Really, Isaak," she said, taking a long pull on her carved wooden pipe. The exhalation shrouded her in smoke, through which her eyes cut like stars. "If you're trying to bring a new dawn to Petersburg, even Felix would tell you opera singers are hardly the place to start."

And now every drawn face and darkened brow in the room had turned toward him.

"You agree, Felix?" Lena said. "Seeing as you're the most experienced tactician in the room, I'm sure we're all hungry for a taste of your wisdom."

He'd prayed he could make it through this first meeting as a passive observer, but clearly that had been too much to hope. He shot Sofia a desperate glance, communicating *Help me* as clearly as he could without screaming. For the briefest moment, he thought her shoulders stiffened in annoyance. A sickening fear, and a familiar one—once again, incapable of following through, of living up to even the most basic expectations—but in another moment it was gone, and she watched him with that same patient, knowing look.

"You know your father better than anyone, Felix," she said. "Imagine that this plan succeeds. The Koalitsiya shuts down every corner of the city, every bit of commerce and entertainment, everything that keeps the jewel of his empire alive. He receives a petition that his people have united to strike and will return to work once he accepts them into his council, once he makes concessions to ease rationing and taxation. Tell me what you think your father will do if that happens."

Felix's mouth had gone very dry. "There's no need to call him my father that many times," he said. "You've made your point."

"What will he do, Felix?" Sofia repeated. "Will he open his doors and welcome their penniless Jewish refugee leader as the new chairman of the State Council?"

Felix bit his lip. He hadn't known Isaak's religion for certain, though he had suspected. Certainly it explained some of the man's urgency. But in the greater picture, that hardly mattered. There was only one possible outcome to the scene Sofia had described. And though the Koalitsiya wouldn't like that answer, they deserved to hear it.

"He'll crush you," he said hollowly. "Completely. Like he's done every protest before you."

The words drained the room of air. Through the thick silence, Felix could hear the rattle and rumble of conversation beyond the door. Business as usual, rippling through the *traktir*. And for the tsar, dismantling a strike—no matter how well organized, no matter how determined—would be just the same.

A man halfway down the table, wearing a patched jacket and narrow spectacles, nodded. His belly was thick and soft beneath his yellow waistcoat, in the pocket of which Felix could see a heav-ily dented watch that might have been valuable once. "Let it be known I never thought I'd say it," he said, in a broad voice that made Felix think of his own childhood tutors, "but the Komarov boy is right. I've been saying it for weeks, Isaak, Yelena. We can take all the principled stands we like, but the tsar has the Imperial Guard and we don't, and that's that. Unless he thinks we can fight back, we're not a danger, we're an inconvenience. And he'll think nothing of destroying every last one of us."

Strong words were meaningless to the tsar. He'd brush aside petitions and peaceful protest with a cloud of cannon smoke. Banish those who led them, to a prison camp in the east or the bottom of the river, anywhere so long as they were silenced. Isaak would be killed, no question. Felix could hear his father issuing the order to his ministers: *The security of Russia comes first. Strike now and minimize the damage. Report back to me when it's done.* It would take less than a day from start to finish. Nothing left but bones and scorched earth.

"So what are you suggesting?" Lena said quietly.

"We need to find a way to make him listen," Sofia said. "What-ever it takes."

The door flung open, causing half the members of the Koalitsiya to rise in alarm. Felix froze—now would have been an ideal moment to own a pistol; why had he not stolen one from the palace?—but as the room's unease faded, it became clear the woman who had just entered did not intend to launch an assault. Small, brown haired, and five or six months pregnant, the woman seemed to be well-known to the group. Not least of all to Isaak, who leapt to his feet in surprise.

"Irina," he said. "I thought you were at the docks today, we would have waited—"

"Love," Irina said coldly, "you need to start explaining yourself very well, and very quickly."

Agitation had dominated Irina's expression when she'd entered the *traktir*, but with every passing second, her face was hardening. It cooled as it passed over Felix, settling to stony anger as her eyes moved to Sofia. Sofia remained unmoved, as if she'd expected Irina's arrival all along. Like a stone solid against a stormy sea, she leaned back in her chair, the stem of her pipe resting against her chin in thought. Not a hair of her braid was out of place.

"You're a member of the tsar's inner circle, I suppose?" Irina snapped, throwing Felix a dark glare.

Felix flinched. "In a manner of speaking," he said. "Less so lately. What have you heard?"

Irina took another step toward him; Felix, without meaning to, edged still farther back. "They're looking for you," she said. "Komarov scum. You and Sofia. And they know you're with us. Give me one good reason I shouldn't hand the two of you over right now, before you call the tsar's fury down on all our heads."

Felix pressed one hand to his mouth. The world tilted drunkenly; even his body didn't seem to be his own. He'd known his father would waste no time sending men after him; he hadn't known they'd followed his trail so closely. A reasonable man would have heard his own damnation coming for him and given up the game at once, slunk back to the palace, and begged to escape the hell that awaited him. A month ago, Felix would have done it. But now, the thought of his father's guards only stoked the fire already crackling between his ribs. If a man couldn't speak up for his own country without drawing half the Imperial Army after him, surely that was a sign his father's rule had gone too far.

Isaak watched him warily, and Felix knew what he was thinking—if Felix was the kind of person who couldn't be trusted, this was the moment he would try to run. This would be the moment for the Koalitsiya to bar the doors, to block his exit. To kill him, if the circumstances called for it. But Felix was finished running. The determination that filled him now was the sort that consumed everything else, leaving only flame and ash where fear might have lived.

"I'll give you more than one reason," Felix said coldly. "First, because I'm not going to betray you, now that you've saved my life twice over. Second, because I know more about the tsar and the way he thinks than you could learn in a decade, and it seems to me you're going to need that. And third, I know his soldiers. What did the man he sent after me look like?"

"I . . ." Irina began. She'd expected him to beg for his life, not try to turn himself into the Koalitsiya's best hope. It didn't matter, though. Even without her answering the question, Felix already knew who the tsar would have charged with capturing him. Who would have needed the stamp of loyalty that came with saying yes.

"A captain," Felix prompted. "Early thirties. A little shorter than me. Dark eyes, short beard, a scar along his brow just here?" He traced a thin line along his own forehead, from his hairline diagonal to the end of his right eyebrow. How many nights had he traced that same line along Sasha's brow with one finger, following the lingering signature of a French soldier's blade? It had seemed like a seam of pure silver after dark, gilding Sasha's handsome face with an unconventional layer of beauty.

Irina nodded, and Felix's last hope that he'd been mistaken crumbled. "He said he'd be back tomorrow night. And that he won't stop until he's found you."

"No," Felix said. "I don't expect he will."

"You want to earn your place in the Koalitsiya?" Isaak said, and all of Felix's authority vanished in an instant, siphoned back into their leader and his words. Isaak's face was impassive, but power flashed through him then. Felix had seen the same flash in Sasha a hundred times. Anger, honed and made deadly with resolve. A wolf hungering for prey.

"Whatever you want from me, I'll do it," he said.

"Take care of the soldier," Isaak said. "I don't care how you do it. But within the week I want you to tell me we've heard the last of him, and he's never coming back."

Felix squared his shoulders against Isaak's suspicion. He couldn't afford to project anything other than certainty. If he wanted to survive, he would have to become stronger. There was no room in this world for the boy he'd been twenty years ago, the one who had gone hunting with the tsar and wept when the bleeding wild boar stumbled to its death in the snow.

He was a man of the people now. And Sasha was his responsibility.

"All right," he said. "Tomorrow night. You have my word."

From the other side of the table, he saw Sofia smile.

18

Marya

The tension spooling outward from Lena settled over the cold apartment like a shroud. Her actions were ordinary, scrubbing at the floorboards with a wadded-up rag while Marya plunged her own into the bucket of rapidly graying water, but there was a venom to each movement that belonged nowhere near such a mundane task. Each swirl of the rag threatened to strip away a layer of wood.

She should have left well enough alone. Lena shared her thoughts in her own time, arriving at the point of vulnerability only after thinking herself into knots on the way there. It was no good trying to shorten the process. But just then, Marya was willing to risk anything to break this awful, sharp-edged silence. She tossed her rag into the bucket with a small splash and sat with her back against the wall beneath the window. A tight channel of cold air whistled through a gap around the glass, piercing through her scarf to her scalp.

"Come here," Marya said, beckoning Lena to sit beside her. "The floor will wait."

Lena flinched, but whether the reaction was surprise or distaste, it was also brief. The look she turned on Marya was perfectly empty. "You want another lecture from Ilya on the virtue of cleanliness, then."

Marya scoffed. "Ilya can hang." This was hardly the tenderness she'd hoped for, but at least Lena was talking. At least it had displaced that terrible silence.

After a pause that seemed to bend like a fishing line, Lena sighed, then came to sit beside Marya. Lena's hand splayed against the floor palm up, and Marya accepted the wordless invitation to slip her own into it. Lena's smile didn't fully manifest, but a shadow of it was better than nothing.

"I don't know what to do," Lena said.

Each word seemed to weigh on her like a suit of iron. Marya wanted to take Lena in her arms, to remove some of that pain and store it in her own heart, but she knew Lena as well as she knew herself. The best course of action was what she was already doing: to sit here with her, hold her hand, and open the door, which Lena would walk through when she was ready, and not a moment before.

"You can talk about it, Lenochka, if you want to," she said. "I don't know what to think about it either."

Lena gave Marya's hand a brief squeeze, equal parts affection and the beginnings of a clenched fist. "I'm worried you do know what to think, Masha."

This was not the response Marya had expected. Marya had heard Lena angry dozens of times—at the tsar, at Ilya, at Isaak, at Petrushka, at an off-duty soldier for cheating at cards. But never at *her*. She'd considered a hundred reasons for Lena's distemper, but never once had she thought it was her. "I don't understand, *kotik*."

Lena pulled her hand away, circling her knees with both arms instead. It felt like an attack, though she'd barely moved. "I know you. I can tell what you're thinking. And you aren't worried about this. Not the way you ought to be."

Marya pressed her palms against her thighs, feeling foolish and exposed. Trying to justify an instinct was like trying to describe the taste of water. "I trust him," she said. "You saw him last night. You saw how frightened he was. How many people have we brought into this place just like him, scared to the bone but ready to do something about it?"

"It's not the grand duke I'm talking about," Lena snapped. "It's *her*."

Marya flinched. The sudden shift stung worse than the cold touch of winter against her back. A thousand guilty associations flooded in its wake: a lingering glance in the university hall, rapt attention in the *traktir*. A kiss as cold and bright as starlight, surrounded by the dark. She was on the brink of losing everything, the one steady place she'd ever had to stand, and it seemed to her she'd taken no conscious steps to cause it.

"Isaak trusts her," she said stubbornly. "That counts for nothing with you?"

Lena laughed. "Isaak's a person, Masha. He's not some kind of magical creature bound by God to see the truth. He can be fooled the same as any of us."

"She isn't trying to—"

"I saw her at the *traktir*," Lena said flatly. "Everything the grand duke said that day, she prompted him to say it, like a mother feeding words to a child. The Koalitsiya is wrapping itself around her finger every minute we let her stay here. Tell me honestly that doesn't disgust you."

Marya stood up, and with a brusque motion Lena did likewise. She towered half a foot above Marya, but the distance between them seemed infinitely greater than that. For the first time, Marya wanted not just to defeat Lena in an argument, but to crush her. To make her see the depth of how wrong she was and beg for forgiveness. It was as if a spirit had soared into her chest, filling her with a hunger for vengeance beyond anything she'd known.

"Maybe someone has to push us, if we're ever going to win. Lenochka, what we're asking for, the tsar isn't willing to give it. It's a fight, and we have to be prepared to sacrifice for it. Aren't you? Didn't you think changing the course of an empire would come with some risk?"

"Risk, yes," Lena fired back. "Not this."

She had never seen Lena so angry before. Yelena Arsenyevna had always been collected, practical, a stone pillar holding up Marya's world. Now, Marya looked into the drawn face of the woman she had cared for—fought beside, loved—and saw only a closed window, curtains drawn and shutters locked. One she itched to break through, with a venom that frightened her.

"We aren't like them," Lena said. "The Komarovs. Isn't that what we've always said we want, from the beginning? A world where our lives aren't expendable, where every one of us matters? What they're asking for will burn it all to the ground. If you're willing to fight like Sofia fights, Masha, if you'll throw lives away to make a point, how does that make you any better than they are?"

The accusation was so nonsensical Marya couldn't form a retort. She'd have laughed at another time: *How is it different, Lena? Would you open your eyes? How could it be more obvious?* Marya pushed a stray lock of hair out of her eyes. "Because we're fighting for something. How can you not see that? They're fighting to keep us down. We're fighting to rise. Sometimes it hurts, and I wish it didn't, but if you aren't willing to—"

"To what? There's not much you aren't willing to do, is there, Masha? You'd kill the tsar himself, would you? Storm the Winter Palace with Ilya's bloodthirsty ex-soldiers and poison the entire family, down to the smallest child? Tear the tsar's ministers limb from limb? If that's what Sofia told you to do? If she said it was necessary?"

Marya did not answer. This was their cause. It was what had brought them together. Both Marya and Lena lived in the same world, wanted the same future, had watched the same people bleed and suffer and die for want of a solution. So what did it mean that Marya knew Lena wouldn't like her answer?

"You can't even say it," Lena said. Her laugh was dry as gunfire, and she reached for the scarlet scarf she had tossed across the table. "I don't know what that woman has done to you, Masha. But I don't like it."

The words, *that woman*, pushed Marya's frustration over into a dark pit of rage, and she slapped the scarf from Lena's hand. It sank to the ground as if through water instead of air, settling in a puddle like a slain serpent. Lena made no move to pick it up.

"Is that what this is?" she demanded. "You're jealous?"

"Jealous?" Lena gave a staccato laugh. "This isn't jealousy. I'd like to sew her up in a sack and throw her in the Neva, and then maybe I'd finally sleep at night. Can't you see what she is? Can't you tell what she's doing?"

"She's what we need," Marya said flatly. "She's helping *me* be what we need."

Lena looked at her a long moment before fastening her overcoat. The scarf lay on the floor between them, forgotten.

"Where are you going?" Marya demanded.

"Out," Lena said, without looking, and she was gone.

Marya stood frozen, listening to Lena's footsteps on the rickety stairs, then the slam of the door. She could picture Lena without effort, her tall form moving easily through the snowy courtyard, dark skin luminous and bitten by the wind. She wouldn't cry, that wasn't Lena's way, but Marya knew how her shoulders would press close to her ears, tension coiling through every muscle. Step by step, moving farther away. Leaving her.

Gone.

Marya sank back to the floor, leaning against the wall. The room felt colder now, shot through with gusts of wind that brushed her like a mockery of Lena's hand. Without meaning to, without ever giving her anger permission to turn into something else, she bent herself double, forehead against her knees. And for the first time in many, many weeks, she wept.

She stood by what she'd said. Sofia was right, Felix was right, and Marya wouldn't have acted differently if given a chance. Marya had agreed long ago to give up everything for the Koalitsiya if the cause asked it of her. Nothing in her own small, unimportant life mattered enough that she wouldn't give it up in exchange for the country's future.

But she'd never thought Russia's future would ask her to give up Lena.

She wept, and it was liberating at the same time that it ached. How long had it been since she'd broken? It was small, and it was selfish, and it was pathetic. But if a person wasn't allowed to be small and pathetic in the privacy of their own grief, the world was crueler than Marya had thought.

"Now what on earth could be the matter?" said a smooth, familiar voice.

Marya flinched and looked up, hastily wiping the back of her hand across her eyes. So this wasn't a private grief after all.

Sofia removed her thick fur hat and closed the door behind her. Her plait glittered with stray snowflakes, rapidly melting in the relative warmth. Faced with Sofia's stunning face, her elegant poise, Marya had never felt more ridiculous, more despicable. Crying over a fight with a lover, with the future of the country at stake.

"I'm sorry," Marya said thickly. "I—"

She started to stand up, but Sofia shook her head, then sat beside her, there on the still-wet apartment floor. More impossible still, she spread one arm over Marya's shoulders, cradling Marya into the curve of her side. Sofia's body was frigid from the cold, but Marya would have welcomed a blizzard with open arms if it meant staying close to this woman, being comforted by her. What was happening was impossible, but if Marya questioned why Sofia—beautiful, powerful, perfect—wanted to be near her, it would all disappear, and she'd be as alone as she'd been before. Let the impossible happen, if only for now.

"Everything important hurts," Sofia said. "If it's worthwhile, it comes with a little pain. Surely you know that."

Of course she did. If she had any fight left in her, she'd have snapped at Sofia for daring to treat her like a fool, like a child, like an idealist who didn't understand the price of what she was asking for. But the confrontation with Lena had taken the wind from Marya's lungs, and she was too tired to care about what she ought to have felt or thought or said. She rested her head on Sofia's shoulder, Sofia's fingers carding through Marya's hair, and for a long, awful, beautiful moment, she allowed herself to cry and be held. No one had seen her fall apart like this in years, not since she'd been a child. Now that she'd begun, she wasn't sure she'd ever be able to stop. Marya leaned against Sofia as if the skin keeping them apart could melt and she could fall into her, stop *being* at all and let her essence be swallowed by this stronger, more powerful woman, who alone could make sense of this mad world.

"She doesn't understand," Marya said finally, her voice thick with the shadow of tears. "I don't know how to make her see. I wouldn't have *chosen* any of this, it's—"

"Why would you have chosen it?" Sofia said. It would have felt like reassurance if not for the warm cruelty that simmered beneath it, a backhand challenge. "If we could shape reality so easily, none of this would be needed. People like you leave their mark by changing the world they're given, not by pretending they were given a different one."

Marya let out a long breath and ran one hand along her mouth. It felt impossibly stupid to explain her own weakness to Sofia. Sofia had no time for nonsense like this, petty personal griefs. Her cold, unforgiving pragmatism was exactly what Marya needed, and it was foolish to second-guess something so essential, so necessary.

"I don't want to lose her over this," Marya murmured. "She's the only one who's ever cared for me like—"

Sofia's laugh stopped her sentence dead. Her hand was still in Sofia's. She felt her own pulse in every finger. It was as if the hand no longer belonged to her, and with another beat of her heart, the rest of her body no longer would either.

"If she only cared about you so long as you were small and cautious and fearful, Masha, she never cared about you at all. That's not love," Sofia said, voice fierce as her eyes. "That's servitude. That's weakness."

Sofia leaned closer, and they were so close now, no space between them. Exposed, and terrifyingly vulnerable. She no longer had any sense at all of who she was.

"Love is freedom," Sofia murmured. The tip of Sofia's finger brushed against her cheekbone, and it jarred Marya like a hammer to the bell of her heart. "Love pushes you forward. It strips away your fear and makes you bold enough to destroy what no longer serves you and take what you need. It's not beautiful, and it's not delicate, and it's not easy. But it's the only thing that drives us, that makes us powerful."

Sofia's lips were inches from Marya's now. There had been a time to pull back, to turn away, but it was long gone.

"And unless I'm very much mistaken," Sofia said, "it's the only thing you're really after."

Marya closed her eyes and let time, pain, the world itself vanish into Sofia's kiss.

19

Felix

The wind tore between the buildings of Krestovsky Island and into the courtyard, a beast that whipped Felix's coat around his legs and plunged its fingers into his heart. He'd dreaded this confrontation from the moment he'd agreed to it. It had weighed on him through the restless afternoon and evening he spent with the Tverskys, their conversations only half registering through his humming nerves. Now, after a day of it, this final stretch of waiting only made his worst apprehensions flare up with double strength. He folded his arms, briefly losing himself in the cloud of his sigh. Would it be worse if Sasha never came, or if he did? Both seemed equally impossible, in this empty courtyard bordered by bitter wind and darkness.

Then he saw the familiar shape clad in dark green moving toward him out of the night, and the fear vanished, replaced by pure determination. This was how he'd sworn to prove his usefulness to the Koalitsiya. He could do it. No one knew Sasha as well as he did.

"Now this," he said calmly, and stepped out of the shadows, "is the least romantic place I can think of for a rendezvous."

Sasha froze with half the courtyard still dividing them. Under the weak light of the moon, the shadows beneath his strong cheekbones reminded Felix of a hollowed skull. Clearly he had expected to find a ragtag collection of angry civilians, weapons drawn. Clearly he had not expected Felix, unarmed and alone. Sasha's pistol hung from his hand, the metal catching the scant light like a shooting star as it dropped from his hand to the snow.

"So it's true," Sasha said, so quietly Felix had to draw nearer to hear. "You did fall in with them."

Sasha had a preternatural ability to keep his emotions from his face. It had always maddened Felix, that insistence on treating his own feelings like a vulgar secret, an approach so reminiscent of his father's. Felix had adapted, learned to read Sasha from the smallest signs. He noted the slight twitch in Sasha's mouth, the firmness in his jaw, and knew them for what they were: an emotion rippling under the surface, like some great whale beneath the waves. Perhaps it wasn't so different from the one coursing through Felix now. Relief, to know the other was safe and unharmed. And a desperate, almost maddening desire to make him *see*.

"They won't come back here, you know," Felix said. He leaned against the building's interior wall, the cold brick a steadying force spurring him on. "My father showed his hand too early by sending you. Now they know this place isn't safe, they've scattered, and he'll have to start his hunt over from the beginning. Surely you knew that would happen when you left them."

The series of movements as Sasha bent, retrieved his pistol, and halved the distance between them was both choreographed and brutal, somewhere between a dance and a battle maneuver. This close, Felix could see that most of the shadows in Sasha's face weren't from the darkness at all. He looked positively hollow with exhaustion. Stifling the urge to run his hand along Sasha's unshaven cheek, he formed fists in his coat pockets instead.

"Your brother's worried about you," Sasha said.

Felix wasn't sure what part of the lie was more laughable: the idea that Anatoli had spent a single minute fretting about anything but the political implications of Felix's disappearance, or the way Sasha hadn't even attempted to claim that the tsar was concerned.

"Tolya sent you," he said. "He and my father."

Sasha didn't deny it. "Given the way you were talking, it seemed reasonable you and the vila might seek out the only organized popular movement worth paying attention to in the city. The implications, when I suggested it, didn't thrill them."

"Don't call her that," Felix said.

"They ordered me to come after you," Sasha said, as if Felix hadn't spoken. "It would have been a quick bullet between the shoulders if I said no. But it might be better, in the end, that it's me and not your father's men. You might listen to me."

All the heroes of the old stories had known the correct order in which to put their loyalties: justice, then country, then love. Doing what was right mattered more than doing what Sasha thought was worthy of him. But this was no heroic tale, and Felix could not count on the comfort of distance or tradition. He would have to look Sasha in the face and tell him it was too late, that the time when Felix might have listened was long gone.

"At least step inside," Felix said. "I know you're tough as a mountain, but my God, Sasha, have pity on a pampered aristocrat. This wind will be the death of me."

As Felix had hoped, Sasha laughed, and the corners of his eyes crinkled with amused compassion. The sheltered prince, constantly caught wrong-footed by the country his family had only ever half ground into submission, unused to the slightest discomfort. Felix had bristled at that look in the past, seen the care in it and extrapolated to pity, to condescension. Now, it felt like a warm embrace on the coldest night.

The back door to the courtyard building opened with little pressure from Felix. The light inside was even worse, and the entryway ended after a few feet in a staircase leading to several stories of narrow landings. Felix mounted the first few stairs and sat, elbows on his knees. Sasha remained where he stood, as if sitting signified dereliction of duty. He ran one gloved hand over his mouth before speaking. Felix couldn't remember ever seeing him quite so tired before.

"I'm glad you came," Sasha said. His voice, which had lost some of its power in the courtyard, sounded more clearly in the enclosed space, like a priest's song in a church. "But I won't lie to you, Felya, your father is angry. Your brother thinks he can talk the tsar down to exile, let you leave in peace. But I want you to be ready for what you're coming back to."

He sounded so certain, so steady, that Felix felt the sick temptation to believe him. How simple it would be to return to the Winter Palace with Sasha at his side, to beg his father's forgiveness and slip back into the life he'd left behind. But that wasn't why he'd come.

He hadn't told the Koalitsiya of his plan, certain they'd have tried to dissuade him if they'd known. But he knew Sasha. And he knew that Sasha, though he'd never listen to Sofia, would listen to him. How many people had died at soldiers' hands by now? How many starved? How many run out of their homes? How many heads crushed beneath the heel of his father's boot, because people like Sasha and Felix didn't have the courage to act? Sasha would see it, if only Felix could find the proper words.

"Sasha," he said, "I'm not going back."

Some last store of hope in Sasha crumbled at this. "I don't understand," he said, an instinctive response Felix knew was a lie. He'd understood this from the moment Felix had left the palace. He'd only hoped that he'd been wrong.

"You see it, too, I know you do," Felix said. He was speaking more urgently now, as if arguments became more persuasive the faster he delivered them. "Why did you become a soldier in the first place? Not because you enjoy fighting."

"Because it's my duty to—"

"Because you had to," Felix interrupted. "Because my father never gave you a choice. I'd think if anyone would see what the Koalitsiya is advocating for and why, it would be you."

"Felix—" Sasha began.

Felix knew trampling the opponent was no way to win an argument, but listening felt like ceding ground. "They're just the same, these people," he said. "They have no choice but to try to bring about something better, because there's only pain in their future if they don't. If it's ever going to change, they have to demand it.

And I can help them, Sasha. Sofia and I, we both can. My family's caused enough pain. I want to be part of something good for once, do you understand?"

It was the first time he'd said it out loud, and the truth of it startled him. To be part of something good. Not the idle, life-loving prince, suited only for a party and a drink and a laugh. A warrior, but on the side of justice, using his power and his brains to lessen the suffering of others, instead of increasing their pain without even noticing. It would make him the kind of man he could be proud to be. The kind of lover Sasha might be proud to have.

"I can't keep hurting people, Sasha," he said quietly. "I can't bear it."

He'd expected Sasha to see the truth in this. Perhaps that flash of compassion that had sparked in the courtyard would kindle into something stronger. He hadn't expected Sasha to draw back as if Felix had struck him.

"And me?" Sasha said. "You seem to have no trouble hurting me."

"That's not—"

"It is!" The words seemed to escape Sasha's throat like an animal bursting from a cage. He again pressed his gloved hand to his mouth, repairing the mask, and when he spoke next, his voice was painfully measured. "You think I wanted this, Felix? You think I wanted to spend my life fighting?"

Felix descended the stairs, reaching for Sasha's hand. "No, that's what I'm trying to—"

"But I did it," Sasha interrupted, brushing his hand away. "And I'll keep doing it, for as long as I need to. Because I know my place, and I know what's right. There's no peace without order, Felix, and if you think the chaos your new friends are preaching will lead to a better world and not a swift execution, you know even less than I thought you did."

"I know plenty," Felix said hotly.

Sasha laughed, like a dagger straight into the core of Felix's pride, and shoved him in the chest. It was the same dismissive gesture Felix had used in the Winter Palace, only with Sasha's strength there was a threat in it as well as disdain. "Do you? The city is on a knife's edge. Every man with a gun thinks he's justified to murder the tsar and move into the palace himself, and when the tsar's own son runs off and starts playing brigand with a witch, who can blame them for thinking it? The longer you're here, the more permission you give them. They'll burn the city down for a chance to destroy your family."

Felix felt the last of his leverage slipping away. "Do you know how these people are living, Sasha?" he tried again. "Do you know what my father's done to them?"

"Of course I know. Better than you ever will."

A thousand accusations rose from the phrase. Of course Sasha knew. When Felix had been growing up in palaces, learning to conjugate French and German, Sasha had been living in this very neighborhood, leaving home at seventeen to earn half a living as a soldier. It was Sasha who'd endured the sideways sneers of Felix's friends in the Catherine Palace, Sasha who carried the haunting memories of another man's war through each waking day and rest-less night. If one person in this darkened stairwell understood fully what it meant to live under Tsar Sergei's rule, it was not Felix.

He'd hoped so desperately it would be different than this. Their goals were the same: peace, freedom, stability. Sasha could have looked on Felix with quiet affection, with the softness he didn't dare show anyone else, as they built a better world together. Per-haps he was a fool after all, to have hoped for that.

"I don't want to fight with you, Sasha," Felix said—then, wryly, as if a joke would do him any good, "I never win when we fight."

Sasha's brow lowered. "Did you ever think there might be a rea-son I always win?"

"You're a trained killer, Sasha, I know the reason."

"That's the difference between us, Felya," Sasha said coldly. "When I sent people to their deaths, at least I knew I was doing it."

The familiar diminutive rose like armor to protect him from

the worst of the accusation. Felix might not know much about war, or about governing a country, but he did know Sasha, and he knew that so long as the soldier tolerated his teasing, didn't retreat behind rank or push him aside with a curt "Your Imperial Highness," Felix hadn't entirely lost. He took both Sasha's gloved hands, and this time Sasha did not back away. He stood rigid, as if the slightest movement might shatter the mask he wore so carefully, might leave him either petitioning the tsar for the Koalitsiya's aims or shooting Felix where he stood. This close, it was impossible to forget that Sasha never set foot in the street unarmed. The pistol at his belt, a knife on his right hip. The finest shot in the Sixth Corps, and Felix had come without a weapon.

"At least talk to them," Felix said. He knew he was begging, but pride was a concern for another day. "I'm hopeless at explaining it, not the way Isaak can. He'd explain how different it is from what you think. He's a good man. Reminds me of you, in a 'could break your neck but most likely won't waste the energy' sort of way."

Sasha's smile cocked at an odd angle, as if amused at the idea of a good man resembling himself. "I've never known you to need someone else to do your talking."

It was almost a joke, and Felix was so relieved he might have drowned in it. "Desperate times. Just meet with him? Isaak will be at the printshop on Liteyny Prospekt most days next week. Tell him I sent you, that you're a friend, and ask him to explain. You don't have to agree with me now, you don't have to break any promises to my father. Just promise me you'll listen."

Sasha pulled his hands away. He looked almost forlorn, wavering on the edge of a decision. Felix had seen him look that way in the past, after a dream that had shocked him awake. Once, the nightmare had been so vivid that Sasha had lashed out in his sleep and kicked Felix from the bed onto the floor. When Felix had clambered back under the covers, Sasha had looked just this stricken, his face just this ashen. Then, Felix had taken Sasha in his arms and traced soft circles down his scarred back until Sasha's breathing slowed. Then, he'd helped deepen the divide between nightmare and waking life, and when Sasha had fallen asleep again, he'd done so with his fingers intertwined with Felix's. Then, he'd known what to do to mend the rift. Now, he could only wait, and hope whatever they'd built together was strong enough that Sasha could trust him.

"I'll think about it," Sasha said curtly. "I promise you that. Now get out of here."

"Sasha—"

"Go," Sasha snarled, and his empty hand flexed toward his pistol. "Before I change my mind about bringing you back."

Felix didn't truly believe Sasha would hurt him.

Even so, he didn't wait to find out.

"I love you, you know," he said, and he bolted past Sasha, into the courtyard.

He didn't stop running even after he hit the street. Only after several breathless minutes did he slow to a walk, when a furtive glance back proved that Sasha had not followed him. The street was empty, except for the few snowflakes that had begun to fall and dust the ground anew with white.

He imagined Sasha standing alone in the staircase, arms hanging by his sides like the limbs of a broken puppet, before turning and walking silently back toward the Winter Palace. To Felix's father.

Or to somewhere else entirely, to think for himself.

Felix knew Sasha better than anyone else. He was certain Sasha had meant it when he said he'd consider.

Now all he could do was wait.

20

Sasha

The next evening, Sasha stood motionless in the Cathedral of Our Lady of Kazan, waiting for a blessing he wasn't sure would ever come. Heavy incense filled the church, dulling his nose and the edges of his vision. The press of people standing around him on every side made the room even warmer, their voices rising and blending into the same chant. He bowed his head, unwilling to face the icons looking down on him. He'd thought the blessing of a priest would give him courage for what would come next, but instead his presence felt like a cruel joke, a hypocrite flaunting his sin in the face of God. The church wouldn't have knowingly invited a Judas to pray among its congregation, but apparently it would allow one to stand and mouth the words, so long as no one made too many inquiries.

He'd already decided what to do. God should have blessed him for it. He was only doing what was right. But standing here beneath this grand icon of an aureole-crowned Christ, God felt impossibly far away.

The movements of the liturgy were as preordained as a military exercise. The end of one prayer transitioned seamlessly into the beginning of the next, carrying Sasha along in its current. His muscles remembered how to worship, the ache of standing for hours to praise and repent, each word as familiar as his own name. It wasn't comfort, not the way he'd hoped it would be, but it was closer to calm than he would have found alone in the city, or in the halls of the palace.

"Monsieur," a man whispered beside him.

Sasha flinched. The man had kept his voice low enough, but the word still felt painfully loud, and in it Sasha heard the unmistakable ring of pity.

"I'm fine," he said, refusing to look.

At the stranger's quiet exhale, Sasha knew his lie hadn't been believed. "Monsieur, please, you look awful, may I—"

"It's nothing," Sasha said, louder than he'd meant to.

A woman standing in front of him, whose headdress indicated she'd skimmed the portion of the Sermon on the Mount extolling poverty, turned to glare at the two men behind her. Sasha bowed his head in what he hoped resembled either reverence or apology until he was certain she'd ceased glowering. The man pointedly faced the altar again, plainly regretting his impulse to offer comfort in a house of God.

The priest's prayer was traditional for the season, but the words passed through Sasha's ears without leaving any meaning behind, as if he'd never heard the language before. He needed God to listen to him now more than ever, but church-sanctioned prayers had no words for the kind of help he needed. Sasha kept his head low, letting his own thoughts drown out the service.

Please, God, forgive me. Forgive me for what I've done, and for what I'm about to do.

As his prayer blended with the soft, swaying rhythm of the cantor, the words took on the power of a refrain, blunted by the cloud of incense. Sasha felt bathed in gold, singled out and terribly seen. The icons around the church seemed to glitter with meaning as he amended the prayer with an earnestness that made him tremble.

And please God, let Felix forgive me, too.

———

It was late by the time Sasha left the cathedral. Not even the most dedicated soldier would have faulted him for retreating from Our

Lady of Kazan to the quarters Anatoli had designated for his use at the Winter Palace. The night cut sharp this time of year, and even someone twice as dangerous as the leader of the Koalitsiya would have gone to ground long ago, secreted in whatever warm den he'd chosen to hide in until morning. Sasha could sleep and know the chase would still wait for him when he woke. But sleep was a thousand miles off tonight. Felix had given him a piece of information, and every hour in which he hadn't used it was another hour he'd have to live with the awful, haunting doubt of whether he should. Better certainty than anticipation. Better action than thought.

The narrow Catherine Canal wasn't far from the cathedral, and Sasha adjusted his path to follow its frozen length. He felt like a child again, so close to the water. Back then, he'd wasted endless afternoons dreaming of stowing away aboard a merchant ship and sailing as far from the city as he could get, toward whatever destiny the stars had fixed for him. And what a destiny it had turned out to be. Far into the wilds of Russia, and into the service of none other than the tsar, only to find himself almost within view of his childhood home, preparing to drive a knife into the back of the man he loved.

Preparing to save him, he told himself firmly. To serve the tsar and put an end to this, one way or another.

By the time Sasha crossed the frozen Fontanka toward Liteyny Prospekt, he had left the unease of the cathedral behind him. No time for qualms or second-guessing now. This, action, was where he thrived. Sidestepping a rushed-looking man barreling toward him in the opposite direction, Sasha ducked down an unremarkable side street, then spotted his destination ahead. He didn't know this part of the city well, but a few pointed questions to the more loquacious members of the Semyonovsky Regiment had given him enough to feel confident in his bearings. The printer's shop sat exactly where he'd been told it would, a narrow building that looked as if it were being squeezed by the two statelier shops on either side. Curtains had been drawn against the front window, but Sasha could see the line of golden light beneath, and now and again the shadow of someone moving behind them—fast, but not secretive. This was the last-minute flurry of activity before packing up for the day, the burst of energy that came from the knowledge that in twenty minutes you'd be sitting in front of your own stove with your feet toward your own fire.

When Sasha entered the shop, the man in the heavy leather apron set down a tray of type and scowled at him. Small wonder: this wasn't the sort of business where a stranger often had an urgent order late at night. Sasha had borrowed civilian clothing from the Winter Palace, a bland black greatcoat that concealed his identity as a soldier, but only so much could be done to make him look approachable. Still, Sasha knew the value of putting up a convincing front. One didn't grow up poor in Petersburg without knowing how to manipulate others to get what you wanted. As he threaded his way around the high shelves and past the ink-stained press, he took care to keep his air deferential, his shoulders hunched and his hands out of his pockets, well away from his pistol. He doubted the printer spent his time actively plotting among violent traitors. More than likely, he neither knew nor cared to know how his employee spent his time when not setting type at the shop. Even so, it never hurt to be cautious. No reason to create a scene before one was warranted.

"We're near closed for the evening," said the printer brusquely. "Unless your business is quick and to the point, you might do better to come back in the morning."

"Forgive me," Sasha said. "I don't mean to keep you. I only wanted a word with Isaak, if he's finished for the evening."

Sasha had only a first name to go by, but the printer's expression—as he'd hoped it would—lost the edge of its suspicion. Still not happy, precisely, but no longer afraid. Apparently visitors who looked at least as disreputable as Sasha often came creeping through this way after dark, on the hunt for a few words with the printer's assistant.

"Tversky!" the printer shouted. Turning back to Sasha, he shook his head, bitter and amused at once. "My God, that man. Does he send one of his friends around every night at this hour to make sure I can't ask him to stay late?"

"I finish exactly what you ask of me, Kyril, and you know it," said a man who could only have been Isaak, emerging from behind a towering shelf of manuscripts. "If you want more dedication from me, pay me for it." A thin, dark man with a shadow of a beard, his eyes flashing even when defending his reputation against this petty slight. There was nothing remarkable about his face, but Sasha knew at once this was the man he was after. He'd seen agitators and turncoats at the front: the kind of men General Dokhturov had pulled from camp and shot like dogs before their dangerous words turned more of the regiment against the tsar's cause. There'd been wildfire in those men's eyes, too.

Isaak leaned against the shelf, sizing up Sasha with a sweep of his eyes. "I'm sorry, I don't think we've met."

"No," Sasha said. He glanced toward the door, feeling more than ever like an amateur actor. But he didn't have to believe his own performance. All that mattered was that Isaak did. "Not yet. But we do have a mutual friend."

"Oh?"

"Sofia told me I should talk to you."

The name tasted like ash in his mouth, but its effect was immediate. Isaak no longer leaned lazily against the shelf. All the power of his attention was fixed firmly on Sasha, the focus of a saint or a marksman. No doubt Isaak was armed, but that didn't worry Sasha. He was the best shot in his regiment; he was more than confident he could outdraw a printer's assistant if it came to that.

"Right," Isaak said, reaching for the gray overcoat he'd thrown at some point atop the shelf. "Kyril, everything should be in order in the back. If it's not, shout at me in the morning. My friend and I have something to discuss."

And there it was. Easy as breathing. Maybe Sasha had been wasted as a career soldier. If he'd ever taken the time to teach himself proper French, General Kutuzov could have sent him behind enemy lines to play the spy, and Sasha could have lured Napoleon himself unarmed and alone into a back alley somewhere. How much faster that might have ended it all. The bell above the shop door tinkled as he held it open for Isaak, following behind him into the street.

Over on Liteyny Prospekt, glass lamps blazed on posts at regular intervals, casting a reassuring glow on any well-to-do passerby after nightfall. But here, even one street over from the main thoroughfare, Sasha's own shadow blended seamlessly into the darkness. He had never felt so invisible, and seldom so powerful. A few scattered candles glowed through the windows surrounding him and Isaak, but the reach of their light failed before long, leaving them isolated like pinpricks in the dark.

"Sonya didn't tell me to expect you," Isaak said. Not entirely off guard, then—the hand in his coat pocket almost certainly held a pistol.

"No," Sasha said, "I don't think she was certain I'd follow through. Another man would be offended by how little she seems to think I'm capable of."

Isaak laughed. "As far as I can tell, Sofia's very good at pretending to be haughty and unimpressed when it suits her. Now, what is it you wanted to ask me?"

A cold, sparkling thrill danced through Sasha as they walked. This was the energy of the hunt, the pure clarity that came at the moment of action. This was one inch closer to Sofia. To the task he had sworn himself to, and would carry out no matter what.

I'm sorry, Felix, he thought, driving the butt of his pistol into the man's temple.

Isaak groaned and crumpled to the street. An ugly red mark already rose on his face, one that would darken to a vicious bruise within minutes. One knee on the man's back keeping him pinned to the street, Sasha dove a hand into Isaak's coat pockets: first one, then the next. Nothing but a few kopeks and a small metal square in the left pocket—a piece of type from the printing press, a curious trinket to steal. In the other pocket, he found the pistol he'd known would be there and confiscated it.

"Isaak Tversky," Sasha said.

The man tried to writhe out of Sasha's hold, but the chill pressure of Sasha's gun against the nape of his neck was enough to still him.

"You are under arrest for your role as organizer and chief agitator of the treasonous collective known as the Koalitsiya," Sasha went on, though against Isaak's silence it felt as though he were delivering the charges to himself. "And you are charged with harboring two dangerous fugitives wanted by His Imperial Majesty Tsar Sergei: Sofia Azarova and Grand Duke Felix Sergeevich. You will be brought to the Trubetskoy Bastion for further questioning, at which point your sentence will be determined. Cooperation will serve you well. Stubbornness will not. Am I clear?"

Isaak said nothing. If Sasha couldn't feel the soft rise and fall of the man's breath under his knee, he'd have thought the rebel was dead. When Sasha pulled him to his feet, Isaak swayed a little, unbalanced from the blow to the head, but maintained his silence. Even with the trail of blood now trickling down his temple, the fire in his eyes had not faded.

Sasha gritted his teeth and steered Isaak away from the shop, one hand grasping the man's collar, the other keeping his gun against Isaak's spine. As he passed the nearest darkened window, he could see both of their silhouettes, cast in the golden light of a distant candle glittering behind. He watched himself shove Isaak forward, barely breathing. Perhaps the figure in the window was the real Aleksandr Nikolaevich and he the reflection, in this world where everything had been inverted and reversed.

You're doing the right thing, he told himself, pushing Isaak northward. As if waiting for the cue, a soft snow began to fall. When his breath fogged in front of him, it hovered there like incense.

21

Sasha

Sasha sat on a ledge outside Isaak's prison cell, his hands clasped between his knees. Over the hours he'd been sitting in this corridor, his eyes had adapted to the darkness, and his surroundings had sharpened: the low ceiling, the rows of locked doors, the desk a short way down the corridor where one of the tsar's officials sat with a single candle, desultorily making notes in a ledger. The sound of the official's pen against the page reminded Sasha of rats clawing at a locked door. The initial rush from the arrest had faded long ago, and now Sasha waited for the prisoner to wake with the fatigued detachment that always accompanied a night watch. At some point, he'd become aware of the smears of Isaak Tversky's blood along his palm, which had crusted and dried there.

Isaak would know how to find Sofia. He might know how to break her. And though Sasha had never employed them himself, he knew there were ways to make a man give up information.

Wearily, he rose from the ledge, his stiff knees aching. The official did not look up from his notes—a soldier supervising his charge in the Trubetskoy Bastion was not news, it was business as usual, and this official had reached his current rank by making what happened behind closed doors none of his business. Sasha drew aside the slat of wood covering the tiny opening in the cell door, though he didn't expect the scene within to have changed. He'd checked on the prisoner every hour since he'd arrived and seen only the unmoving shadow of Isaak's body slumped on the prison cot. Now, though, that shadow was sitting up, one hand to its forehead.

Any weariness that had seeped into Sasha during his long wait was gone now. It might have been midmorning on a brilliant summer's day from the new brightness of his energy. He signaled to the official, who set aside his pen and trotted over like a faithful hound.

"The prisoner is awake," Sasha said. "Open the door."

"Yes, sir," the official said.

"Yes, Captain," Sasha corrected.

The official gave Sasha's nondescript greatcoat a sideways glance before pulling a dutiful salute. "Yes, Captain." He reached into his pocket for the key, which grated in the door as though the locksmith who'd fashioned it never intended it to be used. "I'll be outside. Knock when you've finished."

Sasha nodded. "We might be a moment."

"No hurry, Captain," the official said. "No one here is going anywhere."

With a mute nod—the Trubetskoy Bastion didn't seem like the place for a joke, however grim—Sasha entered the cell.

Isaak didn't look up. No attempt at escape, not even curiosity at who had joined him. The Bastion had that effect on men, or at least so Sasha had heard. This was the prison where the tsar sent men he never wanted to think of or hear from again. Difficult to maintain a fighting spirit in these narrow cells with their arched ceilings and metal cots, the whispers of a century's worth of ghosts presaging what was to come. Isaak held his left arm at an odd angle, pressed tight to his chest. Sasha had given the other guards express orders not to hurt him, but this was their domain, not his, and he wouldn't have been at all surprised if he'd been disregarded. Channeling the unshakable authority of the generals he had known on the battlefield, Sasha stood in front of the cell's single high window. Isaak's eyes were as well adjusted to the dark as his own, and the pale moonlight would be enough. He wanted this prisoner to remember his face.

"Tversky," he said. "Good to see you awake."

Finally, Isaak glanced up. The deep bruise against his temple was Sasha's doing, but the dried blood from his nose confirmed Sasha's suspicion that Isaak's stay in the Bastion had begun brutally. The crusted blood only made the studied blankness in the man's black eyes even more unsettling.

"You're the soldier who threatened my wife," Isaak said, with the matter-of-factness of a shopkeeper naming his price.

"And you're the traitor who wants to dethrone the tsar."

He expected Isaak to deny it—this, after all, was a leap from the information he had. Felix had alluded to acts of protest, which was not necessarily the same as attempted assassination. What he didn't expect was for Isaak to shrug, the movement jerky and careless, devoid of fight.

"So you say," Isaak said. "If you're going to kill me, Captain, do it."

"I don't want to kill you."

"You have an odd way of showing it, if that's the truth."

Sasha didn't blame Isaak for doubting him. He had no reason to wonder whether the soldier with his hand on the trigger had, perhaps, seen enough blood for one lifetime. A thousand dead Frenchmen would have scorned his hypocrisy, but Sasha shoved away the image of blue-frozen corpses the moment it appeared. There were enough ghosts in the Bastion already without inviting his own to join them.

"What I want," Sasha said, leaning back against the wall, "is for you to answer a few questions. Help me, and I'm perfectly capable of helping you."

"I'm already familiar with the kind of help men like you can offer."

"You're a young man, Isaak," Sasha said lightly. "Well-liked by your friends. A bright future ahead of you. I've already met your wife, it seems. You have children?"

It was a shot in the dark, but it met its target as what little color remained in Isaak's face drained away. Sasha had no idea where to find Isaak's family, let alone any inclination to hurt them, but he knew how he must look looming there in the shadows, and fear could make a man do or say things he'd sworn he never would. Another lesson the war had taught him. He supposed he should be grateful for the education.

"Charming," Sasha said. "I don't want to take you away from them. Tell me what I need to know, and you'll be back by the fire with your family before they even notice you're gone. Now. What would I have to do to get your people to surrender Grand Duke Felix?"

Isaak remained motionless on the metal cot. Only the slight hitch in his breathing indicated that he had heard.

"You don't seem surprised I'm asking about a Komarov," Sasha said, changing tack. "I'd think that would at least raise an eyebrow. You spend so much time with grand dukes you forget which ones you've met?"

"I meet all kinds," Isaak said, matching his insincerely light tone—that short pause, it seemed, had been enough to master himself. "You aren't going to frighten me, Captain, if that's the plan. I'm not so easy to scare."

Many men in the Imperial Army had been put in charge of questioning enemy prisoners. With each passing second, Sasha saw why he had never been one of them. The task required brutality and patience, two qualities he seldom managed to use at once. He could stand here for hours making irritated conversation and never gain any useful information. Or he could take Isaak by the throat and choke the answer out of him, which would only result in an unreliable confession and more blood on his hands. His palms were damp with sweat now. It occurred to him—however powerfully he wished it hadn't—that Felix wouldn't even have recognized him if he saw him like this.

"I want to be clear," Sasha said. "I don't want to hurt the grand duke. I want to help him. Though I'm not sure I can say the same for you. I know the way people like you can twist your words, make others believe that you—"

"I'm not trying to twist anything, Captain," Isaak said coldly. "Which you would know, if you listened to what I'm saying, instead of what you expect to hear."

With a pained grunt, he drew himself up off the cot. Even bruised, shaky on his feet, there was power in his stance. What Sasha felt wasn't respect, not exactly, but a dim sense of regard flickered in the pit of his stomach. Isaak's breath came roughly, and it was clear how much the movement cost him. But when he spoke again, the words were soft, almost kind. The last thing Sasha had expected to hear in a place like this was kindness.

"Many of my friends in the city are soldiers," Isaak said, "or at least they used to be. I'm sure you don't believe that, but it's true. Are you from Petersburg, Captain, or are you only stationed here?"

Sasha couldn't have said exactly why he answered. Only that Isaak had spoken to him like he was a person, not a tool in the great machinery of the tsar. Had asked the question as if he cared to know the answer. And it had been a very long time since anyone but Felix had done that. "Yes," he said, "I grew up here."

"And you chose to make your name by serving the tsar," Isaak went on, with only the faintest hint of sarcasm. "I can respect that."

Sasha barked a laugh. "I'm sure you can."

"I can," Isaak repeated, "because I know the sacrifice a decision like that calls for. I can imagine what you've lost."

"You have no idea what I've lost. You don't know a thing about me."

"No?" Isaak said, and for a moment it was as if they faced each other in an army barracks or a *traktir* in the center of the city, anywhere two men with something to argue over might meet to spar with words. "Then don't think you know me either. Do you know what this is?"

With his uninjured arm, Isaak reached up to loosen his shirt collar. Sasha watched in wild confusion as Isaak hooked one finger through the chain around his neck, until a tiny pendant at the end poked free. Sasha squinted, barely able to make it out. Isaak tugged the chain until it snapped, then tossed it toward Sasha, whose hand shot up almost independently to catch it. A thin metal disc, etched with some sort of symbol. He ran his thumb across it, reading it by touch. It faintly resembled a common letter, but the corners were wrong somehow, the proportions unfamiliar.

"It's not Russian," Sasha said dully, painfully aware of his own ignorance. He could almost hear Felix's taunt, *Have you ever opened a book, or do you only burn them to keep warm in winter?* The kind of remark that would have sounded affectionate in Felix's voice, but dripped with loathing in his own.

"No," Isaak said. "Hebrew. But then, I don't suppose you'd have any reason to know that. If you grew up in Petersburg, so far from the Pale."

Sasha raised a single eyebrow. Either Tversky was the bravest man he'd ever met, or one of the most reckless, or both. No wonder he and Felix had fallen in together. They had in common a dogged, maddening unwillingness to recognize how dangerous it was to say what they thought and believed in a place like Petersburg. Ever since a ukase passed by Felix's great-grandfather, all Jews in Russia had been exiled to the Pale of Settlement, a partition at the far western edge of the country, and only those with wealth, high birth, or an aptitude for highly skilled work could secure legal permission to travel. Living as a poor Jew in Petersburg, under the tsar's nose, was a crime punishable by deportation or forced labor, even for a man not currently spearheading a group of political agitators. Isaak was watching Sasha still, a challenge radiating from his silence, daring him to act.

"If there is a point to this," Sasha said, with carelessness tuned to be irritating, "I would suggest you get to it soon."

"You had your war, Captain," Isaak said. He never took his eyes away from Sasha, his voice light but his intensity breathtaking. In the poor light of the cell, his rough beard resembled an old bruise, almost blending with the dried blood from his nose. "My family and I, we had ours. The tsar sent you to the front, to fight and bleed and die for his empire. And the tsar sent his army to my home, too, so my family would bleed and die for his god."

It was not at all the same thing, and Sasha was not interested in pretending to see the similarities. War was unlike anything else under heaven, and his experience of it had caused him enough pain without adding to it the suffering of a people on the far side of the nation whose paths had never crossed his own. Perhaps Isaak wanted him to feel guilty about this. Well, he would have to try harder than that. If the worst experience of Isaak's life was that a few soldiers had behaved roughly around him once, Sasha had stories of his own that would silence the man for good.

"I served honorably during the war," Sasha said, each syllable clipped and precise. "Whatever happened in the Pale, I wouldn't call what you've decided to do in Petersburg honorable."

"No. Honor has nothing to do with any of it." The longer Isaak talked, the more Sasha remembered what Felix had told him, about Isaak's ability to speak. Even like this, captured and beaten, with his back against the wall, the man could string words together with more strength than anyone Sasha had ever met. The dingy cell around them seemed to melt away as if it were the memory, not the scene Isaak spoke of next. "I had a home there, a family, a trade, a new bride. A life, Captain. Until I woke one night to breaking glass and smoke, and a band of the tsar's soldiers holding torches in the street, and the house around me on fire."

Sasha's mouth tightened. He'd seen a similar disturbance play out more than once. His time at the front had kept him far away from the Pale, but soldiers everywhere were superstitious and prone to creating enemies, and war left a man hungry enough to take what wasn't his if it silenced the twist in his belly. He'd seen more than one *izba* lost to flames in his time, more than one family running for safety with what they could carry. The targets had always been poor families, outcasts. People the tsar had no interest in protecting.

"I'm sure the tsar has no idea how many Jews were killed on his orders that night," Isaak said, as if remarking on a curious error in a shopkeeper's ledger. "That sort of thing doesn't make it into the imperial records. What's two fewer people in the world, to the tsar's army? It's only to me they're my parents," he finished, and the mask of composure nearly cracked then, under the weight of the word.

For a moment, Sasha felt his resolve waver. Every Russian had a story of tragedy. Sasha could have told his own, of a poor boy raised along the docks of the tsar's city, a gun thrust into his hands at seventeen in exchange for soldier's wages and a mouthful of food twice a day or near it.

"You see it, Captain," Isaak said. "You don't want to, but you do. What have either of us ever gained from that empire? From that god? That's all I want, for this country to share with us at least a fraction of what it gives to those above us."

Isaak reached out a hand, and Sasha felt his own start to extend toward it. It was like muscle memory, the desire to offer his hand to this man.

This traitor, whose fine-sounding words were no more than that.

Both Isaak and Sasha had made their choices. Sasha had chosen to serve and obey. Isaak had chosen otherwise. Every decision had consequences, no matter which god you believed doled them out.

"I'm going to ask you once more," Sasha said. "Tell me how I can secure Grand Duke Felix Sergeevich and Sofia Azarova. Help me do that, and I will let you live. Continue like this, and I will personally ensure you never see the outside of this cell again. The choice is yours."

Isaak drew himself up to his full height. Even through the blood trickling from his brow, his eyes were steady, and his jaw was set. He'd meant it when he said Sasha couldn't frighten him. Nothing could frighten a man once he'd reached this precipice, this point of no return.

"No," he said simply.

It was as if a lever had been pulled in Sasha's mind. This was no longer a conversation, and therefore the rules of conversation no longer applied. This was a fight for information, the same way war was a fight, or loving a man like Felix had been a fight. And Sasha knew better than most people how to defeat an opponent.

Sasha shot out an arm and gripped Isaak by the throat, choking off a cry of pain.

"That," he said, "was the wrong answer."

What he might have done next, God alone knew, if not for the knock on the cell door. On its heels came an influx of light that, from the corridor, would have been dim, but against the blackness of the room felt like day. Sasha flung Isaak aside, turning away before he could see the man crumple to the floor.

"What?" he demanded of the official now standing in the doorway.

"Forgive me, Captain," the official stammered. "You told me to inform you if any—"

"Out with it."

"It's Lieutenant Suvarin. He's just outside. Said he needs to speak with you."

"Tell him I'm busy."

"I did," the official said. "Several times. He insisted."

Andrei. Damn the man. Sasha had always prided himself on his ability to identify a capable soldier when he needed to. If the determined young man he thought he'd known proved to be an anxious busybody who couldn't wait five minutes to receive fresh orders, perhaps he was losing his ability to read people.

"Fine," he said. "Keep an eye on him. I'm not finished."

As he left, the faint glint of Isaak's silver chain danced in the corner of Sasha's eye.

Andrei waited at the end of the corridor, his arms folded. In the dim light, he reminded Sasha of a creature out of a fairy story, some copper-soldier guardian escaped from the world below. It was not an endearing impression. Sasha strode down the corridor so quickly it felt as though the floor of the prison moved on its own under his feet.

"What in God's name do you want?" Sasha snapped.

Unlike most people on the receiving end of Sasha's ire, Andrei didn't blink. His eyes seemed bluer than ever: the sharp blue of a cloudless sky, under which anyone might feel exposed. "You tell me. Do you mean to kill that man tonight?"

Sasha bristled. "I was—"

"I heard you," Andrei interrupted. "The guards think it's nothing, but I know better than that. And if you take one moment to think, you'll thank me for stopping you."

Forget Isaak. Sasha would have killed Andrei, too, in that moment. "He's their leader, Suvarin. You expect me to just let him go?"

"I never said let him go," Andrei said. "I said don't do anything you'll hate yourself for in the morning."

Sasha took a deep breath, and with the dank prison air came a waft of clarity that had fled from him in the cell. He'd killed in war, of course. But though Isaak was the leader of a faction the tsar himself had declared dangerous, he was also unarmed, alone, and injured, trapped in the dark. If Sasha had gone through with what he'd been on the brink of doing and utterly destroyed the man penned up in a cell like an animal, it would have transformed him into something new, something irreversible.

He sighed, and with the sigh he saw some of the tension drain from Andrei.

"Thank you," he said.

"It's what soldiers do for their brothers," Andrei said, with a half shrug that fooled neither of them. "Or what I wish someone had done for me."

Isaak would be there tomorrow. Sasha could continue the interrogation then, with a cool head. First, he would walk, and then he would rest, and then he could look again with clear eyes. As they always said in the old tales, "The morning is wiser than the evening." Andrei began to lead him through the prison halls, toward the courtyard. It was a clear night, cold and blank, and the purifying air would strip the rest of this rage from him. He would be able to think then.

The scream that came next, from behind the closed door of Isaak Tversky's cell, stopped both soldiers dead.

It wasn't possible. It made no sense at all. But Sasha knew the sound of a dying man when he heard it.

THE BUILDING OF SKADAR

In a distant kingdom, in a distant land, three brothers
set out from their father's home to make their way
in the world. They walked until the bast of their shoes
shredded, until they could feel each rock and root beneath
their feet, but they never stopped their journey for more
than a night. After many long weeks, the brothers came
to an empty plain beside a swift river. The land was good,
the surrounding forests dense with game, and the heavens
themselves seemed to smile upon the spot.

"Brothers," said the eldest, "let us stop here and build our
home. I haven't seen such a likely place in all our traveling."

"Surely others will see the richness of this spot as well,"
said the second brother. "We must build a strong, well-
fortified home, or else others will come and attempt to drive
us from this land."

The youngest brother said nothing. He was a thoughtful
man and seldom spoke unless he saw the need.

So the brothers set to work, hewing great trees from the
deep forest and breaking them into beams to support a
fortress, which they decided they would name Skadar. Each
day, the brothers worked under the heat of the sun, their
sweat running down the beams like sap. Each night, they

sank to the ground and slept as dead men, senseless with weariness. And each morning, when they opened their eyes, their carefully laid beams lay scattered across the plain as if a great storm had struck them, all their work undone.

Seven times seven nights this went on, until the brothers stood surrounded by the wreckage of their future home yet again, and despair hung heavy on their hearts. But just when the eldest brother began to suggest they pack up their tools and move on, a wind rushed in from the forest, and there before them stood a beautiful maiden, silver hair loose in the wind, feet bare in the yellow grass. The brothers did not ask who she was, for they already knew—they had heard from their mother and grandmother that a powerful vila lived in the woods of this region, and they knew at once that this was she.

"Why, brothers, do you persist in trying to build here?" the vila asked.

"We have traveled far," said the youngest brother, "and we are determined to make a home here, with four walls that will keep us safe."

"Be that as it may," said the vila, "nothing you build on this spot will stand. All your efforts to build will be the same as you see here, unless you add one thing to the foundation to ensure its strength."

"What must we add?" demanded the eldest brother.

The vila stood silent for a moment, and then she spoke, her voice at once sweeter than honey and darker than wine.

"A man," she said.

The eldest brother protested that such a crime would go against God, and therefore could not be done. The second brother protested that such a crime would go against nature, and therefore could not possibly be done. The youngest brother shook his head but said nothing, for it seemed clear to him beyond words that such an act must never be done.

Another breath of wind, and the vila was gone. In her place, briefly, stood a pristine snowy owl, which took wing and disappeared into the forest.

The brothers remained quiet, and they did not build that day.

That night, when the moon painted the plain and swept across the swift river, the eldest brother and the second brother exchanged a look, and wordlessly they decided together. They came upon the youngest brother sleeping and pinned him to the earth, the eldest seizing his hands and the second his feet. The youngest brother woke at once, and his cries would have been terrible if anyone but the night-wakeful creatures of the woods had been there to hear them. The eldest bound his brother's hands with thick hempen cord, so that he could not fight, while the second secured his ankles with double-tight knots, so that he could not run. Then, leaving their brother prone upon the plain, they took up their hammers and beams, and they set to work.

"God, have you no pity?" cried the youngest brother. "I've worked beside you every day! Can you do this to your own blood?"

The eldest and second brothers only worked faster.

Before long, they had laid out the foundation of the fortress, with a hollow chamber left in the western corner, fortified on all sides with great stones from the forest. They cast in the youngest brother, still bound, whose cries only gradually softened beneath the cushioning of planks and stone and moss and clay, first two feet high, then five, then twenty. By the time the next sun dawned after the seven times seventh day of construction, the fortress of Skadar stood tall and proud and strong, and the youngest brother's cries had been replaced by the piping remarks of magpies, which feasted upon the insects that scuttled across the grass.

The eldest and the second brother moved into the fortress that morning and looked around their home. The plain was vast and fertile, the river swift and rich with fish. The heavens themselves, they told each other, smiled on the spot. From the forest, a snowy owl sailed out of the trees, heedless of the hour, and perched on the gate of the fortress. There she stayed, day in and day out, for as long as the two brothers lived. After their deaths, the owl would venture away during the daytime, but at night she would return to her perch on the gate and resume her watch.

Even now, it is said, boatmen traveling down the river at night hear cries through the dark as they drift past the grand fortress of Skadar, though whether they hear the call of an owl or the shriek of a man, the stories do not always agree.

22

Marya

A terrible heaviness descended on the little apartment on Preo-brazhenskaya Square, growing every hour Isaak did not return. At first, Marya and Irina reassured each other as they'd done a dozen times before, spinning excuses by candlelight. Perhaps Kyril Ivanovich had left Isaak to finish an urgent order by himself, the unscrupulous old bear. It wouldn't have been the first time the printer had shoved the bulk of his work off on his assistant so he could get home to his own wife earlier. When Sofia joined them midway through the evening, her face stung with the cold as if she'd just walked the length of the city, Marya gestured for her to take a seat at the table, and Sofia fell into the rhythm of trading explanations as though she'd been part of these conversations for years. Perhaps Isaak had stopped off at the *traktir* for a drink and was still shouting at the proprietor about the rights of man. Or perhaps he'd visited Ilya to discuss tactical shifts and lost track of time. He might still arrive at any moment, shamefully late but safe.

The longer his absence stretched, the fewer plausible reasons remained.

Finally, well past midnight, Marya reached across the table and brushed Sofia's hand. "Can you?" she said quietly. Sofia's knowl-edge of the city seemed to be encyclopedic, and though Marya knew someone who knew someone in every quarter of Petersburg, her usual connections weren't likely to aid in a search at this hour.

Sofia understood at once. She nodded, drawing her coat back

around her. "I'll be back before you know I'm gone," she said, "dragging him in by the ear."

"God help him if he doesn't have a good excuse," Irina said, though the attempt at levity fell flat.

A pained silence lingered in Sofia's wake, though Marya tried her best to fill it. She kept her voice light, knowing that Irina was barely listening, the tone mattering more than the words. It was a waiting game, she told herself fiercely. Keep talking long enough, and Sofia would stroll back through the door with Isaak on her arm, and Irina in her relief would give him such a haranguing that wives four hundred versts away would tell the tale of it to their husbands as a warning.

But when the door to the apartment finally did open, the sun had almost risen, and Sofia was alone. Marya had never seen her so grim. Her shoulders were hunched, her eyes downcast. For a long minute, she didn't speak. She hung back, as if the news she'd brought would find no welcome at the table where Marya and Irina sat.

Finally, Irina shoved back her chair with an awful scrape. "Say it," she said. "Whatever it is, tell me."

Sofia closed her eyes and took a shaky inhale, though when she spoke her voice was level. "I looked everywhere," she said. "All the safe houses, the university, the market, everywhere. And then I—I didn't know what else to think, and I went to the Trubetskoy Bastion."

Irina opened her mouth, but almost no sound passed her lips. Only a soft, involuntary groan, as if a knife had darted into her chest and stuck there. For Marya, the effect was worse than if Irina had begun to keen. That wordless noise said, *I knew this would happen*, and in the same breath, *I can imagine nothing on earth worse than this*.

But there could be no mistaking it. That prison only meant one thing.

Marya had never, not for a moment, thought about what she would do if they lost Isaak. He had always been the one to comfort them before distress turned to despair, the one to turn panic into practical action. Whether it was the splintering of a new faction or the threat of imperial soldiers, Isaak would see a crisis and defeat it with confidence and bold words. He was always there, the center that drew them together, and Marya felt utterly unequipped to cope with such a loss without him. There was no one to help her make sense of it, no one to tell her what came next.

The news traveled fast, and before long, half a dozen members of the Koalitsiya had come to Preobrazhenskaya Square, to spend that first long night after the news with Irina. Felix, seated on the floor with the rest of them, his knees curled into his chest as though trying to make himself disappear. Petrushka and Oksana and large, silent Nikolasha, whom Marya was certain she'd never heard speak more than ten words together. All of them had loved Isaak, in their way. Everyone here had called him a friend. Some more than that.

But few had cared for Isaak the way Marya had. And no one's grief could come near to Irina's.

Marya didn't leave Irina's side for a moment that night, and not after, as the next afternoon stretched toward evening. It was better this way. Her own grief could be set aside in the face of Irina's deep, penetrating bereavement. Thank God for ritual in times like this. Marya knew little of her friends' customs beyond what they'd shared with her and what she'd seen on the days of the year they'd retreated into fasting and prayer. But in the face of Isaak's death, Irina was left with a preordained set of behaviors to lean on, and Marya, too, took comfort in being directed through something larger than herself. Irina could sit here on the floor, surrounded by friends, while Marya could drape the windows in cloth to prevent her catching sight of her own reflection. She could bring food: basic fare like kasha and *svekla* sharp with horseradish, the best she could scrounge up with limited supplies, but which at least was familiar enough to eat without thinking about it. And she could listen while Irina spoke. The air through which her voice moved seemed to hang heavy, weighted by the density of Irina's words.

Marya had heard Irina and Isaak recite this prayer before, quietly and in private, every year on the anniversary of Isaak's parents' deaths. Surely the kaddish wasn't traditionally said like this, one soft voice in a darkened house full of others who did not understand the words, isolated from a community of faithful mourners, but Irina had to adapt the custom. Isaak had been buried in the communal grave the tsar reserved for undesirables. There would be no opportunity for their friends to wash his body, no chance to wrap him in a prayer shawl before the casket was closed, no way for Irina to place the first shovelful of earth on its lid. The burial rites had been taken from her, and a week of mourning surrounded by family had been taken from her, and a chance to say goodbye had been taken from her, but she had the mourner's kaddish, if not the numbers required to say it properly, and she would hold on to that until she had no strength left to hold anything.

Prayer was one support for Irina. The other support she asked for now.

"Tell me again," she said. She sat with her spine against the wall and her head tilted back. Marya had never seen her look so tired.

Sofia, across from her, closed her eyes. "Irinushka, I've told you, there's nothing new—"

"I said tell me again."

Marya gave Sofia a sharp, silent nod. She'd known Irina for years. And though this might have sounded like slow torture to anyone else, Marya knew Irina needed this. She needed to hear it, again and again, until she could recite the story verbatim. Only then would she really know it.

A long sigh, and then Sofia began again. The story had been stripped down in the retelling, purely utilitarian now. "When I couldn't find him, I started to fear the worst. I went to the Trubetskoy Bastion, and as I got closer, I saw two soldiers leaving the prison, Captain Dorokhin and one of his men. I stayed in the shadows, and thinking they were alone, the captain was bragging about the prisoner he'd just executed. He . . ."

"Say it," Irina said, when the rest of the sentence did not come.

Sofia closed her eyes. "Captain Dorokhin said the tsar would reward him for making sure there was one less Jewish dog on the streets. The moon was bright. I could still see the blood on his uniform."

Irina reached for Marya's hand, which Marya gave without hesitation. Her friend's grip was so strong her own palm began to ache, but it was a good hurt, from the world of the living.

"Do you know how he did it?" Irina said hollowly. "A knife? A gun? Did it take long to—"

"He didn't," Felix said fiercely. "It's not possible. The guilt of it would kill Sasha."

"For God's sake," Ilya snapped. He gripped Felix's shoulder, hard enough for him to flinch. "Isaak's dead, and it's the soldier's feelings you're worried about? It's not a game we're playing, little prince, not one of your pageants."

Felix shook off Ilya's hand, his face flushed pink with both shame and anger. "I know. But it can't have been Sasha."

"She heard him say it," Ilya said. "He admitted it, and you were supposed to have taken care of him. It's because of you that—"

"Enough," Felix snarled, though the break in his voice was not entirely from anger—Marya thought, for a moment, that the grand duke might cry. Ilya started another retort, no doubt crueler than the last, but Felix tugged on his coat and stormed out of the room before anyone could stop him. The door hung open in his wake before blowing gently shut on the current of air from the drafty hall.

"That isn't helping, Ilya," Marya said coldly.

"Now you're defending him, too?" Ilya demanded. "I could have told you he'd cost us from the first day he arrived. Whatever he says, he was still born one of them."

It shocked her how quickly grief could turn to anger. It raced through her then, sharp, hot, and desperately, achingly alive. "You have nothing to gain by hurting him," she said. "It was the captain who killed Isaak, not Felix. But if you want to give Felix a reason to go back to his father and send the entire Semyonovsky Regiment down on us, by all means, carry on."

Wincing, Ilya turned away. She'd won, but Marya felt no better for it. Isaak had been gone less than a day, and already the cracks within the Koalitsiya seemed deeper, poised to become terrible rifts that could sever the group beyond repair. Ilya was driving Felix away, and now Marya was separating from Ilya. In a week they would be a dozen factions, drifting like floes of ice during a thaw, and all the ideas Isaak had fought for would fade away into silence. She was disrespecting him, tormenting Irina, by giving in to this. Before cruel words she would regret could slip out, Marya left the circle seated on the floor, fleeing for the solitude of the landing outside the front door. She couldn't leave, not when Irina needed her, not when the Koalitsiya was on the verge of collapsing into rubble. But she needed a moment to think. Surely no one would begrudge her that.

For a moment, she wondered if Felix had landed on the same solution, but the stair was empty. The grand duke must have needed more distance than the landing could offer. Relieved, she sank down onto the top step, resting her elbows on her knees.

Isaak Mikhailovich was dead. And part of her—a loud, not-inconsiderable part—wondered if the future he'd dreamed of hadn't just died with him.

He'd always known that leading the Koalitsiya came with risks. They'd talked about it, many times, before he turned up the collar of his coat and set off into the evening. *It's dangerous*, she'd said, and he'd laughed that infectious laugh and replied, *Of course it is, Masha, or anyone would do it. If I'm hurt or I'm caught, so be it, as long as I tried.* There was so much she should have said to him those nights. So much she should have done. If she'd reminded him of his wife, of his unborn child who deserved a father. If she'd kept in closer contact with her connections in the city, worked the people who traded and sold with her, plied Alevtina for news of any emerging threats. If she'd seen it coming.

If, if, if, a hundred thousand *if*s, and her friend might still be alive.

She pressed her knuckles to her lips, willing herself not to cry. Today was a day for grief, but not hers. She was here to be strong, to chart a path forward, to handle what needed handling, not to fall apart. They were all prepared to die for the success of the Koalitsiya, but death had always seemed abstract, romantic even, when discussed in the back room of a smoky *traktir* with a fourth or fifth shot of vodka, when tactics had spilled into broad ideals, a liberated future they would build and share together. Talking of death was one thing. The soft rasp of Irina's voice over the mourner's kaddish was something else.

Isaak. The first of them she'd met, back when she'd known no one in Petersburg. Alone and making her own way with a handful of stolen goods, her father dead a matter of weeks. He'd found her shivering in the shadow of the printer's shop where he worked, trying to keep out of the wind. She'd never forget his stern face melting into kindness as he saw her and reached out a hand, not in pity but in greeting.

Come on, devushka, *you can't stay here,* he'd said, *not in the cold.*

Won't your master mind, she'd asked him, tongue heavy with the chill, and he'd laughed and said, *I have no master, and don't you forget it. Besides, I make a habit of bringing in strays, Kyril expects it by now, stop being stubborn and come inside.*

Isaak, who'd invited her to join him singing a folk song from their childhoods one night and had praised her voice as twelve sorts of perfection, adding on a half-dozen requests for songs that he attempted to harmonize with in his own spirited but imprecise tenor. Who'd stayed awake long into the night just for the pleasure of sharing her company, trading lewd jokes, quoting philosophers she'd never heard of until she'd thrown a hunk of stale brown bread at his head to get him to stop. Isaak, her friend.

Isaak, buried in a shallow grave behind the Trubetskoy Bastion.

She brushed the beginnings of tears from her eyes, furious with herself for letting them start. Lena would find out soon, if she didn't already know. And then, in the one place Marya dared to hope for comfort, she would have to face Lena's judgment. Lena, who had warned her what this would cost.

Marya felt rather than heard someone join her on the landing. She turned, half expecting her thoughts to have conjured Lena, but it was Sofia who looked back, eyes soft with concern. Of course. No one else could move so quietly. No one else gathered here tonight, Marya realized, would have been compelled to comfort her. The Koalitsiya loved her, and she loved them, bound together by shared hope, but none of them would look at the situation and think Marya was the one who needed someone to share the load.

"I'm all right," Marya said, hearing the waver in her voice that betrayed her as a liar.

Sofia nodded. "I can always count on you for that."

Marya Ivanovna with the heart of stone. She hadn't been that way with Isaak, with Irina, with Lena. She'd let herself feel, let herself want, let herself hope. And look where it had gotten them. Sentiment only led to weakness. With the Koalitsiya as fragile as it was now, weakness was a luxury Marya couldn't afford. Irina was in no state to lead them. Ilya would leap at the chance, but he would wrench them farther from the path Marya and the Tverskys had charted.

No, if the Koalitsiya was going to survive this, Marya would have to lead it.

The thought was enough to send her spiraling. Her breath came too fast, and sparks danced at the edges of her vision. Full already with grief, there was no room for the fear, and it spilled out in every direction, overflowing.

Sofia took Marya's hand and pressed it firmly, and then she was no longer breathing at all. No longer needed to. It was as if Marya's chest had been torn open, her heart and lungs removed and a great chasm left behind. It was terrifying. It was intoxicating. It was terrible and delicious at once. Sofia's eyes looked like wine held up before a fire, like molten gold poured from a crucible.

"I should have been there," Marya said quietly. "I should have known, somehow. I should have stopped them."

Sofia's smile was soft and melancholy, though she didn't speak. Instead, her free hand trailed a slow path along the outside of Marya's thigh. It was the least appropriate moment for sensuality, and yet it grounded her, reminded her that while Isaak might be gone, she was still here, she still lived. She wanted to pull away, and to beg Sofia never to stop.

"It's going to change now, you know," Sofia said. "Irina will see it, too, once the shock fades."

"I don't know how we can go on without him, Sonya," Marya said, tasting the diminutive on her tongue for the first time. It had always sounded so natural when Isaak said it, like a brother to an older sister. It sounded entirely different coming from her. "I can't be what he was. I don't know how."

"You don't have to be him," Sofia said fiercely. "You're enough on your own, Masha. And you already know what you need to do. They can't take what they've taken and not pay. Blood for blood. It's the only way animals survive in nature, by refusing to become prey."

Vengeance. It was vengeance Sofia promised. And there surging in front of the fear: a hunger, fiercer than any Marya had felt in her life.

"Yes," she said, and then again, louder. "Yes. They'll pay for what they've done. I'll make sure of it."

"We'll make sure," Sofia said. "Together."

The words were spitting fire, but Sofia's hand across Marya's brow was soft, as soft as the kiss she leaned in to take without invitation. Marya, breathless, let Sofia's strength seep into the void grief had dug within her. This kiss was a solemn vow, a promise. This was a kiss that swore to kill.

Sofia tasted of salt, of vodka laced with frost. Her hair was soft beneath Marya's fingers. It was like kissing on the exposed edge of a mountain, wind whipping them nearer to a fall, every nerve alive. Let it be magic or madness, so long as it always felt like this. Sofia's kiss became oblivion, wiping away death itself, erasing every inch of the world that was not this. Sofia's hands were as bold as the rest of her as they eased Marya back against the wall, in the moonlight through the window. Her hands moved to the hem of Marya's skirt. Moved beneath it. Cold fingers against the inside of her thigh. This, now, was something else entirely.

"May I?" Sofia murmured.

The "no" was half formed on her lips already. Shock howled like a wind through the emptiness of her, startling away the thrilling comfort of the kiss and leaving only the familiar, constant low tide where in others heat and yearning might have lived. Marya's body didn't know what to do, it didn't know how to *want this*, a quirk that Lena had always understood and never pressed her on, would never have pressed, not here, not when every nerve under her skin cried out in fear and pain and loss.

But Lena was not here. And this wasn't about want. This was a need.

"Yes," she whispered. *Yes. I will give you anything, so long as you take me away from myself, swallow me inside you, make me nothing and somehow* more.

Sofia's cold hands brought a wave of warmth with them now. Her kiss grew stronger, more insistent, even as her hand skimmed the length of Marya's leg beneath her skirt. Marya pushed aside her misgivings and grasped for the former feeling of the kiss, the sense that they subsisted on one shared breath, every secret contained between them. There was no room to think, nothing left in the world but the cold trail of Sofia's palm sweeping upward, caressing the inside of her thigh.

Sofia had clearly made love to other women before, but her experience was a gift rather than a cause for jealousy. Oblivion was the goal, not taking command, and it was the easiest thing in the world to disappear into the thicket of Sofia's breathing and follow

her confident hands. Along the bridge of Sofia's nose was a scattering of freckles—barely there, so faint they were only visible from
inches away. How much simpler, how much more beautiful the
world would have been if nothing else existed but that expanse of
freckles, the peace of that small and intimate constellation.

And then the pulse between her legs, warm from the firm
pressure of Sofia's fingers. Drowning, deafening, foreign but not
unwelcome. The world narrowed to the width of two fingers, the
circumference of a traced circle. Heat began at her core and spread
outward, thinning the air, until she was stifling a whimper like a
child waking from a nightmare—no one could hear them, God, no
one could hear, and she silenced herself through force of will. Plea-
surable and invasive, intimate and at the same time nothing at all
to do with her. She thought it couldn't build more, and then it did,
and did, until the shuddering peak of it tore out all the breath she
had left. The sigh hung there in a haze, almost solid. Proof that
something altogether impossible had happened.

Marya leaned back against the wall, drained. Bewildered. As if
she had dissolved into emptiness and was capable of anything.

After a long moment, Sofia pressed a single kiss to Marya's forehead, like a scribe sealing a letter. The brush of her lips seemed to
spark with stars.

"Come back inside," she murmured.

"I can't." Marya gestured at her flushed face, her eyes still pink
with tears. The empty shell that had once been Marya couldn't go
back in that room, couldn't claim her part of their shared grief.
The void she had become belonged nowhere, could look at no one.

"All right," Sofia said, squeezing Marya's shoulder. "But come
back tomorrow. They need you."

There was nothing to say to that. No words left for agreement or protest. Sofia smiled softly, then disappeared back into
the apartment, leaving the door cracked. Through the gap, Marya
could hear the rasp of Irina's voice, tracing the contours of the
same prayer again and again.

She pressed the tips of her fingers to her closed eyes, then turned to the window. It was nearly sunrise, and the dirty glass caught the lightening sky of near dawn. She ran her fingers through her disheveled hair and settled it into a loose plait. It was only too easy to move without thinking, the automaton that had once been her preparing to re-enter the world.

They need you.

The movements curt and efficient, she bound her hair beneath her black scarf and tugged on her coat. Out. She had to get out, away from her friends and their terrifying, impossible need. The air grew colder with every stair she descended, and the frigid door handle made her palm ache even through her glove. She pulled it open, preparing for a burst of snowy wind against her eyelashes. She would walk along the river until she could think properly. Then they would plan, then they would decide, then any number of actions. But first, she would become herself again.

Instead of the empty courtyard she'd expected, the shadowed face of Yelena Arsenyevna looked back at her from the threshold. Lena's right hand was still extended, reaching for a door that was no longer there.

Marya fell back half a step without meaning to. There was nothing inside her, not even the mechanics to feel shame. She couldn't run. Couldn't speak. The shock of Sofia's fingers still cold against her inner thigh, lips still sparking with Sofia's kiss, Marya looked at Lena as if at a stranger. Lena's expression was dark and worn, and for a moment Marya was certain she knew everything, but she caught herself before beginning to explain—Lena's grief was not for Marya, Lena's pain had nothing to do with her.

"You heard," Marya said. Her voice sounded unfamiliar, the words someone else's. *I love you*, she wanted to say, and *I'm sorry*, and *He's dead and I don't know what I'm becoming*, but the voice that had taken possession of her throat was incapable of such honesty. As she stepped away from the residual warmth of the building and joined Lena in the courtyard, somehow the distance separating them remained exactly the same.

"Of course," Lena replied. "I came as soon as I did."

Lena looked as terrible as Marya felt. The shadows under her eyes were deep, and the whites were tinged pink, much as Marya's must have been. Lena started to extend a hand, but Marya made no move to take it, and she abandoned the gesture halfway through.

"Are you all right?" Lena said.

A word from Marya and that guarded look would break apart. Say *I'm not all right* and she could collapse back into the arms she knew, let Lena's warmth and the familiar smell of her, spice and sweat and heather, let the entirety of Lena gather her up and put the pieces of her back into their whole. All she had to do was say it.

"I'm fine."

Lena sighed and folded her arms. "I'm glad I can tell you alone, at least." Her brows lowered, but there was still a spark of hope in her eyes. One Marya wished wasn't there, knowing that she didn't deserve it. Every moment Lena looked at her like that threatened to bring the world crashing back, make it all impossibly sharp and real again.

"Tell me what?"

"I'm leaving," Lena said. "Tonight."

The word landed like a fist through a windowpane. "But . . ."

No words would come beyond that. Only a loud humming from deep within her chest, making each rib tremble. Lena couldn't have meant *leaving*, not truly. She was *Lena*. No matter what cruel words had gone between them, no matter how deep their wounds, Lena would always be the one constant in a mad world. Without Lena, there was no home to return to, no center around which to rebuild herself.

"My sister is still in Riga." Lena's voice gave no sign of hurt or regret; the way she held Marya's gaze told a different story. "She's always said she'll take me in if I need her to."

Marya forced her body to move forward, reaching for Lena's hand. "But you don't need to."

Now it was Lena's turn to snatch her hand back. "I do. This isn't what I agreed to, Marya. It's not what you agreed to either. Without Isaak, we can't—"

"We can," Marya cut in. "We have Sofia. We have Irina. There's you and me. We can still do this. We have to, Lenochka. In his name, if nothing else."

"Masha, don't you see what she's doing to you?" Lena said. Almost pleading now. Marya couldn't tell if the cause of the shine in Lena's eyes was Isaak or herself. "You need to go, before it gets worse. Come with me. Come with me and be safe, please."

"Lena—" Marya began.

"I'm going, one way or another," Lena said flatly. "I only came to tell you and Irina. Go or stay, that's your choice, and I can't force you. But I won't be part of this, not what it's going to be now. I'm finished. Are you coming?"

Marya stood staring a long moment. Looking not at Lena, but at her bootprints in the fresh snow.

"Marya?"

She had to speak. She had to decide. The silence choked the life from her thoughts, and the emptiness in her chest roared.

"Go, then," she said. "But Sofia needs me."

She felt the words land from a great distance, watching both herself and Lena from the vantage point of a snowflake, of a bird circling overhead. It was nothing to her if Lena's lips parted in shock, if Lena blinked to keep back tears. Marya had pledged herself to Sofia, to the Koalitsiya, to the emptiness within her that left room for strength of purpose and nothing else. If Lena thought liberty could come without a price, perhaps she had always been too naïve to do what was necessary. A loss like that didn't bear thinking of, and so she would not think of it, and that was all.

"Find me," Lena said coldly. "If you change your mind. I hope you do. And tell Irina I'm sorry."

Without another word, Lena tucked her gloved hands in the pockets of her soldier's greatcoat. It took only a few strides of her long legs before she had covered the length of the courtyard and rounded the corner. She didn't look back.

Somehow, despite it all, Marya had expected her to.

23

Felix

He had done this. The thought stayed with him no matter how far he walked, no matter how fiercely he prayed for the death he deserved to find him. It dogged Felix through the night, chased him along the river, and finally shoved him into the filthy *traktir* on Sredny Prospekt, where the proprietor pushed a bottle of liquor in front of him and let him seal his own fate with it. He poured two fingers of vodka and shot them back before filling his glass again, this time high. There wasn't a drink in the world that would bring him oblivion as fast as he needed it, but he intended to do the best he could with what he had. Chasing emptiness, until that cruel thought stopped whispering its accusation—its truth—in his ear.

Felix had told Sasha where Isaak could be found, and now Isaak was dead.

He pressed his eyes closed and slumped forward, fingers nested in his hair, shoving back tears. He hadn't earned the right to cry. The Koalitsiya had trusted him. Isaak had trusted him. And he'd led the wolf straight to their door, on the foolish hope that Sasha might have a scrap of decency under that hard heart of his. His fists tightened in his hair until his scalp ached. He'd given Sasha the chance to prove himself, to build a new future, and Sasha had proven himself to be exactly the monster the Koalitsiya thought he was. So be it. Sasha had chosen the empire, and Felix had chosen the people. He would give everything he had to this movement, because this wasn't talk anymore. This wasn't childish idealism.

No, Felix was angry now. Angrier than he had ever been. And this was the kind of anger that demanded action.

The drink poured fast and steady, until he wasn't sure whether the glass of vodka in his hand was his fourth or his fifth. It hardly mattered—the sooner he could escape who he was, the better. Felix had little practice caring for people outside palace walls, but Isaak had managed to see potential in Felix that even he hadn't realized was there. Something more than the small-minded dilettante his father had always dismissed. More than what Sasha had always seen, wasted potential needing a firm hand and careful guidance. Isaak saw a different future for him: a man worth listening to, who could be believed in. Two things Felix had never been before.

Two things he would be, come death or pain or the end of the world, for Isaak's sake.

He raised the glass to his lips again, thudding it empty against the table a moment later. Tonight, he would drink and hate himself and hope to forget. Tomorrow, the real work would begin.

———

Felix woke with his cheek stuck to the dirty table, a half-finished glass near his forehead. The bottle was empty, but even so, his head felt clear, as if his new certainty of purpose had shielded him from the worst effects of drink. After a few mouthfuls of blisteringly cold water and a quiet apology to the owner of the *traktir*, who had let Felix sleep through the night in an undeserved show of kindness, he'd mastered himself enough to return to the apartment on Preobrazhenskaya Square. Sleep had honed the anger in his breast to the tip of a spear, and the winter air acted like a whetstone against it.

The mood of the apartment now could not have been more different from when he'd left it. The time for stricken mourning had passed, and he could hear raised voices even from the landing, brazen and reckless. The snatches of conversation audible from the stairs were enough to condemn every man and woman in their number if the Imperial Guard happened to catch wind of them.

Compared to the squalor of Preobrazhenskaya Square, the Admiralteysky District looked like a fantasy spun up by a romantic painter. Velvet curtains glowed around the edges from the warm fires burning behind them, and the streetlights glittered like anchored stars atop their poles. Even the streets had been cleared of snow and slush, leaving the dozen-odd members of the Koalitsiya room to walk three abreast through the empty thoroughfare. Though they could see the silhouettes of Petersburg's finest citizens moving behind their curtained windows, the streets themselves, that night, belonged to the people.

Felix walked near the head of the pack, in step with Marya and Ilya. In his right hand, he held aloft a torch. The flame licked the air behind him as they moved, leaving a smeared trail of light across their faces.

Felix's father had tried to inure him to violence as a child, dragging him along on endless hunting trips that invariably ended with Felix flinching away from the death stroke. He never understood the thrill of stalking something unprepared and underdefended, holding its death in your hands. Preordained slaughter was execution, not sport. But as the night air filled his lungs, he began to wonder whether what had disgusted him hadn't been the violence so much as the senselessness. All that blood, staining the snow crimson, and for what? What had anyone gained from it except a worthless trophy?

This, now, was for a purpose. If the hunt had felt like this, Felix would have understood what his father found to love in it.

It was madness, planning an attack on an undefended house in the Admiralteysky, but the energy coursing through Felix hardly allowed him to question the wildness of the act. It was as if someone had drained his body of blood and replaced it with quicksilver. His vision seemed heightened to an impossible degree, every flake of snow drifting to the ground perfectly defined. The night itself smelled like gunpowder.

All men had a limit to how much pain they could bear, and Felix and the Koalitsiya had found theirs. Let the tsar and his ministers know what it felt like to live in fear.

He hadn't visited this house in years, not since the tenure of the previous chairman, but his feet would have remembered the way even if the group hadn't been bearing him along in its current. His father always reserved the grandest houses in the finest district for his ministers, and by long-standing tradition, the chairman of the state council lived in this well-appointed three-story home. Bezkryostnov would have decorated it splendidly, this baroque oasis, tucked away on a quiet street where danger seldom dared to tread.

Desperate times, though, gave danger permission to roam.

He tilted his head back, tracing the length of the faux-Grecian columns along the façade of the house. It was the ideal target for an attack of this kind, a direct assault on the minister responsible for law enforcement, and practically unguarded compared to the state buildings that crowded Palace Square. Through the curtained windows, soft light revealed moving shadows, passing back and forth on the second story. Too many to be simply the chairman and his wife, the silhouettes too elegant to be the staff. Perhaps Bezkryostnov hosted a soirée that evening. Felix could picture it without effort, having attended dozens of similar events himself. A hired string quartet in the corner of a private ballroom, endless bottles of the finest vintages, and for entertainment dusty old men recounting embellished tales of their long-ago military exploits against the Turks or the Swedes for the umpteenth time.

The first makeshift missile flew past Felix like a shooting star. Rocks and bits of brick at first, enough to shatter the windows, but makeshift torches almost as soon as the broken glass began falling like rain. He'd known it was only a matter of time until they'd gone too far to turn back, but knowing it was nothing compared to watching the surge of light as the flames found fuel to feed on. Damask curtains, carpets imported from Persia and Constantinople, vapid French landscapes painted in oil and displayed in gilt frames. First the fire, then, moments later, the screams. Not pain but panic, a shrill cry as the guests' peace shattered like so much window glass. Felix felt the fire cast a glow against the planes of his upturned face. He could only imagine what he looked like to the rest of the Koalitsiya: the tsar's eyes, the tsar's nose, the tsar's cheekbones, painted in flames. At least now the empire would think twice before crushing another member of the Koalitsiya beneath the heel of the state. This animal bit back.

Another crash, a furious swell as the fire took proper hold of the second story, and then it was as if the spell suspending the Koalitsiya had broken. The noise of the outside world surged back, startling Felix out of himself. Pounding footsteps, shouts from elsewhere in the dark, and there, cutting through it all, the unmistakable cracks of rifle fire. Far off, but not far enough.

"Soldiers!" Marya roared.

Felix hurled his torch—it spun wildly before skittering to rest against the front door, flames eagerly climbing the varnished wood. Without waiting to see if the others followed, he bolted into the night, away from the sound of gunfire. He wasn't slow, but Marya tore past him like a deer on the move, darting forward and between buildings, into the shadows. He followed her as best he could, despite the rising stitch in his side. Behind them, the crackle of flames remained constant as a snare across a battlefield.

They wouldn't be caught. The Koalitsiya was the people, was the city itself. How could his father's soldiers hope to stop an entire city now that it had come alive?

Minutes later, the streets opened before him, and he found himself near the north bank of the Moika, which wandered through the Admiralteysky in lazy ribbons. He skidded beside Marya, who had stopped to catch her breath. Her eyes caught the reflected lamplight the way the icy river did, throwing back sparks. Behind them, back toward the smoldering wreckage of the chairman's house, Felix heard shouts, and the report of pistols. He shared a look with Marya, whose black eyes fixed grimly on his.

"This is what you asked for, isn't it?" she said. "Isn't this what we wanted?"

Was it? A scream, high and piercing in the night.

"It won't bring him back," Felix said softly. "But they won't forget this."

Marya looked back, and for a moment it was as if she'd forgotten Felix stood beside her at all. Her hand clenched around nothing, and Felix wondered briefly what, or whom, she was thinking of, as the gunshots rang louder.

"It won't be enough," she said. "Not on its own."

He could still smell the smoke on the night air. Felix let out a long breath, and the warmth against his lips reminded him of ash. The city trembled around him, tinder waiting for a spark.

"But I don't want to find out what else in this city can burn," Marya murmured.

A final gunshot, and then silence.

24

Marya

The smell of smoke didn't leave her memory for days. Every time she closed her eyes, she saw flames dance across her closed lids. Every nerve in her body felt exposed, twanging wildly at the smallest hint of danger. Every beat of her heart ricocheted like gunfire. No one died that night, somehow, though it had been a narrow escape. The chairman and his guests had fled through the back into the courtyard before the building succumbed entirely to the flames, or so reports said, and the worst anyone had to complain of was superficial burns and lingering smoke in the lungs. The Koalitsiya had been equally lucky. Oksana had twisted out of the way just in time—it was her scream Marya and Felix had heard— and the guardsman's bullet had only grazed her scalp. It bled like all head wounds bleed, until Marya was certain there couldn't be any blood left in Oksana's body to lose, but with pressure and time it proved to be only a scratch.

Marya didn't think they could count on being lucky again.

She'd hoped—foolishly, maybe—that after the initial shock, Irina would stand up and take the authority Ilya had tried to wrest from her. Isaak's loss would ache to the bone, a pain that would last as long as Irina lived, but both the Tverskys had sworn themselves to the Koalitsiya. Irina couldn't stand back and let fantasies of revenge destroy everything she'd worked for, cost their makeshift family even more lives. She wouldn't leave this weight to fall on Marya's shoulders alone.

Or so she thought. With every passing day, she wondered if she understood this new Irina at all.

They'd gathered that afternoon in an abandoned shop front off the Apraksin Market, where the regular wave of people making half-legal transactions provided a convenient screen to shield even the most dubiously licit activities. The shop windows had accumulated so many months' worth of grime that the filtered light inside reminded Marya of a cave. Perhaps three dozen people had crammed themselves into the small space, displacing a season of cobwebs and dust. Marya had tried to urge Irina toward the front of the crowd, but it was like trying to guide a statue. Irina remained at Sofia's side, which she had barely left for more than a moment since the night of Isaak's memorial.

Marya glanced down at their interlaced fingers. "They need to hear from you," she said.

The lines around Irina's eyes softened briefly. She started to open her mouth, and Marya allowed hope to rush in—they might still turn this tide, they might still step back from the edge. But Sofia tightened her grip on Irina's hand and spoke with the sternness of a priest.

"We're past words."

Irina nodded. Her expression was stone again.

Marya wanted to argue, but Ilya had already clambered on top of a handful of overturned crates at the far side of the shop, where he stood next to Pyotr Stepanovich. There wasn't time now to fight. If Irina couldn't say what needed saying, then Marya would do it for her. With one last, pleading look at Irina, Marya turned and plunged into the crowd, until she could almost reach up and brush the hem of Ilya's trousers.

"We did our best," Petrushka was saying, "but the bastards got away without a scratch. They're kicked, but they're not down."

"Not yet," Ilya said, and the crowd stirred into life.

Marya saw those who, like her, shifted uncomfortably at the thought of what Ilya might mean. But another part of the crowd—just then, it seemed to her, the larger part—pressed closer to Ilya like sea on shore, hungry for whatever words might fall from him next, whatever plan. The crowd had hung on Isaak's words just this way, but the people in those crowds had never seemed like feral beasts, all claws and teeth and vengeance. She had never been afraid of another member of the Koalitsiya before this moment.

Ilya pressed on. "They won't hide behind their palace walls now that we've shown them we're ready to fight. They'll want to be the ones who strike next. And we won't let them, will we?"

"We have everything we need," Petrushka roared. "Half the soldiers in the city are hungry for a chance to defect. We're one last push from an army—"

The word shook Marya from her silence. "And what then?" she yelled. Petrushka and Ilya both looked down to her with narrowing eyes, and more than one voice around her muttered in discontent. "How much blood is enough? How many are you planning to kill?"

The crowd started to shout, but Ilya raised one hand, and the room fell silent. It was enough to make Marya's stomach turn, that instant obedience. She craned her neck to see Irina standing silent at the door, her face an utter blank.

"As many as it takes," Ilya said.

Half the crowd erupted in a call for blood.

———

They drifted away from the market after the crowd had broken up, Irina and Marya and Sofia. Marya wanted to be furious with them, but her friend's drawn, shadowed face drove out her anger, leaving a different sort of unease. She couldn't maintain her outrage, not when Sofia still held Irina's hand so tenderly. It was late afternoon, and the sun had just disappeared behind the second horizon of the cityscape, though a few stray beams of light reflected off the snow and made Marya squint.

"Irochka," Marya said softly. "When's the last time you've eaten?"

Irina didn't answer, which was answer enough.

Sofia and Marya exchanged dark looks. There was work to do, a brewing disaster to avert, but the first order of business was to make sure Irina didn't collapse of exhaustion and malnourishment in the street. She allowed herself a flash of selfishness—this was what she was made for, comforting a grieving friend, clearing the way for a proper leader to command, not trying to do all of it at once while it fell to pieces in her hands—but only for a moment. This was the role she had, if not the one she'd asked for. No one would do it but her.

"Stay here," she said, setting off at a jog back into the market. "I'll be right back."

She darted back to the food stalls that lined the Apraksin Market, where *shchi*, buckwheat cakes, and various pastries and dumplings could be bought for a few kopeks. Weighing her options, she haggled her way into a half-dozen pirozhki wrapped in paper, each filled with spiced potato and cabbage. It wasn't much by way of a meal, but it was fast and warm and inoffensive, and she harbored hope that she might persuade Irina to eat it.

When she returned, Irina and Sofia sat side by side on the steps of a deserted shop, their knees angling toward each other, Sofia speaking quietly. Dressed in black and stern faced, the two of them looked like they had broken off from a nearby funeral. They both fell silent as she approached, Irina avoiding her eyes. Unsettled, Marya pressed the paper-wrapped pirozhki into Irina's hand and sat on the step below them.

"Eat," she said. "For the baby, if not for you."

Irina sighed, but she took a bite, and Marya was forced to consider herself satisfied. They sat in silence, watching the sun settle into night. People passed in groups of two or three, heads bent against the cold as they hastened to finish their purchases before darkness fell in earnest. In their averted eyes, Marya intuited a secrecy she knew rationally wasn't there, a spark of division, the false promise of violence. This must have been the way Isaak had moved through the world, haunted by this same simmering mistrust. Small wonder his face had often been so tired.

"You have to speak to them," she said finally. "Before it gets worse."

Irina made a slow performance of finishing off the first piro-zhok, delaying the need to speak. A small, spiteful part of Marya envied her the luxury of her grief: to be able to sit there, silent, while the remains of the Koalitsiya limped on without sparing a glance for her. How much easier it would have been if someone she could trust was standing beside her, willing to shoulder the weight of it all. Sofia leaned over, resting one hand gently on her knee, and Marya couldn't be sure if the feeling that rushed through her was gratitude or anger.

"I don't want it to be true either," Marya said. "It was always meant to be him, not us." She didn't dare speak Isaak's name aloud. "But it has to be someone, or the Koalitsiya will break apart. You can already see it happening. Ilya's pulling them one way, and Lena leaving has made the moderates think about splitting off in the opposite direction." She tried to convince herself that saying Lena's name was meaningless to her, caused no more pain than any other word. "They need someone leading from the front."

"And what do you expect her to do about it?" Sofia said coldly.

Marya stared. Irina still would not meet her eyes, but Sofia looked boldly at her. It was like searching for recognition in the face of a stranger. "The Koalitsiya is fracturing because it doesn't know who to follow," she said. "But they'll follow Irina. It was her vision as much as Isaak's. We can still do what we set out to do."

"They killed Isaak, Masha," Sofia said. "You think people like that will give up their power because we ask for it?"

"Irochka," Marya said, reaching for her hand—a gesture that was not returned. "It can still be the way we wanted it to be. It doesn't have to be like they're describing it, all blood and death and whatever man's left standing at the end."

"Doesn't it?" Irina said grimly. She looked at neither of them, but at the last gleam of daylight swiftly melting from the street.

"Of course it doesn't," Marya said, cursing the waver in her voice that made her sound uncertain, compared to Sofia's unshakable confidence. She stood up, hoping the extra inches would lend her the authority she was grasping for and missing. "Isaak always talked about—"

"Isaak loved to talk," Irina said. "Look how far that got him." She set aside the wrapped pirozhki and turned to face Sofia fully. For the first time since Sofia had arrived with the news, a different expression had transformed her once-vacant face. Not grief. Not emptiness. Not hopelessness.

Anger.

"We've tried it Isaak's way," Irina said. "We've tried peace, we've tried reason. He tried to guide us gently into a better world, and they killed him for it. Maybe that's the only language they understand. An eye for an eye, a man for a man."

Marya shook her head. She suddenly felt very small, set against these two women in black speaking of blood. "You don't talk like this. This isn't you."

"It's a new world," Irina said, looking at Sofia. "And I'm starting to learn who I am in it."

"I think you should leave, Marya," Sofia said. She took both Irina's hands, and the two women stood, their shadows long and inhuman in the last beams of daylight. "Let the two of us talk alone for a moment."

"But—"

"Go, Masha," Irina said.

Arguing with her would have been like contradicting a gravestone. Marya hesitated a moment more, looking between them with rising dread. But this was Sofia, not some nameless menace. This was Sofia, who had sat with her the night of Isaak's death and sworn they would find their way forward together. Sofia's aims matched her own. They always had. And she would only agitate Irina further by staying.

"Think about it," she said finally, her voice barely more than a murmur. "I'm your friend. I only want to help you."

"We know," Sofia said gently, with a soft smile. "It's all right. I'll find you later."

It was foolish to be reassured by such a simple phrase, but she clung to it with everything she had. The night was falling fast, and she could see, as Irina did, the impossible allure of someone else's certainty. Anyone would crave a commanding presence like Sofia's when their heart was so full of grief. Anyone would take the hand of someone who understood, if it was offered.

"I'll be at the apartment," Marya said quietly. "Come find me when you're ready."

"We will," Sofia said.

Irina said nothing until Marya turned, tearing herself away from the two women half bathed in shadow. When she did speak, Marya was just near enough to hear Irina's first words, before the faint rumble of the city washed the rest away.

"Tell me what to do."

25

Sasha

The Bolshoi Kamenny hummed with the chatter of rich, well-connected people taking their seats. Several minutes remained before the first notes of the overture would fill the theater, making this the prime opportunity for Petersburg's best connected to stay abreast of the week's gossip. There was plenty of it, of course—rumor had it that the Sheremetevs' servants, inspired by the attack on the chairman's house, had turned every horse in the stable loose into the streets, punctuating their long-standing petition for higher wages. Here, though, such news seemed distant and insubstantial, as fanciful as any drama enacted for a paying audience. Above, warm light spilled from the chandelier suspended from the painted ceiling, illuminating the stage, but the five tiers of boxes and the sweep of floor seats below them were the true attraction for these people. The production to come—*Orfey i Evridika*, Sasha had gleaned as much from the snippets of conversation around him—was incidental. The most important reason to attend the opera was to see others, and to ensure that one was seen.

Sasha's task tonight was simple. All he needed to do was stand here, at the back of the tsar's box, and let no one in or out without the tsar's express permission. Tensions in the Winter Palace were higher than ever after the Admiralteysky attack, and Tsar Sergei was taking no chances. Tensions would have been higher still if the Komarovs had known how long Sasha and Andrei had stared at Isaak's body in the Trubetskoy Bastion, blood still seeping from the knife between his ribs, as if a clear and comforting explanation would present itself if they only waited long enough. An inquest was underway, though Sasha had heard the whispers—*a waste of time, he must have killed himself, stolen Captain Dorokhin's knife to avoid torture*. A plausible explanation, if it had indeed been Sasha's knife they'd pulled from the dead man's chest. No, Sasha knew better than to dismiss this death as a suicide. A man he had apprehended, a man under his watch, had been executed. By his own people? By his enemies? In either case, a failure. And he would not be caught with his back turned again.

Sasha funneled his awareness down through his core, through his legs, and into the soles of his feet, focusing on his connection to the earth. Isaak Tversky was dead because of his negligence, but the lapse would go no further. If the tsar and the tsarevich saw the increased ferocity of his focus, the doggedness with which he executed orders, they'd have thought the cause to be appropriate loyalty, not the cringing, cowardly guilt of a broken man trying desperately to undo what he had done.

In front of Sasha, the tsar kept his attention on the still-empty stage, while the tsarevich and the tsarevna sat shoulder to shoulder, speaking in lowered voices. More accurately, Catarina was speaking, while Anatoli managed a nod and an encouraging hum at periodic intervals. Of the three royals in the box, it was obvious the tsarevna was the only one with even the barest affection for opera as an art form. Both men's interests were of the active sort, and the tsar, in particular, seemed to consider entertainment of any stripe a distraction from more practical matters of state. Nevertheless, Petersburg expected its rulers to display a taste for the finer things, embrace the worldliness of Russia's grand empire. And in a time like this, with agitators snatched off the streets every evening and the chairman's house in ashes, with the bruises of war still tender and dissent growing bolder, it was doubly important to prove to the city that the Komarovs weren't afraid.

And so, the opera. And so, the extra guards.

Beside Sasha, Andrei stood with his hands laced behind his

back, trying not to fidget. The young lieutenant seemed even younger here, his handsome face ill at ease behind the crisp trim of his mustache. Kopenkin was positioned outside the door, and others had been stationed at regular intervals throughout the building, which ought to have been enough to ward off the minimal dangers native to the theater, but if anyone were to slip past them, Sasha and Andrei would be ready.

"Stand still, Suvarin," Sasha muttered—the lieutenant's nerves were grating his already-frayed ones. "It's an opera house, not Borodino."

Andrei flushed. "I'm sorry, Captain. It's just—"

"I know what it is."

Andrei had seen it, too, the pool of blood across the cell floor. If a man could be killed under guard in the most secure prison in Russia, then safety was hardly assured in an opera box.

Sasha bit the inside of his cheek past the point of pain. The prison was not the only memory that troubled him. He'd been to this theater once before, the year before Felix's exile, by express and secret invitation of the grand duke himself. Felix had thought it a great joke, seeing the stoic, fearsome soldier sitting stiff-backed in an opera box, not understanding a word of the Italian comedy unfolding in front of them.

"I don't know why I bring you anywhere, Sasha," Felix had said at the interval, as his hair caught the light from the chandelier in a way that made him look like he'd stepped out of a fairy tale. "You can't let yourself enjoy anything."

"It's only fair," Sasha had answered. "You enjoy everything too much. I keep the universe in balance."

And Felix had scoffed as though Sasha were the most ridiculous person ever to walk the earth, and he'd leaned over and kissed him—fast enough that the men and women in the neighboring boxes hadn't even noticed, but long enough that Sasha could think of nothing else throughout the entire opera, only *Felix brought me, he asked me to come, he wanted me here, he kissed me, there, under the light of the chandelier, he kissed me first.*

The man in his memory bore almost no resemblance to the nervous fugitive who'd waited for him in a snowy courtyard not long ago. The Sasha who had kissed the grand duke under cover of darkness was nothing at all like the haunted soldier who stood here now, looking down at the crimson carpet and seeing only remembered blood. It was as if they stood on opposite sides of the same mirror, looking at a future neither of them would ever have.

"Just endure it," Sasha said to Andrei. "It will be over soon."

Andrei nodded and corrected his posture to mirror Sasha's. The lights dimmed, and the chatter below the imperial box quieted first to a murmur, then to a hush. The conductor bowed to the audience, accepting polite applause, and then the overture spilled across the hall, violins and horns followed by the smooth sweep of flute and oboe. After an interminable time, the curtains parted, and the opera began in earnest.

It was agony. Even though the piece was in Russian, Sasha still couldn't understand a word; the lyrics spilled by too fast and then a moment later too slow, and the briefest spell of inattention was enough to render the whole story incomprehensible. If he'd been in the audience, he'd have kicked his feet up and snatched a half hour of sleep, or passed the first act whispering snide remarks to whatever fool had persuaded him to come. As it stood, he remained stern and motionless at the door, as if he were a statue instead of a living, breathing guard. His task wasn't to feel comfortable or enjoy himself. It was to stay alert, and feel nothing, and ensure that danger kept its distance.

The music shifted, and Sasha heard the rustle of spectators leaning forward as the soprano—Evridika, Sasha suspected, though he hadn't paid enough attention to be certain—took the stage alone. She looked otherworldly, standing in a sweeping black gown with a cloak of whisper-soft silk trailing behind. Even the stage lights filtered down, from full light to a pinprick, like high noon seen from the bottom of a deep pit. The singer's voice rose, elegant but desperate, though Sasha could catch only isolated words, which flew from the song like ravens. The glint of opera glasses flickered through the high boxes, the audience's gaze following the woman as one. Sasha watched as Evridika arced one arm toward the ceiling, the note soaring from her throat like an arrow. The arm was elegant, but the fingers were wild, splayed like claws. Like the hand of a dead man clutching his chest while blood spurted between his fingers, grasping a knife that had surged on its own from the darkness to pierce him.

Sasha swallowed hard. It was an opera. Frivolous entertainment for the well-heeled. If anything darker lay beneath it, it was only because his own memory had put it there.

"Captain," Andrei said sharply, at full volume.

Sasha heard it, too. Voices outside the box.

It was as if the opera had disappeared, the theater transformed into the hush before battle. He raised one hand in warning, bidding Andrei stay by the tsar's side. With the other, he loosened the pistol from his belt, felt the reassuring weight of the full chamber. In all likelihood, it was nothing. A rude theatergoer hurrying to relieve himself in the middle of the aria. But he wouldn't risk the safety of the tsar on likelihoods.

"Tolya, what—" Catarina began, as Sasha faced the door with his pistol at the ready. Sasha ignored her. Steady hands, both eyes open. As he'd been trained.

"You there," Kopenkin shouted beyond the door. "Stand down, or—"

"Please," came a woman's voice, and Sasha felt the terrible pitch of his nerves ease slightly—threats, in his experience, did not begin with a woman's voice or the word *please*. "I only want to speak to His Imperial Majesty, just for a moment."

"Get away from the door," Kopenkin snarled.

"Only a word—"

"That's an order."

"Very well," the woman said. "Your choice."

What followed was the unmistakable sound of a gunshot.

"Captain—" the tsar said.

The door opened, and a woman stepped over Kopenkin's body

into the box. Perhaps thirty, thin limbed and not ill featured, wearing a long tan coat that hung open to reveal the curve of her pregnancy. Beneath it, her shirt was worn thin at the neck, the embroidery coming loose in places, and her skirt ended an inch too high on her ankles. Dark haired, with a spray of freckles across the bridge of her nose, lips pressed thin. In her hand, she held a dented dueling pistol. It was as if her eyes had already looked on hell.

The woman from Krestovsky Island. The rebel who had refused to answer his questions, alongside the eight-fingered man. He recognized her in a breath.

The woman held her pistol steady, though it was not a soldier's steadiness. In the theater below, voices began to rise. The singer onstage continued, and the orchestra did not falter, but a faint murmur of alarm drifted from row to row.

There was no time to think. Sasha sighted his pistol and fired.

In the same moment, a searing pain shot through his right shoulder like a hot iron.

He cried out and stumbled back. In a moment his sleeve was sticky with blood, the pain almost too sharp to think. From below, he heard the singer scream. A panicked Andrei turned to him, but Sasha shoved him aside, starting to raise his gun again, and his dry mouth formed the words *No, the tsar—*

The box faded, then sharpened, until he saw it all in brutal color.

Sasha's shot, knocked sideways, had grazed the woman's left arm.

With her right, the woman raised her pistol and fired a second bullet directly between the tsar's eyes.

Everything stopped. The gun in Sasha's hand might have been unloaded for all he was capable of shooting it. Anatoli roared like an animal, rage where Sasha's nerves had betrayed him into shock. The assassin cocked her pistol again, preparing for a third shot, but Catarina, with frightening speed, leapt from her seat and flung herself between her husband and the gun. The movement was just distraction enough for a pair of ushers to charge into the box, two strong young men who pinned the assassin's arms to her sides. Her impassive expression was that of a woman already dead.

"Lights!" Anatoli shouted. "Lights, *nom de Dieu*, some light!"

Sasha heard the orchestra falter, then stop. Lights began to rise. From somewhere to the side, another scream. Sasha could barely hear it over the sound of his own harsh breathing.

"No," he heard Andrei say. The soldier knelt beside the tsar, cradling the back of his head. Blood wept through his fingers and into the scarlet carpet. Anatoli shoved Andrei aside and now bent over his father's unmoving body with a horrible, unearthly keening, a howl. Catarina knelt at his side, afraid even to touch him.

Forcing himself into motion, Sasha leaned against the wall of the box for stability and scanned the audience, which was just beginning to understand what had happened. Rich men and women, the upper crust of Petersburg glittering with diamonds and pearls. So many faces he didn't recognize.

And one he did.

There, directly across from the imperial box, as though she'd placed herself there to secure the best view. Sofia Azarova, just as he'd last seen her at the Winter Palace, dressed in black, every inch as composed and impassive as the assailant. He could have sworn, for a sickening second, that her eyes met his and the corners of her lips inched toward a smile.

Checkmate, Captain, he heard her say in his ear.

"Captain," Andrei said.

He turned and saw the lieutenant, the vision hazy, his hands drenched with the tsar's blood.

"You have to sit down, Captain, you can't—"

"Not now." He turned back so quickly his vision tilted.

The box was empty. Sofia had disappeared, as if he'd imagined her. But the satisfaction on her face had been real. Not even in Sasha's cruelest dreams could he have imagined an expression like that.

His hands slipped from the edge of the box, and he cursed, sinking to his knees, catching his wounded arm against the wall as he did so. The pain surged until he felt the scarlet carpet rushing up to meet him, and then he felt nothing at all.

———

Sasha awoke on his back in a bed he'd never seen before, in a room that, though not particularly elegant by imperial standards, could have belonged nowhere but the Winter Palace. He tried to sit up, but the fire in his arm pushed him back again, and he collapsed against the pillow with a low groan.

"Don't be stupid, Captain," Andrei said from a chair beside the bed. "You've been shot. Lie down."

Sasha gritted his teeth against the pain. His uniform had been removed from the waist up, and a mass of clean bandages stemmed the flow of blood from his shoulder and upper arm. A loose linen sling kept his right arm secured to his chest. It had been hours since the opera, then. Enough time for someone to find a doctor. God knew how much chaos had already ripped through the city in that time.

"What happened?" he said, trying again to sit up, more gingerly this time.

Andrei reached for a pillow and tucked it behind Sasha's back for support, easing him upright. It was a curiously tender gesture from Andrei, who had always fulfilled his duties with such professional detachment. The gentleness made Sasha's heart sink. Soldiers like Andrei reserved their kindness for the dying and those who would be better off dead. He'd seen it at the front.

"They removed the bullet, and the wound's been disinfected and stitched," Andrei said. "Nothing too severe, God be thanked, though you left plenty of blood at the Bolshoi. You'll get full use of your arm again if you're careful."

"Not me." Sasha's left hand clutched the blankets, while his right hung uselessly in its sling. "The tsar. What happened?"

Andrei's face darkened. "Tsar Anatoli questioned the assassin himself."

Sasha's blood ran cold. Tsar Sergei had been under his protection, and now Tsar Sergei was dead. If it had been any of his men in this position, Sasha would have signed their death warrants without flinching. The tsarevich—Tsar Anatoli now—would be within his rights to have him arrested, executed or shipped out at first light to a labor camp, and no one would challenge the order.

"They didn't shoot her?" he said. The Anatoli he'd seen in the imperial box hadn't seemed like a man disposed to mercy. That howling, inhuman rage.

"The theater was already on the edge of panic without publicly executing a pregnant woman in the imperial box," Andrei said drily. "Besides, they thought she might give up the others."

"And?"

"They got her name," Andrei said. "Irina Aaronovna Tverskaya. But they couldn't get anything else. Loyal as dogs, these rebels."

Sasha closed his eyes. Tverskaya. Isaak's black eyes flashed back to him, obscured with a slowly seeping trail of blood.

You have a wife? Children?

He'd done this. He had sent her husband to his death. Given her a reason. And now the tsar was—

"She's dead now," he said.

Andrei's laugh was bitter. "You've been unconscious for a day and a half. Of course she's dead now."

Irina's body would be at the bottom of a pit somewhere, if any ground in the city had thawed enough to dig a grave. Maybe the same pit as her husband. If not, what would they do with it? There were options, of course. Tricks Andrei's senior officers in the Semyonovsky Regiment had always known. Anyone the tsar didn't want could always be disposed of. Sasha's dizziness returned with the thought. He pressed his lips tight and waited for the vertigo to pass. Maybe he could persuade Andrei to sneak him a flask of rum. Anything to blunt the awful weight of his own self-loathing.

"They've already started planning the coronation," Andrei said. "They want it soon, after the funeral, once it's safe for the tsar to travel to Moscow. I don't expect we'll be invited."

"No," Sasha said grimly. "I imagine not." He shifted his shoulder to relieve the stiffness in the joint, wincing.

If only he'd died when the bullet pierced him, as Kopenkin had. Died honorably, laying down his life for the tsar, and made a clean end of it. They heaped people like that with posthumous titles, erected monasteries in their honor. All it took was a good death. The bed felt more like a prison with each moment, as the sound of wind sweeping across Palace Square drifted in through the curtained window.

"God help us all," Sasha said. He crossed himself and turned his face to the wall.

Part III

FIRE

AND ICE

26

Felix

Bracing his palms against the windowsill in what had once been the Tverskys' apartment, Felix watched his father's cortège pass through the breaks between buildings on the opposite side of the courtyard. The pageantry, he observed as though from a great distance, was remarkable, equal parts magnificent and austere. As it should be: the choreography of a tsar's funeral had been rehearsed and perfected over centuries, until no doubt the metropolitan of Petersburg could have coordinated one in his sleep. Perhaps no one had expected to resurrect the ceremony so soon, not with a tsar in the prime of life, but that was the comfort of tradition: prescribed steps to fall back on in moments of pain. Each sledge in the procession had been draped in black, and heavily armed guards marched two abreast on either side. Though he couldn't see it, he knew the elaborate carriage in the center of the train, its gilded wheels slipping and sticking in the packed snow, held his father's body. From here, the cortège would wind its way through the city, across Isaakievsky Bridge, through the northern neighborhoods, and finally to Petropavlovsky Cathedral, where the bodies of tsars had been interred since the foundation of Petersburg. As he watched, it felt as if the procession passed through his veins instead of the streets.

It had been two days since news of Irina's attack at the Bolshoi Kamenny had reached Felix. Since then, all factions of the Koalitsiya had kept their distance from him, as if his connection to the imperial family could spread like some disease. Left to himself, Felix had slipped into a twilight sort of existence, neither dead nor alive but merely present. He wore the same clothes he'd been wearing the night of his father's death, and his hair was a disaster, made that way by more than a day of pushing his hand through it. The old Felix would have been ashamed for anyone to see him in a state like this. But that Felix, or at least part of him, had died when his father did.

Marya, beside him, laid a hand on his shoulder. She alone, it seemed, remained able to look at him. Sometimes he wondered whether she blamed herself for what had happened almost as much as he blamed himself.

"It seems like the entire city has come out," she said.

"I know." Felix's voice was as rough and cracked as his lips. When was the last time he'd had anything to drink? When was the last time he'd spoken? He couldn't remember doing either since his father's death.

"I'm sorry," she said quietly.

"Are you?" he shot back, though without malice. "If Irina had escaped, would you still be sorry?" He worried his bottom lip with his teeth, though he'd been doing so often enough that even the lightest touch sparked pain. That had been unnecessary. He knew what his father had done. Marya had declared him her enemy, and not without reason. Felix, too, had chosen a side. But still, it had been his father.

Marya flicked the nail of her index finger with her thumb, resulting in a soft *click* that jarred Felix's nerves. "You could go to the cathedral with the rest," she said softly. "No one would see you in a crowd this size."

His first instinct was to laugh, his second to ask if she was mocking him. The city swarmed with guards, and every one of the late tsar's ministers and officials would be on alert for the traitorous grand duke and his companions. Walking out of this room and into a street teeming with soldiers would have been the equivalent of signing his own death warrant. But his next thought, which came later but stayed longer, was that however mad and suicidal the gesture might be, he had to make it. Now that she'd said it, he would be unable to think of anything else.

"We won't get caught," Marya said, seeing him hesitate. "I promise. If you want to go."

Felix didn't speak. For a moment, he feared he would cry. He couldn't weep, not in front of her—if he let himself begin, he would never stop. But Marya had offered, and she didn't make offers she didn't mean. She, too, had lost someone dear to her. She'd been deprived of two chances to say goodbye.

Finally, he cleared his throat and wiped the back of his hand across dry eyes.

"All right," he said grimly. "Let's go."

Felix hadn't seen so many people in one place since his brother's wedding, and the terrible silence of this crowd made it appear twice the size. The streets were choked with bodies, all moving in slow, sober unison behind the cortège. A handful of them, those with more means than the rest, wore formal mourning, but most of Petersburg was poor enough to own only one set of winter outerwear, and the wind bit cold at this time of year. Here, so far from the head of the crowd, it hardly even resembled a mourning procession, this drab-colored crush of people moving in the wake of the hearse. Felix tugged up his scarf to better obscure the lower half of his face, and Marya kept close beside him, her shoulder brushing his arm every few steps. She must have found it revolting, showing even this much grace toward the departed soul of the tsar. That she said nothing was a mark of her affection for Felix, and he felt the warmth of it, unsure whether he deserved it but unwilling to give it up.

They followed the crowd toward the cathedral, so slowly Felix hesitated to move forward for fear of clipping a stranger's heel. The street was subdued, lowered heads and hushed voices, but even soft noise was comforting after the silence of the empty apartment. This was what a funeral was for, a chance for the bereaved to spill out their grief and know there would be others to collect what you couldn't carry. Felix could have wept with relief, with hate, with any number of emotions he didn't yet know how to name.

Ahead of them, the spire of Petropavlovsky Cathedral jutted into the sky like a white blade through flesh. The angel atop the spire might cut an opening to heaven if they only stretched their arm an inch farther. Felix wanted to follow the crowd to the walls of the fortress, to see the carriage rattle from the slush to the cleared stones. He couldn't enter the church, not without consigning himself to swift arrest, and though he yearned to at least catch the sound of the priests laying his father to rest, he knew better than to tempt fate by walking under the shadow of that fortress, within reach of that god.

The crowd began to part, pressing to the sides of the street to leave the center clear. Marya took Felix's arm and pulled him aside, under the lip of a stone building that served as an extension of the fortress armory. He followed without protest, like a child woken from a nightmare, and watched the current of the procession split down the middle, body after body, citizen after citizen. The bells in the cathedral had begun to toll the hour. The midpoint of the day, as if predicting everything to come after the interment of Tsar Sergei would be a slow declension into shadow. The bells sounded beautiful at first, high and low tones ringing out the dense harmony they'd been forged for. Then other bells from other churches around the city added their calls, drifting in from all directions. The idea was a chorus raised in mourning, but a thousand bells clashing out of tune added up only to noise.

Then, as though the bells had summoned them, he saw Anatoli and Catarina, walking through the new path in the center of the crowd.

Their mourning garb was the finest that could be procured, Anatoli's black greatcoat lined round the collar with fur, Catarina's hat and cape of sleek sable. His narrow face was stung pink with cold, and she held his hand with a level of commingled tenderness and resolve that Felix had never seen from her before. There, surrounded by the Imperial Guard, in the shadow of his wife, moving toward the body of their father, Anatoli looked terribly small. Heat rushed to Felix's face, and the corners of his eyes began to sting. He shouldn't have come here. This was a mistake. Anatoli's grief was pure, and the people filling these streets had all come to share it in the same uncomplicated way. He didn't belong here, the traitor and the outcast, unwelcome and unnatural as the ghost at the feast.

When Anatoli turned to look directly at him, Felix couldn't have moved if there'd been a gun at his temple commanding it.

It was the first time he'd seen his brother since the night he'd escaped from the Winter Palace. Felix felt as though he'd aged twenty years since then. Tolya, somehow, had aged backward. Dressed all in black with that serious expression that did not suit him, he looked exactly as he had fifteen years ago at their mother's funeral, when the brothers had stood beside each other on the cathedral floor between lines of tombs in marble and precious stone, mosaic angels looking down from the high vaulted ceiling, large eyes black and sorrowful. Felix had been thirteen then, dressed in deep mourning and keeping as close to fifteen-year-old Anatoli as he could while they followed the procession. The tomb of the Tsarina Natalya Fyodorovna, to its right an empty space that would one day house her husband. To its left, the marble tomb of Felix's grandfather, the gold Orthodox cross atop it catching the morning sunlight. Felix could smell the musty odor of mourning clothes dragged out of storage, could feel his brother's clammy palm. Sensed the pressure of a thousand counts and princesses and ministers watching the two boys with enough pity to drown in, *Those poor princes, to suffer such a loss so young.*

For fifteen years, Felix had thrown all his energy into forgetting that day. So, he knew, had his brother. And here they were again, an impassable gulf between them this time, yet both thinking the same thought: *I blame you for this, but no one understands how I feel like you do.*

How many times had he mused that his mother would have

approved of the Koalitsiya's aims? The tsarina's commitment to giving alms to the poor, her long walks through the city of Petersburg. Her connections to the city's liberal institutions, the reformist ministers and clergymen. The fights that raged in the imperial apartments after the tsar met with his council, fights Felix and Anatoli had always pretended not to hear. Would Anatoli remember those moments, too?

Catarina, noticing where Anatoli's attention had fallen, whispered in his ear, but Anatoli barely acknowledged her. There in the mass of the crowd, tears threatening but forbidden to fall, Felix raised his right hand and crossed himself, willing Tolya to read his thoughts.

Please. Be the person I know you are. Be the brother I remember.

Another nudge from Catarina, and then the pair moved on, and there was nothing but this unremarkable street, and these unremarkable people, and Marya beside him, tugging at his sleeve, recalling him to the present. He shook his head, and they broke off from the procession, back the way they had come. With every step, the thought repeated, louder each time.

Be the brother I remember.

All that night and the following morning, Felix drifted. It seemed that two voices hissed at him incessantly, shattering his peace and pulling him in opposite directions. Sofia, on his right shoulder, reminding him of the torture that had undoubtedly befallen Irina, the darkened prison that had echoed with her scream, her wish for a death that could not come soon enough. A hunger for justice, and if justice was out of reach, vengeance to take its place. It was what he owed them, these people who had kept him safe.

And on his left shoulder, Tolya. His brother.

He shared the plan first with Marya, surprising even himself with the show of faith. Marya believed in him, had treated him kindly since the death of the Tverskys, but even so, she'd known him such a short time. What he was about to suggest could sound dangerously like betrayal to the wrong ears. And yet, with every-thing at stake, it was Marya's opinion of his plan he wanted. After all, she was the closest person the Koalitsiya had left to a leader—other than Ilya, who was hardly the person to consult. And much as Felix wanted to make his mark, he would never be a commander. Relying on the weight of his family name to earn the role would only make him more like his father, like the tsars who had come before. Marya was Felix's captain now, and if she gave him an order, he would carry it out.

"Do you think he'll listen?" he said.

Marya steepled her fingers and pressed the tips of her thumbs to her chin. The gesture cast odd, barred shadows across her face. Felix thought of the deep creases in an old woman's brow, or the reflection of prison bars.

"You know him better than I do," she said.

Felix shook his head. The sigh that escaped him belonged to a much older man. "Two years ago, before I left Petersburg?" he said. "Yes, I knew him then. Now? I'm not sure. But if there's even a chance—"

"If there's a chance," Marya said, decided, "then you have to try."

27

Sasha

Once, a summons to the tsar's study would have been the honor of a lifetime. Now, Sasha suspected it might be the last order he ever received. The door was open when he arrived, revealing the same gilt and paneling and sturdy furniture that had adorned the space when the previous tsar had occupied it. The simple consistency was unnerving. He hesitated on the threshold, rocking forward onto the toes of his boots. Entering felt obscene, like walking into a tomb before the coffin had been nailed shut.

"Come in, Captain, and close the door," Anatoli said sharply.

With a silent prayer, Sasha did.

The new tsar stood against the long picture window overlooking the north grounds and the Neva, the curtains thrown back to let in the night. In his mourning clothes against the black sky, Anatoli seemed to be little but a face and a pair of hands, a ghost floating untethered in the domain of his dead father. Until recently, Sasha had served the tsar only from a distance, but even so, it was impossible to deny the resemblance between father and son. Their posture, their bearing, their somber expressions, all of it was the same, the similarities even more striking than they were with Felix. If Anatoli were broader across the shoulders and peppered some gray through his hair, Sasha might have believed that the spirit of Tsar Sergei had visited them that night.

The tsarina sat in an armchair near the window, hands folded in a way that might have been delicate were it not for the whiteness of her knuckles. Since the assassination, she had scarcely left her husband's side. Sasha would never forget the sight of the graceful Prussian princess lunging between her husband and the assassin's pistol, her instinct to defend the tsarevich more finely honed than his own had been. He envied her that clarity, that uncompromised loyalty.

"You called for me, Your Imperial Majesties," Sasha said softly.

"We did." Anatoli did not acknowledge Sasha's genuflection, nor give him permission to rise. Sasha did so regardless, with great trepidation. Kneeling before these people felt like offering up his neck to the sword, and though he knew he deserved it, the animal part of him wasn't ready to go quietly yet. "I wanted to ask what you think I ought to do with you."

Sasha's mouth tasted acrid, like he'd licked silver. Knowing the shot was coming didn't make it easier to look down the barrel of the gun.

"Put yourself in my husband's position," Catarina said, as if Sasha wasn't already agonizingly aware of their position. Her face was pale and very drawn, and it seemed she had not slept or eaten properly since the hellish night at the opera. Sasha had seen people run this ragged during the long nights after a battle, when the threat of nightmares alone was enough to make a man volunteer himself for one watch after the next. Those were not people one could count on for kindness. "Imagine that a soldier under your command was ordered to protect your father. Imagine the entire country trusted him with that one simple task. And then imagine somehow that your father is dead, you yourself alive only by the grace of God, and the soldier responsible for protecting you both escaped with little more than a scratch. What would you do, Captain, if you found yourself in that position?"

Pain flashed through Sasha's injured arm, but he kept his expression as stony as before. Catarina was right. A scratch. It was irrelevant, utterly irrelevant, in the face of his larger failure.

"What would you do, Captain?" Catarina repeated.

He licked his dry lips. "I would order that soldier killed, Your Majesty. Anyone would."

That was it, then. He braced himself for a blow, for the door to burst open and a pack of guards to seize him and fling him into the same cell he'd consigned Isaak to. It took everything he had not to cringe away from the new tsar, to stand tall and accept the punishment he deserved. But instead of issuing the command, Anatoli scoffed.

"Soldiers," he said to Catarina, with the same disdain another person might use with the word *animals*. "I told you, that's all the imagination they have. Kill or be killed. I thought you were different, Captain. It's why I haven't had you arrested yet."

Sasha blinked. "Your Majesty?"

Anatoli paced from the window, stalking like a hunter between the trees. "You're more use to us alive than dead, Captain. You know my brother. You know the city. The Imperial Guard trusts you, as does the Semyonovsky Regiment. We can't make use of any of that if I put a bullet in your brain."

"But I want to make myself very clear on this point," Catarina said. "So do listen carefully." She rose from the chair to stand beside her husband; seemingly without thinking, he reached to take her hand. "We need you, but I do not like you. And I do not trust you. You give me a reason to believe you're giving us anything less than every bit of dedication you have, and I will have you on your way to a *katorga* to spend the last of your miserable days hewing iron out of rock with your bleeding fingernails. Am I clear?"

Sasha bowed. Each breath seemed like a miracle, a beat of borrowed time. "God bless you, Your Majesties."

"God's blessing is not my concern at the moment," Anatoli said curtly. "I want to bring order to my city, and if God could do that with a blessing, he'd already have done it. I need you to—"

A soft knock on the door. Anatoli scowled. "What?"

The door opened, and a frightened-looking footman poked his

head and shoulders into the room. Sasha had seen that expression before, on sixteen-year-old boys facing their first line of enemy soldiers. He and the other officers had once taken grim bets on their new recruits, who would rise to the challenge and who would soil themselves before the charge began. "Someone here to see you, Your Imperial Majesties."

"Do I look as if I'm in a mood to receive visitors?"

Sasha fully expected the footman to bolt. But whatever visitor had come at this hour must have been nearly as frightening as the new tsar, for the servant stood his ground.

"I told her you were indisposed, Your Majesty," the footman said. "But she insisted you'd want to hear her."

Catarina glanced at her husband, who nodded. Little secret what they were thinking—Sasha knew it, too. A woman, unaccompanied, demanding an audience with the tsar, was an uncommon occurrence under ordinary circumstances, let alone in times like these. And all three of them must have suspected which woman it was most likely to be.

"Send her in," Anatoli said tightly. Sasha started to edge toward the door, but Anatoli shook his head. "You stay here, Captain. Consider it your first chance to prove your renewed loyalty to my family. I assume you can still shoot left-handed."

Sasha nodded mutely and took a step back, hand resting on the end of his pistol. The door opened fully, and a familiar snow-pale woman, dressed like a wandering spirit in a long black coat lined round the collar with fur, strode into the study.

It took all of Sasha's self-restraint not to shoot Sofia on sight. She had taken care to remove her usual mocking smile—indeed, she looked positively sober, and her curtsey was every bit as deep as was proper. If Sasha hadn't known her, he'd have thought the deep shadows under her eyes stemmed from grief, or remorse, or fear. But he knew her far, far better than that. Her deferential mourning looked grotesque, given his knowledge of what she was and what she wanted, an ill-fitting and uncanny mask. This woman, though he didn't know how, was to blame for the death of the tsar. She had stolen Felix from him. Sasha wouldn't let her destroy the only Komarovs yet to fall into her trap.

"Your Imperial Majesties," Sofia said. She held her curtsey long enough that Sasha could imagine her knees trembling. "Please accept my prayers for your health, and my sincerest grief at the news of your loss. Russia's loss."

"Get up," Anatoli said curtly. "You've made it clear what you and my brother thought about my father. Unless you're here to throw yourself on my mercy and beg for life in prison instead of immediate hanging, I can't imagine why you've come."

Sofia stood, though she never raised her eyes from the ground. Humility hung over her like a too-large coat, begging the spectator to wonder what was hidden beneath. "I hope you know I've never borne you any ill will, Your Majesty."

"You've given me no reason to believe that."

"Then let me give one now," Sofia said, and her eyes flicked up. It was like staring down a wolf at the edge of the woods, eyes yellow and luminous. "I've come here to warn you about your brother."

Without thinking, Sasha took a sharp step forward. "The brother you twisted and manipulated and then abandoned to the rebels who killed his father? That brother?"

"Captain Dorokhin," Catarina said severely. "I do not recall the tsar giving you permission to speak."

He snapped his mouth shut. The rebuke was justified, but that did not silence his deep and rising unease as Anatoli approached Sofia. The tsar's brow was furrowed in what Sasha deeply hoped was distrust but feared might well be interest. Sasha wanted to pull the tsar away, lead him somewhere far from here and make him see the danger of this creature's persuasive words. But there was nothing he could do but watch.

"I saw my brother yesterday," Anatoli said coolly. "At the funeral procession for our father, alone. If you were so concerned about his intentions, that seems like a curious place to leave him unobserved."

The tsar eased down into the armchair Catarina had abandoned, straight backed and imperious, looking startlingly like his father. Catarina remained standing, one hand on his shoulder. Sofia did not move, as was proper, but Sasha couldn't help but feel an air of threat in her poise. It was easier to lunge into an attack from one's feet, and he did not want to find out firsthand how fast a vila could move. Would to God she'd give him an excuse to fire on her. He would not miss again.

"Felix has asked me to keep my distance," she said. "I didn't feel it would serve my cause to cross him."

"I imagine you're about to tell me why that is," Anatoli said. "I suggest you stop being coy and tell me what you've come here to say. I'm giving you an audience because I need information, but you'll find that while my brother may be a credulous idiot, I am not."

Sofia ducked her head in another half curtsey. "Of course not. That's why I've come to you. Felix can't see that it's gone too far, he's lost all sense of—"

"Of what?" Anatoli cut in, before Sasha could open his mouth to voice his own protest. "Of what you and that pack of rebels told him to do? I know my brother. He's a selfish, stupid child who never had a thought in his head that wasn't about drinking or whoring until you turned up on his doorstep."

A flash of loyalty, long stifled, surged in Sasha. Felix had been selfish, had at times been frivolous, but he'd never once been stupid, never that, and never purposely cruel. It was what Sasha had always loved best about him, that fearless gentleness, that absolute refusal to consciously cause pain to another that had seemed, in Sasha's eyes, like the most impossible and magnificent quality in the world, even more so because of where he had come from. Felix lived in a reality that brushed against Sasha's but never quite intersected with it, one where the ultimate goal was to be happy and to sweep up as many other people into that happiness as he could manage. Felix wasn't a pawn, and he wasn't a weapon. Anatoli, as his brother, should have known that better than Sasha did.

But it was Catarina who interrupted. "Let her finish," she said, gripping Anatoli's shoulder when he started in surprise. "I know he's your brother, and that makes you want to forgive him anything, but remember why your father sent him away. It wasn't on a whim."

"So you've said," Anatoli replied wearily, but instead of arguing the point further, he gestured curtly at Sofia with one hand, indicating she should go on.

"I did ask the grand duke to join the Koalitsiya in the beginning," Sofia said, and again that artificial humility kept her eyes on the carpet, making her expression impossible to read. "I hoped he could be our connection to the palace. We spoke at Tsarskoe Selo about how we could work with you and your father, gradually sway the council to enact political reforms. That's all I ever proposed. Reform. Gradually. Within bounds."

"Is that so?" It was impossible to tell from his voice whether Anatoli was considering Sofia's words or mocking them.

"It was never meant to be like this," she went on. "It was that Tverskaya woman who turned matters violent, she and her husband, and Felix was pulled into their orbit. There was nothing I could do. And I think the death of your father broke something in him. He doesn't think he has anything to lose. I came to you today to tell you this honestly, Your Majesty. Felix frightens me."

Sasha could have laughed at the idea that anything on this earth could frighten Sofia. But Sofia had not made this speech in an attempt to convince him. She'd made it to convince Anatoli. And the tsar had turned to look over his shoulder, back at his wife, who nodded.

"Your Majesty," Sasha began.

"Captain," Anatoli said without looking. "If I want the opinion of the man who not only failed to apprehend my brother but also let my father bleed out in an opera box, I assure you, I will ask for it. Until then, I suggest you do as you are told and remain silent."

"But—"

"Silence."

That hadn't been the voice of a frustrated man irritated at an interruption. That was the edict of a tsar, whose word was God's law and who would impose his will on anyone within his reach, at whatever cost. Anatoli rose, the medals across his breast glittering like the room's gilt molding in the firelight. He looked like a holy warrior, all gold and flame and coiled strength.

"I knew the rebels wouldn't stop with my father," he said, turning back to Sofia. "Even though Tverskaya is dead. Everyone knows I'm their next target, and I've fully prepared the Imperial Guard for that eventuality. The Semyonovsky Regiment will tighten its fist on the city by week's end. But you're asking me to believe the grand duke is considering violent treason, and that kind of accusation demands proof. Felix is my brother. Surely that counts for something."

"Felix belongs to the Koalitsiya now," Catarina said. "You've seen what they'll do, Tolya. Surely you know that's beyond blood."

Anatoli sighed and allowed his eyes to close briefly. "You think he'll kill me." His voice was flat, emotionless. Sasha couldn't tell if his tone signified disbelief or resignation.

"I think if you don't do everything you can to stop him, the risk will be on your head, Your Majesty," Sofia said.

Sasha couldn't disobey the tsar again, not with the tsarina's threat of exile and forced labor so fresh. But to see Sofia standing there, bold and beautiful and lying, every word of it a lie, drummed against the edges of his reason. He had never felt such deep hate in all his life. It terrified him to the core and made him yearn to be the terrible assassin Felix no doubt thought he was, if only to end this once and for all.

"Your Majesty," Sasha tried, once more, softly. "Please."

Anatoli did not look at him. His attention was all on Sofia, her angular face, her amber eyes. Her false words, telling the new tsar everything he already feared in his heart to be true. "Tell me what you think I should do," he said.

Sofia swept another low curtsey. When she straightened up again, her mouth was sober, but her huntress's eyes were gleaming.

"Of course, Your Majesty."

28

Felix

In Felix's memory, the Summer Garden was the most beautiful place in Petersburg. He had passed more childhood afternoons there with Tolya than he could count. They'd always been under the close watch of some half dozen of his father's guards, who had received strict orders never to let the tsarevich or the grand duke out of their sight for an instant, but even so, being allowed to roam under the sky had been the purest, most elemental sort of freedom. The gardens had something wonderful to offer every season, and Felix had loved them all equally: the fresh lilacs and roses of spring, the pond they could boat across in summer and crisscross on their skates in winter. Though it was the oldest and finest garden in the city, it had always felt like the brothers' secret. The one place they could escape the grim majesty of the palace and, for a few hours at a time, be simply two boys, doing what they liked.

It had been wishful thinking to suppose that the memory of those long afternoons might make Anatoli more disposed to listen to him now. These were Felix's own memories that joined him as he walked alone between the rows of snow-covered hedges, as he let his gaze wander across the frozen pond. He had no way of knowing how his brother might recall the same moments, or how the feeling might be tainted by what had passed between them since. Still, he'd chosen the location for a reason, one Anatoli would surely have guessed when the messenger arrived at the gates of the Winter Palace with a letter in Felix's handwriting and one of the buttons from his greatcoat, adorned with the imperial double eagle, to prove its authenticity. The gardens were neutral ground, neither the palace nor the web of streets where the Koalitsiya made its home. There was a chance it might work. If Anatoli came.

He wished he could have brought Marya with him, if only for the strength that came with having someone at his side. But his brother would not respond well to any implications of ambush. This had been Felix's idea. This was his responsibility. Whether this gambit succeeded or failed, no one's head but his own would be at risk for it.

A flicker of movement at the end of the path caught his attention. He had expected to face his brother flanked by a dozen guards, with no fewer than five pistols each aimed at his heart. But somehow, Tolya had come alone.

The only sound in the garden was the crunch of Anatoli's boots against the fresh snow as he halved, then quartered the distance between them. Whether it was from the two long years of Felix's exile or a conscious effort on Anatoli's part, he didn't know, but Felix couldn't read his brother's expression the way he once could. Tolya's mouth was pressed tight, and his eyes were shadowed, as though he hadn't slept properly in days. It had been a long time since Felix had come across a mirror, but he had little doubt he looked the same. It was not a sign of brotherly affection, this bone-deep weariness, but it was a feeling they held in common, and that was a place to start.

Anatoli stopped with ten feet still separating them. His breath drifted from his nose in small, regular pants. It reminded Felix of a horse, waiting for the command to lunge forward into battle.

"You came," Felix said softly.

Anatoli's lip curled. "I have nothing to hide. And I'm not afraid of you."

He could see the crack just beneath Anatoli's mask of imperiousness. The suddenly orphaned boy surprised at the sharpness of his own hurt. Felix clenched his fists in the pockets of his greatcoat, pretending that instead of his nails digging into his own palms, he had reached to take his brother's hand.

"I told my guards to stand back at the gate," Anatoli said, though Felix had not asked. "The smallest sound of trouble, and they'll be here in a moment. Before you get any ideas."

"I'm surprised you didn't bring them with you," Felix said. He made a show of removing his hands from his pockets, spreading his empty palms.

"There's more than one of them who would shoot you on sight. I thought this might be wiser, if you actually intend to talk."

Felix didn't doubt that for a moment. That the vast majority of the imperial household wanted him dead seemed so obvious it wasn't worth remarking on. "How are you?" he said instead.

Anatoli laughed. "How dare you ask me how I am," he said. "You killed him. You'd have killed me. I ought to have you torn apart."

Only a desperate, foolish faith in his brother kept Felix from running. That, and the knowledge that his brother was a fair shot himself and would not hesitate to fire on a fleeing traitor. He could feel as much fear as he liked, but if Marya's faction was to succeed, if they were to build a future not steeped in any more blood than had already been spilled, he would have to play this perfectly.

"But you haven't killed me," he said simply.

"Not yet."

"You knew I'd be coming alone. You could have ambushed me. Could have killed me as soon as you saw me, but you didn't. And I think I know why."

"Because I've never been firm enough with you," Anatoli snapped. "Just as Catarina always says. I forgive you for everything, and look what comes of it."

"Because you know I'd never do it," Felix pressed. "You know I'd never mean to hurt him. Look at me, Tolya. You'll see it's true."

Anatoli said nothing. He stood across from Felix, there at the end of the barren lane that during another season would have bloomed with flowers beyond count. Felix couldn't be sure what

Anatoli saw in his face. Speculation was too terrible, the risk too high, and so he set it aside. Instead, he took in his brother's furrowed brow, the cares of authority no doubt adding new lines every day. Stray snowflakes tangled in his lashes before melting like tears from the warmth of his skin. His brother's face, beside him in the cathedral, as the lid of the tomb closed over their mother.

He knew. No matter how deep the rift between Felix and their father had grown, Anatoli knew that Felix would never willingly have created that scene again.

Anatoli cleared his throat, and when he spoke his voice was thicker than Felix was accustomed to. "So. You asked me here to talk. Hadn't you better start talking?"

Felix heaved a breath and tried to imagine he was speaking only to his older brother, not to the new tsar of all Russia, not to the man who could put him to death in a moment if the mood struck him. "This might be the first time you've ever asked me to talk *more*, Tolya."

"Believe me, I regret it already."

Felix smiled faintly—now, that was the brother he knew. "Do you remember when we used to talk about what your rule would be like?"

Anatoli laughed like their father now, almost brutally. "You mean when I was eight and promised when I was tsar, no one would have to study mathematics? I don't think childish games will make your point."

"There was more to it than that. Don't you remember? Walk with me."

Anatoli took a step back, his trust visibly shaken. He set his jaw, and Felix watched him fight the urge to glance over his shoulder, to call for the guardsmen waiting at the front of the park. "Why? So your rebel friends can spring out of the snow and gut me like they killed our father?"

"*Bon sang*, Tolya, no, so I can *talk* to you. Would you stop acting like you're on the brink of being martyred?"

The silence hovered there like a feather, drifting toward the ground without landing. Then Anatoli, without saying a word, began to meander along the snowy path, Felix following only steps away.

He and Tolya had loved each other once, though it had been years since either of them had shown the other anything resembling affection. They were brothers. They were blood. Tolya, who had taught Felix how to ride at the family's country estate in Gatchina. Who'd gotten roaring drunk with Felix the night before his wedding, leaving them both brutally hungover throughout the whole endless ceremony, each fighting the urge not to laugh as the priest droned on about temperance and fidelity. Who'd stayed awake with Felix before their mother's funeral, arms around each other's shoulders in silence, watching the shadows move and stretch along the floor. Tolya, his brother.

"The day after we arrived in Tver," Felix said. "I was fourteen, and you and I went hunting with Papa, and he caught that poacher in the woods. Do you remember what you told me that day?"

"I wasn't aware you found my words worth memorizing, *petit frère*," Anatoli said dryly, keeping his gaze on the path.

"You said that when you were tsar, you'd never punish a man for doing what was necessary to live. I never forgot that."

Anatoli's brows contracted. "That's what you want me to think? That woman killed Papa because it was necessary? You're farther gone than I was told."

"Not her," Felix said doggedly, though not without a memory of Irina's quick temper, her wry humor, her voice murmuring in prayer for her husband found dead in the tsar's prison. "You've already condemned her. The rest of the city didn't kill Papa. They're only trying to do what's necessary to live."

Anatoli stopped walking near a fountain that would shoot up like a splendid geyser in springtime. It resembled a tombstone now. "Is your band of anarchists so poorly organized that one woman could want to fill the streets with blood and the rest would happily take bread and salt at my table? Don't be naïve, Felix. Every traitor in your camp would run me through with a bayonet if they could."

Now was not the time to think about Ilya's coal-black eyes, hungry as the chairman's house succumbed to the flames. Nor was it the time to think about what had risen in his own heart at the same sight. "They want dignity and freedom," he said, "and the means to live. That's it. If you spent the time among them that I have, you'd know that. What they want isn't much, but they'll give everything they have fighting for it. The brother I know wouldn't make them fight so hard. He'd see that a tsar who gives freely is better loved than one who stands firm."

He reached for his brother's hand, but Anatoli twisted away, disgust curling his lip and chilling his voice. "Don't touch me," he said. "Don't you dare speak of what a tsar should do. Did you come here to tell me that Papa deserved what happened to him?"

"No," Felix began, and how was it possible that this conversation had gone so wrong so quickly, and where were the words coming from in the back of his mind, in a voice that sounded like Ilya's: *Of course he deserved it, after what he's done to Russia? A quick death was too good for him.* "I'm not saying that. I'm trying to help you. I know you, Tolya. You didn't want to be tsar yet, not like this. But if you take this chance, you could be brilliant. You could be what we need. You could save us all. My God," he murmured, as much to himself as to his brother, "you have no idea how much I want you to be the one who saves us."

For the briefest, most fleeting of moments, it seemed almost that Anatoli wanted it, too. His lips parted, and Felix could hear the unspoken words on his tongue, how easy it would be to simply whisper *yes*. Yes, he would say, and then Felix would reach out and fold his brother in his arms, and they would weep there in the Summer Garden for their father, and for their mother, and for every bitter loss they had felt, separately and together. Then they would stand tall and return to the Winter Palace, the determined new tsar and his loyal younger brother, and with their councilors and ministers and generals and representatives from the people they would plan a different kind of future, one built for peace and not for vengeance. One simple *yes* and they could do all of it. The deaths that had brought them here would never lose their sting, but they wouldn't have been for nothing, they would have laid the foundation for a better future, then.

Anatoli's expression hardened. The hands that might have reached out curled into fists, and he took a step back from Felix, whose heart congealed into something rigid and cold. Above them, a songbird cried for its mate from the leafless tree, its music sounding tinny and unnatural without its partner's harmony.

"You really do think I'm a fool, don't you?" Anatoli said. "They said you'd try to win me over. Try to make me turn my back on everything Papa stood for and throw in my lot with your band of traitors. Well, let me be the first to tell you this, little brother, if no one else has. I'm not the soft-hearted puppet you think I am."

Felix flinched. *They?* He only had a hope of success if he was speaking to his brother directly, if someone hadn't poisoned the earth before he could plant in it. "Tolya, who have you been—"

"Don't call me that." Anatoli had always shouted when he grew angry, but he wasn't shouting now. It would have been better if he had, anything but this low, cold rage, this awful, familiar loathing. "I came as you asked because despite all advice, I thought Papa's death might have opened your eyes. I thought you might be willing to own your mistake and come back. Clearly I overestimated you."

It was all going wrong. It was all slipping away, and there was nothing Felix could do to stop it, nothing but watch it happen.

"If I see you again, *petit frère,* I will have them kill you," Anatoli said. "You or any other member of your Koalitsiya. You threw in your lot with traitors and murderers, and now you'll face the consequences."

"Just listen to—"

"Go back to your friends," Anatoli said, already turning away. "Tell them I expect a full and unconditional surrender by tomorrow morning at dawn. If I don't receive it, you'll have no one but yourselves to blame for what happens next."

There was nothing left to say. He could only watch Anatoli slowly retreat down the path of the gardens, until his brother was a black smudge among the leafless trees, and then a moment after that he was nothing at all. Felix stood alone, then tilted his head back to look at the sky, an endless sheet of gray, filtered light falling indiscriminately through the clouds over the barren park. The wind in the silent garden reminded him of whispers, faceless voices passing through the palace halls.

29

Marya

While she'd known that the hours and days in the wake of the tsar's funeral would be a time of confusion, she'd thought they would be given a moment, at least, to breathe. Clearly she'd underestimated the power of tradition. The lid had scarcely been placed on Tsar Sergei's tomb before Tsar Anatoli assumed the duties and authority of his father. His formal coronation would take time to orchestrate, but for the practical matters of ruling a people, there was hardly a beat of disruption between father and son. The elder Komarov brother even looked like his father, with the same high forehead and proud nose. If Marya hadn't seen the funeral procession wend its way through Petersburg, she might have thought the death of Tsar Sergei had been a mad dream, disproven upon waking.

When the tsarina had died—though that had been years ago, when Marya was only fourteen—the city had swelled with sympathy for the two young princes, those somber-faced boys whose mother had been torn from them too soon. Anatoli must have remembered that, from the way he assumed his new role. Turning his own grief into political theater might have struck some as distasteful, but he'd have remembered the last time he'd lost a parent, and he played public sympathy like someone who had seen its power once before. To say nothing of how much stronger the effect was this time, when his father had been murdered in front of him, leaving him to assume a throne he had not expected to take so soon. Even Marya almost felt sorry for him, though the feeling didn't last long. She, too, had lost a father, and the country had continued on undisturbed.

Even if public opinion hadn't landed so strongly in Tsar Anatoli's favor, Marya knew, the Koalitsiya would have struggled to find its equilibrium in those first days of the new regime. Irina's suicidal act of defiance had shaken members of both factions, enough that even Ilya and Pyotr Stepanovich seemed to lose their footing. For Marya, it was more loss than she thought she could bear. Her two best friends, within days of each other, and their unborn child, too. Felix's initial overtures to Anatoli had ended in abject failure, but there was still a chance the seed Felix had planted might grow, might still result in a different kind of tsar than his father had been. If there was a chance Irina's sacrifice might bring a more humane emperor to the Winter Palace, then she would pray for it every night and every morning, and she and what remained of the Koalitsiya would wait. There was work still to do, after all. She could visit the pawnbrokers of Petersburg and bring in a few rubles to feed herself and Felix and the other members of the Koalitsiya who clung to her, now that neither Isaak nor Irina were there to center what remained of their group. Life had to carry on, even as it crumbled.

Today, three days after the tsar's funeral, she was dealing with an irate pawnbroker who kept a shop just south of the Catherine Canal. As a rule, she tried to avoid Nikita Fyodorovich as much as possible, as neither his personality nor his prices were any great enticement to spend time in his company. But Alevtina had become especially nervous at the idea of pawning stolen goods after the death of the tsar, and while this collection of engraved silver spoons hadn't exactly been obtained by legal means, they were nevertheless burning a hole in the pocket of her greatcoat.

"You wouldn't offer that price to a dog, Nikita, so don't insult me that way," she said, leaning both elbows on the counter.

Nikita ran two fingers along his mustache. "Times are hard, Masha."

"Times have been hard since Petersburg was a swamp," Marya

shot back. "After a hundred years, the excuse runs a little thin. Look at them again and tell me they're not worth more."

He scowled at the spoons in Marya's hand. "Unless you've brought me another pair of eyes to look with as well, the offer stands. If you don't like it, try for a better one elsewhere."

On another day, under other circumstances, she'd have dug in her heels and negotiated for a better price, but the deaths weighing on her heart left her short on patience. She shoved the spoons back in her pocket and prepared a vicious retort, one cruel enough that it would have startled Isaak if he'd been there to hear it.

The bell above the shop door startled her out of speaking.

Both Marya and Nikita stared at the man silhouetted in the doorway, dressed in the green and red of the Semyonovsky Regiment. The shop was small, and the soldier's shoulders could almost touch both sides of the doorframe. One hand hung loose by his side, the palm perhaps twice as broad as Marya's. The other held a pistol. Once Marya spotted it, she could not tear her eyes from it.

"Can I help you?" Nikita said. His voice, belligerent moments ago, had faded into an obsequious shadow of itself.

The soldier did not move. He reminded Marya of a golden eagle she had seen once as a child, its claws wrapped around the outstretched arm of the Bronze Horseman. The bird had remained perfectly still except for its eyes, which seemed to take in every moving soul beneath the statue. The stillness had only made the bird more threatening, its perfect poise an illustration of the terrible movement possible in an instant.

"You're in violation of an edict from the tsar," the soldier said.

Marya darted a glance at Nikita, who had gone deathly white. "What edict is that?" she said. "This is a legal business."

"By order of Tsar Anatoli," the soldier began, as if he'd recited the words that were to follow a dozen times in the past hour, "all Petersburg citizens are to clear the streets between the hours of six in the evening and six in the morning. Curfew stays in place until the threat against the imperial family has been fully uncovered and eradicated. Violation of curfew is considered a criminal offense."

The only sound was the steady tick of the half-dozen clocks crowding Nikita's shop, insistent and mocking. The punishment for a criminal offense needed no elaboration, no matter who was now tsar.

"The assassin was arrested at the scene, I thought," Marya said carefully. It felt like a betrayal, using the word *assassin* when what she meant was *Irina Tverskaya, my friend, who you and your men killed, along with her husband and her child.*

The soldier scoffed. "The tsar isn't foolish enough to believe the assassin worked alone," he said. "And his mad brother's on the loose as well. Get yourself home, *devushka*, before you find yourself tangled up in danger that doesn't concern you."

Her mouth had gone very dry. If this soldier only knew how deeply this danger concerned her. The curfew must have gone into effect only hours before. How many members of the Koalitsiya had been left exposed and uninformed in the streets of Petersburg that night? What might they say, under pressure from the Komarovs' brutal questioning? She could feel Nikita's terror radiating from behind the counter. The pawnbroker might not have known in exactly what circles Marya ran, but he could sense how much danger they both now faced. There'd been enough death of late without adding this man to Marya's tally.

"Yes," she said, ducking her head. "Of course."

The soldier took half a step to the side, granting barely enough room to pass. She could feel his heat against her as she slipped by, smell the sour scent of his breath. Every moment, she expected a hand to close over her arm, the cold kiss of a pistol against the small of her back.

The moment she reached the blessed cold of the street, Marya gathered her skirts and ran.

Tsar Sergei had been severe. Cruel. Distant. Under his watch, people had starved, people had died, while he and his ministers sat in their gilded palaces and held balls and hunted in the same woods where peasants who voiced even the slightest opposition were apprehended and shot without trial. Under his watch, poor men had fallen under French guns while rich men talked strategy behind a screen of cigar smoke. But Tsar Sergei had been predictable. An observant man could always anticipate what he would do next. He listened to his ministers, to tradition.

Unlike Anatoli Sergeevich, who played by no rules now, and called down the wrath of hell.

Since the night the new tsar instated his curfew, the evening streets had become eerily silent, a dead man's veins drained of blood, occupied only by the most daring lawbreakers and the hungriest rats and birds. The Koalitsiya had abandoned the apartment off Preobrazhenskaya Square—the specter of surveillance there made it difficult to breathe—and fractured into fragments, and Marya didn't know where to find half its members now. She stayed with Felix and Oksana and a few others in a small room near the Haymarket, where they sat each night saying little and watching the lamps cast shadows on the bare walls. The stillness was agonizing. Worse yet were the sudden bursts of noise: raised voices, smashed glass, the whip crack of gunfire. Worst of all was the silence that followed.

Curfew was only the beginning of Anatoli's response to the death of his father. Soldiers wandered the streets in packs, stopping people for questioning with no warning and no justification beyond the quickness of the suspect's walk or the quality of their overcoat. More than one man stumbled home just before curfew with his clothes torn, eyes blackened, and nose bloodied, fully aware that his injuries were a sign of getting off lightly. Still more simply vanished, lost to the void of the tsar's prisons and labor camps. After one particularly bloody series of arrests, Marya forbade Felix from setting foot outside the apartment. If the tsar's soldiers caught sight of him—the renegade Komarov, responsible in part or in whole for the murder of the former tsar—Anatoli couldn't devise a death he'd consider painful or slow enough. Felix put up no protest at all, which felt worse than if they'd had to physically restrain him. It was clear he held himself personally responsible for failing to sway his brother, and the guilt of it had begun to eat away at him. It was awful to see the energetic, passionate man that had once been Felix Sergeevich fade into the shadow he became, haunting the corners of their one shabby room, picking at hangnails until his fingers bled.

An officer of the Semyonovsky Regiment stationed on every street corner in the city would have been hard enough, but Anatoli's retaliation did not stop there. After a week of curfew, strict rationing crunched the city, until the allotment of food for a family of four became barely enough to sustain a single grown man. So it was that when Marya heard of the Imperial Army's early February raids in the Pale of Settlement—in Mogilev, in Minsk, in Kovno—she couldn't be certain whether the twisting feeling in her stomach was primarily hunger or guilt. The capture and execution of two Jewish rebels, one of whom had assassinated the tsar, was more than cause enough for Anatoli and his ministers to tighten the empire's fist on the Jewish communities within its borders. Marya listened to the stories of burned villages, salted earth, murdered children, but did not allow herself to weep. Irina would have had no patience for useless tears. She would have demanded action.

She and Isaak would have demanded exactly what they always had, which was nothing more or less than justice.

———

"I know what I'm supposed to do," Marya said to Sofia one night in mid-February, late enough that the sounds of skirmish and gunfire in the street below had died to low murmurs. "But I don't know if I can do it."

They sat in the corner under the light of a single oil lamp, Felix and the others sleeping on the opposite side of the darkened room. Sofia's amber eyes looked as deep as the grave. Marya hugged her knees so tightly her elbows ached, but despite her desperate need to be held, Sofia did not offer, and Marya did not ask. It was hard not to think of that day near the Apraksin Market, when Sofia and Irina had sent her away, when her friend's face had taken on the hollowness of a martyr. She didn't blame Sofia—no one could convince Irina to do anything she hadn't already decided to do, however persuasive they might have been. But the possibility of comfort she always felt near Sofia had turned cold, as cold as the rest of this rapidly unraveling world. No time for gentleness tonight. Tonight, she had to decide.

"If you know what to do, then you can do it," Sofia said. "Thought and action are the same now. You're already holding them together, leading them, every day. Doing what has to come next isn't any different."

Marya rested her cheek on her knees, looking past Sofia to the lamp resting on the table behind her. In the glow she saw Irina's wedding ring, the silver chain around Isaak's neck. She saw hundreds of thousands of people she had never met, engulfed in flames, screaming, cut down in the snow. Sharper than imagination, clear as prophecy.

"We've lost so much already. And I can't be responsible for more, Sonya. I can't."

Sofia made a soft sound of disagreement, almost disappointment. She stood up, taking her long black coat from the chair and snaking in one arm. It was selfish to wish she'd stay—Sofia had been a transient presence during these first weeks of Tsar Anatoli's reign, arriving for a meal and a hurried conversation before disappearing back into the thick of the city. Keeping the remnants of the Koalitsiya alive and informed demanded time and attention, and without Sofia's help Marya would have been in a constant state of terror, wondering which of her friends had fallen to the new tsar's soldiers. But even so—even with the new shadow that had fallen over Sofia's presence—part of her still wished Sofia would linger. It would have been such a small gesture for her to offer a flash of tenderness, if only to break up the darkness.

"The ones responsible for pain are the ones who take, Masha," Sofia said. "Not the ones who try to stop it. You aren't to blame for what the tsar has done."

Marya's heart ached. She no longer knew whether the ache was loss, regret, hate, or hope. In the past days, they had become impossible to untangle. "I am if I fail."

Sofia smiled and rested one hand on Marya's shoulder, her body already angled toward the door. It seemed a profoundly unusual moment to smile, but there was so much comfort in the curve of her lips that Marya couldn't bring herself to question it. There was such hope in that smile, such confidence, and she would do anything to lay claim to a fraction of that certainty. "You won't fail," she said. "Not you."

She had nothing to say to that. The leadership of the Koalitsiya had fallen to her for lack of anyone else, after it had lost its true leaders one after the other. It was a false inheritance, not a destiny. She was no chosen hero, visited by spirits and guided from the cradle to lead. She was only herself, only Marya.

But perhaps that could be enough.

"There might still be a chance," Marya said quietly. "If we can make the tsar see. Felix still thinks we can. And I'll never forgive myself if I don't try."

Sofia nodded, then let her fingers trail along Marya's shoulder, across the back of her neck. Marya closed her eyes, trembling. In a moment, Sofia would be gone again, and Marya would be here, seeing a hundred possible failures flicker before her in the glow of the lamp. But right now, this second, she was not alone. And Sofia's presence brought with it a powerful, burning faith, one that was beyond Marya's power to argue against.

"You won't fail, Masha," Sofia said. "Just wait and see."

THE QUEEN OF THE OWLS

There once was a king with four daughters, each resourceful and clever and ambitious, and their father was as fond and proud of them as if they had been sons. Over the years, suitors came before the court to plead their case to wed the four princesses, and the king, trusting his daughters' wisdom, allowed each to choose the suitor she liked best. In time, the eldest princess gave her hand to the bold King of the Falcons, the second eldest chose the shrewd King of the Eagles, and the third eldest married the daring King of the Ravens. The king, proud of their choices, waited for the youngest princess to select her spouse, but year after year passed, and no suitor won her favor.

At last, the youngest princess came to the king and said, "Father, I am lonely here without my sisters. Let me go out into the world and visit them, and perhaps I shall find a suitor on my travels that pleases me better than those who have yet come before me."

The king gave his consent, and the princess made ready and set out toward the lands ruled by the King of the Falcons.

On the way, she came across a vast open field where the grass was trampled and stained with blood. The broken bodies of soldiers littered the field, their armor crushed, their weapons lying beside them where they had fallen. The bold-hearted princess was alarmed but not frightened, and when she saw a cluster of white tents pitched at the northern end of the field, she made for it, holding her knife close.

As she approached, the flap of the largest white tent opened, and out stepped a beautiful queen in silver armor, a saber at her side. Pure white wings stretched from her shoulders, finer and more lovely than the drab black and brown feathers that had adorned the wings of the elder sisters' suitors.

"Who are you?" asked the princess.

The queen smiled and stepped forward, her bare saber catching the sunlight. "I am the Queen of the Owls," she said. "My army and I are resting here after defending our land from a band of rebels, who broke their word to their queen and betrayed us. We have reinstated order and shall depart for home tomorrow. And you? Are you here by your own will, or does someone compel you to seek me out?"

"I am royal in my own right," she replied, "and no one but my own heart compels me to you."

The response pleased the Queen of the Owls, who invited the princess into her tent. They lay together that night with great tenderness, and in the morning they were married there on the field of battle, the grass still discolored with the blood of those who had defied their queen.

Soon, the Queen of the Owls brought the princess back to her palace, and they lived together peacefully and happily for many months. But as the seasons turned, discontent broke out in the east of the kingdom, and the Queen of the Owls prepared to depart and make war again. The day her army was to set out, she took the princess into her arms and bid her farewell.

"I will return as fast as I am able," she said, "but while I am gone, this palace is yours as much as it is mine. Rule in my place, and tend to the kingdom's affairs as you see fit. Only do not open the locked birch cabinet in my private rooms, for it is essential that you never see what lies inside."

The princess agreed and kissed the Queen of the Owls, who departed that evening at the head of a glorious army, her saber flashing in the setting sun.

For some weeks, the princess did as she was told. Still, thoughts of the locked birch cabinet never left her. Each time she passed it, her curiosity grew, until one day she took the Queen of the Owls' great chatelaine and fitted the key into the lock.

Within, she found herself face-to-face with an impossibly old man, dressed in rags and bound hand, foot, neck, and waist by twelve strong golden chains. The man's skin was taut and dry as a drumhead, and the princess could see the angles of his bones beneath.

"Take pity on me, sister, and give me a drink," said the man.

The princess's heart ached in sympathy for the old man, and she swiftly returned with a wooden cup, which she held to his mouth.

He swallowed its contents without pausing for breath and begged again with his tight cracked lips, "Take pity on me, sister, and give me a drink."

She did as she was told, and once again the old man drained the cup and begged for another. After he had drunk a third time, he flexed his arms and legs, and the strong golden chains shattered into uncountable pieces. The princess drew back, but the old man had already caught her wrist with his strong, ancient hand.

"My thanks, sister," he said, "for your foolishness and curiosity have unleashed Koshchei the Deathless, as your wife knew you would, and now you will never see her or your sisters again."

And he soared through the window in a terrible whirlwind, holding tight to the princess's wrist, and carried her off to his palace, where she still sits today, imprisoned in a tower, waiting for the moment when she might seize some advantage and escape. And as she sits alone, she asks herself why—not why the Queen of the Owls had set her such a test, but why she was cruel enough to condemn her with a kiss.

Marya

The day dawned clear and cold. Marya couldn't remember the last time the sky had been so pristine, pale blue feathered with clouds like a bolt of fine silk. It felt as if God was blessing the plan she'd staked her last hope on and had made an effort to show it. On another day, she'd have dismissed that thought as soon as it appeared, but with her nerves racing until she wondered if her veins might burst, any reassurance, however foolish, was welcome.

Already, word had traveled farther than she'd dared to hope. In the broad square stretching in front of the Winter Palace, the people who walked behind her numbered in the thousands. Three thousand? Five? The kind of perspective needed to estimate numbers of this magnitude was beyond her. Never in any of the Koalitsiya's previous actions had she seen a crowd like this. They'd always dealt in terms of dozens. But with the new tsar's grip on the city tightening by the day, more people than ever before had felt the urgency of making themselves heard.

The crowd moved through the city in a wave, inexorable and endless. In it, Marya knew, walked the people the Koalitsiya had reached in their days of preparation for this demonstration. Workers. Mothers. Priests and their congregations. Farmers and serfs from outside the city—word had traveled far and impossibly fast. A motley collection of the dispossessed, all brought together by two shared emotions, the strongest there were: fear, and hope.

Felix walked beside Marya, his jaw clenched tight. She'd told him he could remain behind if he chose—the new tsar was his brother, whatever else—but Felix, from guilt or conviction or something harder to define than either, had insisted. He'd thrown himself headlong into preparations with determination bordering on monomania, readily becoming the right hand she needed. He'd helped Marya draft the petition to the tsar, his elegant hand making the almost-treasonous assertion look like art. *On behalf of the people of Petersburg, we denounce the violence that took the life of His Imperial Majesty Tsar Sergei. In return, we ask you to denounce the violence against us. End your retribution, lift the foot from our necks, and you will find what we want is the same. A safe, prosperous Russia, food on our tables, and no fear for the lives of those we love. We are all God's children, Your Imperial Majesty. Treat us so, and there's no limit to what we can achieve together.* He'd written that part without any direction from her: if anyone knew what kind of argument might pierce the heart of the new tsar, Felix did.

The petition that followed had been a cautiously balanced list of conditions, smaller demands culled from the vision Isaak had shared in his speech before the scuttled general strike. An end to rationing and curfews. Clear charges and a trial after every arrest. An immediate condemnation and enforced end to the pogroms still raging in the Pale. Nowhere near the universal liberation they had dreamed of, but even so, Felix had looked at her while writing the list and said, with the ghost of his old humor flashing through, "Ask for the emancipation of the serfs while you're at it, Ryabkova. And why not ask him to give you wings? He's beating the city into the ground and you think he might agree to legal reform?" But if the new tsar made any concessions—or even gave any sign that he'd considered their petition—it would prove that Anatoli could be negotiated with. That progress through policy was possible. That life, as the Koalitsiya had always believed, could become better without bloodshed.

Under Marya's direction, the Koalitsiya had circulated the petition widely, encouraged people to read it aloud on every corner and in every church, until each soul marching with them this morning could have recited it by heart. They hadn't had a direct channel to the palace, but every wall in Petersburg had ears, and a mouth with which to tell the tsar what those ears had heard. No doubt a dozen soldiers had already repeated it verbatim to the new tsar.

Yes, by now, the tsar knew what they wanted. But a written petition could be ignored in a way a grand gesture could not. And with this many people, she was counting on making an impression. She took a deep breath, then released a sigh. Felix, beside her, gripped her hand.

Too far in to turn back now.

Palace Square stretched across the vast heart of Petersburg, the white-and-yellow Winter Palace to one side, Nevsky Prospekt to the other. She'd walked through the square hundreds of times, hardly giving it a thought, but today, the space was alive. The crowd reached the square and spilled out like a river rushing to the sea. Craning her neck, Marya could see the gate cordoning off the palace, and flanking it in steady lines the unmistakable green of soldiers' uniforms. If she turned her head slightly, she could see the brilliant sunlight reflect off dozens of rifles, which leaned against dozens of shoulders. Felix saw them, too, and tightened his grip on her hand.

The crowd had been given strict instructions: there was to be no violence today. They were to deliver their petition to the guards, say a collective blessing for the tsar and tsarina, and after an hour of peaceful demonstration—long enough for a select few to speak, and to let the tsar comprehend their sheer numbers— move together through the city to Our Lady of Kazan, where they would pray for a favorable outcome. But no one could say what the tsar had told his soldiers.

Please, she thought—the word a prayer of sorts, though she was not certain the intended audience was God. *Let this be right. Let me not have made a terrible mistake. Let him listen.*

She could only imagine what the square must have looked like from above, where Anatoli and Catarina no doubt watched from a secure room in the palace. A mass of citizens, disorganized but earnest, some holding aloft crudely made flags, others bearing the triple-barred Orthodox cross or their own household icons—some even with paintings of the late Tsar Sergei, there having been no time to produce any of the new tsar. And opposite them, a phalanx of armed soldiers, guns at the ready.

One, a serious-looking man on horseback with his right arm bound to his chest in a sling, seemed to be staring through her, grim as a rider guarding the gate to hell. Felix inhaled sharply, and she saw him staring at the injured soldier as if he'd laid eyes on a ghost. The soldier, too, appeared unsettled. He shifted the rifle over his back to hang less heavily on his injured arm, his face drawn and bloodless.

She nudged Felix with her shoulder. "That's him?" she murmured.

The determined set of Felix's mouth was answer enough.

The captain—Sasha, Felix had called him—seemed stricken. As if time stood still for him, and the bodies of the crowd had melted away, and no one remained but him and Felix and their own private pain. But he was only one soldier, and even if Felix could make the stone heart of this killer soften, it would do nothing to sway the rest of them. The Semyonovsky Regiment had been given commands, and they would carry them out. She could tell from the way they stood, with the confidence of men who didn't consider themselves responsible for what would happen next. They were devoted soldiers, these men, and loyal to their tsar. If this turned bloody, if they died here, their families would think they died well.

God willing, it wouldn't come to that.

Each lungful of breath mingled before them, until it seemed to Marya that Petersburg itself was breathing, the massy bulk of the city drawing in air and then holding it. The scene hung on a knife's edge, alive with anticipation.

And then—from where, Marya couldn't see—the voices started to rise.

She glanced to Felix, whose eyebrows lifted toward heaven. She hadn't planned this. But there they were, as undeniable as the gleaming rifles ahead: the voices of first two, then ten, then dozens, a chorus of voices lifted up in song.

The melody was clumsy, but Marya felt a shiver pass through her as it grew stronger, gaining resonance and depth. She knew the words—everyone did, the song as much a part of the fabric of the country as the soil, the river, the air.

How glorious our Lord is on Zion, no tongue can explain.

Sung in times of victory, in times of celebration, as a blessing. A song to praise the tsar and his country, and all that God had made. A song of peace.

Tsar Anatoli, from inside the fine walls of the Winter Palace, must have heard. If he peered from the balcony through the gap in the curtains, he'd see the people spread before him, their flags and icons. The children—God, they'd brought children, Marya could see them now, as if the music had pulled a screen from her eyes— waving crudely made paper flowers. Lost among them, the tsar's younger brother, collar turned up to his ears, face drawn. And all around, the hymn rising in the clear winter sky, like celebrants at a christening, or mourners at a funeral. Marya and Felix stood in the wave of the song, waiting. Knowing that one way or another, something was about to break. All it would take was one small push.

And then—with a jolt of yearning and the sick certainty of the damned—she saw Sofia, standing at the center of it all.

Sofia, who held a pistol in her hand.

She wore her hair loose, and the wind ruffled it, scattering it around her shoulders. The fingers around the pistol were curled almost like talons. Marya could see her inhale, a predator luxuriating in the scent of prey. And Marya knew then, without a doubt, what Sofia was about to do.

"Don't," she whispered. Sofia was yards away, another face in the endless crowd, and Marya's voice sank immediately beneath the swell of song.

Somehow, though, Sofia turned toward Marya, as if she had heard.

"Don't," Marya said again.

Sofia only smiled.

It's time, her expression seemed to say.

And then, with that hooked smile still on her lips, Sofia Azarova raised her pistol to the sky and fired.

31

Felix

The song shattered with the echo of the gunshot. The crowd flinched; the line of soldiers trembled. For a long, awful half second, the stillness of the grave hung over Palace Square. Felix had just enough time for a single thought: an isolated, horrified *No.*

Then, with a noise like a great ship being rent in two, stillness gave way to chaos.

The square had teemed with people even before the shot—now, there was not enough air to breathe, let alone space to stand. Panicked men and women and children, dressed in dull-colored, shabby coats, shoved their way toward the open street. Others lunged in the opposite direction, men with fire in their eyes, the hunger for blood coaxed out of them at the sound of gunfire. They drew their own pistols—of course they had come armed, Marya had commanded that the protest remain peaceful, but commands meant nothing with stakes so high, with a crowd this large and her leadership so new—and now citizens had their guns aimed at soldiers, who had all aimed their rifles in a single fluid line.

Felix didn't know who had fired the first shot, but it didn't matter. This wasn't an attack, no coordinated volley. This was rage that had waited long enough and would now fill any crack open to it. Voices swirled around him, cut from their context but vicious even when isolated. One voice, clear as moonlight, *Down with the tsar*, and then another, one that brought the taste of bile to the back of

Felix's throat: *Kill them all*. There was no way to stop this now. The city had burst open, and anything could break free.

His city. His home. His fault, all of it, for letting it get this far. And Sasha.

He couldn't see the line of soldiers anymore, not above the writhing crowd. Sasha was somewhere out there in this madness, injured, alone. He twisted round, desperate for a glimpse of him, enough to know that Sasha was still on his feet, that he hadn't been hurt. There was no time to remind himself that Sasha's safety was none of his concern, no time to think of the reasons he should want Sasha dead. There was only perfect, panicked clarity that if he lost Sasha now, he would truly have lost everything.

Beside him, Marya's black curls flew free from her scarf, her eyes wide and face ashen. She gripped his forearm almost hard enough to bruise.

"Felix, we have to go!"

He tried to wrench himself free of her. He couldn't run away, not when Sasha . . .

But her grip on his arm was firm, and somehow Marya pulled him through the edge of the crowd, into the streets surrounding the palace. Behind him, Felix heard the crackle of gunshots. Impossible to know which side had fired. More and more people poured into the narrow street Felix and Marya had darted down, until the crowd filled the road and pressed against the buildings on either side.

"I have to go back," Felix heard himself say, though his voice was so weak even he wouldn't have listened to it. "Sasha's back there, I have to go—"

He froze, Marya still holding his arm. A half-dozen soldiers rounded the corner, their leader on horseback and the rest on foot. No one moved. Felix stared into the shadowed eyes of a guardsman no more than seventeen, the sparse beginnings of a mustache on his upper lip. His mouth opened, but no words came out. The soldier was terrified, as frightened as Felix. Neither of them knew what to do. A woman's wail pierced the air from somewhere behind him.

Then the mounted soldier gave the order to fire.

Panic filled the street. There was nothing Felix wouldn't do to get away, no wall he wouldn't climb, no stranger he wouldn't shove down to save himself. There was no reasoning with fear like this. He pushed backward, diving away from the guns, his body moving on its own like an animal with its leg in a trap. Buffeted this way and that, he staggered, nearly fell, forced himself to keep going. There wasn't enough room for a retreat. This was every man for himself, and the devil take the hindmost. Waves of people rose in every direction, shoving others aside, pressing against walls, barreling into Felix as they ran, and he into them. No ideals now, only the desperate creature inside them all, clawing for another moment of life.

If Felix had been stronger, he might have been able to steady himself. He might have run forward instead of back, wrested a gun from one of the soldiers and tried to force the chaos into order. But he wasn't that person. He never had been. A woman shoved him, and he stumbled, caught himself with one hand against the wall of a building hemming in the narrow street. His palm left a smear of blood against the stones. From behind, someone clutched at the back of his coat for balance, the tug so hard he stumbled. It was hard to breathe, hard to see, hard to think. A shoulder crashed into his side, and with nothing to brace himself against this time and his balance already shaky, Felix pitched forward, his head catching against the stone wall. He cried out and landed on his knees, then flat against the frozen ground, arms shielding his head in a futile grasp toward safety.

He would die here, then. He would die in this dirty street on the south bank of the Neva, and Petersburg would burn.

It should have been frightening, but it wasn't. The sound of the stampede around him felt muted, as if through a thick blanket of fur, and in place of the noise drifted a curious calm. Maybe it was easier this way. When the streets cleared and soldiers found his body pulverized in the slush, maybe they would let him rest near his father's tomb. Maybe they would lay Anatoli's bones there, too, whether his brother died today or in sixty years. In a century, in two, they would be no different from the Komarov fathers and sons who had come before: united, strong, silent.

"Felix! Run!"

A hand closed tight around his collar, and Marya's strong arm heaved him to his feet. She pulled him along with the current of the crowd, barely keeping her own balance, and flung her full weight against the front door of the building Felix had nearly been crushed against. The door crunched inward with a sound like breaking bones, and they both charged through it, tracking snow and blood across the floors. Felix's body still didn't feel tethered to the ground. Everything hurt, and nothing did. A soot-stained icon crashed from the wall as they ran, landing facedown in front of the hearth. Thank God there was a back door, or they'd have escaped into a worse trap than the one they'd left. They poured through the door into an alley where the air was still enough to breathe. Screams drifted from the street.

Marya's scarf had been torn away, and her face was smeared with dirt and blood. Had she been hit in the nose? She pinched the bridge with two fingers, breathing through her mouth. Blood trickled from her nose down her wrist, leaving branches and spikes like the stem of a rose.

"You're bleeding," she said.

Dully, Felix brought a hand to his forehead. A hot slick of blood dripped from above his eyebrow. He brushed it away with the back of his hand and tried not to think about the stain it would leave behind. He'd had his head smashed against a wall, almost been trampled—his nerves would remember that in time, and the pain, when it registered properly, would be impossible to ignore. But right now, it was as if he were still floating above his own body in that crush of people, waiting for the blow that would kill him.

Marya glanced back. The sound of screams and gunfire filtered through the empty house. A scattering of frantic people who'd followed their lead barreled through the door and ran down the alley, like rats racing from a sinking ship. "Someone has to stop this."

Felix spat against the snow. The spit came out streaked with blood. "How?"

Marya did not meet Felix's eyes. Instead, her gaze drifted toward the sky. As if the answers they needed might descend on brilliant wings. "She might be able to."

Felix knew at once whom she meant. If only he still had faith enough to feel the hope that Marya seemed to. Sasha's grim face returned to him, his narrowed eyes, that plea from their days at Tsarskoe Selo, a time that seemed a hundred years ago now. *Send her away.* If he had, if he'd listened then, how different the streets might look now. "If she could, she'd never have let it start," he said. Another shot, this one farther away but the sound still distinct. "It's too late. She's lost control."

Marya shook her head, though her already-pale face went even paler. "She's the only one left who has any control."

"What do you—"

"She fired the shot, Felix. She has a plan, I know it. And I have to find her."

Before the weight of this could penetrate Felix's brain, Marya turned and ran north, toward the river. Felix could only watch her go. For the first time in longer than he cared to admit, he whispered a small prayer after her.

Please, he thought, *let Marya be right. Don't let this be the end of everything.*

32

Sasha

Hell had broken loose in Palace Square. Behind him rose the high gates of the Winter Palace, firmly locked. Around him, on all sides, shouts, screams, gunfire. Clouds of smoke drifting in the same patterns they'd formed at Smolensk, at Maloyaroslavets. He felt his horse begin to spook, hooves dancing to the side, and he pushed his feet back in the stirrups, forbidding the animal to rear. The horse was terrified, but Sasha's mind had gone perfectly calm. He could run from war, but he couldn't escape it. It was in his blood, and it would find him wherever he went.

The city was collapsing, but he was not at all afraid for himself. With death roaming the square, he could only think of one person, and that person was Felix. Felix, who had been manipulated the same as any of these people, won over with useless words of liberation, then hemmed into this bloody square. Felix, who might already be dead, killed by gunfire or trampled by the crowd. Felix, whom Sasha still loved, like a fool, with all his heart.

War gave men clarity of purpose. The omnipresence of death made it obvious what a person could and couldn't bear to lose. And with gun smoke again billowing through his lungs, he knew in his bones that a world without Felix wasn't a world worth defending.

Captain Batishchev, commander of the Semyonovsky Regiment, roared an order, and the line of soldiers raised their rifles as one for another volley. With the disorienting impermanence of a dream, Sasha alone sat still on his frightened horse while every soldier raised his weapon, every eye sighted. On the other end of the rifle mouths, working men with poorly maintained weapons mounted their own charge, not backing down an inch. It was as though the mass graves at the front had been excavated and their dead set free to wander the city. Blood slicked the cobblestones like a velvet carpet.

No, he thought, shifting in the saddle, still trapped in the split second between the order and the volley. No, he had sworn his life to protect the new tsar, but he had never sworn to do this. Never promised to fire on his own countrymen. On civilians, not invading soldiers. Never vowed to make the city he loved become a terrible echo of the years he fought every day to forget. And he had never consented to sacrifice Felix for the tsar's safety. Nothing—no emperor, no oath—was worth such a cost.

"Captain Dorokhin!" Batishchev roared.

Sasha met his commander's eye without speaking. He could only imagine how he must have looked. The only soldier not to draw arms, staring out from the front line, arm in a sling, face harrowed like someone already dead.

To hell with his oath. Sasha kicked back with his heels, and the horse, with a frightened whinny, lunged forward, driving a path through the crowd.

At any moment he expected a bullet to thud between his shoulders. This wasn't simple failure to obey orders; this was desertion, in the middle of an armed riot. If word reached the tsar of what Sasha had just done, death would be a mercy. He knew the punishment for treason: one hundred strikes of the knout, followed by forty years' exile and labor in the Nerchinsk *katorga* in the far east. It was a sentence meant to kill twice. The odds of a man surviving forty years in Nerchinsk were next to nothing, even if he managed to endure the capital punishment, which no man could. So be it. He'd been on the brink of his own death every day for thirty-one years; by now the threat had begun to lose its sting.

His seat on horseback gave him a better view of the shifting crowd, but seeing the chaos did not show him how to quell it.

Already, as he pushed farther from the palace, he could see bodies trampled by horses or beaten into the pavement beneath him, corpses bearing the marks of booted feet, eyes still staring wide. Friends, family, mothers, sons. Bile rising in his throat, Sasha dismounted, then let loose the reins. The horse, tasting the barest snatch of freedom, seized it at once, shying backward before taking off at a canter westward, away from the sound of gunfire. Sasha sent a small silent prayer after the animal. It would have to find its own way to safety now.

His injured shoulder screamed with every step, but he didn't slow. Bullet wound or not, he couldn't allow himself to falter. All he could do was tell himself to be strong, and repeat it until it became the truth.

He knew his orders. But he didn't know what to do. Didn't know how to exist at a time like this, fleeing citizens and cold air alive with screaming, blood on the pavement of his streets. The war with the French had been bloody, but at least there had been the pretense of difference between ally and enemy—not this, neighbor against neighbor.

Sasha thought back to that body lying sprawled in the snow in the royal park at Tsarskoe Selo, hair falling in a liquid curtain over her face, and he clenched his fist, heedless of the pain racing through his arm. It had all started in that moment. Would to God he'd left Sofia to die in the snow where he'd found her. Or would she even have died? Would whatever fiend bore her have come to her aid, suckling her back to life with milk black as hell? The stories said a demon couldn't be drowned, but no one ever said whether it could freeze.

He drew his pistol, holding it steady in his uninjured left hand. Thank God the assassin at the Bolshoi Kamenny had bet incorrectly that Sasha was right-handed. Around the corner, raised voices drifted toward him, screams neither of pain nor of fighting. No, this was the sound of jubilation. And beneath it, the pop and hiss of something that might have been fire. Sasha could see the glow up ahead, a faint corona emerging from an alleyway.

Sasha barely understood the person Felix had become, but of one thing he was certain: Felix had taken the rebels' cause on as his own, and he would be at the center of this chaos. If Sasha ever meant to find him, the only way was to plunge into the heart of it. He held his pistol close, the barrel still tilted toward the ground. At Maloyaroslavets, he'd killed four French cavalrymen five minutes after a bayonet had sliced his right arm. He'd trained for this. He was twice as dangerous injured as most men whole.

And he'd be damned if he let Sofia destroy everything he had left.

33

Marya

Whatever monster this day had given birth to, Sofia would be at the heart of it. Marya had known it at once, from the brutality latent in Sofia's smile. Sofia had never shied away from danger, and she would not begin today. But chaos like this had no heart. It grew from everywhere at once, each mad branch with a mind of its own, breaking off into new tributaries with each cry in the frozen air. Marya ran through the rat's nest of streets, haunted by the ghosts of screams and shattered glass, alert for a flash of silver hair or the swish of a black coat. Sofia might have been anywhere. There was no telling what she might be doing.

Power went both ways, Marya told herself firmly. If she could start this, then she could stop it. And if Sofia would listen to anyone, it would be her.

She burst out onto the northernmost end of Dvortsovy Proyezd, where the street opened on the south embankment of the Neva. And as Marya stood there, looking out toward the river, she knew at once where Sofia was.

Because the Winter Palace was burning.

It was as if God had descended on the city. Flames raced around the edge of the palace first, catching the ornamental wood and pale-yellow paint until the whole structure shone like an icon above a glowing censer. People ran from the crumbling palace, children screaming in their mothers' arms, a wild stream of people pouring away from the wreckage. A pair of horses nearly ran Marya down as they charged past dragging a fire pump on a two-railed sledge—pathetically small, useless against a conflagration of this size. All around her, soldiers turned from the skirmishes in the streets and raced back to the palace, following the sledge. The Winter Palace looked like the straw dolls burned at Maslenitsa. It looked like a watch fire during the war. It looked like the end of the world.

Marya ran against the crowd, in the wake of the fire pump, toward the flames. She shouldered people aside as they rushed for safety, keeping her head low. She had no plan, no idea of what she would say, what she would do.

Reaching the banks of the Neva, Marya saw her at once, as if she'd been meant to.

Sofia stood on the frozen river, watching as the Winter Palace shot flames into the sky. She was alone, wearing the long fur-lined coat Marya had come to think of as part of her body, a sort of second skin. Her loose hair rippled like a flame itself, the soot and ash doing nothing to dull its brightness. She had folded her arms across her chest, weight shifted over one leg, and her coat flowed out behind her like the tail feathers of a great bird. Sofia had never looked less human than she did now, like a spirit of wind and ice. Though she didn't turn, Marya was certain Sofia knew she was there.

Sofia had told Marya to be the leader the Koalitsiya needed. And with the world on fire around her, that was what she meant to do.

Marya clambered down the bank and crossed the ice with steady steps, toward Sofia.

34

Felix

No matter how far Felix tried to run from Palace Square, he couldn't escape the fighting. Gunfire sang around every corner, and lingering anywhere risked discovery, so he stayed on the move, darting this way and that, losing himself in a city that no longer looked like home. To his right, the dark river curled like a hand around a throat, smoke pouring into the sky above it from some unseen fire. Petersburg was full to the brim with death, and he was not capable of stopping it. He was no hero, no commander, no tsar. He was a twenty-eight-year-old idealist who'd stumbled into the end of the world, and if he died today, he would die alone.

Glass shattered nearby, and Felix spooked like a horse. Driven by a sort of wild-eyed fatalism, he took off running, not to safety but in the direction the sound had come from. Be who they think you are, he told himself. Be the kind of person who tries. Marya wouldn't run away, and neither would Sasha, and neither should you.

Around the corner, no soldiers waited for him, no packs of fleeing strangers. This was a new sort of crowd. Disorganized, rowdy, a group of shabbily dressed men who roamed the streets like wolves. As he watched, one took up a rock and hurled it through a shop window. Felix ducked out of sight, shoulders pressed against the wall of the nearest building. Even from here, he could hear their laughter, and the sound of shattering glass. One of them began to sing, a military drinking song Felix had heard Sasha sing once before, a holdover from the long nights before Borodino, before Krasnoi. There was a note of wildness in this song now, loose and drunk on the taste of gunpowder. Perhaps this man had once been a soldier, too. Perhaps any excuse to watch something burn would have been enough. Down the street, the smash of more breaking glass, and the report of shots.

Felix heard his own breath loud in his ears. The Petersburg he'd grown up in had been nothing but masked balls and state dinners, glittering palaces and princesses who flattered his every vanity. Nothing substantial, nothing real. He could never have imagined what a broken man would do when someone gave him a taste of hope and put a gun in his hand. They would tear him apart, given the chance.

Well, let them try. Marya was doing what she could to put a stop to this. Now it was up to Felix to do the same.

In a gesture that was either very brave or very stupid, Felix pulled away from the wall, toward the men whose shadows shivered in the sunlight, and placed himself between the crowd and the fire. A brick sailed from one of the men's hands over his head, through the upper window of the building, followed by a gust of fire as the curtains in the shattered window caught the tongue of flame. Felix ducked, buried a cough into the sleeve of his coat. His voice when he spoke was as strong as he could make it.

"You have to stop this."

"And why is that?" sneered the man at the head of the group.

Felix took another step toward the crowd, feeling the heat from the flames rush through his chest. "Because I'm a grand duke of the Komarov family," he said, reaching for every drop of authority he'd ever seen his father wield, "and I command you to."

Silence. The man stood staring. Those behind him exchanged sideways glances. Then the man laughed, loud and wild like a dog howling into the night.

"Right, and I'm Bishop Nikon. Get out of the way, before you get yourself hurt."

Felix rooted his feet to the pavement. "I'm the tsar's brother and a leader of the Koalitsiya, and you're in no position to give me orders. Stand down. Now."

The man spat at Felix's feet. Felix flinched. He had never been spat at before. Mocked, yes, laughed at, discounted, ridiculed, cuffed, hit, shoved, almost trampled, but never spat at. These men whose cause had cost him his family, for whom he'd given up every-thing, they hated him.

"Get out of the way," the man said. "I won't tell you again."

Felix didn't move. Even if he'd wanted to, he wasn't sure he could. The sensation of staring down the barrel of a gun had left him hollow.

He felt the man's fist connect with his nose before he saw it move.

Stars exploded behind his eyes. Felix cried out and staggered, fell heavily on his side. Hard ice and stone cut against his hip and shredded his palm. For a moment, the world flashed brilliant white. He pressed one hand to his nose and felt a strong gush of blood seeping through his fingers. Broken? No doubt. And no time to think anything else, before a booted foot drove into his ribs. He gasped for breath, his lungs shriveling. He couldn't speak, couldn't breathe, but he could hear.

"There's a reward, if he's who he says," one of the others said—his voice drifting from above. "The old tsar had a reward out for his head, but the new one will take him, too."

"You'd follow the tsar's order?"

"No one said the reward's for him alive," the man said. "I don't care which Komarov I kill, as long as it's one of them. Even better if it pays."

Felix tried to drag himself to his feet, but a boot stomped on his splayed hand until he heard his fingers crunch. He let out a howl, an animal sound, pathetic. It was too much for his already-aching body to bear. He'd never really known pain, not the kind that shot bright and sharp, not the kind you couldn't will away. Sasha should have taught him how to bear it. Should have taught him how cruel the world could be, how every corner of it could want you dead.

Another kick, and then another. He shielded his head with his arms, knees curled to his chest like a crab stripped of its shell, and let one last scream tear out of him. One way or another, this nightmare would end. When he woke, he'd find out what came after death—or better yet, he wouldn't wake at all.

Another blow to the head, and the world trembled.

35

Marya

Sweat beading into her eyes and chilling her clothes, Marya moved slowly, swallowing down panic as her shoes gripped the snow crusting the frozen river. Sofia had not turned away from the flames, still standing equidistant from both banks, and Marya could see her expression only in profile. What she needed was for Sofia to turn. The moment she did, Marya would be able to see her face clearly, and then she would know if Sofia, too, was scrambling for a way to undo the damage. If she had come today with a plan, however she had misjudged it. If there was anything to be done.

"Sonya!" Marya shouted.

With a grand, slow movement, like a countess revolving through the paces of a dance, Sofia turned.

Bathed in the light of the palace, Sofia's skin seemed as golden as her eyes. The hint of a smile curved her mouth. Everything about her was as poised as if she'd been etched in brass, without a single furrow in her brow. There was no alarm in her as the city crumbled around them. There wasn't even surprise.

Part of Marya wanted to revolt against it. Part of her was screaming that it couldn't be possible, not Sofia. Sofia, the woman who saw the pain of others clearer than anyone. Sofia, who had held Marya and kissed her as if the world was ending, kissed her as if she would have become one with her. Who had touched Marya, strengthened her, wanted her, given her the courage to lead. Sofia, who had recruited Irina into a suicidal assassination, who had fired into a crowd and stood now watching as the Winter Palace burned.

Lena had tried to warn her. She'd said it plainly: *I won't be part of this, not what it's going to be now.* Marya hadn't listened. And now they were here, amid the blood and flames. It was as if Sofia had plunged a knife into Marya's stomach.

"The streets aren't friendly just now," Sofia said, and there was no mistaking it now, that smile. "Better for you to get out of here, Masha. Before it gets rougher."

As if there were any safe places to retreat to now. But the traitorous corner of Marya's heart still leapt at the words, the offer she foolishly yearned to believe lay within them. A cold dismissal, or a plea for Marya's safety. Indifference or love. It was impossible in that moment to tell which.

"Sonya," Marya said, raising her voice to be heard above the crowd. "Please. You can stop this. I know you can."

Sofia's smile dipped slightly. The soft, distant cooling of disappointment. "Why would I want to stop it? It's what we planned for."

A shot rang out to the south, its echoes rippling across the river. Marya flinched. The ice, though thick, felt horribly unsteady beneath her. Was the heat from the burning palace enough to thaw the waters? It might be better if it were. If the ice gave way and she sank beneath the cold pressure of the Neva, it wouldn't matter that the woman Marya had been so convinced she loved now stood cold as a predator, that the cruelty in her smile belonged to a beast rather than a woman. It wouldn't matter how wrong Marya had been, and how much she had wagered on that losing bet.

"Don't you see what's happening? We talked about freedom, Sonya, not—"

"Not what?" Sofia said. "Not victory? Not success? I worked so hard to get you where you are now, Masha. Don't throw it away over some temporary pain."

"Temporary—" Marya repeated. She took another step forward,

despite her fear. "People are dying. People have already died. Isaak and Irina never wanted this."

"Of course they didn't," Sofia said coldly. "But it never mattered what Isaak wanted. All that matters is what the country needs. I made sure of that."

Marya's mouth tasted like ash. Now wasn't the time for polite words, for personal grief. But she had never expected to hear Sofia say Isaak's name with so much disdain. As if Marya had tried to invoke her pity for a beast led to slaughter. Somewhere far beneath the surface, Marya could still see the Sonya who had held her while she cried, who had run those long fingers through her hair and told her she was worthy of love, of happiness. But that person was sliding farther away by the moment, until soon only this cruel apparition would remain. This unfamiliar woman and her cold words: *I made sure of that.*

"You don't mean it," Marya said.

Sofia's smile sharpened, her hair flickering like feathers in the wind. "Oh, Masha," she said. "What a wonder you could be, if you only learned how to see what's right in front of you."

She drew herself up to her full height, and there was a terrible light in her eyes now. The same light Marya had seen in Isaak when the liberatory spirit flowed through him, but warped, sharper, almost feral. There was nothing Marya could say to this kind of belief. Nothing she could say in the face of what came next.

"I killed him, Marya. I thought you of all people would have figured that out."

It wasn't true. Sofia had tried to save him. Sofia had left the apartment that night and searched every corner of Petersburg, had hidden in the shadows of the Trubetskoy Bastion and heard the soldier, Felix's soldier, confess to the murder.

So Sofia had said. And there was no proof but her word.

"You had already done it," Marya whispered. "That night, the first time you came back, you'd already killed him. You let us sit there, waiting for him to come back, and you knew."

"Isaak and Irina brought the Koalitsiya together," Sofia said, her voice light but her eyes endlessly deep. "I value them for that. But neither of them had the courage to do what needed to be done. They played their parts, and then I disposed of them."

The words landed like a blow to the stomach. She was too stunned to feel anything. No person had the strength to understand a betrayal that deep. "Why?"

"To make room for us."

Marya shook her head. It was never meant to be her. None of this should ever have fallen to her.

And wasn't that exactly what Sofia was saying?

Understanding dawned like a bloodied sunrise. Stories through the ages spoke of people elevated beyond reason, chosen by someone greater than they. The witches of the wood chose their companions. Saints chose their holy warriors. The vila chose their princes, their future kings. In none of those stories had the natural order of succession ever mattered. If there was an obstacle in the way, that obstacle would be removed, so that beings with supreme power could shape the future they wanted.

"Why?" she said—a foolish question, and one that hardly mattered now.

"Because I knew you could do whatever it took," Sofia answered. She moved forward, reaching for Marya's arm with a tenderness that belonged nowhere near the flames still licking the sky behind her. Marya drew back, and though Sofia's eyes widened faintly with surprise, she did not try again. "I thought it could be Felix at first. But once I met him, I could tell he'd never have the strength. He could only ever be part of the solution, never the whole. The first night I met you, after Isaak's speech, I knew you understood it. How they'd poisoned the country down to its roots. How there was only one way forward from here."

Marya tried to speak, to form the words *How dare you*, to say *You've lied to me about everything, who I thought you were, what I thought we could be, you said you loved me but you were lying from the start, I've given you everything my friends my hope my city and in return you gave me* this, *this hell I never asked for or wanted.*

"You knew change always happens this way," Sofia said. "In flames, at the tip of a sword. That's how Russia drove out the Golden Horde. That's how the Komarovs bent the land to their will, watering every field with blood and damming every river with bodies. They wiped out the powers that came before them by burning it all to the ground and building again from the ashes. Except we've seen where they went wrong, and we won't make their mistakes."

A terrible sound came from behind them, the sound of snapping wood and shattering glass.

Marya's shoes cut swathes of clear ice from under the snow as she turned. The flames must have reached the beams supporting the second story of the Winter Palace, or perhaps it had spread across the floor. The building gave a great lurch, a dying man gasping for breath, and then sagged, the roof of the east wing collapsing through the third floor to the second. Burning debris clattered to the street like rain. The screams grew louder. Another fire pump raced down the street on a horse-drawn sledge, soldiers rushing after, as if anything could still be saved from wreckage like this.

The Winter Palace collapsed, and Petersburg burned.

Marya hated the tsar as much as anyone. The palace was nothing to her. She shouldn't have felt this way watching it shudder and fall, this deep, bitter hurt, this anger. But these were human lives. Mothers, fathers, children, friends. Isaak. Irina.

Her life.

"You lied to me," she said. "From the first minute. You told me you loved me, that you'd fight for us. And all along, you just wanted to watch it burn."

She'd half expected Sofia to laugh in her face. She'd expected that bitter mouth to tighten. She'd expected Sofia to lunge toward her and tear her across the face with her nails, until her white hands came away red. What she didn't expect was for Sofia to shake her head, eyes wide, and reach out for her.

"Believe me, Masha, I get no pleasure from this. But it has to be done. And I think you know that."

Marya looked at Sofia's extended hand like an adder in tall grass. "You have no idea what I think."

"Don't I?" Sofia murmured. They were a step away from each other now, so that Marya could have leaned forward and run her cheek along the dark fur of Sofia's coat. Could have let herself be swallowed by that warmth, that power. "You want a new world. It's what you've always said. And that's what I'm trying to make."

Marya was hardly hearing the words anymore. Sofia took another step forward, golden eyes alight with eagerness and reflected flame.

"That's the beautiful thing about fire, Masha," she said earnestly. "It's what lets new growth break through. The Komarovs are driving this country into ruin, but after their world burns, imagine what will be left. More light. Richer soil. More to go around. If you want something new, you have to clear away the old. It's always been that way."

There were a hundred responses Marya ought to have made to that. She'd said time and again that the demonstration in Palace Square was to be peaceful, but she wasn't naïve; she'd tucked Isaak's old pistol into her belt before they left. She had to act, had to decide, had to *do*. Her mind told her hand to move, but her hand stayed where it was, useless. A coward's hand. Would she let this happen because it was Sofia who asked her to? Because it was Sofia who offered it?

Maybe she would. Maybe the seduction of being chosen as a hero, the promise of the power to decide for herself, for others, would be enough to persuade her to look the other way. She had never been less certain what she was capable of.

"It's a new world, Masha," Sofia said. It was the same voice, the same tenderness as when Sofia held her in those strong arms, brushed away her tears. It was the same as that night, and it was nothing at all like it. "A world without tsars, without war, without cities or slums or serfs or palaces. The grand forests and open steppes, the shores of the sea, the way it was a thousand years ago, was always meant to be. Imagine who you could be, in a world like that."

Her voice was rising now, with the lilt of a dreamer. Freedom. Beauty. Light. A vision so compelling, so entrancing that for a moment Marya would have sacrificed anything, become anyone, to believe in it. Sofia's hand came up to rest on her shoulder, and the urge to take Sofia in her arms was as strong as the urge to shove her into the burning palace, let the flames have her.

"Don't you see? You're not like the rest of them, Masha. These tsars and their petty nobles, even your friends and their small-minded protests, they're not like you. They don't know what the world could be like. But you do."

Alight with fire and pretty words and horror, Sofia seemed less human than she ever had. Like a creature from legend, an ancient spirit hungry to watch something beautiful burn.

"I'm not like you, Sonya."

"You are," Sofia urged, taking another step nearer. Only inches separated them now. She could almost feel the gust of Sofia's breath. "So much more than you know. You could build something beautiful. The world as it was before men with power tried to bend everything to suit them. We can make that happen. It's already in motion. The price is already halfway paid."

Marya felt hot tears building and forced them back. When she'd lain awake at night, spinning out her own private dreams, the goal had been safety, and happiness, never this. But what better way to secure safety than by destroying everything that might threaten it? Wasn't Sofia right, in her way? Couldn't they make it happen?

As Marya watched Sofia there in the light of the Winter Palace, she saw the future as clearly as she saw the city on fire before her. She saw herself, standing tall in rich furs with diamonds on her fingers, the angel of Petropavlovsky Cathedral at her back, Marya and Sofia and the whole world at their feet, a new world, for people like them. A world free from the selfish tyranny of powerful men, a new beginning, all beings equal. Cities crumbling, palaces given over to ivy and rot, the sea rising up to erase the tsars' palace from its shores. All it would take was a fire, the way God had once sent the flood, to clear the slate and start anew. She could see them standing there, her own black hair tangled with Sofia's white, twin rulers of a newborn country that bowed to no one, and the land around them in flames.

It was freedom. It was magic. It was a way out—not the way she'd envisioned, but a way, and she could take it and finally breathe the air of a free woman.

It could have been heaven. Hell, from another angle. She no longer knew which way to look.

Marya took one step back, then two. Sofia extended one hand toward her, inviting her back, long fingers spread wide.

Isaak, leaving nothing but a bloodstain against the stone floor of his cell. Irina, executed in the tsar's fortress. Lena's set jaw and wary eyes, whispering, *This isn't you*, urging her to think, to realize, to *decide*.

She had decided long ago, though she hadn't realized it. And Sofia, extending an open hand, had also extended an opportunity.

"No," she said.

Then the pistol was in Marya's hand, and Sofia drew back, and as she squeezed her eyes shut to give herself courage, the shot rang out over the frozen water.

The scream was immediate and unbearable. Marya pressed her eyes closed and bolted, praying to keep her footing on the snow-dusted ice. She did not look back. The image of Sofia sinking to the ground, blood staining her white fingers as she clutched her chest, filled every part of her, a sense deeper than sight. Her heart pounded until it felt as if a demon were being torn out through her chest.

"I'm not like you," she said aloud as she reached the far bank of the river. "I'm not."

When she looked back, between the smoke and the shifting firelight, she couldn't be sure if the shape on the ice was a body or a shadow. Above, a snowy owl let out a mournful cry and rode the wind eastward toward the city limit. One wing hung awkwardly, barely holding the bird's weight. It was gone in a moment, disappearing into the clouds that draped the sky like a rich woman's scarves.

Before her, the Winter Palace was in ruins. Its frame had crumbled, but flames still shot skyward from the maimed skeleton, dangerously close to the surrounding structures. It was only a matter of time before the fire would spread, leaping from roof to roof, catching anything in its path. Beyond the flames, gunshots still echoed, undercut by the thunder of hooves against snow as the Semyonovsky Regiment imposed its version of order.

She ran, and she hardened her heart against her own sorrow, as all around her the city burned.

36

Felix

The taste of blood seeped over Felix's tongue, and he let it, feeling the warmth of his own life in his mouth. It was like his body had opened itself up to end it all quicker. His father was dead, his home was in flames, he was alone, and his city had become a vision of horror. If this was how it ended, so be it. He cringed into the filthy street and let the blows rain down on him, while flashes of white danced in front of his closed eyes.

And then, just like that, it stopped.

"What in God's—" one of the men began.

The crack of a pistol, near enough that Felix felt his skull rattle. He kept his eyes pressed closed, shielding himself in darkness. It didn't matter what was happening above him. If they were going to shoot him, it only meant a faster death. Footsteps cut through the silence after the shot. Distantly, he heard his own small whimper, high and sharp, like a prey animal half killed. He bit his tongue and forced himself to be silent. Death with dignity, at least.

"Get back," said a new voice. Different from the others. Lower, softer, and more dangerous. "Step away from him, and go."

"And you'll make us, will you?" one of the men sneered.

A second shot rang through the street.

"If you think killing you will make me lose a minute of sleep, you overestimate yourself. Get out of here."

Felix opened his eyes, but the world around him remained blurry. Only colors, brightness and shadow, and rapidly moving shapes—men fleeing into the smoky street. Warning shots only, then. Somewhere, dimly, Felix found it within himself to be surprised at the restraint. One shadow moved closer, and Felix screwed his eyes shut again. Then the approaching shape spoke, its voice rough but not cruel.

"My God, Felix."

The crunch of snow, louder. Felix felt a gloved hand brush against his cheek with unexpected tenderness. Without meaning to, he leaned into the touch. The hand faltered but did not pull back.

When Felix opened his eyes again, Sasha's face was inches from his. Relief and anger mingled in his heart.

Sasha was alive, but he was not well. Up close, it was more obvious that his face was ashen and grim, smeared with dust and heavily shadowed under the eyes. His beard, once trimmed with the sharp attention to detail he applied to everything, was now an overgrown wreck. The wicked part of Felix took a vicious pleasure in seeing that the injury to his right arm seemed to pain him. His flash of yearning for Sasha during the stampede had come from his gut, but this—this was his head, which knew better.

"I knew you'd change your mind about killing me," Felix said.

Sasha scoffed, though his dark eyes remained soft. "Usually, when someone saves your life, you thank them. But take your time."

Sasha had saved Felix from a pack of rioters who wanted him dead. Sasha had stood shoulder to shoulder with Anatoli as the new tsar rained terror on Petersburg. Sasha had arrested Isaak Tversky and sent him to his death, maybe carried out the sentence himself. Sasha had hunted Felix with the relentlessness of the loyal soldier, and now he knelt here, brushing the hair from Felix's brow. None of it made sense, and the dull ringing between Felix's ears only made it worse.

Felix clutched his ruined hand to his chest, twisting away from Sasha's touch. Even the smallest movement sent a sharp wave of vertigo through him. Impossible to judge how much damage the rebels had done. Equally impossible to stifle the whimper that escaped him. Sasha's face froze in alarm. As though suddenly aware of what had passed between them, he did not reach out to offer help.

"You killed him," Felix said, still doubled over against the pain. "I should have known you would."

Sasha blinked. The words seemed to bounce once against his forehead before sinking in. "There was an assassin, Felix, at the theater, everyone knows—"

"Not my father," Felix cut in. "Isaak. I told them it wasn't you, but it was, wasn't it?"

Sasha opened his mouth but made no reply. Felix could see ghosts lingering just behind his eyes. It could have been a sign of guilt or of innocence.

"No," Sasha said hoarsely, though it seemed he needed to convince himself as much as Felix. "It wasn't. Felix, now isn't the time. You have to get out of here."

Felix laughed. "Right. I'll just be on my way."

"Can you stand?"

"I don't know. Give me your damned arm."

Without waiting for permission, Felix gripped Sasha's left arm with his own, uninjured right hand. He hauled himself to his feet, leaning heavily on Sasha's shoulder when his legs buckled. Everything hurt. The blood rushed to his head, then drained to the soles of his feet. Blood everywhere. His father, sealed in a tomb. Blood in the streets, blood in his mouth, the whole world tilting wildly, blurring and then rushing back with terrible sharpness—

Felix swayed, dropping to his knees, and vomited into the street.

Sasha stood awkwardly three feet away while Felix crouched there, head between his knees, shaking. It was several minutes before the worst of the spell passed. He wiped his mouth roughly on his sleeve.

"I'll interpret that as a no," Sasha said. He bent down and draped one of Felix's arms across his shoulders. "Don't be stupid,

Felix. What are you going to do, bleed out in the street? Let me help you."

Like the coward he was, Felix was already leaning on Sasha before the offer came, allowing the soldier to bear most of his weight. He still hadn't ruled out the possibility that the next ten minutes would be his last. But there was the way Sasha had said his name, imbued with a gentle familiarity he'd feared was lost. And God, he wanted to *live*.

"All right," Sasha said—the strain in his voice was audible, but Felix pretended not to hear it. "Where can you go? Is there somewhere that's safe?"

What a question. Safe? If it wouldn't have hurt so much, Felix would have laughed. His father was dead, his brother wanted to kill him, and the home he'd known all his life had just burned to the ground. Nowhere was safe in Petersburg, certainly not now, with thick plumes of smoke rising to the clouds from endless fires, with shouts and screams and gunshots tearing the city, every soldier except for this one prepared to shoot him on sight.

The memory returned all at once, so strong he felt it in his blood. He'd been lying in bed beneath his grandfather's bearskin, before the war, watching the summer rain pound the high casement windows. Dozing, luxuriating in the warmth of past pleasure, thinking only of how lovely it was to be alive, and to be here, with nothing expected of him that he wasn't happy to deliver. With one hand, he'd gently run his fingers down Sasha's spine, tracing each vertebra, as if he could read a beautiful future in the nicks and scars along the soldier's skin. And Sasha had smiled at the touch and leaned closer into him, and when Felix had kissed his shoulder Sasha had sighed and whispered his name, so quietly it sounded like a prayer: *Felya*.

Tsarskoe Selo was fifteen miles from Petersburg. It was more than he could walk, certainly in a state like this. But he couldn't think of anywhere else worth trying.

"Yes," he said. "But I need you to find me a horse."

37

Sasha

After Petersburg, the quiet of the tsar's woods seemed like a fairy tale. Sasha's mind still held echoes of screams, of gunfire, but there was nothing to threaten them here. Only the smooth untouched snow, the rustling of bare branches, the crunch of hoofbeats in fresh powder, the perfect silence of the night air.

No one had dared stop Sasha, in uniform still, as he forced his way through the city and demanded the horse of a frightened cavalry regular, not even with a ragged man leaning on his good shoulder. A few curt words, a terse salute, and barriers melted away before him, soldiers falling over themselves to let him pass. Sasha had pressed the horse on at a gentle pace. Every nerve in his body itched to kick the animal into a gallop, but Felix had slumped forward half asleep the moment they cleared the city. A slow, awkward progress, then, with his good arm around Felix's waist steadying him and the reins looped around the wrist of the other, relying almost entirely on his legs to guide the animal in the right direction. It was lucky the horse he'd found had been trained for the cavalry; compared to the hellish barrage of cannon fire, two half-broken men holding on for dear life must have been a light burden.

The Catherine Palace hadn't been built for the likes of Sasha, a traitor now twice over, and yet the palace's gilded cupolas rising through the break in the leafless trees inspired a curious sense of relief. This wasn't home—it never would be. But it was a place he'd once felt hope, and might again. He nudged Felix awake as they reached the stable south of the palace, then dismounted, catching Felix before he fell from the saddle. Either the past hour had given Felix time to recover some strength, or he'd sworn not to accept further help from Sasha—either way, the grand duke kept on his feet while Sasha bedded down the horse in a vacant stall. The remaining servants must have kept to the warmth of the palace, not expecting royal visitors at such a time of unrest. Still, some thoughtful groom had left fresh straw in a few of the stalls, and it was short work to gather a bucket of snow that would soon melt to fresh water. Bare minimum of duty done, he gestured toward the door, through which a small stretch of the gardens separated them from the palace itself. Felix led the way. Sasha followed close behind, ready to offer an arm if it was requested. It was not.

This tasteless, extravagant palace had never been more welcome: its judgmental portraits, its marble floors, the gilt molding that made each wall look like an elaborate confection of pastry and sugared icing. It felt like an eccentric old relation: sometimes cruel, and decades out-of-date, but family still. The halls were quiet, though Sasha could hear low voices in conversation from deeper within the palace. A pair of footmen, he suspected, taking advantage of the empty halls to get properly drunk in one of the tsar's finest parlors.

"*Merde*," Felix snarled, and Sasha barely managed to steady him before his knees gave way. Felix flinched at the touch, but Sasha was past the point of worrying about that.

"Here," he said, "lean on me."

"I don't—"

"Don't be a child. There'll be plenty of time for you to hate me later, but you aren't getting up those stairs without me."

"Oh God," said one of the footmen, rounding the corner with a half-empty bottle of wine in his hand. "Your Highness." His companion appeared beside him a moment later, equally as horrified. Trapped between the impulse to bow and the competing urge to run away, the two servants stood there utterly frozen, their mouths half open.

Sasha, generously, chose to help them decide. "Get out of here," he barked, "and leave us be, or I'll put a bullet in both your backs."

With a small squeak from the second footman, the servants were gone. With luck, they would tell their companions about the mad soldier roaming the halls, and the rest of the staff would keep their distance. Even so, they had been seen. Felix couldn't travel today, not injured as he was, but it was no longer safe to stay an hour longer than necessary.

Felix's weakness, for the moment, outweighed his pride. Saying nothing about the interruption, he allowed Sasha to steer him up the stairs and through the abandoned corridor, tracing the way through muscle memory rather than sight. How many times had he walked this path in the night, following an unspoken invitation over dinner, drawn on by Felix's stray glance or pointed smile? Now, anger poured from Felix in silent waves, until Sasha felt that breathing near him was an imposition.

The door to Felix's bedroom stood open, the space blessedly empty. It looked like a jeweled replica from another time, the bearskin stretched over the bed, the crystal decanter of rum on the sideboard still half full. The hearth stood cold and fireless, but the room was out of the wind and warmer than the street in which Sasha had found Felix curled in on himself, bleeding, breathing raggedly, beaten half to death.

He would not think about that now.

Felix sagged back into the bed the moment Sasha drew his hands away, sinking his head into the pillow. The grand bed looked laughably decadent compared to the thin, tired man in the filthy overcoat lying on top of it. Felix's hair was a mess, and his boots had left tracks along the floor to the spot where he had collapsed. His narrow face was deeply bruised, he cradled one hand as though holding the bones together, and his eyes were closed. But when he opened them again, Sasha knew, they would glitter the deep blue of stained glass.

Whatever else, God, he'd missed those eyes.

Sasha pulled the chair from the corner near the bed and sat

back, watching Felix breathe. Up close, it was even worse than he'd thought. What he'd taken for mud across Felix's brow was in fact a crust of dried blood, and the bruise that darkened his cheek made Sasha wince to look at. His gut response wavered somewhere between self-loathing and indignation. From the beginning, he'd said it would come to this. It was Felix who owed him the apology, who should have been on his knees begging for Sasha's protection and forgiveness. Felix had no right to flinch away from Sasha's touch when the blame for everything that had happened, everyone who had died, could be laid squarely at his feet.

Isaak Tversky in his narrow cell, black eyes flashing hatred. Tsar Sergei, brains leaking onto the crimson carpet. No, perhaps not all the blame.

"Sleep," he said quietly. "It's all right. No one will hurt you while I'm here."

He might have spoken to the encroaching night, for all Felix listened. The grand duke's breath was already deep and regular. The furrows in his brow did not smooth, on edge even in sleep. Peace, Sasha knew from experience, would be some time in coming.

"No one will hurt you," Sasha said again, this time to himself, a promise.

He couldn't have said how long he sat there in silence, watching Felix's chest rise and fall. All he knew was that when he finally stood, every limb ached, and the rest of the light had faded, leaving him to walk the palace in the silver shadow of moonlight. Each of his steps echoed like the call of a cantor in a cathedral. He caught sight of one maidservant at the far end of the hall, but she disappeared into shadow as he drew closer, and he heard the decided snap of a door closing. Clearly word had spread, a temporary pact of mutual avoidance silently agreed upon. The palace felt impossibly vast, made even bigger by the knowledge that it was occupied. He refused to let himself think of ghosts, or of the sound of wings. Far better, in a moment like this, not to think at all.

Feeling eerily as though he'd returned to the front, Sasha filled a basin with snow from the courtyard. Freshly fallen, it melted cleanly over the fire he'd lit in Felix's hearth. The fresh sheets in the clothes press tore easily into strips, so white they made Sasha ashamed of his own dirty hands. Then, moving slowly, he eased Felix's injured hand away from his body. Felix flinched, but he did not wake.

He would never forget it as long as he lived, the sensation of Felix's palm in his own, held as tenderly as a baby bird, as he bathed and splinted the shattered hand. With each brush of the torn sheet, the blood and dirt melted away and stained the water in the basin brown. Two fingers were indeed broken, but not badly, and with proper tending, they would heal completely. Then, with a sense of both daring and guilt, Sasha dipped another cloth in the basin and washed clean the cut on Felix's brow.

Felix stirred at the touch, and Sasha froze. Too afraid even to take his hand away. He felt suspended in a moment of judgment, pitched evenly between salvation and flame.

And then Felix sighed, and leaned his head against Sasha's hand, and his brow smoothed over. Even through the filth that clung to Felix's clothes after weeks spent God knew where, there was still the familiar current of his scent beneath it all. Something warm and expensive that reminded Sasha of the nights they'd stolen in this same room, silk sheets and borrowed wine. Even after all this time, being near Felix still felt like home.

He didn't sleep at all that night. Instead, he sat awake, combing one hand through Felix's hair, waiting for the sun to rise. It felt like penance. It felt like communion. More painful than tears, more tender than a kiss.

It was not forgiveness, which he did not believe in, not anymore. But it was hope. And that, in some ways, was even more precious.

———

Felix slept the entire night through, and well into the morning. It was enough to make Sasha wonder when Felix had last allowed himself to let down his guard and rest. Had it been their last night together in the Winter Palace? Sasha himself hadn't been at ease long before that. He wasn't sure he'd ever sleep soundly again. Even so, it was a relief to watch the steady rise and fall of Felix's breath. A promise of what peace was possible, even if not for him.

Time had lost its meaning here, stretched oddly with nothing to mark it, but the sun had passed its highest point of the day and was descending again before Felix began to stir. It was like looking backward through time, back to the countless mornings when Sasha had woken first and sat up in the morning light, waiting for Felix to rub the sleep from his eyes and smile at him. *You can stay in bed with me, you know*, Felix would have said wryly. *You'll make me self-conscious if you're not careful, think my looks have gone off.* He could have laughed, remembering. He could have cursed himself at the same thought.

Because when Felix woke to see Sasha sitting at his bedside, his eyes—as Sasha had known they would—widened. Deep set and shadowed, and terrified. Sasha wanted to run, to leave this palace and lose himself in the trees, let the fresh-falling snow erase his tracks. He'd deserve it, for being the kind of man who made others draw back in fear. Murderer. Traitor. The tsar's loyal executioner.

But Sasha was stronger than his own shame, stronger than Felix's fear. For Felix, he could be stronger than anything.

He remained seated, keeping a careful distance between them. His good hand he kept palm up on his knee, far from any weapon. His injured arm had begun to itch, and if he'd been a braver man, a better man, he'd have asked Felix to help him change the bandages, ensure the wound did not become infected. As it stood, he'd sooner lose the arm than ask.

Felix sat rigid in bed, every muscle tense. The silence was so unlike him that if Sasha hadn't known better, he'd have wondered whether the rioters in the street had cut out his tongue.

"How do you feel?" Sasha said finally.

Felix laughed hoarsely. "Oh, grand. Never better. Let my brother know I'll be perfectly well to stand trial."

Sasha stared. "What?"

"He's here, isn't he?" Felix gestured toward the door, and the long shadow of his arm arced along the floor with it. "Anatoli and his men? You might as well tell them to come in. If I'm going to die here, I'd rather do it fast. You know I'm awful at waiting."

Sasha would not cry. He wouldn't. It was as simple as that. "It's just you and me, Felix. I'm here for you, not because of the tsar."

The disbelief in Felix's face was to be expected. Sasha deserved that distrust. They'd chosen their sides, and that couldn't be erased by a feeling of tenderness, no matter how strong. But here, alone, without the tsar's orders at his back or that woman's relentless whispers in Felix's ear, it was possible to see just how thin the line separating them was. What had either of them wanted? Peace. To be safe. To be right. Here, in the stillness and the quiet, perhaps he could come to see the path that led to Felix's choice, and Felix could see his.

"I'm not going back to the tsar's service," Sasha said, looking at his knees. "That part of my life is over."

"Of course it is." The wry gleam in Felix's eye was sharper than before, tempered now with the bitterness of an older man. "Sneaking me out of the city was treason, Captain. Go back now and my brother will have your head. Don't pretend you're deserting for noble reasons."

The self-flagellating part of Sasha's mind gave way to a wash of self-righteousness. "And why do you think I came for you? You might think treason is a thrilling adventure, but I don't."

Felix's surprised laugh echoed through the quiet room. There was a rusty air to the sound, as if it had been a long time since Felix had laughed aloud. In the time since they'd last seen each other, Sasha had thought repeatedly of Felix's laugh, and the way it rang through the halls during their golden days in this palace, when Sasha had loved Felix, would have done anything for him. This harsh laugh bore no resemblance at all to the old one.

"*Mon Dieu*, Sasha, is this you trying to say *I love you*?"

The blood rushed to Sasha's face. He forced himself to take a deep breath, waiting until the tallest wave of emotion had passed. His task here was difficult enough. Giving in to his feelings would not help.

"Felix," he began. "What I'm trying to say is—"

"Don't."

"I swore my loyalty to your father, and I don't regret that, but I never wanted, I never meant—"

"I mean it," Felix cut in. "Don't. You regret where everything has left us, but you don't think you were wrong. You turned my brother against me, took away my last chance at ending this peacefully. You did this."

The nascent apology vanished, burned away by indignation. It would only hurt him, but before he could stop it, he heard himself saying, "And you? Even now, you're still making excuses for her."

"For who?"

"Sofia!" How had this gone so wrong so quickly? One minute before, he'd been ready to concede anything if it meant Felix would love him again; now, his thundering voice had left Felix wide-eyed and frightened, and still he pressed on. "She came to the palace and convinced your brother not to negotiate with you. She said the Tverskys had poisoned your mind, driven you past reason with their violence. I can't prove it, but I know she was the one to kill Isaak, I *know* it. She's never wanted to help you. All she wanted was the empire burned to the ground. I've told you that from the first day she arrived, and even now, after I've saved your life, you'd still choose her over me?"

Felix closed his eyes, and his fright and anger seemed to melt away, leaving nothing at all in their place. He sank back against the pillows and turned onto his side, facing the wall. The movement made him appear older than Sasha had ever seen him. His bandaged hand rested atop the bearskin, the white fabric spotted gently with blood. The bleeding had stopped at some point during the night. Soon, the bandage would need replacing.

"I think you should go, Sasha."

The dismissal was not a request, but Sasha hesitated one moment more.

Two possible futures stretched in front of him, each as vivid as the other. In one, Felix turned to him, with quiet fear in those dark blue eyes, and Sasha accepted the wordless invitation that was not quite an apology, nor quite forgiveness. They would lie beside each other on the bed, Felix beneath the bearskin and Sasha on top of it, and as afternoon spilled back into night the inches between them would come to feel like nothing, and with the warmth of Felix's body near his, Sasha would think of the words that could put back together something so utterly broken.

Sasha chose the other path, and left.

38

Felix

He drifted into another uneasy sleep after Sasha left him, and when he woke next, it was evening again. Under the moonlight, he decided to chance rising from bed, testing the strength of his legs. The thick-piled rug felt unnatural under his bare feet when he finally did, as foreign as a plush bed of ferns in a tropical jungle. He went slowly, one step at a time, steadying himself on the furniture with his good hand. At some point, Sasha had returned, alerted no doubt by Felix's soft grunts of effort at every movement. He stood near the door, half in and half out of the room, watching Felix's progress. The captain kept his arms folded, though Felix knew if he demonstrated a moment of weakness, a single wavering step, Sasha would be by his side in an instant to stop him falling.

He did not falter, and Sasha remained where he was.

By the morning, he felt himself growing stronger, and he allowed himself to stray farther from his bedchamber, into the heart of the palace. He wandered the corridor by the light of a single candle in a brass lantern—even in daylight, the estate's shadowed corners were impenetrably dark, and the servants, warned off by Sasha's forbidding appearance, had all decided to keep their distance, leaving the lamps unlit. He hadn't realized until now how many mirrors the Catherine Palace held. Endless walls of glass had seemed beautiful, mesmerizing, back when he'd had nothing to fear. Now, Felix was his own eternal companion, his own face the one he caught from the corner of his eye. More than once, he flinched at the sight of himself: his own disheveled hair, the fading bruises, the healing gash on his brow.

Worse still, when he caught sight of himself at the proper angle, it wasn't his own reflection that stared back, but his father's.

He ought to have rested—Sasha certainly thought so, though Felix made a production of ignoring him—but he could no more sit still than fly. Even the whistle of wind across the grounds was enough to startle him. The smallest noise caused him to quicken his stride; moving slowly felt like vulnerability, though he was safe here for now, or as safe as he could be. His steps disturbed a cloud of untended dust, which fluttered around his ankles like cannon smoke.

So many ghosts in these halls. In this passage, he and Sasha had once stolen a kiss, the taste of wine sweet on Felix's tongue. In this house, Felix had been a rich, powerful young man with a lover who adored him, a family who ruled with an eternal fist of iron, and a lifetime of happiness within his grasp. In this park, he and Sofia had once wandered, spinning tales of a grander future.

Here, he had chosen where to place his trust. And everything had followed from there.

At first, he deluded himself into believing he could simply choose not to think about it, but in a place as full of ghosts as this, it became impossible to avoid the memories. The convincing firmness of her voice as Sofia described the suffering brought on by his father's reign, the flattering picture she'd constructed of Felix as a new, enlightened leader. She'd known what he wanted to hear and executed a note-perfect performance, steering him toward chaos, pressing a thumb on the scales to ensure the bloodiest possible outcome. She'd gone to Anatoli days after Irina's death and denounced her alleged friend as a mad traitor. Had she truly killed Isaak with her own hands and then returned to the apartment to deliver the news herself? Every moment he'd believed he was taking charge of his own life, he'd merely been a pawn in a different game. It was enough to make him despise himself.

And yet.

What did it mean that he'd been so eager to believe in the future she'd described?

What did it mean that part of him still did?

Sasha had called her a wicked, inhuman creature from the moment they met. Vila. Witch. Demon. Felix had been the one to dismiss the idea, and the decision had brought them here. Perhaps Felix had been wrong from the beginning. A woman with power beyond what he could understand, come to twist the story of Russia for her own ends, the way the vila had chosen their heroes and warped their fates to succeed.

How comforting it would have been to know that a vila had fated this, that he was not responsible for his own actions. What a weak, pitiable thing to wish.

As Felix drifted through another of the Catherine Palace's mirrored halls, he kept his face low and his collar turned up. Even so, eyes followed him as he passed.

―――――

"We can't stay here," Sasha said that afternoon, from the door to the library.

Felix remained where he was, nestled in an armchair with a book open on his lap. He didn't know what the volume was and didn't care to know: the printed letters swam in front of his eyes every time he glanced at them. But it was a screen to hide behind, and if Sasha refused to leave him in peace, he needed one.

"Tomorrow, if you're well enough to travel, we should go," Sasha went on. "Now that the servants have seen us, it's a matter of time before the tsar hears where you've gone. It isn't safe."

"Of course it isn't safe," Felix said. The moment the chaos in Petersburg died down—the moment Anatoli meted out enough justice in the city to satisfy his anger—the new tsar's soldiers would turn their attention to the missing grand duke. Anyone who had ever met Felix would think to scour the Catherine Palace first, even without a household of servants as witnesses. Now wasn't the time for petulance and stubbornness. Now was the time to move. But Felix hadn't had a clear idea in his head since the riot. It was as if someone had smeared the heel of their hand across his thoughts before the ink was dry. He knew he had to leave, but it was impossible to feel the urgency, not in this maze of ghosts and mirrors, his mind trapped in whatever twilight this was.

Grief, said a voice in his head that sounded like Marya's, but knowing the word was of little use.

"A ship from Petersburg is out of the question," Sasha said. He took another step into the library as he spoke. Tactics and practicalities had always been where Sasha excelled, and dealing with the issue at hand gave him the confidence to push through Felix's silence. "The city will still be crawling with soldiers. And we can't exactly buy places in a troika to Smolensk, not without someone noticing who you are."

Felix closed the book and set it aside. "I'm sorry," he said coldly. "We?"

Sasha blinked. Clearly he hadn't expected Felix's hollowness to give way to anger. It showed how little he understood Felix, what a small fraction of his heart the captain had ever truly known. "I thought—"

"I'm sure you did. You brought me here from the city and everything's finished, everything's forgotten. Is that what you thought?"

He meant the words to chill, and they did. But it surprised him how dearly he wanted that ludicrous situation to be possible. To lose himself in Sasha's arms and let someone else take responsibility for making decisions. It would have been so easy to give in, to become the person he'd been six months ago, without a care or thought. But that man was gone now. And the Sasha he'd loved then was gone, too. He looked into Sasha's face, those black eyes hard as chips of flint: determined, not angry. Sasha stood beside him now in the well-appointed library, but all he could see was Captain Dorokhin standing steady at Anatoli's side, rifle across his back, blood dripping from his upturned palm like a waterfall.

Sasha had saved Felix's life. He'd risked his own safety to get Felix out of Petersburg. That had to mean something. Didn't it?

"Felix," Sasha said. He knelt awkwardly—his splinted arm had healed somewhat, but without full use of it, his balance was still shaky. Felix watched him move from the corner of his eye. He'd already seen enough of what Sasha considered loyalty. "Felix," Sasha said again, and this time the unexpected hoarseness in his voice made Felix turn, more from disbelief than anything.

Sure enough, Sasha's eyes shone. He was not weeping; Felix couldn't fathom a world in which Sasha wept. But even coming this close was terrifying, and it set Felix's chest aching.

"I know it can't ever be the same," Sasha said. "Too much has happened for that. But I'll tell you what I do know. What I knew the second I heard that shot in the square."

A gunshot Felix's own credulousness had brought on. The end of Sofia's plan, patterned with Felix's fingerprints. Torn between shame and anger, he sat in silence, listening.

"I've made mistakes," Sasha said, clearing his throat, as if to dismiss the taste of understatement. "We both have. But no matter what, I would never hurt you. I can't. There's nothing I won't do to keep you safe. From your brother or from anyone else."

In those words, Felix heard a different man. An older one, and more familiar. This was the man he'd known before: awkward and practical to a fault, brave, resourceful, strong, tender beneath it all. The man Felix had trusted with his life, and not only because he had no choice, but because he wanted to. Was it a resurrection, or the brief visit of a ghost? Impossible to say.

Felix stood, and Sasha leaned back as if from a flame. With Sasha still on his knees, Felix felt a terrible rush of power, one that carried a bitter aftertaste, like turned wine.

"I'll leave at dawn," Felix said. "I'm taking the horse. Once I make it to Primorsk, I should be able to buy passage on a ship. I look like a dog that's rolled in its own shit, no one's going to suspect it's me. And a handful of the hideous jewels in this house will get me the money."

"From there?" Sasha said quietly.

Felix shrugged, moving toward the door. "Who's to say? The world is open."

"And . . ." Sasha began.

There was no need to hear the rest of the question.

"I don't know yet," Felix said from the doorway. "I don't know."

The last time Felix had left Tsarskoe Selo, he'd helped Sofia into one of the imperial carriages, wrapped in fine furs, as Sasha sat on horseback and debated putting a bullet through her heart. Now, Felix stood alone, bundled in an ill-fitting overcoat and two scarves he'd dug from a wardrobe, bringing with him only what he could carry in a single haversack. His shadow drifted long across the snow in the rising light.

He knew, without turning, that Sasha stood behind him. Waiting.

Felix inhaled the frozen morning around them. He turned, and though the sun hadn't yet crested the palace roof, the glow from the horizon cast shades of pink and yellow across the blue paint and bright gold. The palace wasn't Felix's home, not really. But it was where he'd built a life. It was where everything had fallen apart.

It was the point from which everything might begin again.

He lowered his gaze to where Sasha stood, awkward as a schoolboy, hands hanging uselessly by his side. And in an aching moment that felt like the most terrible form of grace, Felix extended one hand toward Sasha.

"I can't lift you onto the horse, Sasha," he said. "If you're coming, you'll have to help."

It was as if life had been breathed back into Sasha's body. He was at Felix's side in an instant. Without a word, he unbuttoned his thick overcoat and draped it over both their shoulders, cocooning the warmth of their bodies within it. Felix sighed and welcomed the heat. Inside this nest, the wind outside didn't matter, not if at least one piece of what they'd broken could be mended again.

"Where to?" Sasha murmured as they entered the temporary shelter of the stable.

Felix sighed. "Paris," he said. "He won't find me there."

Sasha winced. "Of course. Nothing like taking sanctuary with the enemy."

"The war is over, Sasha."

"Even so."

For a long moment, neither of them moved to mount the horse. It wasn't hesitation; they were long beyond that. The old custom of taking stock before departing on a journey, even now, when every minute weighed the scales of their life one way or the other. It felt like a decadent indulgence with the threat of detection growing stronger every moment, but together they wordlessly decided to permit it. In a matter of hours, days, weeks, they would be on foreign soil, and God knew what would happen then. Let them enjoy one last deep breath of home.

Felix felt the soft brush of Sasha's hand against his shoulder. It wasn't much, but it sent a clear message: *Breathe. Be calm, and get through this. I will keep you safe.*

Perhaps. Or perhaps this time, Felix would protect himself.

"Are you ready?" Sasha said.

"Absolutely not," Felix said, before mounting the horse. Sasha swung his leg over and sat behind him, his straight posture shielding Felix from the worst of the wind. In front of them, the horse's breath steamed in the pink-tinged morning.

"Do you even speak French?" Felix said, an afterthought.

Sasha laughed quietly, a low rumble against Felix's spine. "Some. Badly."

He leaned against Sasha, careful to avoid the still-tender shoulder. "Lucky you, then, that I'm an excellent teacher."

A twitch of Sasha's heels, a click of his tongue, and the animal moved forward, carrying them into the early morning woods, and to whatever lay beyond.

THE GOATHERD, THE VILA,
AND HER DEATH

Far beyond the thrice-tenth kingdom, a young woman lived near the woods and earned her living tending goats. Her work was hard, but she was an honest woman and pretty enough, and so the goatherd had her share of suitors. But however handsome or rich or wise they were, the goatherd never found one to her liking, and so she carried on alone without feeling as though her life lacked anything at all.

This went on until the dawn of her name day, when a stranger appeared at the edge of the woods. The goatherd was struck immediately by the beauty of her visitor: the unknown woman was pale and bright as the morning, with hair finer than the richest silver and eyes tawny as an owl's. The goatherd was enraptured, and the vila—for such, of course, she was—took advantage of the moment's weakness to seize the goatherd and whisk her to a palace in the woods, so far and so deep within the tangled trees that no one could hope to find her.

With every passing day, the goatherd pined for her home and her friends and her freedom. But she was clever, and she knew the way to outsmart the vila was not to fight her or outrun her. Instead, she was as sweet a wife as anyone had ever known, and she fawned over the vila when she returned each evening from hunting.

"You're in a fine mood," said the vila one night, running her hand through the goatherd's hair.

The goatherd repressed a flinch at the touch and spoke softly. "I'm only relieved you're home again, my love. So many beasts live in these woods, and you'd been gone so long I'd begun to think you had been devoured and I would never see you again."

The vila laughed, the sound high and cold as bells. "Foolish woman, don't you know my death does not lie with wild beasts? From everything save my ordained death I am as safe in the world as you are here in my palace."

"But what is your death, then?" the goatherd asked, taking care not to sound too eager.

The vila kissed the goatherd lightly on the temple, as a fond master might pat his dog. "My dear, you need not worry. My death is far, far away. In the sea there is an island, and on that island there is an oak. Dig beneath that oak, and you would find a coffer buried, in which rests the body of a hare. Slit open the hare, and you will find a duck; slit open the duck, and you will find an egg; crack open the egg, and there you would find my death."

The goatherd feigned joy that the vila's death was in so distant and secure a place, and like a thoughtful wife saw her captor to bed. But the moment the vila had drifted to sleep, the goatherd climbed through the window, stole the finest horse from the stable, and rode as fast as thought to the sea. The horse was a strong swimmer and soon brought her to the island, and from there it was short work to unearth the coffer, and the hare, and the duck, and at last the egg. The goatherd cradled the little egg in her hands, then cracked it open and swallowed it whole, feeling its slick membrane slide along the walls of her throat. Then, still under cover of darkness, she mounted the fine horse and rode back until the animal was slick with sweat and foam. She was in bed beside the vila before dawn.

When the first rays of sunlight danced across the vila's fine face, the vila yawned and rolled over, gracing the goatherd with a smile.

"Good morning, little one," said the vila.

"Good morning," the goatherd replied, kissing the vila warmly.

The moment the goatherd's lips touched the vila, the egg began its work. The vila's fine features tightened and distorted, until her skin resembled tanned leather pulled over a skull. The lovely white hair dried to straw, and the amber eyes flashed with a great burst of light before extinguishing like stars. For one terrible moment, the goatherd was lying in bed beside a desiccated, bleached skeleton, as ancient and grim as the grave. Then the skeleton dissolved into dust, which scattered with the wind that curled through the open window, and nothing remained but the faintest imprint of a woman's body on the linen sheets.

The goatherd took the horse that had saved her life and rode him back to her house at the edge of the forest, where her friends celebrated her return. She never became rich, and one could argue that she never became happy, but she was free for the rest of her days, even though she never stopped tasting the vila's death on her tongue.

39

Marya

A week after the protest in Palace Square that had spiraled into a riot leaving forty-three dead, an event already being called Red Monday, the streets were clear of all evidence. The very next day, bodies had been removed from the snow where they had fallen, the tracks of booted feet and shod horses smoothed over, as if the carnage had never been. Several buildings still bore the scars of the violence, their shattered windows boarded over, their jewel-toned paint smeared with ash, but these, too, would be mended before long. Petersburg was too vain to allow such a crack in its countenance to linger. Even the Winter Palace, which had sustained the worst of the damage, had begun to emerge from its own ashes. Workers toiled night and day at the restoration, awkward scaffolding rising around it like the wreck of some great ship, the sound of hammers falling at all hours. Tsar Anatoli would spare no expense, financial or human, to restore what had been taken from him, making the seat of his empire even finer than before.

In two months, in three, it would look as if the Koalitsiya had never existed at all. As if the people's march on the Winter Palace had been some mad dream. The same imperial family would still move through the same stately rituals it always had, splendidly dressed automatons passing from state dinner to ball to council meeting, bowing and glittering in the light.

But as Marya stood at the edge of Palace Square and watched the workmen's hammers swing and descend, she knew the effects of the Koalitsiya's work would last long after its physical traces were gone.

She folded her arms, hugging her overcoat tighter to her. It was winter still, and would be for weeks more, but the air already carried a hint of something milder. If Marya closed her eyes, she could imagine that the evening would be dotted with fireflies, crowned by the scent of lilacs.

Isaak and Irina were both dead. So was Tsar Sergei. Neither Marya nor the new tsar in this charred, wounded palace would soon forget that.

Marya closed her eyes, and in time with the strikes and clangs of the palace in the early stages of its resurrection, she began to hum. Tsar Anatoli had been unyielding in his retribution after Red Monday, and anyone even suspected of taking part in the day's events could expect the swiftest, severest punishment. But as she let the song that filled her mind escape into the air, it never occurred to her to be afraid. It was an old song, and a familiar one. And daring to think of it at such a time made her feel newly alive.

How glorious our Lord is on Zion, no tongue can explain.

The longer she hummed, the more she knew: this music had never belonged indoors, confined to formal state occasions and patriotic pomp. It belonged here, in the square, to the sound of hammers and the call of voices. Here it could expand until the hymn started to thrum with the power of an exhalation, a folk tune ancient as the country itself, the wild dances Marya had known in her youth. She could see it even there in the open street: the fire they'd stoke in the stove in the corner, their elderly neighbors watching and clapping from the sides of the room as Marya's father took up his violin and whipped the crowd into a dance, and the feet of a dozen men and women kicked up clouds of dust in a flurry of laughter.

It sounded like freedom. And freedom was the kind of song that carried.

Petersburg's memory was longer than the Komarovs gave it credit for. The tsar and the tsarina would paint over any footprint the Koalitsiya had left behind, but the indentations would be there still, just a layer of frost away. Perhaps it had not been their time now. Perhaps the ground had been too frozen for seeds to thrive. But their sacrifice was not for nothing if it tilled the soil and opened space for new roots.

Every fire left room for new growth.

It was not for nothing. It was for the future. Someone else, years from now, might remember that a group of people before them had given their lives for the question of freedom, and that thoughtful citizen with the long memory might turn from the past toward the future, and set themselves the task of finding a better answer.

The last notes of the song drifting away under the endless rhythm of the workmen, Marya sighed and turned in the direction of the harbor. A woman stood at the end of the street, watching her in return.

Frost-colored hair against a black fur-lined coat, more striking than the most expensive gown. Eyes that glittered like a promise. Eyes that had always known her, and always would, better than she would ever know herself. Lips bending into a smile that contained impossible promises of power.

Marya blinked, and the street was empty. Only milling workmen and tight-packed snow, the usual backdrop of the city.

Though more than a mile still separated her from the frozen harbor, Marya imagined she could smell the salt sea nevertheless, hear the cry of a gull. Spring whispered in the air. Soon enough, the ice would melt, and the ships would drift back to Petersburg, their masts weaving through the waves like a forest on the move. Soon, traders would wend their paths across the Gulf, weary birds perching on their broad masts. There would be room on one of those ships for a woman traveling alone.

No one would remember Marya Ivanovna's face in Petersburg. No one would ask questions about a woman looking to leave the city in the aftermath of tragedy, searching for a quieter life somewhere to the south, in Riga. Somewhere a familiar face waited, and might be persuaded to forgive.

She would find Lena. She would try again.

Let the dead bury the dead—life was here beneath the sky, and with all the defiance she had, she would have to live it.

With one last look at the palace, Marya turned away and disappeared into the tangle of streets beyond the square. Behind her, the sound of hammers drifted like the chimes of church bells. The peal of a city both mourning and proclaiming victory. Wounded, but not finished.

Waiting.

HISTORICAL NOTE

While *Let the Dead Bury the Dead* is an alternate history describing characters and events of my own invention, it was inspired by real people and events. The following note highlights some of the real-life history within the fiction—though this is just a starting point, and the real stories of Russian history in the early nineteenth century are well worth learning about in their own right.

Though the Koalitsiya is fictional, popular rebellion was on the rise in the wake of Russia's 1812 war against Napoleon, largely for the reasons I've described. Fending off the French summoned a tremendous surge of patriotism and unity from Russians of all walks of life, and the country's peasants fought and died beside its well-born officers in significant numbers. At least four hundred thousand Russian soldiers were killed or wounded that year—the equivalent of the entire population of Saint Petersburg at that time—with seventy thousand of those losses attributed to the one-day Battle of Borodino that Tolstoy describes so hauntingly in *War and Peace*. After this tremendous sacrifice, and the proof that Russia's common people had been as instrumental as its nobility in turning Napoleon away, returning to the highly stratified, oppressive social structure of the day-to-day empire was a difficult pill for the country's peasants to swallow.

One result of this discontent was the Decembrist Revolt of 1825, during which a contingent of some three thousand rebel troops faced off with the Imperial Army in Senate Square, demanding that Russia institute a constitutional monarchy to fill the void left by the death of Tsar Aleksandr I. I've modeled the Koalitsiya and its climactic demonstration after this group, though it's not a one-to-one reproduction: Ilya is inspired by the Decembrists' military background, while Isaak draws on the movement's philosophical, intellectual undercurrent. The Decembrists, though of a higher social class than my Koalitsiya is, were likewise unsuccessful, with their ringleaders subjected to execution or exile. Still, this uprising was one of many cracks in Russian autocracy that eventually culminated in the 1917 revolution. (It also lent its name to the Portland indie rock band the Decemberists, which has nothing to do with Russian history, but which I did listen to extensively while writing this book.)

In many ways, my fictional Tsar Sergei is modeled after Tsar Aleksandr I, who successfully delivered Russia from the threat of Napoleon and then alienated his people through a series of increasingly conservative decrees and scuttled reforms. Anatoli and Felix bear some resemblance to Nicholas I and Grand Duke Constantine Pavlovich, who found themselves on opposite sides of the Decembrist Revolt after the death of Aleksandr I: one faction fought for Nicholas as autocratic tsar, while the other wanted Constantine as a constitutional monarch supported by an elected parliament. Granted, Nicholas and Constantine were Tsar Aleksandr's younger brothers, not his sons, and the question of that succession was a lot more complicated than I've made it in this book, but the root of my invented conflict grew from this moment: the fissure where divine right to rule splits a family down the middle.

The parallels only go so far, though. Tsar Aleksandr I was not a particularly strong personality, and moreover he wasn't murdered. He died of typhus at age forty-seven (or faked his own death and roamed the countryside incognito as a hermit until age ninety, depending on whom you ask, but once again that's another story).

The death of Tsar Sergei is a mirror image of a later historical assassination: Russian prime minister Pyotr Arkadyevich Stolypin, who was shot by a leftist revolutionary during a performance of *The Tale of Tsar Saltan* by Nikolai Rimsky-Korsakov in 1911. I also drew on the assassination of Tsar Aleksandr II, who was killed by populist bombings in 1881. His son, Tsar Aleksandr III, responded to the death of his father with a brutal police crackdown and a flurry of oppressive policies, much as I've depicted Anatoli doing.

Isaak and Irina's experience in the Pale of Settlement was inspired by my own ancestors' lived experience in what is now Lithuania. I'm deeply grateful my own family made the decision to emigrate, which is the reason I'm sitting here writing this historical note today, but I wanted the Tverskys to stand in both for them and for those who stayed. This period in Jewish history is rich with bravery and tragedy, often in the same breath, and its stories deserve to be told more broadly.

Which leaves Sofia. The figure of an outsider with alarming power whispering in the ear of the tsar's family is a familiar one, whether in the person of the Siberian holy man Grigori Rasputin or the religious mystic Baroness von Krüdner, who exerted a powerful shaping influence on Tsar Aleksandr I after the Napoleonic Wars. Sasha's inherent distrust of Sofia is reflected in historical reactions to both Rasputin and von Krüdner. Given that the tsar was seen as God's emissary on earth, any person able to exert an undesirable influence on him was often seen as beyond God, beyond the earthly. I've leaned into this notion by embracing the Slavic folktale, examples of which I've adapted and reimagined throughout this book. The vila herself is a figure primarily found in Serbian folklore, though I've also drawn on other sinister women from pan-Slavic folktales: the rusalka, Baba Yaga, the warrior queen Marya Morevna, and others.

Slavic folklore is rich and exciting territory, and if you enjoyed the versions I reshaped here, you'll love the real thing. Though often dark and at times brutal, they are a powerful representation of the mindset I've tried to capture in Marya, Felix, and Sasha. One that knows no matter how grim or hopeless the world may seem, there's always another story worth sharing—one that, in the next telling, might turn out differently, or at least show us a different way to try again.

ACKNOWLEDGMENTS

I'm so lucky to have a team in my corner who are as talented as they are kind. My editor, Carolyn Williams, for guiding me forward with grace and insight, and for being the kind of champion every author hopes to find. My agent, Bridget Smith, for your ongoing belief in me and for always telling me when I can do better. Everyone at Doubleday who helped make this book a thousand times better and more beautiful: copyeditor Amy Ryan, cover designer Emily Mahon, cover artist Roberts Rurans, production editor Victoria Pearson, marketer Lindsay Mandel, publicist Tricia Cave, text designer Pei Koay, and production manager Peggy Samedi. Thank you for your effort, skill, and craft.

Extra-special thanks to three readers who godparented this book: Juan Martinez, who cheered me on through the ugly first draft and helped me find the joy again; Olesya Salnikova Gilmore, whose authenticity read sharpened the lens of this book in countless large and small ways; and Aubyn Keefe, whose friendship and legendary literary eye lifted me out of many pits of despair. A million thanks aren't enough.

Thanks to Alissa Gulin, Ann Foster, Audrey Fierberg, Bridget Roche, Claire and Al Keefe, Colby Dockery, Dan Cabrera, Erika Carey, Jessica Ross, Katie Brill, Kim Ellsworth, Kristen Field, Lana Wood Johnson, Minh Nguyen, Molly Lyons, Nina Kryza, Sara Connell, and Val Utter for hyping me up, helping me weather the hard times, and unfailingly answering my horse questions. Squad goals, truly.

Thank you to the booksellers, librarians, reviewers, and readers who gave *A Tip for the Hangman* such a warm and generous welcome. I hope you love my second rectangular child as much as I do. She's all yours.

Thanks to my siblings—Danielle, Adam, Jason, and Taylor—for rallying around my wild author adventure, and to the extended family for all your love and support. Thanks also to my cat Mina, who did not help with this book in any way.

Finally, my parents, for showing up at every virtual event, accepting that I'm never going to give that Rasputin biography back, making me laugh, and being the kind of people I aspire to be. I love you. Thank you.

Allison Epstein earned her MFA in fiction from Northwestern University and a BA in creative writing from the University of Michigan. A Michigan native, she now lives in Chicago, where she works as an editor. When not writing, she enjoys good theater, bad puns, and fancy jackets. She is the author of *A Tip for the Hangman*.